Dear Mystery Reader:

Only two female writers have ever won the prestigious Shamus Award for Best Novel: Sue Grafton and the author of the book in your hands right now, S. J. Rozan. Rozan's novel, *Concourse*, earned an enormous amount of critical praise, culminating with this distinguished and well-deserved honor.

In *Mandarin Plaid*, Lydia Chin and Bill Smith are back for another fast-paced mystery. On a case that draws them into the high-stakes New York fashion world, our favorite P.I. duo travels through Chinatown's sweatshops, Manhattan's wealthy Upper East Side and deep into a world of prostitution, drugs, and murder in New York's seedy underground.

S. J. Rozan is not only one of DEAD LETTER's finest writers, but a rising star in the mystery world with a truly original voice. If you haven't checked out a Rozan mystery, now is the time!

And don't miss S. J. Rozan's next mystery, *No Colder Place*, now available in hardcover from St. Martin's Press.

Yours in crime,

Joe Veltre
St. Martin's DEAD LETTER Paperback Mysteries

Other titles from St. Martin's **Dead Letter** Mysteries

MANDARIN PLAID

S. J. ROZAN

St. Martin's Paperbacks

MANDARIN PLAID

Copyright © 1996 by S. J. Rozan.

All rights reserved. No part of this book may be used or reproduced in any manner whatsoever without written permission except in the case of brief quotations embodied in critical articles or reviews. For information address St. Martin's Press, 175 Fifth Avenue, New York, N.Y. 10010

Library of Congress Catalog Card Number 96-8499

ISBN: 0-312-96283-5

Printed in the United States of America

St. Martin's Press hardcover edition/September 1996
St. Martin's Paperbacks edition/August 1997

10 9 8 7 6 5 4 3 2

For Willy and Simon

ACKNOWLEDGMENTS

The author is grateful to

My agent, Steve Axelrod
My editor, Keith Kahla
every writer should be so lucky

Jim Finney, Royal Huber, Ellen Kornhauser, Jamie Scott,
Lawton Tootle, and Betsy the Plotmeister Harding

Susanna the Other Plotmeister Bergtold

Helen Liu and Beebee Lam, who let me in

John Leffler, who loaned me books both seminal and germinal

Steve Blier, Hillary Brown, Bart Gulley, Sally Helgesen,
Julia Moskin, and Max Rudin, who put up with a lot for this one

Sui Ling Tsang, a great coach

Deborah Peters, a great genius

and
Helen Hester, because, and Nancy Ennis, anyway

MANDARIN
PLAID

One

It's not that I don't like spring in Madison Square Park—I'm a fan of the fat little buds on the trees and the sun sparkling off the puddles. It's just that I'm not usually strolling through here with fifty thousand dollars, looking for the right trash can to drop it in.

My footsteps crunched gravel on the curving path. The air was chilly, but the soft March sun grazed the back of my neck. Snowdrops and bright crocuses were up everywhere.

The sweat tickling my spine had nothing to do with the weather.

Squirrels chased each other down trees and over spring-soggy grass. The dogs in the early-morning run chased each other, too, while their owners chatted by the fence. The fresh breeze smelled sweet.

My skin prickled.

I kept my eyes jumping, trees to paths to dogs and their owners.

On a bench up ahead, Bill Smith, my sometimes-partner, pretended to read a book. He had a thermos of coffee beside him, which was a good thing. His job was to watch my back, and then, when I was out of sight, to watch the trash can until someone came to withdraw my deposit. That could take a while.

The client hadn't asked for that, but my brother had.

1

* * *

When I'd met Genna Jing and her boyfriend, John Ryan, at my brother Andrew's loft the night before, all they wanted was someone to make the drop.

"I would do it," John Ryan said. He sipped white wine as he and Genna sat hip-to-hip on Andrew's angular 1950s sofa. "But Genna doesn't want me to. And I certainly don't want her to. Then someone reminded Genna she had a friend whose sister was a private eye."

Ryan was blue-eyed, well-tanned, wearing a black T-shirt under a poplin suit the color of dark honey. His short wavy hair was the same color. Genna Jing, beside him, had the silky hair, porcelain complexion, delicate features, and tiny ears of the classically beautiful Chinese.

I don't have those, though my mother has always said I'd be almost pretty if I'd let my hair grow and keep my mouth shut. And wear skirts more often.

Genna Jing was wearing a skirt, a tight knee-length one with a slit up the side, and a short-sleeved silk blouse with a Mandarin collar—a clichéd Chinese vamp outfit, except both pieces were plaid. Different plaids. I wasn't sure whether my mother would have approved, or not.

"Brad told me," Genna said. "My secretary. He's a friend of Andrew's. Do you know him?"

"No."

"Well, he was looking for a job when I was looking for a secretary, when I started on my own. Andrew put us together." Genna Jing indicated my brother, doing something precise in the stainless-steel kitchen across the loft.

My brother Andrew is four years older than I am, good looking, with a smooth forehead, a sharp nose, and eyes that, if you ask me, twinkle like our father's used to. We have three other brothers, and nobody else's eyes seem to do that. Andrew's a photographer. With equipment as exacting and precisely kept as he is—lenses ground and polished in Switzerland; carbon steel tripods that wouldn't jiggle in an earthquake; lots of different 35 mm, 4"× 5" and

8" × 10" camera bodies each just right for a different kind of film—he produces images, sometimes things and sometimes people, of such sweet and chaotic darkness that they can take your breath away. My mother just thinks they're confusing, but Andrew's very much in demand.

"It's just a drop?" I asked Genna Jing and John Ryan. "Leave the money where they said and walk away?"

"No way, Lyd," Andrew called, clinking ice into two 1965 World's Fair glasses. In demand or not, and even though he was the person who'd brought me this client, he was beginning to annoy me. "Listen, you guys," he addressed the pair on the sofa. "When you said you wanted to meet my sister I thought you wanted something *investigated*. You know, researched, phone calls and stuff. What you're asking her to do—"

"Is what I do," I finished. Actually, I'd never done this before, but every P.I. I know has been asked to make a shady payoff at some time or other. It's one of the services the profession offers.

"Lyd—"

I threw Andrew my steeliest look. He's the brother I use that look on least often, so it sometimes works. He frowned, but he closed his mouth and went back to slicing limes. I turned to the pair on the sofa. "Then what? They pick up the money, and you get your sketches back?"

Genna glanced from John Ryan to me. "I don't think they'll give them back," she said. "They'll probably just throw them away."

"Wait, I don't get it. Someone broke into your studio and stole your sketches, right? For your line for next spring?"

She nodded. "The first full spring line for my own label, Mandarin Plaid."

"And you're paying fifty thousand dollars but you're not getting them back? What's the money for?"

"Well, it's not like the drawings are originals or anything." Genna spoke with the unease of a polite person who doesn't want to patronize her listener by explaining the obvious. To me, though, this wasn't obvious.

"You mean you have copies?"

"These days, everything is done with copiers and fax machines."

Genna gave me a small smile. "There are no originals anymore."

"Then why pay the ransom at all?"

"Because if I don't pay," Genna said, squeezing John's hand, "they're going to ruin me. They'll abort my career before it starts."

"How?"

"They're going to sell them. To Mango, or Bizniz, or someplace like that."

She said this seriously, her voice soft with that damper of shame that comes when someone is about to do something bad to you and you can't stop them.

I knew those names: national chains of inexpensive, up-to-the-minute clothes. I shopped in them, because I liked the styles and the prices, but I didn't shop there often, because my mother scorned anything I bought from them as "bad cloth, bad sewing." Then she'd fix me with a meaningful stare and announce, "Only a fool thinks cheap saves money."

Andrew, the lime slicing completed, came over and handed me my Swedish sparkling water, something I know he goes all the way to the Upper West Side to buy. He leaned back in a molded plywood chair of the same vintage as the sofa.

"They'd buy them?" I asked. "Stolen designs?"

Genna didn't answer right away. John took it up.

"Sure as hell," he nodded. "I don't know how much you know about the fashion business, but it's cutthroat. Right now, Mandarin Plaid's ready to take off. We've been getting a lot of press lately. People are expecting big things from Genna. Her first show is next week, Market Week."

Andrew broke in to say to me, "Market Week is when—"

"When the designers show next season's clothes. In the big tents in the park behind the library," I finished. Andrew's my favorite brother, mostly because he assumes I'm a total idiot less often than the other three do; but he still does it sometimes.

Genna gave me a raised-eyebrow look of understanding. John just nodded. He must not have any brothers, I thought.

"I'm not doing the tents," Genna said. "I'm not big enough. A friend is lending me his loft. But I've invited everyone, and there's been some talk. It could be okay."

4

"Bigger than okay," John said. "It's going to be huge. Enormous. Gigantic. But if Genna hits with this line for fall, and then a chain like Mango or Bizniz starts putting out Genna Jings for spring before we do, it'll be a disaster."

The magnitude of this was beginning to shape up for me. I asked another question. "Now that the sketches are stolen, why don't you think they'll sell them to Bizniz or somebody anyway, after you pay the ransom?"

"We thought about that," John said. "But it's risky. They might run into an honest person at Bizniz. Surprise! Then what?"

"And you don't think they'll take that risk?"

John shook his head. "I don't think they're pros. In fact, to do a thing like this I think they have to be a little crazy. There have to be easier ways to make a buck, don't there? Even illegally."

I wasn't sure. So far, this seemed pretty easy to me.

"They might try to sell them out of spite if Genna doesn't pay," John went on, "but I don't think they'll risk it if she does. Anyway, in terms of risks, that's one I think *we* have to take."

"Do you have any idea who they might be?"

Genna shook her head. Her hair brushed her shoulders and settled perfectly back into place, but it seemed to me that something in her eyes didn't.

"It had to be someone who knows I'm about to have my first show, but that's no secret," she said. She sipped at her wine. "And someone who would know what to take. But that could be anybody."

"Not really anybody," I said. "How did they know where to find what they wanted? That they weren't grabbing up rejects? You said your alarm went off but they were gone by the time the cops got there. That's quick work. It means they knew just what they were doing."

"By the time *I* got there," John put in. "I beat the cops by five minutes."

"But what's the difference?" Genna's voice, steady and controlled until now, began to quaver. "Even if we knew who it was, I'd have to pay, wouldn't I? Unless we could find them and get the sketches back right away. And be sure they hadn't copied them." She bit her lip and looked away.

John wrapped his arm around her shoulders. "It's okay, Gen," he said softly. To me he said, "She's right. They want the money tomorrow morning. The most important thing is to stop them. Then to get Genna's show done. *Then* to find out who these bastards are."

"I'm sorry," Genna said to me, with a weak smile. "I'm not usually like this. But I'm just exhausted. I've been pushing so hard to try to get the show done. Things keep going wrong, people backing out at the last minute—it's been a nightmare. But this is the worst."

John kissed Genna's pale-silk forehead. He turned to me. "Can we just do this?" he asked. "Can you just make this drop, and we'll worry about everything else later?"

"Yes," I said, over Andrew's "No." His was louder, but mine was firmer. Narrowing my eyes at my brother, I went on, to Genna, "But if someone did this to you now, why won't they do it next season, even if you pay them? And over and over?"

"They won't be able to." Genna swallowed and brought her voice back under control. "It's the timing. If my show's successful—"

"Which it will be," John said.

She smiled gratefully at him. "Which we hope it will be, then I'll be established. After a few seasons it doesn't matter if Bizniz or Mango or anyone is selling things that look like Genna Jings. It's only in the beginning, if the spring line of Mandarin Plaid looks like something they already have at Bizniz, that I'm in trouble. Then my investors would pull out, and I'd never have a line."

That reminded me of another question. "The ransom money," I said. "Where's it coming from? From your investors?"

"Oh, God, no. It would be a disaster if they even found out about this. They might lose confidence, no matter what we did. They'd pull out."

John said, "Genna's getting the ransom from me."

At that, Genna's face changed. She looked down at Andrew's polished wood floor. "No, I'm not."

"Genna . . ."

"I got it already." Her words were so hurried I almost missed them.

Ryan didn't miss them, but it took him a minute to know what to do with them. "You *what?*"

6

"John, I told you I wouldn't take your money, and I don't want to talk about it now." Genna turned to me. "I borrowed the money. It's right here."

She drew a thick envelope from her metallic handbag. "It's in fifty-dollar bills. That's what they wanted." She handed the envelope to me. It was heavier than I would have thought.

"No," Andrew said as I took it. "Lydia's not doing this."

"Andrew," I said sweetly, "buzz off."

"Lyd, this could be dangerous."

"It won't be. And you sound like Ted." I figured that would stop him. Ted's the oldest of us and pretty stuffy. Andrew doesn't like to sound like Ted.

Andrew opened his mouth again. "And like Tim," I added, just to be safe. Tim's the youngest of them, the brother between me and Andrew. He's a lawyer. Nobody likes to sound like Tim.

"Give me the details of the drop," I said to Genna, putting the envelope in my briefcase.

"Genna," John broke in. I could hear the effort it cost him to keep his tone reasonable. "Where did that money come from?"

"We'll talk about it later."

"You *borrowed* it? What the hell did you do, max out your credit? Genna, baby, are you nuts? You're going to need that as soon as things get rolling."

"John—"

"Baby, what's wrong with you?" John pleaded. "I've given you money before. What's your problem now?"

"That's an investment." She didn't raise her voice; if anything, she spoke more quietly. "Every penny of that money is accounted for. If Mandarin Plaid hits, you'll get it all back. And more. If not, it'll be a great deduction. But I don't think you can deduct ransom payoffs."

"I'm not sure," I said. Andrew gave me a you-really-*are*-crazy look. "No, what about kidnap ransoms?" I defended myself. "That's the cost of doing business. So's this."

I might have been right and I might have been wrong, but it was clear I wasn't speaking to the issue.

"John, I don't want your money. That's not who I am." Genna gave John a look so steely I found myself hoping the one I'd given

Andrew was as good. I liked her for it. Not all Chinese women have a look like that. My mother considers it unseemly. "We've had this argument before and I don't think Andrew and Lydia need to listen to it."

John didn't speak, but his eyes held Genna's as though he was willing her to do what he wanted. Her face was calm, and she didn't look away. The contest was silent and brief. John Ryan suddenly gave up, and stood.

Wineglass in hand, he strode through the room to the open front windows, moving as though he had to force his way. He glared into the street, one hand on a window frame. Genna turned to me with the look women give other women when their men are misbehaving.

When she spoke, all she said was, "Can you do it?"

"Of course," I said.

"Lyd—"

"I took the job, Andrew."

"I know. I know." He sounded resigned. "But at least don't do it alone, okay? Take Bill with you?"

"Ma would kill you if she heard you say that."

"Ma will kill me and chase me through all the caves of hell with a cleaver if you get in trouble and it's my fault."

"That's true." I grinned.

"Who's Bill?" Genna asked.

"Another investigator, someone I work with a lot. Sort of my partner."

"Your mother doesn't like him?"

"She hates him."

"Let me guess: he's not Chinese."

Genna and I smiled, the same smile.

Then Genna's faded. "I don't know," she said. "They said to keep this quiet. I don't know if it's a good idea to bring in so many people. Will you feel safer if he's there?"

"Not safer." Dispel that thought right away, that Lydia Chin might need someone to keep her safe. "Dropping money that someone's waiting for isn't likely to be dangerous. The bad guys will be as interested as we are in having things go smoothly. But if Bill were

8

there, he might get a chance to see who makes the pickup."

"They said no cops," John growled, from the window.

"We're not talking about cops. Not to grab the guy, just to have a look at him. Even if Bill doesn't follow him—" which I knew he would, especially if I told him to, and probably even if I didn't "—he can describe the guy to us. Maybe it'll turn out to be somebody you know."

"What if it is?" John asked testily, looking out over the purple spring evening on Twentieth Street. "What are we going to do about it?"

"That will be up to you. But at least you'll know."

Which is how I came to be in Madison Square Park on a bright March morning, heading for the fifth trash can in from the corner, which Bill had already scoped out so he'd know where to plant himself.

Madison Square Park, which spreads north and east from Twenty-third and Fifth, is a happening place in the early morning. Rising young executives hurrying to work maneuver around dog-walkers and their dogs, while others, whose positions in their companies are either more secure or more hopeless, sit drinking coffee and chatting before they go on. Some of the benches are occupied by the homeless, who stretched out on them the night before and are in no hurry to move anywhere. At this time of year, this early in the morning, half the park is in shadow from the tall buildings on Madison, while the sun billows through the budding trees and into the other half. The line between the two halves keeps moving. If you watch you can see it.

My instructions, which Genna had gotten over the phone, were to leave the envelope in the can and keep walking. I'd been given a time, 7:30, and a warning: no funny business. The thief had been told I was a friend of Genna's who was doing this for her because Genna was spooked. I didn't know if he believed that, but I didn't care. I was too annoyed that, although this was my case, Bill was going to have all the fun.

Once I dropped off the money I'd have to follow the instructions to make myself scarce; to the client, a successful operation meant having the exclusive rights to her own sketches again, and my first responsibility was not to jeopardize that. I'd probably head back to Chinatown and my office, where I'd call Genna, report in, and then sit and wait for Bill to call me.

Bill, meanwhile, would be waiting for, spotting, and then shadowing the bag man all over town.

I looked at him, up there ahead on his bench, probably full of adrenaline already, edgy to start the cat-and-mouse. He hides that rush better than I do—he's been in this business longer, and he's got more self-control in general—but I know he feels it.

I was feeling a little of it myself as I neared the trash can, even though I completely expected nothing at all to happen. Reaching into my pocket to pull out the envelope, dropping it casually on yesterday's *Post* and a half-eaten hot dog, I felt that jumpy sense of triumph you get when an important job's successfully done. Plus that irrational disappointment that now there's no more to do, that now it's over.

That's the part I was wrong about. It wasn't over.

I heard the bang and whine as soon as I'd turned away from the can. Instinct took over from thought. Something caught me in the face as I dove behind a tree. I rubbed at it: a splash of mud thrown up by the impact of the bullet. The second shot sprayed gravel from the path into the air. Dogs barked and howled. Executives hit the dirt. Screeching birds wheeled into the sky. People ran and yelled and ran some more.

I crouched in the mud and forced myself to count to sixty. I gave it up at five. My heart was pounding and time took forever.

I peered out. Around me were people lying still like fallen park statues. Even the squirrels were hiding; nothing moved. Somewhere at the other end of the park a dog was barking, over and over. At that end people were running and shouting. I looked for Bill. His book was lying alone and open on the bench, its pages flipping forlornly in the wind. No third shot came. I emerged from behind my tree.

In the distance, approaching fast, I heard the wail of a police siren. People stirred and stood. I moved a little way from my tree and blended into the quickly gathering crowd. I examined the faces around me. Fear, anger, and confusion bathed them all. I glanced into the trash can.

The envelope, of course, was gone.

TWO

By the time the detective on the case arrived, the scene had picked up quite a crowd. Dogs sniffed each other suspiciously as their owners whispered questions. Executives brushed dirt from the fronts of their business suits, glanced at their watches, and frowned, but didn't leave. Everyone peered around everyone, in case there was something to see. The cops wouldn't say anything; the crowd asked its own questions and answered itself, with stories that grew wilder and wilder. A shooting, everybody knew; but where was the body? Gone already; too disgusting to look at, riddled with bullets. Drugs. Gangs. Terrorists.

The detective was a big, thick, sour cop from the Thirteenth Precinct. I watched him bark questions and orders at the uniforms, squint irately at the bullet they showed him, snap back at civilians asking questions. He elbowed his way through the crowd as though that was the part he enjoyed. "Shooter in the park in the goddamn morning," I heard him mutter as he lit a cigarette. "Jesus, I'm glad my granddaughter don't live in this city."

Chainsmoking, he waited for reports from the uniforms talking to people over by the stand of trees the shots had come from. They'd already interviewed those of us standing closer. I'd told them the truth, when they got to me: I'd just passed the trash can, heard the first shot, hid behind a tree. I hadn't seen the shooter and couldn't even tell them exactly where he'd been.

As the uniforms came back with their reports, the grim-faced

11

detective snarled at the crowd again. His eyes swept over me, moved on, came back.

Okay, Lydia, I thought, time for you to go, as his attention was taken by a patrolman with a question. I turned to leave and saw Bill behind me, hanging at the back of the crowd.

He'd obviously been watching me, because he gestured me over as soon as he saw I'd seen him. The crowd had thinned out by then; I wondered why he hadn't come through it, or at least called my name.

"Are you okay?" he asked as I reached him.

"Why were you sneaking up on me?"

"Not on you. Come with me, before—"

I didn't get to hear before what. What I heard was a shout.

"Hey, you! Smith!" It was the detective. He made Bill's name sound like an accusation.

I looked at Bill. "Before that?" I asked.

He shrugged.

The detective plowed through the crowd to reach us. "So," he said, planting his feet as though the park were swaying but he was intending to stay put. His heavy tweed jacket reeked of cigarette smoke, and his face radiated disgust. He looked Bill up and down.

"And here I thought I just had the asshole du jour." The detective's words were addressed to Bill, as though no one else was standing around us. "Just your average wacko taking target practice in the park. But no, Krch. You got a better-than-average asshole. You got someone brings Smith out. Who's your girlfriend?" he asked abruptly.

Bill sighed. "I was just trying to get to know the lady, Harry. You don't be careful, you'll ruin my social life." He leered in a friendly, lecherous way down at me.

I looked from Bill's leer to Krch's scowl. I scowled, too. "Don't wolly. You luin it all by yourself. Clazy Amellican." I wheeled around and righteously stomped away.

I headed north along the path, still stomping, kicking pebbles out of my way. I had to stop myself from punching a tree. An easy job, a job I'd promised my favorite brother wouldn't be dangerous, had ended in gunshots. At *me*. The client's money was gone. Pumped with adren-

12

aline, I had made myself stand quietly and watch as the cops came up with nothing. And now my own partner—not even my partner, my employee, someone I'd hired!—had told me to go get lost while he talked to Detective Harry Krch.

Of course, there was a good reason for that one. There had to be, or he wouldn't have done it, which is why I'd played along. When I'm not furious with the world for shooting at me and at myself for being a stupid, incompetent, hopeless excuse for a private eye, I know that Bill thinks highly of me and would never just sweep me under the rug and take over my case.

And when I stopped being furious, I would remember that.

I halted in a sunny spot at the edge of the park, near a particularly bright splash of crocuses. I took some deep, calming breaths, which didn't work, and thought about my next move.

Bill and I have this thing we do when we're working together and we get separated. Whoever can leave heads a few blocks north of where we'd been. You find a place, sit and wait, and after a while the other one shows up.

Trying to think like Bill trying to think like me, I considered the options.

There were benches, of course, all through the park between where he was and where I was. I could plunk myself right down and wait for him here; but Krch might notice Bill finding me, and since Bill had clearly made an effort to suggest that we didn't know each other, it seemed I ought to at least find out why before I gave the game away.

Bill had seen me stomp away east on the park path. I could settle in the first coffee shop north up Madison, which was on the east side of the park. Bill would eventually find me there, but I wasn't sure I could sit still over a cup of tea in the mood I was in.

I looked around. Across Madison and up two blocks was a big gray building with a small gray plaza. It had wide steps up into it and planters with ivy and budding trees. You could pace back and forth or sit on the planters and swing your legs and consider the evil, not to mention the incompetence, so deeply ingrained in the human soul.

I headed there.

The walk, which I took very fast, soaked up some of the jumpiness. I marched up the sidewalk between looming, shadowed buildings on one side and, on the other, buildings with sunlight blazing off their windows, obscuring what was inside as completely as the shadows. As I went, I examined, weighed, and dismissed the possibility that the shooting, as Krch had suggested, was just some home-grown loony taking target practice in the park, and that the payoff had actually gone as planned, with the thief seizing the opportunity to grab his envelope in the confusion.

Not likely. Coincidences happen all the time, but not when you need them.

I reached the plaza slightly out of breath. Good. Exercise regulates the system. All around me, business-suited figures of both genders trotted up the steps and into their offices, where they would go through another peaceful, secure nine-to-five day where no one would shoot at them and they wouldn't lose track of fifty thousand dollars of their client's money. A delivery man took the steps two at a time, carrying someone's breakfast, singing to himself. Speeding up the sidewalk, a bike messenger narrowly missed a kid on rollerblades shooting the steps.

I wished I had my skates myself, to work off my nerves while I waited for Bill.

I circumnavigated the plaza, then crisscrossed it, then divided it into quarters and traversed each one. I bought a cup of hot cocoa from a sidewalk cart and tried to warm myself up with it as I paced. Come *on*, Bill, I thought, as I passed from sunlight to shade and back to sunlight again, watching the stream of office workers grow to a torrent as nine o'clock approached.

When my cocoa was gone and Bill still hadn't shown, I called Genna. I'd been holding off because I'd wanted to talk to Bill first. He might have seen the shooter, or the guy who took the money, or something. But Genna must be beyond jumpy by now, sitting by her phone. I hated to call a client and tell her I wasn't sure what was going on, but I hated worse to do nothing at all.

The phone was snatched up before the first ring was over. "Hello!" Genna's voice demanded.

"Genna, it's Lydia."

"Lydia! My God, what happened?"

"There was a problem." I leaned into the phone's metal enclosure, trying to drown out the noises of passing traffic. "Do you know already?"

"I got a call," she said. Her voice was high and fast. "I was waiting for you, but it was them."

"What did they say?"

"He said, either I was being way too cute or I was real unlucky, but either way it was too bad for me. He said he'd call again if he decided to give me another chance. Lydia, what's he talking about?"

"Someone took two shots at me after I dropped the envelope."

"*Shots?* They shot at you? My God, are you all right?"

"Yes. But when the dust cleared the envelope was gone."

"Gone? Someone took it?"

"Someone must have. And I guess what the guy on the phone was telling you was that it wasn't them."

She was silent, but someone in the background wasn't. "Get on the phone in the conference room," Genna said, not to me. "It's Lydia."

A pause, a click, then, "Lydia? It's John. What the hell is Genna talking about? Shots? What happened?"

I repeated the story. "Someone else must have known," I said. "If the thieves called you and they don't have the money, this must have been a hijacking."

"But who?" John said. "Who else knew, besides you and me and Genna and Andrew? And Brad, but my God, he was the one who suggested hiring you."

"And he doesn't really know," Genna said, from the other line. "He thinks we hired Lydia to investigate the robbery. I didn't tell him about the ransom demand."

"Well, what about that other detective?" John asked. "The one working with you. Lydia, how well do you—"

"Well," I said shortly. "Did you guys tell anyone? Anyone at all?"

"No," said Genna.

"No way," said John.

"Well," I said, "it doesn't have to be us. It could be them."

Genna asked, "What do you mean?"

15

John answered her before I could. "That they double-crossed each other, Gen. Right, Lydia? They stole the money from each other?"

"Yes," I said. "Or one of them was blabbing in a bar to the wrong stranger about his clever plan."

"What's going to happen now?" I could hear a thin edge of hysteria creeping into Genna's voice.

"I don't know," I said. "But it sounds like your thief didn't get what he wanted."

"No. And he said he'd call."

"It'll be okay, Gen." John was firm and gentle. "Money was what he wanted. When he gets over being mad, he'll call and ask for more money."

"But it's gone." Genna seemed on the verge of tears. "The money's gone."

"Genna, that's not a problem. You know that."

"John—"

"Genna, baby, one problem at a time, okay? I know how much you hate the idea of my money. But this is your whole damn career, Gen. Can we not worry about the money right now? Lydia, what happens next?"

"We wait for him to call," I said in my most in-charge voice. "When he does, call me at my office. We'll work out a plan from there."

"Thanks, Lydia." Genna sounded grateful.

John said nothing, and we hung up.

It was another ten minutes before Bill turned up. I'd been about to give him thirty more seconds and then go do something when he came loping across Madison Avenue. Stopping my pacing, I glared at him across the plaza.

"Buy you a drink?" he called.

I nodded. He transacted the business at the sidewalk cart, carried over two steaming cups, leaned against a planter, and grinned.

"Clazy Amellican, huh?"

"Why did you do that?" I demanded. "Get rid of me?"

He pulled a cigarette from his jacket pocket. "Krch and I go back a long way. He thinks I'm the offspring of Satan and a snake. You obviously didn't want the cops to know who you were or you wouldn't have been just another face in the crowd like that. I was trying to protect your secret identity, Batman."

Humor was a mistake, right then. "The money's gone," I snapped.

"I saw."

"Did you see the guy who took it?"

He shook his head. "I was chasing the shooter."

"Your job was watching the money!"

He gave me a strange look. "Lydia? Someone fired two shots in a busy park. At *you*. I'm not going to sit around and wait to see what happens next."

"No, you're going to go charging off like some comic book superhero chasing the bad guys—"

"—while you're trapped behind a tree not able to do anything. Which is what you're really mad about." He sipped his coffee. High overhead a silver jet streaked west. He followed it with his eyes.

"You're right," I finally said.

"I know."

"Do I have to apologize?"

"No." He grinned. "But you really should wash your face."

I'd forgotten about the clump of mud that had hit me. I rubbed at my cheek. "Better?"

"No, but more adorable. You want to hear about the shooter?"

I nodded.

"Red and tan baseball jacket, dark baseball cap, jeans, sneakers. Light-skinned. I chased him half a mile up Fifth and never saw his face."

"Rats. You couldn't ID him?"

"No.

"Where did he go?"

"East at Thirty-fourth. He was gone by the time I got to the corner. I told Krch about it; maybe he'll send someone to see if he ditched the gun. I'm not sure he believed me, though."

"What did you tell him you were doing in the park?"

17

"Reading *War and Peace*." He riffled the pages of the book sticking out of his pocket.

"I'll bet he didn't believe that either." I leaned against the stone planter, staring at a big fluffy cloud high in the sky. "I called Genna," I said. "The thieves had called already. At least, one of them did." I told Bill about my talk with Genna and John. "John Ryan proposed you as a possible source of the leak," I added, at the end.

"That's gratitude for you. I haven't even *taken* a leak since early this morning."

"If you want to remedy that, don't let me stop you."

"You couldn't. But first tell me what we're going to do now."

"Now? What can we do now?" I realized I was snapping at Bill again. I controlled myself and said, "I'm going back to my office to wait for Genna to call."

"And I'm going home to wait for you to call."

"What makes you think I'll call you?"

"If you didn't call me, who would you blame when things go wrong?"

"First of all," I said with great dignity as I stood up, "nothing else is going to go wrong. And secondly, I'm Lydia Chin. I can blame anybody I please."

And I walked away, head held high, at a stately pace, leaving Bill to clean up the cups and napkins at the planter we'd used as a breakfast table.

THREE

I had paperwork to do in my office anyway, which meant I'd have something to distract me while I waited for Genna's call. I usually have paperwork to do in my office. I try to keep even with it— Bill's always ahead of his—but the best I can do is to make piles: *Now, Soon, Later*. Then I don't do any of it until *Immediately*.

18

I got out of the subway on Canal and walked east toward Chinatown. My office is just west of Chinatown's unofficial but long-standing border. Over here, the electronics retailers, leather-and-jeans discount places, and job lot stores on the ground floors have English signs. More and more now, though, even this far over, the upper-floor signs are in Chinese: doctors, of Western or Chinese medicine; lawyers, especially immigration experts; acupuncturists, architects, accountants. The sweatshops are expanding in this direction, also. You can tell which ones they are because the windows are soaped or grimed or stuck with translucent rice paper, so you can't see in.

My office is a room and a bathroom I rent from a travel agency on Canal. I have no windows on the street, and my name's not on the street door. Nobody who sees you come in here has to know that you didn't step directly into Golden Adventure to find out whether there's a boat to Shanghai, but instead continued down the hall to admit to Lydia Chin that you can't solve your problems by yourself.

Chinese people hate to admit that.

But Genna had admitted it. And look where it had gotten her.

At the end of the hall I unlocked my office door and curled my lip at my piles of paperwork. A lot they cared. The red light on my phone machine was lit, so I rewound to hear my messages. There was a total of one, from Andrew. "How did it go this morning? Call me."

Sure, Andrew.

Later.

I went into the bathroom and washed my face, as Bill had recommended. As I dried off and put on some moisturizer, I thought, So this is what a private eye looks like when she's lost fifty thousand dollars of her client's money.

The thought disgusted me. I went back to my desk.

The phone rang.

I yanked up the receiver and said, "Chin Investigative Services," in English and then in Chinese.

It answered in English. "Lydia? It's Genna. I wasn't sure you'd be back there already." Her voice was subdued, a little tentative.

"I'm here. Did they call?"

"No. Not yet. Can you come up here?"

19

"What's wrong?"

"There's something I think I should tell you. Can you come now?"

And leave these piles of paperwork? "I'm on my way."

Genna's studio wasn't far from Andrew's loft, in an ex-industrial building in Chelsea, with huge windows, wood floors, and slow elevators. On the ride up I glumly considered what had occurred to me as soon as I'd put down the phone: Genna was probably going to fire me. Why not? She could have lost her fifty thousand dollars all by herself; it would have been cheaper. Who needs a brainless P.I. whose partner chases a distraction all the way up Fifth Avenue while she cowers behind a tree, missing the real action taking place at the trash can ten feet away? If I were Genna, I'd fire me.

The elevator stopped, and I got out to face my fate. Mandarin Plaid Studios had the right-hand front piece of a jigsaw puzzle of studios and offices carved out of the top floor. The door was glass; I could see into the bright, polished space while I waited for someone to answer my ring. Above the receptionist's desk, at which no one sat, four discreet plaques told me about the awards Genna had won for her work. On one wall a long series of photos overlapped each other, taking you down a country road inch by inch. A huge round clock with no numbers and little stubby hands filled a lot of the opposite wall.

It was Genna herself who finally came to the door; no one else seemed to be around. "Thanks for coming up," she said. "I'm sorry you had to wait. Brad—you know, my secretary, Andrew's friend— and my assistant are out to lunch, and John's down in Chinatown, at the factory. I'm the only one here."

She smiled, a slightly nervous smile. Well, the decent Chinese thing to do would be to put her at ease by talking about something besides what we were here to talk about. I asked, "You have a factory producing your things already? Where John is now?"

"No, not yet," she said. Her smile turned grateful; she understood what I was doing. "But if orders come in from the show, we have to be ready. When you're new you don't have any leeway to deliver late, or short the order. There's a particular factory we want to use. Roland Lum, do you know him?"

I considered. "I think I knew his father. Roland took over that factory in the last year or so, when his father died?"

"That's right."

"All right, then I know who he is. He's the oldest son, a few years older than me. He was a friend of my brother Elliot's. I remember his father. Big spender, big reputation in Chinatown. He used to send baskets of sweets to his kids' classes at school at Chinese New Year. The rest of us were jealous."

"Well, the son's in charge at the factory now," Genna said. "He'd committed to working with us, but then he told me he'd gotten a big offer he couldn't turn down, and he dropped us. He does high-quality work, though, so I want to get him back. John's been trying to persuade him."

"I'm surprised," I said. "I'd have expected him to sell the factory. I thought he'd be a doctor or lawyer or something by now. Something professional and clean, not a factory owner."

Genna and I both knew what we meant when we talked about "factories": the smudged-window sweatshops where women—most of them new here, most of them illegal—work twelve-hour days in rooms that are hot in summer, cold in winter, where the whine and shriek of twenty, fifty, a hundred machines never stops.

My mother had been one of those sewing ladies all my life. I'd done my homework in the corner on piles of cotton scraps, while the machines whirred and the radio, almost inaudible, played high-pitched quavering Chinese music. I'd snipped threads on winter afternoons after school so my mother could put out more pieces because all the work was piecework. I'd played chasing games between the machines with Andrew until Willy Leng, the owner of my mother's factory, caught us, yelled at us, and stuck us in his office to practice writing Chinese characters until my mother's shift was over. Usually my brother Tim was already in Mr. Leng's office, doing extra-credit homework.

"Well," Genna said, "but that factory's the family business. He's the oldest son. I guess he had to." She showed me into a small, sunny conference room up front. "Would you like some coffee?"

"Do you have tea?"

"Of course."

I looked around as Genna went to get my tea. Thick-pencil sketches of skirts and shirts and dresses were pushpinned onto the walls next to photos of models. Fabric samples draped and pleated and spread over them. Buttons and braid and other sorts of things my mother calls "trimmings" were stuck everywhere. The combinations they made were startling. A crinkled gold fabric flowed over what looked like melting seashells; I guessed they were buttons. Five different heavily textured leather scraps were pinned to a lucious creamy white wool. Shiny black silk with a shimmering, disappearing pattern, like ripples in a pool on a moonlit night, was crisscrossed with metallic strips of silver, gold, and red.

"I wondered about your work," I said to Genna when she returned.

"Many people do," she said dryly.

"Oh." I took the mug of tea. "I didn't mean it that way."

"That's okay. I wonder myself." She was wearing a loose blazer in a thick, tweedy men's fabric, a big-collared white shirt open at the neck, and a skirt of the same fabric as the jacket. The skirt was so short that the jacket was longer. The Suit according to Genna Jing.

"I work with whatever I'm interested in," she said. "Mostly that seems to be things that set up expectations and then do something different. My work is really strange sometimes. I'm lucky I found people who want to back me. I wasn't sure I would."

"Well, I like it," I said. "Though I don't think I'd look good in it."

"Of course you would." Genna was emphatic. "To wear clothes like this all you have to do is look like you meant to. Attitude. You can do attitude, right?" She went on without waiting for an answer, which I thought was a good thing. "This here, the gold?" she said. "It's for an evening gown." She pointed to the photo next to it, a head shot of a model with a cap of short pale hair and a you-can't-touch-this, don't-even-try expression. "Andi Shechter," Genna told me. "She's going to wear it in my show. Lots of attitude. But the color would be great on you, too. One shoulder bare. In fact," she narrowed her eyes, looked at me as though she were seeing something new, "have you ever modeled?"

"Me? I'm only five-one. And my mother says I walk like a truck driver. Sometimes like a truck."

"That could be fun. People should move in clothes. The models, when you see them in magazines—did you know they're all safety-pinned and Scotch-taped together where you can't see it? It's totally fake. Then they stand still and don't breathe. And then you go to the store and wonder why you don't look like that in those clothes."

I'd never wondered. "Actually, my mother makes most of my clothes. Or else she alters what I buy."

"No kidding? Did she make this?" Genna inspected the lapel of my midnight-blue linen jacket. "She's really good."

"Her mother taught her to sew in China. And she's been sewing in Chinatown for thirty years."

We were both settled at the conference room table by now, where a spring breeze floated in the open windows, stirring the fabric samples. I felt a brief moment of embarrassed silence. Then we both spoke at the same time.

"Well—" said Genna.

"I'm—" I said.

"Wait," I said. "Let me go first. I'm really sorry about what happened this morning. It's inexcusable. Bill and I both should have been more awake. If you don't want us on this case anymore, I'll understand." Only it'll kill me, I thought, not to have a chance to fix things up and redeem myself.

Genna gave me a surprised look. "People shot at you. It wasn't your fault."

"It's something I should have thought of and been ready for. That's my job. I'm sorry."

"Oh," said Genna. "Well, thank you. But I'm not firing you, if that's what you think."

"You're not?" My heart soared. Sunshine poured into the room; a bird chirped outside the window. Okay, Lydia, I scolded myself. Get yourself under control. You have a client. Pay attention. "Then what's this about?"

23

"I said on the phone, there's something I want to tell you. I should have told you yesterday, but John thinks I'm being ridiculous. He talked me out of it, I guess. I thought it didn't matter, because once I paid, it would be over. But now the police are involved, and it's not over."

"The police are involved in the shooting, but we didn't tell them about you."

"I know that. But they might find out. Anyway, maybe I am being ridiculous, but I'll feel better if I tell you."

"Well, then, tell me."

Her elegant hand—French-tipped today—picked at a thread in her jacket sleeve. "It's just that I think I know who's doing this."

"You do? You know?" Close your mouth, Lydia, don't stare at the client. "Why didn't you tell me yesterday? Who?"

"Well, I don't *really* know. John says it's completely farfetched, and I thought, what's the difference? Even if I'm right, I'd still have to pay. Actually, I don't know why I'm telling you now. Except Andrew said—"

"Andrew." I'd forgotten about my brother. No, more like repressed him. "Does Andrew know what happened this morning?"

"Yes, he called me, and I told him. Was that wrong? Did you want to tell him yourself? I'm sorry; I should have thought."

"No, no, it's fine." I waved away the question of who should be telling Andrew something I was sure he could live a long and happy life never knowing.

"Didn't he call you? He said he was going to."

"He did," I said guiltily. "He left a message for me to call him, but I didn't yet. I'll bet he's upset."

"Upset?" Genna's smile was wry. "He said something about locking you up until this case ends. He said when you get taken like this it makes you madder than a hornet and stubborner than a mule. He said you hate to lose."

"Andrew always had a weakness for clichés," I said in a superior way. "You can tell from the fifties furniture." Secretly I was pleased. I didn't think Andrew meant those things as compliments, but they sounded like compliments to me.

"He said you wouldn't stop now until you found out what was

24

going on, whether you had a client or not. He's afraid you'll get into trouble doing that. He said you had before."

"What Andrew thinks of as trouble," I said in a professional voice, "is just part of my job. It's—"

"You like it, don't you?"

"My job?"

"The trouble part."

She was looking at me in a strange way. Worry and recognition were mixed in her eyes, and something that might have been pride; but I had the feeling none of those things was for me.

"Yes," I said carefully. "I guess I do."

"I thought so." The strange look passed. She shook her head. "I don't understand that, myself. I'm not big on risk."

Involuntarily, my eyes went to the odd fabrics and outrageous sketches stuck on the walls. Genna's glance followed mine. "That's different," she said.

"I'm not sure."

Genna looked appraisingly from her work to me. "Maybe you're right," she said slowly. Then she sat up straight; suddenly she was all business. "Anyway, Andrew said you wouldn't stop, no matter what. So I thought I could at least tell you what I was thinking."

I waited silently for Genna to tell me what she was thinking.

"Do you know what a show producer is?" she asked.

"Like on Broadway?"

"No," Genna said. "For a runway show. Sort of like on Broadway, but their role's a little different. They're consultants; you hire them to take care of everything but the clothes."

"The music and the lighting, that sort of thing?"

"Yes, and also the shoes, and the accessories. And the makeup and the models. To pull it all together, to give your collection a 'look.' The way it works, the producer would study your work, then say we should use so-and-so and so-and-so, they'll wear your things well. And we'll put everyone in white patent leather army boots, we'll use that with everything. Very pale on the makeup, with black-rimmed eyes for evening. Et cetera. You see?"

"I never knew that. I guess I thought the designer did it all."

Genna smiled. "All I do is the clothes. Believe me, that's enough.

Of course, you want to work with a producer who understands you. Someone who's in tune with what you're doing. I thought I'd found someone like that about six months ago, a producer named Wayne Lewis."

"You thought," I said. "But you were wrong?"

"I'm not sure if I was when I called him. I'd known Wayne from other jobs I'd had in the industry, although I hadn't seen him in close to a year. I remembered him as the kind of person who inspires confidence. He always had an answer to everything. He could come on strong, but I wanted a strong hand running things, especially this first time. So I called him."

"But it didn't work out?"

"No, it didn't. He came on even stronger than I remembered, and short-tempered, which was new, although he was always a little impatient. He was unreliable, never on time for meetings. He had some really good ideas, I thought, about the collection and the show, but he was so difficult to deal with that it wasn't worth it. I was actually relieved when he quit."

"When was that?"

"About three months ago. I think I might have fired him if he hadn't. But one day he called and said he couldn't work with us anymore, sorry, good-bye."

"I wouldn't have thought you were that hard to work with."

"I don't think I am. But John can be difficult. He wants things to happen fast, and then he wants the next thing to happen. He loves action, not planning and details." She smiled softly. "I think it's one source of the trouble between John and his mother."

"They don't get along?"

Genna's silky hair swayed as she shook her head. "And I'm the other reason. That's why this has all got me so upset, Lydia. John's mother thinks I'm after his money. She wants me out of his life. She absolutely hates it that he works here. He's what they call in the business the 'outside man,' you know? He deals with all the *stuff*, so I can concentrate on design. Anyway, I'm hoping if my line takes off and I have money of my own, maybe she'll feel better about me."

"Is he . . . is it a problem between you that his mother feels that way?"

"Oh, no. John cares less about it than I do. He says let's just get married, and the hell with her. But I don't want to do it that way. My mother-in-law. I'd like to get along with her if I can. Am I making sense?"

I smiled. "To me."

She smiled also. "I thought so, and I'm glad. Andrew and I have talked about it, and he gets it, but John just doesn't."

"I think," I said, trying to be cross-culturally understanding, "that where he comes from, 'mother-in-law' carries a different meaning."

"I guess so," she agreed. "But anyway, that's not why I asked you to come up. I'm sorry. I really don't like it when other people assume their personal problems are interesting to me, and here I am acting as though mine are interesting to you."

"But they are," I told her. "That's why I'm in this business. Everything about everybody is interesting to me."

"Really? I'm not sure if that makes you lucky or unlucky."

"Me either. But the more I know about you the more likely I am to be able to help solve your problem."

"Well, I don't think knowing what my future mother-in-law thinks of me is going to be much help in getting my sketches back. But what I wanted to talk to you about was Wayne."

"Because you think he might be behind this."

"He could. He'd know what to take, and he'd know this kind of threat would work, at just this point in my career. After all, it had to be someone in the industry. I didn't think he hated me that much, but old wounds grow over time, don't they?" Genna didn't look at me as she said that.

"Have you had any contact with him since he left?"

She shook her head. "I didn't even get a call for a reference. I was kind of glad about that. I don't know what I would have said."

"Do you know where to find him?"

"I have his home address. He works out of his apartment."

Genna got up to get the address for me. As she did, the studio door opened to admit three people in joking conversation. A thin, short-haired woman sipped something iced through a straw between her bright red lips. A broad-shouldered, goateed young man with

27

three earrings up the side of his left ear flopped down at the front desk. That must be Brad, I thought. And John Ryan, glancing into the conference room out of what seemed like habit, stopped when he saw us. The smile fell from his face. He stepped into the room. Softly he said to Genna, "They called?"

"No."

The conference room had a sliding glass door; John pulled it shut.

"They didn't call?"

"No."

"Then . . . ?" John looked from Genna to me, obviously waiting for an explanation of my presence.

"I asked Lydia to come up," Genna said. "I wanted to tell her about Wayne." Her manner seemed defiant to me, almost defensive.

"Wayne? Wayne Lewis?" John raised his eyebrows. "Well, I think you're barking up the wrong tree with that one, but go ahead. Do you need me? I have some calls to make."

Genna shook her head. John kissed her, smiled at me, and left.

"He didn't say it was ridiculous," I told Genna after the sliding glass door was shut again.

"No. But he doesn't believe it."

"Why not?"

"He thinks Wayne is washed up. Burnt out and all talk. He doesn't think he'd have the nerve to do something like this, or the creativity." She sighed. "Maybe he's right. I don't know. I don't know anything, except that I have a million things to do to get my show together, and less and less time to do them in. Let me get you Wayne's address, and then I'd better get back to work."

We went out to the receptionist's desk, where the guy who must be Brad was typing on a computer keyboard, talking on a phone tucked onto his shoulder. You're going to pull a muscle like that, I thought, as Genna flipped through a Rolodex. I stood in front of Brad until he glanced up from phone and keyboard and noticed me. "Lydia," I mouthed, pointing at myself. Brad's face lit in a warm grin. Without missing a beat, he half lifted from his chair and offered me his hand. After we shook he sat again and went immediately back to talking and typing, with an apologetic shrug and a smile at me. I smiled back.

I took the paper Genna handed me and promised to keep her up-to-date on whatever I did. As the elevator drifted to the ground floor I mused over the fact that, while waiting for someone to call and ask for a second fifty thousand dollars in exchange for her whole future, Genna Jing seemed able to concentrate on doing a million things.

F O U R

The address Genna had given me was in Greenwich Village, a nice walk from here on a spring day. I called the phone number, to make sure Wayne Lewis was in.

"Lydia Chin?" he said, when I introduced myself. His voice was raspy and his words quick. "Do I know you?"

"No," I said. "But I'd like to come see you. I won't take up much of your time. I'm in the neighborhood."

"You mean now?"

"Yes, if it's convenient."

"Sorry. I'm on my way out. What's it about?"

I'd planned carefully what I was going to say, and I said it. "I work for Genna Jing, Mr. Lewis. She has a problem she thought you might be able to help with."

"Genna Jing? She wants my help?" He laughed a short, unpleasant laugh. "You have to be kidding. Tell her to forget it. As a matter of fact, tell her to go to hell."

"It's a fairly serious problem," I went on. "Even if you don't have a solution, I was hoping you might be able to suggest someone who would."

"Why the hell would I? With all due respect, Ms. Chin, Genna's

29

not my favorite person, and her boy toy Ryan even less. If they've dug themselves into a hole right before Market Week, I think it's great."

"They haven't exactly dug this hole, Mr. Lewis, but they're willing to pay to get out of it."

"They'd have to pay a hell of a lot to get me to pick up a shovel."

"Fifty thousand dollars?"

There was a long pause. "That must be one huge goddamn motherfucker of a hole."

My mother would wash your mouth out with soap if she heard you talk that way to me, I thought.

Then she'd wash out my ears.

I said, "May I come discuss it with you?"

"In fact," he mused, ignoring my question, "I bet that kind of money could get you out of a black hole. A blackmail hole. Don't you think?"

"Not blackmail," I answered. "Blackmail's a crime, and crimes interest the police. This problem, on the other hand, can be solved without police involvement. Though I have to say that the police, from another angle, have become interested. If the problem isn't solved soon, they may get more deeply involved than anyone might want."

"You know, Ms. Chin, I'd almost think you were threatening me, if I had any idea what the hell you were talking about."

"I'd like to come tell you, Mr. Lewis, and I'd like to do it soon."

"Oh, would you? Well, you know, half of me wants to tell you that I really don't give a shit what you'd like."

"And the other half?"

"Wants to find a way to get in on this fifty thousand dollars, especially if it's Genna Jing's."

"So, may I come over?"

"Please, be my guest. But not now. I have an appointment I can't break. Say four o'clock?"

"That's the soonest you can manage?"

"Lydia Chin. That's a Chinese name, right?"

"Yes—"

"Amazing. And they say the Chinese, especially the women, are self-effacing and shy. Where the hell did a pack of pushy little dictators get a rep like that? Four o'clock, lady. I'll see you then, or not. Up to you. And don't forget to tell Genna Jing I said to go to hell."

Wayne Lewis hung up on me.

I called Bill.

"Hungry?" I asked.

"For your company? Always. Did they call?"

"No. And I meant for lunch."

"You have to be kidding. It's half-past two."

"I haven't eaten yet. I'm starving."

"That's too bad. I had a turkey club. Roast turkey, right out of the oven, you know that great oven smell? Crisp bacon, thick juicy tomatoes. Mmm. Lots of mayo. On rye. Did I mention the bacon? And for dessert—"

"That's too bad. I was going to buy you dessert."

"Buy me coffee, and I'm your man."

I wasn't sure the investment was worth the return, but I told him where to meet me, and hung up.

New York right now is flooded with new coffee bistros, lots of glass and chrome, tiny spotlights, and huge photographs of gritty urban scenes. There are so many that they can't possibly all last. In the meantime, you can get a good cup of coffee, or, more to the point as far as I'm concerned, tea, on almost every block in some neighborhoods. The Village is one of those.

The place I'd picked was playing classical music, something with sweet violins and a fast-moving piano, as I settled myself at a window table. I don't know much about music, but it sounded good to me. If I really wanted to know what it was, I could ask Bill when he came in. If I really wanted to ask him.

I ordered goat cheese with roasted peppers on a baguette—much better than a turkey club, any day—and a pot of mango tea. The waitress had a ring through her nose. Her midriff was bare so I could see the crown of thorns tattooed around her belly button. She had a very nice smile and brought my tea right away.

I was drinking it, wondering if I could avoid my brother Andrew completely until after the thieves called again and I had a chance to do this right, when Bill arrived.

"So," he said, "what's new?" He kissed my cheek. I let him, which I thought was fair of me.

"You mean, since I got shot at this morning? Nothing much."

"They haven't called? Have you talked to Genna?"

"As a matter of fact I just came from there."

"Where?"

"Genna's. She asked me to come up. Actually she wants me to model for her." I stretched the truth for him.

"Model what?"

"Nothing I'd let you see, so wipe that grin off your face. And what she really wanted was to give me the name of our suspect."

"She has a suspect?"

The nose-ringed waitress brought Bill's coffee. He glanced at her tattoo with what may, I suppose, have been scholarly interest; he has a big fancy one himself, on his left arm. I narrowed my eyes at him until he was through looking.

The waitress left. Bill tried his coffee. "I thought they said they had no idea who was doing this." He didn't mention my narrowed eyes.

"Well, Genna does. A guy named Wayne Lewis. He's what they call a show producer. He used to work for her. She says John thinks it's ridiculous, which is why she didn't tell me yesterday. I even got the feeling that's why she wanted me to come when John wasn't there, so he wouldn't get all bent out of shape when she did tell me. But a funny thing happened."

"What?"

"John came in while we were talking. She told him why I was there, sort of with a chip on her shoulder, but all he said was, 'Well, I think you're wrong.' Then he kissed her and went away to do some work. He didn't seem annoyed or exasperated at all."

"Maybe she's wrong about him. People often assume other people will react in ways they won't. Like if someone sees a man examining a woman's tattoo they might think he's interested in the bare skin all around it."

"Who would think that? But I had the idea that they'd already talked about Lewis being our guy, and she knew how John felt."

"Maybe he's reconsidered."

"Maybe." I put down my teacup. "Anyway, if Genna's wrong about John maybe she's wrong about her suspect. But I called him." I recounted my conversation with Wayne Lewis.

"What do you think?" I asked, when I was done.

"I think he sounds like a nasty creep."

"Which Genna more or less said."

"But I don't know if he sounds like our man."

"No, me either." I finished my tea and gestured to the waitress for our check. She smiled the nice smile again and brought it over. "He didn't deny it hard enough," I said to Bill, opening my wallet. "But he also didn't jump on the offer. Unless he's a superquick thinker and a really subtle strategist, I think he might be just what he sounds like."

"A guy looking for a way to cut himself in on a free lunch."

"Exactly. But I thought you might want to come along and check him out."

"I sure do. You mean," he said, as the waitress came and took my ten dollars, "you're not sticking me with the check, like the last two times?"

"I assumed you'd kill me if I did."

"Well, you're right about that. But then you make wrong assumptions so rarely."

In order to preserve his illusion I didn't tell him about the assumption I had made, on the way up to Genna's, that he and I were about to get canned.

"There's something else," I told Bill, as we strolled through the narrow Village streets beneath trees that were just starting to unfurl bright green leaves. "About Genna."

I had phoned Genna before we left the bistro, to find out if the thieves had called again, and to tell her we were on our way to Wayne Lewis's. She told me there had been no call. I promised to let her know as soon as we'd met with Wayne.

"What about her?" Bill asked.

"I'm not sure. It just struck me that she wasn't nearly as upset today as I would have expected her to be. She's pretty well focused on her show. I mean, I know it's the biggest thing in her life right now, but I think I'd be kind of distracted if someone with a gun had taken my borrowed fifty thousand dollars and someone else was about to call any minute now and ask for more."

"Or else ruin your career."

"Or else that."

"You know what else I'd like to know?" Bill asked. "Just because I want to?"

"What?"

"Where she got that fifty thousand dollars."

I looked at him in the dappled sunlight. "She borrowed it. John was angry that she'd maxed out her credit."

Bill didn't answer. I was quiet for a while also, thinking.

Wayne Lewis lived in the ground-floor apartment of a house on a street near the river. When these were private houses the ground floors were the kitchens. Only service people came there; they were lowly spots. Now they were highly desirable garden apts., quiet st., West Vil., near riv. & trans.

It was just after four when we turned the corner, the hour in the spring when the sun sparkles in yellow-orange glints off the water as it starts inching lower over Hoboken. The early flowers in peoples' window boxes swayed happily in the breeze, and the fronts of the brick houses all glowed honey-colored.

The other thing that glowed was the red and blue lights on the police cruisers and the orange ones on the ambulance in front of Wayne Lewis's house.

Bill and I stopped short at the end of the block. We stepped back a little, as out of sight as we could be and still see what was going on. Not that anyone was noticing us. All the cops—about half a dozen— were watching the EMS techs roll a covered gurney across the sidewalk and load it into the back of the ambulance.

Where they'd brought the gurney out of was the ground-floor apartment.

"Do you know any of them?" I whispered to Bill.

"The cops?" He searched down the street, shook his head.

"Then wait here." I popped a piece of chewing gum in my mouth, slipped on my sunglasses, and sauntered down the block.

It was a quiet neighborhood. Cops and ambulances had brought people out. I surveyed the crowd, settled on two teenage girls in baggy pants and untied basketball shoes.

"Hi," I said. I grinned a laid-back, gum-chomping grin as I came up beside them. "Like, what's happening?"

"Guy got killed," one of them told me. She said it with an I'm-a-big-city-kid-I've-seen-it-all-before toss of her head that her wide eyes, fixed on the gurney rolling into the ambulance, disputed.

"Killed? For real?" I popped my gum with a loud crack. My mother used to hate it when I did that as a kid, but I kept at it because it's something none of my brothers ever figured out how to do. "You mean, like, someone killed him?"

"Shot him," the girl agreed. "Three times." She cocked her finger into a gun, stuck it in her friend's ribs, went, "Pow pow pow."

Her friend slapped her hand away. "Come on, Geri, that's not funny!" They both giggled.

"Who?" I asked. "Did you guys see it?"

"Uh-uh." Geri sounded disappointed. "We heard the cops talking."

The door slammed shut on the ambulance with a final clang. I said, "Geez. Who was he?"

"Some guy," Geri said. "He lived down there. His name was Wayne something."

"Who killed him?" I asked. "Did they get the guy?"

"Uh-uh. Some lady upstairs called the cops 'cause she heard the shots, but I guess the guy figured he was good to go."

"Yeah, like he's really gonna hang around and wait for them," the other girl drawled sarcastically.

"Well, he could've." Geri was defensive. "Like if he was a psycho or something."

"Yeah, like if he was you."

The girls shoved each other and giggled again.

"So did, like, anybody see him?" I asked. "The guy who did it?"
Both girls shrugged; neither answered.

"I knew him," Geri's friend suddenly said, not looking at anyone. "That Wayne guy. I used to see him, like, walking his dog. I wonder what's gonna happen to the dog?"

The two girls looked at each other. For the first time they seemed upset.

The door to the ground-floor apartment opened, letting out a man with a wary walk and a bad suit. I figured he must be the detective on the case.

"Geez," I said to the girls. "Wish I could hang, but I gotta go. See ya."

"See ya," they answered absently, watching the ambulance pull out and the cops rearrange themselves.

I sashayed back up the block to where Bill lounged on someone's front stoop, looking down, out, and oblivious. I walked right past him. As I rounded the corner he rose and ambled after me, as though a pint of cheap wine was calling him home.

He waited until we'd made another turn and were headed east before he caught up with me. By then I'd gotten rid of the gum. I took off the sunglasses when he fell into step beside me.

"It was Wayne," I said, not waiting for him to ask. "He's dead."

Bill said nothing for a minute, then asked, "How?"

"Someone shot him."

We reached Seventh Avenue before either of us spoke again. Traffic stopped at the light and then went. Pedestrians crossed this way and that way, cut in front of the traffic, and hopped up to the curb. Store windows glittered in the late sun. A woman singing to herself walked a huge white dog past us as we stood on the corner.

"Damn!" I said suddenly, softly, and about nothing.

Bill touched my shoulder, gave me a squeeze, and took his hand away again.

"Okay," I said, "all right." I looked around at all the people coming and going, straightened myself up. "We'd better go see Genna. I think I'd like to tell her about this before she finds out some other way."

We took the subway back to Chelsea; just a few stops, but faster than walking. Holding a stainless steel pole while the subway car roared and rocked, we talked about Wayne Lewis's murder and what it could mean.

"It sort of fingers him as the double-crosser, doesn't it?" I said. "And his partner didn't like it. Which would explain why nobody called Genna yet with a new arrangement. He was busy killing Wayne."

"Or the partner was the double-crosser. They fought about it and the partner killed him."

"That could be too," I admitted. "Either way, I'll bet Genna doesn't hear from them again."

"No," Bill agreed. "Being a shakedown artist's one thing, being a killer's another. Even if the killer hasn't got the money, I don't think he'll expose himself by asking for more."

The train raced around a curve, throwing me off-balance. I grabbed the pole.

"But," I said, "what if Wayne was just the thief, with no partner, and the hijacker was somebody else sort of piggybacking on Wayne's racket? Isn't that possible?"

Bill considered that. "And he killed Wayne because Wayne knew who he was?"

"Or something like that. Bill?"

He watched me, waiting.

"The hijackers?" I said. "There had to have been at least two of them."

He nodded. "One shooting, the other to grab the envelope."

"So this could be more messy than it looks."

"I'm almost sure it is."

We rode Genna's slow elevator up to the big glass door. Brad buzzed us in and waved us to wait as he grabbed the pencil from behind his ear and scribbled down a message from the phone mashed against his other ear. He hung up the phone, slipped the pencil back behind his ear, and stuck out his hand to me.

"Hi!" he said with a smile. "I'm Brad. Sorry I didn't get a chance to meet you before. How's it going? Brad Hadley," he told Bill, offering him his hand next. Handshaking didn't stop Brad from other movement. He snatched up the phone as it rang, asked it to wait, and zipped around the desk to show us into the conference room. "Genna'll be in in a minute. How's Andrew?"

"Fine," I said.

37

The phone rang again. Brad grabbed the receiver behind me, asked it to hold a minute, pressed the other blinking button and told it he'd be right with it, replaced the receiver, and shrugged. "I'd love to talk." He grinned. "But I guess I can't. After Market Week? Maybe we can get together with Andrew?"

"Sure," I said. "Great."

"Okay," he said as the phone rang again. "See you." He ran back to his desk.

"It's past five," Bill said to me as we watched Brad's figurative dust settle. "Don't these people go home?"

"Not before Market Week," I said, as though I'd known that all my life.

Bill turned his attention to the fabric, the trimmings, and the sketches pinned to the walls. "This is what she does?"

"Uh-huh."

He surveyed the walls silently, examining each grouping, each strange combination.

"That crinkly gold stuff, up here?" he finally said. "That would look great on you. Maybe pajamas."

"It's for a man's suit," I told him haughtily, but I don't think he believed me.

I heard the quick tap and soft pad of footsteps, Genna's flats followed by John's wing tips. Genna and John, both looking harried, came toward the conference room in whispered conversation. Inside, John slid the glass door shut.

"Lydia," Genna said, with an uncertain smile. "I thought you were going to call."

"We have to talk," I answered. "Genna Jing, John Ryan, this is Bill Smith, my partner."

Bill shook Genna's hand, then John's. His smile was noncommittal. Genna returned the smile, maybe a little mechanically. John gave us both a frown.

"What's this about?" John asked. "You can't believe how wild it is around here right now. We don't have much time."

"You'll have time for this," I said bluntly. "Wayne Lewis is dead."

Genna's porcelain face drained of all color except the color that was painted on. She groped for the chair beside her, for support.

John Ryan didn't move. Finally, as though he hadn't heard, as though he were still waiting for me to say whatever it was we'd come to say, he asked, "What?"

"Someone killed him," I said. "Shot him. I don't know when or who, but they were taking the body out when we got there about an hour ago. Genna, you have to go to the police."

"No!" That was a small but quick and definitive burst of sound from Genna. She swallowed. "No," she repeated, her face still colorless, her voice soft but clear. "I can't. If this gets around in the industry it'll ruin me, Lydia. First the theft, then murder . . ." She trailed off, looking at nothing across the room. "I've worked all my life for this. And it's almost here. I can't give it up now."

"You sure as hell can't!" John put a firm hand on her shoulder, turned to me angrily. "How do you even know Wayne was really involved in this? It was just a suspicion of Genna's. She was probably wrong. He wasn't the type. And people get killed in New York all the time."

"Have the thieves called again?" I demanded.

"No," said Genna, in a shaky voice. "No, they haven't."

John looked quickly at Genna, then back to me. "So what?"

"If I were an extortionist and I hadn't gotten my fifty thousand dollars I'd call again. Unless I found out my partner had double-crossed me. If I killed him and took the money back, then I wouldn't call again."

John and Genna were both silent.

"Genna," I said, pressing, "there's a killer out there. He's got your money and he's killed for it. If you don't do everything you can to stop him, then you're responsible for whatever he does next. The next scam, the next death. Whatever he does."

Color flooded Genna's cheeks, hot, high color. "I'm not!" Her eyes flashed. "It's not my responsibility! It's not my *fault!*" She spun, yanked open the glass door, dashed past Brad to her office.

John moved slowly to the door and pulled it shut again. He turned to face us.

"This is too important to her," he said. "You can't ask her to throw it away like that."

"That's not what we're asking," I answered. "We're asking her to help find a killer."

"And throw her career away in the process."

Bill, who had said nothing since we'd come here, now said calmly, "Are you sure that would happen?"

"What?" John's voice was impatient.

"Are you sure Ms. Jing's career would collapse if this became public?"

"Of course. Her investors would disappear in a flash."

"Why would they?" I asked. "Isn't a little scandal good for business?"

"A little scandal, people jetting off to Rio with other people's wives, sure. But murder? Who's going to put money into someone involved with that?"

"No one's saying Genna was involved."

"Oh, come on, Lydia! *You're* saying it: he stole her sketches, now he's dead."

"That's not—"

"Not what you meant? Oh, really? But if you had half a million dollars to invest, don't you think you'd be looking for somewhere else to put it?"

I'd never thought about looking for a place to put half a million dollars. I said, "If Genna doesn't go to the police, this might come out anyway. Wouldn't that be worse?"

"It won't come out, because Wayne didn't steal Genna's sketches and there isn't anything to come out. If Genna gets mixed up in this it'll ruin her for nothing. By tomorrow they'll find the guy who killed Wayne, and it'll turn out to be some trick he picked up on the pier."

"And if they don't?"

"Then it will take them two days, or they'll never find him. So what?"

"Even if he was involved," I said slowly, "you don't care if they find his killer, do you?"

"No," John said bluntly. "He wasn't involved. But if he was, no, I don't care. It's not my problem. Genna's my problem. This is her time, and no one's going to screw it up for her."

My eyes traveled over the walls, the suede and the silk, the black netting and white wool. Bill was silent, waiting for me. My case, my move.

"If Wayne Lewis was involved," I said, turning back to John, "*if,* then we have information that could be the difference between the police catching his killer or not. We can't not give it to them. We have licenses to think about, John."

"Then I guess you'll do whatever you have to do," John said angrily. "Though maybe you should think about something besides your licenses. Maybe you should think about the fact that Genna's not the only one around here with a name to protect."

I felt Bill tense, but he said nothing.

"What does that mean?" I asked tightly.

"Just that private eyes who botch an easy job and then run to the cops might have a harder time finding the next job, if it gets around." He looked deliberately from me to Bill, then back. Then, as if this were just the end of a disagreeable sales meeting, he looked at his watch and said, "We'd better wrap this up. I have to be at the factory in the morning." He paused, to make sure I'd get it, then said, "In Chinatown." He slid the glass door aside. "Look," he said, "I think it would be better if you don't come back here. Just send your bill, we'll take care of it."

My face flushed hot as Genna's had. "It was Genna who hired us," I said.

John looked at me for a beat. He said, "Wait." He stalked out, down the hall, into Genna's office.

Bill leaned against the wall, hands in his pockets, his whole attitude so careless and casual that I could tell he was boiling mad.

"I'm sorry," I said.

His eyebrows went up. "What the hell for?"

"Getting you in a bad situation."

"It's what I live for." He pushed off from the wall and crossed the room to stare out the window.

I wanted to say something else to him, though I wasn't sure what it was, but John and Genna emerged from Genna's office and headed toward us. Genna's face was still pale and her makeup was new. Walking into the conference room she didn't look at John, but she was able to look me in the eye as she said, "John tells me he doesn't think there's anything else you and Mr. Smith can do for us, Lydia. I think he's probably right."

"Genna—"

"I'm grateful for everything you've done and tried to do. I'm sorry it worked out like this." She held my eyes for another second, then turned to go.

I said, "What if they call again? The thieves?"

Genna stopped but didn't turn. John said, "If they do, we'll think about it."

That was about as much nothing as I'd ever gotten from anyone, but I had no way to answer it.

"Thank you," Genna added, still without looking at us. "Seriously, thank you." She left the room.

"I hope," said John pointedly, after she was gone, "that your next case goes better than this."

He walked from the room and disappeared into Genna's office, leaving us to find our own way out. Brad, on the phone, gave us a raised-eyebrow smile, and I smiled back. No need for Andrew to hear about this.

Neither Bill nor I spoke on the ride down. Bill lit a cigarette as soon as we left the building. I watched him shake the match and throw it away.

"I'm sorry," I said again.

"Knock it off. Let's get coffee."

It was purple dusk in Manhattan. Cars stood headlight to taillight on the crosstown streets waiting for the avenue traffic to stop and give them a chance. Bill and I walked up the block to Fifth and found another of the new coffee bistros three storefronts in.

We settled, he with his espresso and me with my keemun, on tall stools at the glass counter in the window.

"This stinks," I said.

Bill didn't answer. He knew I didn't mean my tea.

"We're going to the cops," I said. I tossed my head. "The hell with John Ryan."

"What would you do if I weren't involved?"

The question was unexpected, and made me look up from my

42

tea to meet Bill's eyes. His face was completely serious; no jokes, no anger. I knew he already knew the answer to the question he was asking.

That was the only reason I told him the truth. "I wouldn't go to them," I said.

"Because if you do, Ryan will do a hatchet job on you. On us; but it would be worse for you than it would be for me."

I nodded glumly. That was true. I was much newer in the business than Bill. I didn't have repeat clients going back years, or a reputation that might be able to ride out a wave of bad talk. In Chinatown, especially, respect was critical; being young, and a woman, I already had two strikes against me there. And Ryan, through Roland Lum's factory, was connected in Chinatown.

"But if we don't go to the cops we could be in trouble," he went on. "That would be worse for me than it would for you." 'Be in trouble' is one of those phrases that only has one meaning, like 'if anything happens to me.' 'If anything happens' is a euphemism for 'if I die,' and 'be in trouble' is a P.I. euphemism for 'lose my license.'

Which to some P.I.s is the same thing.

I knew this was true, too. Young and new, I might be able to bluff my way through an investigation. Gee, officer, I didn't have any idea my client's case was related to this murder . . .

But Bill wouldn't. He'd been around too long; he'd cut too many corners, skirted the edge of trouble too often. No one would cut him any slack.

"If you went to the cops," Bill said, "it wouldn't be to spite Ryan. It would be to protect me."

I felt my cheeks flush. I looked away. "I got you into this."

"I took the job. I'm a grown-up."

"You didn't know it would mean this kind of trouble."

"No." He grinned. "But I was hoping. Listen," he said when I made an impatient noise, "let's forget that for now. Answer this: if your honor and my license weren't up for grabs, what would you do?"

I drank my tea. It was a reasonable question; I tried to think about it reasonably.

"I wouldn't go to the cops."

"Why not?"

43

"Because," I said, "because there's something else here besides what we're seeing."

He nodded. "Go on."

"They're hiding something." Until I heard myself say that I hadn't been sure I was thinking it. "They were anxious to pay up yesterday," I went on, thinking out loud, "and so nervous they hired us to handle the drop. Today I've been shot at and someone's been killed. That ought to be even scarier, but they're not nervous anymore, except about the idea that this will come out and ruin Genna's big chance. The thieves haven't called again, but no one seems to be worried about what they'll do with the sketches. Obviously there's been a change from then to now, something we don't know about."

"And what's your inclination?"

"To look into it."

"Rather than going to the police."

"Maybe not rather than. Maybe before. Just to make sure."

"Of . . . ?"

"Of whether there's any faint chance John could be right. That going to them could ruin Genna without helping anybody."

"Because you don't want to ruin her."

"No, I don't."

"Because you like her."

"Shouldn't I?" I said defensively. "Just because she's hiding something and she fired us and her boyfriend threatened us, is that any reason to dislike a person?"

"Not for one Chinese woman to dislike another."

I looked out the window and sighed. "You're right. I'm being ridiculous."

"I didn't say that."

I turned back to him. "You like her, too?"

"No," he said. "I like you."

I felt my cheeks grow hot again.

"You want to know why?" he asked.

"No."

"Okay, I'll tell you. Because you're beautiful. Wait, don't throw that," he said quickly as I hefted my teacup. "The real reason is, be-

44

cause you have two reasons not to go to the police and you were going to do it anyway. For me."

"Well, really for me," I said.

He gave me a skeptical look.

"So I wouldn't feel guilty when you lost your license and ended up on the street corner with a cup and I never put a quarter in it."

"You wouldn't put a quarter in my cup?"

"My mother needs them for the laundry. So if I look into this on my own—just a day or two—will you lie low until then?"

"No."

"Bill—"

"*We* look into it. On *our* own. That's my last offer."

"I don't want you to be messed up in this any deeper."

"You should have thought of that before you met me. Now," he said, standing, "I'll go get us a refill so we can make a plan."

He threaded his way through the crowded cafe. I watched him, his familiar, fluid walk, the easy set of his shoulders, the way his eyes covered the room as he moved through it, looking everywhere without seeming to look anywhere in particular. Deep-set eyes in a worn face, a face even I couldn't call handsome.

Even I? What's that supposed to mean, Lydia? I demanded. Why should you, as opposed to anybody else, expect to think of Bill as handsome?

Of course, there wasn't any reason, and I turned my thoughts stubbornly back to the case while I waited for my new cup of tea.

F I V E

While I thought, I stared through the window and watched the parade of people on Fifth Avenue. This far downtown, in Chelsea, Fifth Avenue isn't the glamour-and-glitz address it is up-town; but it's taken on a new identity in the past few years, a cutting-edge, creative-professions sense: architects, ad agencies, designers, photographers. Like my brother Andrew, I thought guiltily. I really had to call Andrew.

Later.

The people walking by my window were dressed for the neighborhood. I saw a lot of black, a lot of heavy boots; short, mussed-up hair on women, long flowing hair on men. A smudgily made-up young woman with hair the white-gold color of morning light leaned against a lamppost. She wore a leather jacket open to reveal a cropped, ribbed top above painted-on black pants. Smoke would come out of my mother's ears if I ever tried to leave the house looking like that, but it was the height of fashion.

"You know," I said, as Bill handed me my fresh cup of tea, "there's something we'd better put out on the table."

"You mean," he said, sliding back onto his stool, "the fact that our ex-clients may well have killed Lewis themselves?"

"So you do think it's possible?"

"Sure it is. Objectively I'd say it's likely."

"Objectively," I agreed. "But I don't think so, and you don't either. Why not?"

"You, because of the ancient mystical solidarity of Chinese womanhood. Me, because I saw her face when you told them."

I ignored his first remark, as I usually try to do when he talks about Chinese womanhood. I said, "And *his* face."

"And his," Bill agreed. "Peculiar reactions."

"I thought so, too. But why?"

"I've seen guilty people trying to fake it," Bill said. "And innocent people stunned by that kind of news. This was neither."

I nodded. I haven't seen as much as Bill, don't have as much experience to go on. But my gut feeling was the same as his.

"But it's still possible," I said, "that they killed him."

"Or one of them did."

I didn't ask the next question. But Bill answered it anyway.

"Let's wait," he said, "and see how things look." He sipped his espresso. "So? Have you decided what we're going to do?"

"How come I have to decide?" I complained. "As the considerably more experienced member of this team—in addition to being

46

considerably older, I might add—don't you have to at least advise me?"

"Nope."

"Oh." I squeezed some lemon into my tea. "Well, to start with I'd like to know more about Wayne Lewis."

"And I'd like to know what killed him."

"Three gunshots," I said. "Pow pow pow."

"From what gun?"

I clinked my cup back into my saucer. "I'm behind, aren't I? You want to know if it was the same gun that shot at me this morning."

"If it wasn't, it doesn't prove anything. If it was, it knocks the unrelated-crimes theory out of the box."

"Okay," I said. "Can you look into that while I look into Wayne?"

"Sure. There must be somebody on the Department who's still speaking to me. Or maybe I'll just call Krch and discuss it with him." He grinned.

"What is it between you and him?" I asked. "I thought you got along with most cops."

"Most cops are decent people."

"Not Krch?"

"I don't know," he said. "Maybe he was once. Maybe he still is." He lit a cigarette, toyed with the burnt-out match. "The case we met on, he framed a kid in a homicide. He was sure the kid had done it but he couldn't prove it, so he set him up. The kid was a trash-talking jerk, but he wasn't a killer. I worked for the kid's lawyer. We had a face-off, the kid was released and Krch was transferred. He wasn't busted back to patrol, but he'll never make Second Grade."

"You were able to prove Krch had set the kid up?" I asked.

"No," Bill said. "I framed him."

Bill went back to his apartment, which is also his office, to make phone calls. My plan was to head off to Wayne Lewis's old neighborhood, to see what I could see, but first I needed to call my mother.

My mother and I have a deal. I live at home, in the Chinatown apartment where Andrew, Tim, and I were born. Ted and Elliot were

47

born in Hong Kong while our parents waited to come here, which gives them some sort of special status in my mother's eyes, though I've never been sure why. My mother's allowed not to admit that I live there because she needs help carrying groceries up the four flights of stairs and changing light bulbs and washing windows. Until she's ready to move in with Ted's family in Flushing, someone needs to keep an eye on her. We've proposed the move, my brothers and I. It'll take her a few years to get used to the idea. Then one day she'll announce, as though she'd just thought of it, "Chinatown is so crowded now, it's hard for you children to come visit me. I'll move to Flushing. Ted and Ling-an can fix up the basement. Make what they call a mother-in-law apartment," she'll add, nodding sagely, to show her children that there are certain things you need to know to get along in America, and she knows them.

Meanwhile, while she adjusts to the idea, Ma gets to claim I'm still at home only because I can't make a decent living at my unsuitable profession.

For my part of the deal, I get to keep whatever hours I need to keep, and I have a right to not answer any of her questions I don't want to answer.

As a Chinese mother, though, she has the eternal, inalienable right to keep asking them.

I went to the pay phone by the cafe's front door and dialed home. I stared out the window and idly watched the pedestrians weaving the fabric of the evening, crossing in front and behind, warp and weft, interlocking, becoming parts of each other's lives, permanently but in ways they would never know about.

"Hi, Ma," I said when my mother answered the phone. With my mother, of course, I spoke Chinese. "Anything up?"

"Up," she grumbled. "What could be up? The sky, the clouds? The sun was up, but it's down now. It will be dinnertime soon."

"I know," I said. "I won't be home for dinner, that's why I'm calling. I'll be a while, but is there anything I should pick up?"

"No," she said. "Nothing I need. Unless you want oranges, or water spinach with the fish tomorrow."

That meant: buy oranges and water spinach.

"The stands will be closed by the time I get downtown," I said.

Outside the window, a bus swooped down, scooped up some passengers, and took off again. "I'll go out in the morning."

"All right." Her voice hinted that if she died before morning from lack of water spinach, the whole world would know why. "But call your brother."

"Which brother, Ma?" I asked, thinking, Come on, Lydia, if you read your mother's mind like a good Chinese daughter you'd *know*. Which is what my mother thinks, too.

"An Zhong."

Oh. Andrew.

"He's anxious to speak to you, Ling Wan-ju. He called here and he called your office, in case you were working."

I bit my lip to keep from saying, I *am* working, Ma. "Did he say what he wanted?"

"He wanted to speak to you," she said, sounding amazed that I needed any more than that before I'd jump to fulfill an elder brother's wish.

"Okay," I said. "Listen, Ma, I may be late tonight, so . . ."

I stopped. Outside the window, the woman in the cropped top pushed herself off her lamppost to grab the arm of a man who had just rounded the corner. He was startled, then seemed to relax as he recognized her, though he didn't look pleased. She murmured something to him, then waited to see how he would react.

She was familiar to me somehow.

He was John Ryan.

He glanced around him, then at his watch. He took her arm and they hurried down the street together.

"Ling Wan-ju?" My mother's voice jumped in my ear. I'd almost forgotten her. "What were you trying to say?"

"I've got to go, Ma," I said. "Don't wait up. I'll call An Zhong," I added quickly, without saying, Someday.

I hung up and scurried out, catching sight of John and the woman waiting for the light at the next corner. I stayed about half a block behind them, threading through the moving pattern of the night. I was thinking, I knew it, John. I knew you had something to hide.

They went two blocks, then headed west another two, not seem-

49

ing to say much as they strode along together. In the middle of the next block, they ducked into a club called Donna's.

I knew about Donna's, though I'd never been there. You see the name in the paper, on that page in the Sunday *Times* where they tell you the coolest newest thing going on. A lot of the time it's going on at Donna's, and it's fashion people, models and designers and, I supposed now, outside men and show producers, who are doing it.

John had nodded to the wide, unsmiling doorman, who seemed to know him. The doorman had inclined his polished bald head and pulled open the door, and John and his cropped-top friend had disappeared inside. I wondered how I, your basic nobody, unknown to any doorman anywhere on earth, was going to get in. Well, Lydia, I suggested, the truth never hurts.

But first, a little quick change.

Not that there was much I could change. I stepped into a doorway up the block, leaned over and ran my fingers through my hair, trying to disturb its normal stick-straight, blunt-edged look as much as possible. I felt my gun in its waist clip poke me in the ribs when I did that. Maybe I should keep lipstick in a holster, too, for occasions like these. Hair thoroughly mussed, I unzipped my leather jacket, unbuttoned my shirt one button past where decency would suggest, and made the collars of both stand up. Then I put on my sunglasses and marched forward.

"Herro," I said to the doorman in a breathy, Chinese-accented voice. "Mr. John Lyan, is he here yet? I am Chin Ling Wan-ju." That was the part where the truth came in.

"Mr. Ryan's here." The doorman said suspiciously, "Who did you say you were?"

"Chin Ling Wan-ju. From Hangchow." I smiled so he'd know I wasn't offended at not being recognized. "He is with the beautiful blonde American woman? She is here also?"

"Andi Shechter? Yes, she's here."

Andi Shechter. That's why she was familiar. The you-can't-touch-this model who was going to wear Genna's crinkly gold dress.

"Good," I said to the doorman, trying to sound much relieved at this news. "I may enter? I am not too late?"

"Too late?"

"My plane, so late from Bali, I almost missed connection at Milan. Then circling your Kennedy one hour before landing! Mr. Lyan asked to meet him here at six. I am late, afraid he will be gone."

"No, they just got here."

"Oh, so lucky! Thank you so much, I will light incense for you, for your plane never to be late." I smiled and stepped around him as he moved, scowling slightly, aside. He opened the door almost automatically. I felt him watch me for a few seconds, then turn back to the street and let the door close.

Now I was inside Donna's, and a smoky dark place it was, too. I thought everyone except Bill had given up smoking, but I could see I was wrong. Very thin young women stood at the bar or sat on big soft armchairs holding cigarettes in one hand and glasses of clear sparkly water in the other. Some of the men were smoking too, though not as many. The music was the Rolling Stones, loud enough to cordon off the conversation at the next table but not loud enough to pound.

I looked around for Ryan and Andi Shechter. I thought I spotted her, but when I moved a few steps closer, it turned out to be another blonde woman in a cropped top and tight pants. I scanned the room again, and finally there they were, beyond the bar, deep in conversation beside a low table.

Well, Lydia, I thought, I'll bet this is one place where you can order a Perrier and no one will think you're a wimp. So I sidled up to the bar and ordered, positioning myself on a bar stool from which I could see John Ryan and Andi Shechter but where they weren't likely to spot me.

The bar stool next to me had been empty when I sat down but it didn't stay that way. Wavy dark hair, teak-wood tan, collarless white shirt buttoned to the neck, no tie, linen jacket: very au courant, totally up to the minute, and all he could think of to say was, "You're new here, aren't you?"

What I thought of to say was, *Oh, please,* but it occurred to me that I'd be even less likely to be spotted if I were in conversation with someone than if I were moping at the bar by myself.

I gave him an impersonal smile. "Yes, this is my first time here."

"Who're you with?"

Boy, I thought, they don't waste time around here, do they? I shrugged.

"Well," he said, "if you don't have anyone yet, I'm always looking for a new face."

I sipped my drink to keep from laughing out loud.

Then he handed me a business card.

Oh, Lydia, you really are an idiot, I told myself, as I read, "Everest Models, The Peak of Perfection."

"Ed Everest," he said, offering me his hand. His handshake was limp, so I made mine that way, too. Maybe that's how they do it in this business. "It's a small agency, only top-quality girls. On the way up. You're a little short," he said, looking me over the way you would something you were about to buy, "but I handle a lot of exotics, I could probably do something with you. You have a different look, could be good. What's your name, sweetheart?"

"Mishika Yamamoto," I told him.

"Mishika," he said, nodding approvingly. "That's good. We'll drop the rest. What've you done? Any runway?"

I shook my head, trying hard to think of modeling jargon I could use in this ridiculous conversation.

"Doesn't matter," Everest said. "I can teach you to walk. I can teach you the outfits, anything you need. You have a great head." He reached out, traced a finger lightly through my hair from my brow to the back of my skull, lingering on the bluntness of the hair at the nape of my neck.

"Thank you," I said, shrugging my shoulders, shifting in my seat.

Everest smiled and watched me move. "A great head," he repeated. "Any tattoos?"

"No," I said.

"Too bad. That's hot these days, especially on the Oriental girls. Well, we can always do temporaries if we need them. Why don't you bring your book by tomorrow? You have a book? Doesn't matter, I probably wouldn't use it anyway. Photographer we use, he's a brilliant guy, goes a little further than most of these wusses, gets an edge. I like my girls to have an edge. You, Mishika, you have an edge. I can see it."

I didn't say anything, but Ed Everest smiled again, as though he'd gotten the answer he wanted. "Call tomorrow," he said. "I have a full plate but tell my girl that Ed said he wants to see you." He was peering deeply into my eyes, totally focused on Mishika and her modeling future. Then his gaze was suddenly distracted, catching a glimpse of someone across the room. Probably it was someone more important than I. Well, who wasn't?

Ed Everest left his bar stool, squeezing my shoulder, saying, "Great, sweetheart. Mishika. Great. Looking forward," and wormed his way through the crowd to find another face.

Well, I thought as I sipped my drink. Well. That's two people already today who want me to model. My mother would be so pleased.

The bar stool next to me, so recently emptied of Ed Everest, now took on another occupant, a black-haired, red-lipped young woman in a cropped top and tight pants. Is this a uniform, I wondered, or is it just that no one but a model is willing to take the risk of showing that space above the waist where most of us have at least a tiny little bulge of flesh?

The red-lipped woman lit a cigarette and cocked her empty glass at the bartender. He brought her another Perrier. Holding the cigarette not at her fingertips but down lower, between her knuckles, she took a drag, sipped her drink, and, without looking at me said in a raspy voice, "You're new."

I already knew that, I wanted to say, Ed Everest told me. But instead I smiled and said, "Yes. Mishika."

"Mishika," she repeated. "Yeah, okay. I'm Francie. Listen, Mishika. I don't know what you know, but you probably don't know much because you're not dressed right and you're not made up right and you need some work on your hair. Okay? So you're new." She drank some Perrier, leaving a voluptuous red stain on the glass. "What you need to know is, stay away from Ed Everest."

"He was just here," I said.

"What the hell do you think I'm telling you for?" She waved her cigarette impatiently. "He said he could help you, right? Said your look is different but he could do a lot with it, right? Tell me, Mishika, you see anyone else rushing over here to do you a favor and make you famous?"

I had to admit that I didn't.

"No one will." Francie sucked on her cigarette. "It doesn't work like that. Anyone who tells you it does is lying. Ed's clients," she said, turning her eyes on me for the first time. They were an intense, luminous green, a contact lens green. "They're not so interested in how you look *in* the clothes."

"Why are you telling me this?" I asked, still not completely sure what she was telling me.

"You don't believe me? You think I'm trying to screw up your career or something? You think I'm trying to keep him for myself?" She gave a short, nasty laugh. "Ed doesn't want me. He doesn't specialize in white girls."

She swigged down the last of her Perrier and climbed off the stool. "Suit yourself. Most girls don't want to hear it. But don't say I didn't try."

She pushed through the crowd. It parted to let her pass and closed up seamlessly after her.

I stared after her thoughtfully. Then I turned my attention back to John Ryan and Andi Shechter. They were still alone together, still talking, but Ryan's gestures, the tilt of his head and set of his shoulders, had taken on a tinge of impatience. The bar stool next to me stayed empty, so I was able to sip my Perrier and watch.

The music had changed from the Stones to 2 Live Crew, yesterday's bad boys blending into today's. It was louder now, less melody, more beat. Andi Shechter pressed out one cigarette and lit another. Her lips seemed tinged with a hard smile; she appeared to be enjoying herself.

Ryan ran his hand through his hair. He looked around wordlessly. Pulling a moneyclipped thickness from his pocket, he seemed to ask a question and she seemed to answer. He seemed to be unhappy with the answer. He said one more thing as he peeled some bills, folded them over, and handed them to her. He stood and walked away without looking back.

Hmm, I thought. Not quite what I expected.

I picked up my Perrier and headed over.

Donna's was more crowded now, a crush of young, leggy, beautiful bodies. The music had changed again, to the weird, dreamy harmonies of a rising indie group called Saturnine. I threaded my twisty way through the room with a lot of bumps and "excuse me's," until I finally broke free from the tangle of people to emerge into the area where Andi Shechter sat. The two chairs across the low coffee table from her were occupied, but the one beside her was still empty. I settled myself gingerly in it and smiled tentatively at her.

"Hi," I said. "Is this okay?"

She looked at me, surprised, as though she hadn't noticed me sitting down. She shrugged.

"Aren't you Andi Shechter?" I asked.

Her stare was blank, a little unfocused. She said, "Yeah."

"I've seen your work. I really like it," I said, hoping that was how models talked to each other.

She smiled, a different, surprised little smile, one that softened her face. The softness made her look startlingly young. Maybe that was why it faded so fast, so she could go back to looking like a grown-up. "Thanks," she murmured.

"I'm Mishika," I said. "I'm new."

Her smile came back, but this time it wasn't soft. It was the hard-edged one she'd smiled at John. She pulled on her cigarette. "I know."

"Everybody seems to," I sighed. "It's my clothes, right? And my haircut?"

"Don't worry, honey, you'll catch on." She spoke idly, not particularly interested in me or my problems.

"That man you were talking to," I asked tentatively, "was that John Ryan? Who works with Genna Jing?"

She looked directly at me for the first time. "Yeah. That was him. Why?"

"I'd love to work for her," I said wistfully. "I'd love to wear her stuff. Do you know if they have all their girls for their show already?"

Andi Shechter stared for a moment, then laughed. "Go for it, honey. Get your agent to call. Maybe you'll get a gig. John's into Oriental girls these days."

I was trying to decide how model-wannabe Mishika Yamamoto would answer that when another thin pale woman in a cropped top and tight pants—she must not be new—burst through the crowd abruptly. It was Francie, I realized, formerly of the bar stool next to mine. She threw a quick, dismissive glance at me, then crouched beside Andi Shechter's chair. She asked Andi urgently, "Did you hear what happened?"

The pounding of the music and the loud edginess of the talk and laughter around us made her have to almost shout, but this was obviously the start of a private conversation. So Mishika drank her Perrier, shifted politely in her seat to face away from them, let her eyes search the room, and listened very hard.

"What do you mean?" Andi almost-shouted back.

"What happened," Francie repeated. "Did you hear? Wayne's dead."

"*What?*"

I chanced a quick look.

Andi's eyes were wide. She leaned in closer. "What the hell are you talking about?"

"Shot," Francie said. "This afternoon."

"Oh, shit!" Andi said. "Oh, *shit!*" She took a long drag on her cigarette, then stamped it out hard in the ashtray. "What the hell are we supposed to do now?"

"We have a choice?"

Andi stared, then shook her head. "Oh, what, the Peak of Perversion? Fuck Ed, I'm not going to Ed."

"Where are you going to go, then?"

"Someplace else. I'm not going to Ed."

"Yeah," said Francie. "Whatever. If you think of something better, let me know." She stood, looked at Andi, then plunged back into the crowd.

"Shit!" Andi said, to no one. The smoke from her cigarette curled toward the ceiling. She stayed like that for a few moments, unmoving. Then, suddenly, she jerked to her feet, yanked her purse from the chair, sliced through the crowd, and was gone.

Six

I jumped up and tried to follow, but I had more trouble with the crowd than she did. I got tangled up with a grinning man who seemed to think our mutual misunderstanding about who was stepping left and who was stepping right was pretty funny. Almost yelping with frustration, I finally broke free and made it outside. I looked up and down the street but didn't see Andi. I turned to the doorman, who was scowling professionally.

"Excuse me, please," I said, retrieving the Chinese accent. "Miss Andi Shechter, do you see where she goes? So foolish, the address she gave to meet her I have lost."

Without breaking the scowl, he nodded toward Eighth Avenue. I hurried down the block, but it didn't do me any good. By the time I reached the corner, she was gone—maybe north, maybe west, maybe into a cab and far away.

I stood on the sidewalk, just breathing. The cool spring air tasted as good as a glass of ice water on a summer day. A good long walk, that's what I needed, to clear the smoke from my lungs and my brain. For the second time that day I headed down from Chelsea to the Village, toward Wayne Lewis's place.

After a few calming blocks of Eighth Avenue traffic, I found a pay phone and called the answering machine at my office. "Three messages," it said, in the nasal electronic voice that always sounds like it's scolding me. I played them back.

The first was from Andrew. So was the second. "Lydia, *call* me! What's the matter with you?"

What's the matter, indeed. I listened to the third.

"Miss Chin, this is Eleanor Talmadge Ryan." The voice was an older woman's, firm and clipped. "Please call me at your earliest convenience." Then came the number. Then came the hang-up click.

Ryan, I thought. My goodness. I spent my last quarter doing as told.

I introduced myself to the voice that answered the phone. That voice went away and got another one, and I introduced myself again.

"Miss Chin," the firm and clipped tones pronounced. "Thank you very much for calling. I'd like to see you."

"Ms. Ryan," I said innocently, "I'm afraid we haven't met . . . ?"

"You know my son John," she said, in a voice that suggested that disingenuousness might not be the way to go with this one. "And it's *Mrs.* Ryan, if you don't mind." I got the feeling that it was *Mrs.* Ryan whether I minded or not.

"Yes," I said. "I know John."

"Of course. Now, can you come up?"

"Tonight?"

"I would appreciate it. Unless you have plans?"

Which I would change if I knew what was good for me, the subtext went.

Luckily I hadn't had any plans that sounded more interesting than this.

"All right," I said. "Give me time to make a call. To change my plans." See, lady, Lydia Chin can play this game, too. "Where shall I come?"

"To my home." She gave me an Upper East Side address, I promised her I'd be there in half an hour, and we hung up.

I ran into the deli on the corner, got a cup of tea and more quarters, and called Bill.

"Hi," I said, swallowing a mouthful of tea when he answered the phone. "I smell just like you."

"Manly?" He sounded impressed.

"No, of stale tobacco. Guess who called me?"

"Your brother Andrew."

Taken aback, I said, "How do you know that?"

"Because he called me, too. He wants to talk to us. He says he has something to tell us."

"I'll bet he does. Whatever it is I don't want to hear it, because I know what it is. He's going to yell at me. If you're there he'll yell at you, too."

58

"If he yells in Chinese I won't care."

"I'll translate, so you'll have to. Anyway, forget him; I'll talk to him later. No, this was better. John Ryan's mother."

"No kidding."

"Ummhmm," I said through my tea.

"How did she get to you? And what are you eating?"

"I'm drinking tea. And I don't know. But she knows I know John, and she wants to see me. Now."

"Are you going?"

"Are you serious? But first I wanted tell you what else happened. And to find out what you found out."

"I found out nothing. Mike's going to call me back on the guns. Nothing else interesting's turned up yet, either."

"That's because you were in the wrong place. Where I was, things were *very* interesting." Finishing my tea, I told him about John and Andi, Andi and Francie, Ed and Francie and me. I had to put three more quarters in the phone to get through it all. "They sounded upset that Wayne was dead, Andi and Francie," I said at the end. "But I'm not sure it was because they liked him. Andi didn't even ask Francie what had happened, who had killed him."

"Do you—" he started, but an electronic voice broke in, demanding more quarters.

"Give me your number, I'll call you back," Bill said.

"No, ask me later," I said. "I have to go anyway. I'll call you."

He barely had time to say, "Okay," before the telephone, in a huff, cut us off.

As I hailed a cab on Eighth Avenue it occurred to me to wonder whether the rude phone and my disapproving answering machine might be cousins.

The Ryan homestead was in a blocky red-brick building on York Avenue, the eastest of the Upper East Side. The building was of the age that's always vaguely referred to in New York as "prewar." A uniformed doorman opened a glass door for me into a softly lit lobby. A half-dozen polished antique chairs and two end tables stood very carefully in their places on the marble floor, as if they'd lose their jobs if they got out of line.

Behind a counter a concierge waited to hear what I had to say.

"Mrs. Ryan, please." I emphasized the *Mrs.* maybe a little more than I absolutely had to. "I'm Lydia Chin."

"Mrs. Ryan's already called down," the concierge told me, his face a polite blank. "East elevators."

At the east elevators another man in a uniform turned a key so the elevator would go, and sent me up.

The lobby on the twenty-third floor was carpeted, softly lit, and tiny. Only three doors opened off it. In a building this big, that told me something about the apartments.

I saw that what it told me was true, when the door to 23A was opened by a square-shouldered, gray-haired woman in a wool skirt and low-heeled shoes. Behind her, the foyer gave way through an arch to the living room. Spindly wooden chairs and velvety sofas clustered on an acre of white wool. Above the huge marble fireplace an oil portrait of a balding man with a nice smile and a proudly handsome woman with icy blue eyes watched everything that went on, including my entrance. Beyond them, at the end of the room, spread a stunning view of the East River.

"Miss Chin?" the square-shouldered woman said. "If you'll follow me, please. Mrs. Ryan is expecting you."

We walked down a thickly carpeted hallway hung with framed prints of fruit and flowers, past a series of rooms whose open doorways I peeked into but whose uses I couldn't keep up with. The floors that weren't carpet were polished dark wood, parqueted in intricate patterns. I recognized the formal dining room by the long table and sparkling chandelier, and the study by its leather chairs and its shelves of leather-bound books, although I thought the oil portrait of two golden retrievers broke the serious mood a little.

At the end of our walking tour I was ushered into an enclosed terrace, glassed on three sides. From it the lights across the river glowed close and clear. Traffic on the highway, which I knew was a tangled snarl of honking horns and screeching brakes when you were in it, from here flowed in a silent, serene ballet of white and red lights. The bridges arched over the river, barges floated under the bridges, and everything was peaceful, purposeful, and under control.

This glassed-in terrace, I thought to myself as my guide left, would have made a nice winter garden, a conservatory.

But there wasn't a single thing growing in it.

"Miss Chin." A voice leapt into the room from behind me. It announced my name as though it were telling me—and would tell me only once—something I didn't know. "Sit down," it instructed.

I turned around, in time to watch a tall, unsmiling woman stride through the doorway onto the terrace and seat herself on a heavy, expensive-looking wood garden chair. I recognized her from the portrait over the fireplace, though her short, silk-white hair had been darker then.

She folded her hands and faced me, obviously expecting something. Her icy blue cashmere sweater and slacks were too much like her eyes for coincidence. In the wave of her hair and the blue of those eyes, I saw John Ryan.

She watched me with an air of controlled impatience. I wasn't sure what she was waiting for, but the last order she'd given was for me to sit down, so I did. The chairs, I found, were as solid as a boulder and about as comfortable. The back of mine was too deep and the arms too wide apart for someone my size. I had two choices: slouch or perch.

I perched.

The woman's face resolved from expectation to satisfaction. That order carried out, she was ready to continue. "I'm Eleanor Talmadge Ryan," she stated, as though for the record. "I want to speak to you about my son John, and Genna Jing."

"I'm pleased to meet you, Mrs. Ryan," I said, although the phrase suddenly rang more frivolously time-wasting than it ever had before. "But I'm not sure what I can do for you. I don't know John or Genna very well. We only met yesterday."

"You're a private investigator they hired," she said bluntly. "I want to know why."

Boy, I thought. If this woman treats money the way she treats words, no wonder she's rich.

"I'm sorry," I said. "I'm not sure how you know that, but I can't tell you anything beyond it."

"Of course you can. What you're saying is that you won't. How I know is not your business, but so that you'll appreciate how serious I am I'll tell you that I pay to be kept up-to-date on my son's activities."

I swallowed to keep my jaw from dropping. "You pay people to spy on John?"

"I am John's mother, Miss Chin."

Well, yes, I thought. But.

However, relations between mother and son were clearly not the subject under discussion, and I wasn't anxious to be told something else wasn't my business.

"Have you asked John about this?" I was pretty sure she hadn't, but I was interested in hearing her answer.

"Don't be coy, Miss Chin," she said coldly. "If I'd wanted to speak to John I would have called him here."

Called, I thought. Summoned. Commanded. Required the presence of. Hi mom, I'm home.

I said, "It was actually Genna who hired me, Mrs. Ryan."

"Genna Jing," Mrs. Ryan said, articulating carefully, as though she didn't want me to miss any of this, "is a woman with whom I would prefer my son not be associated. I am willing to pay rather more than you might expect for anything which will help separate them."

"Excuse me?" I didn't exactly stammer, but I didn't quite sound like the queen of cool, either.

"My son," she said, "is a wastrel and a dreamer. He understands the value of very little. He is in some ways like his father, but for all his faults, my husband never forgot who he was or where he belonged." She smoothed her perfectly smooth slacks and continued. "John is my only child. I have largely written him off." She said this as if it were just one of the many choices available to mothers concerning their children, like buying him a new suit or sending him to college.

"However," she went on, "his children will be my grandchildren. I have hopes for them. Children can be taught, perhaps schooled with a firmer hand than John was; that was my mistake, I believe." She frowned, as though trying to understand where she'd gone wrong in a recipe and why her cake had fallen.

"And you would prefer," I said, not quite able to believe what I was hearing, needing to test it out, "that John's children not be Genna Jing's?"

"I have nothing personally against the young woman. I've never even met her. But surely you can see how unsuitable a match like that would be."

"No," I said, "I really can't."

"Oh, please don't be deliberately obtuse, Miss Chin. My son and Genna Jing are from completely different backgrounds. They cannot possibly have anything in common."

"Don't you think that's up to John and Genna?"

"I absolutely do not. An immigrants' child, raised among you people, and John—they would find out for themselves in a matter of months how little they share."

"Then maybe you should let them do that," I said hotly. "And for your information," I added, remembering what Andrew had told me, "Genna's from a fancy suburb of Chicago. Oak Park. She went to boarding school and a private college. And she's got her own business."

What are you doing, Lydia? I demanded, furious with myself. *Those things aren't the point anyway.*

"A business," Mrs. Ryan continued, acknowledging my anger in no way whatsoever, "which, without adequate capitalization, will never survive. I believe that's what Genna Jing is after from my son."

I pulled in hard on myself, trying to match her cold control. "His money?"

"Would it be the first time a woman made love to a man for money? Many women make a profession of it."

"Mrs. Ryan—!" So much for control.

"I really don't care to hear your comments, Miss Chin." She backhanded the air in front of her as though she were shooing something away. "My son, for his part, is no doubt attracted to the glamour he believes he's found in the circles in which Genna Jing travels. John has never understood the difference between true elegance and cheap glitter."

Oh, but you're wrong, I said to her inside my head, seeing Genna's face, the straight line of her back, her small, well-kept hands.

I think John understands true elegance very well.

Mrs. Ryan said, "I'll give you a thousand dollars to tell me why you were hired."

My eyes widened before I could stop them. That was more than I'd gotten for being hired.

"No, thank you," I said, trying to sound as cool as if I were turning down a cup of tea.

"Five thousand, then. This is not a negotiation. Dealing with you is worth five thousand dollars to me. Beyond that it's easier to see if I can get the information elsewhere. Your partner, for example. He may have expenses you don't have and might welcome some extra cash. But consider this: if someone is going to sell me this information for five thousand dollars, why should it not be you?"

"Mrs. Ryan," I said, trying to be professional and keep the fury out of my voice, "you may be able to buy this information, but not from me. And not from Bill. Our reputations rest on keeping our clients' business private. It would be extremely shortsighted of us to take this offer."

"Is that so?" she said thoughtfully. "Well then, I'll amend it. For five thousand dollars I'll buy the information from you and not disclose where it came from. If I'm forced to go elsewhere for it, I'll let it be known to my son that you were here, and it came from you."

She sat facing me, waiting for my answer, her face expressionless. What she'd just said to me—the threat she'd made—was cruel, but she didn't seem to be taking any joy in it. Nor did she seem to have said it reluctantly, as if she were forced by circumstances to be meaner than she'd like to be. It was just a tactic, a way to apply pressure to increase her odds.

I could have sworn that an icy breeze had gusted through the glassed-in terrace, but the terrace was covered and controlled, and no wind had caused the chill I felt.

"Mrs. Ryan," I said, standing, "I'm sorry I can't help you." I turned to walk from the room.

"Sit down," she ordered me.

I turned again to face her. "No."

Then I left, walking as soundlessly down the carpeted hallway as I had come. Well, Lydia, I thought, between mother and son you might be looking for a new career. But at least you've had the satisfaction of seeing something very few people probably get to see: the expression on Mrs. Ryan's face when someone tells her "no."

SEVEN

I called Bill from the closest phone booth I could find.

"How was she?" he asked. I pressed the phone to my ear to block out the whoosh and honk of traffic.

"I hate her," I barked. "She's rich, mean, and nasty. She thinks she owns everybody. If I'd stayed another minute she would have called me a Dragon Lady."

"What an opportunity. Why'd you leave?"

"So I wouldn't lose my temper. I almost told her my ancestor Genghis Khan had sent me to collect white slaves and ship them back to China, and she was going to be first."

"Genghis Chin," he said. "Why did she call you?" His voice was calm and familiar. I took a breath and tried to get my anger under control.

"She wanted to know why John and Genna hired us," I told him.

"And she didn't ask John because . . . ?"

"Because she thinks he'll lie to her."

"To his own mother?" Bill sounded shocked. "I'll bet you never lie to your mother."

"It wouldn't get me anywhere. She offered us five thousand dollars."

"Jesus Christ. For what?"

"The answer."

"I hope you took it."

"I wouldn't touch it. She'll be calling you."

65

"I'll endeavor to give satisfaction. Did she say why she cares so much?"

"She thinks Genna's after John's money. Now that Genna's got John in her evil clutches she's afraid there'll be hordes of slanty-eyed children calling her 'grandma.' She's desperate for something to stop that."

"She told you that?"

"Oh, what, you think I'm overreacting? Putting words in her mouth?" I demanded.

"No, I didn't say that."

"Well, I'm not! She said she didn't want one of 'you people' quote unquote to be the mother of her grandchildren."

"Ah: family values."

"Stop it! You just don't get it, do you?" I stomped my foot in angry frustration, twice as frustrated that Bill couldn't even see me do it.

"Lydia?" His voice was tentative. "Are you okay?"

"No, I'm not okay! Why should I be okay? A woman who spends more at the hairdresser in a month than my mother ever made in a year just told me I'm not good enough for her son—"

"Not you. Genna."

"It's the same thing! She probably wouldn't even be able to tell us apart. Because, you know, we do all look alike."

"Not to me."

I stopped, rubbed my forehead, and sagged against the side wall of the phone enclosure. "I know," I sighed. "I'm sorry. It's not your fault. It's just . . . I don't know. You act as if this weren't a big deal. Like I should just get over it and make jokes about it. You have no idea how it feels!"

"No," he said quietly. "I suppose I don't. But I didn't mean to make it worse."

"I know," I said again.

The traffic light changed; cars began to slide by. Nobody crashed into anybody else.

"Bill?" I said. "Let's just talk about business for a while, okay?"

"Okay. Tell me this: How did she know who you were?"

I took a breath and prepared to talk about business. "I don't know. She says she has ways."

"Winning ones, I'm sure."

"Oh, right. Like blackmail." I told him about Mrs. Ryan's closing threat.

"That's not blackmail," Bill said. "It's extortion."

"Don't get technical with me! It's a cold-blooded dirty strong-arm shakedown. I didn't like it from John, and I hate it from his ice-queen mother!" I stopped ranting for a moment. "She explains a lot about John, doesn't she?"

"Does she make you like him better?"

"No. But I can see why maybe he can't help himself. Family values," I said.

"Well," Bill said, "I don't think it's a threat to worry about. Whoever told her who you were obviously doesn't know why we were hired, or they'd have told her that, too. Where else is she going to get that information, except from me, John, Genna, or Andrew?"

"Andrew?" I hadn't thought of that, but of course it was true: Andrew did know why we'd been hired. "He'd never—"

"Not if he knew he wasn't supposed to. But someone will have to tell him that. That means someone will have to call him."

"What's it to you?" I bristled.

"Not a thing," he said. "But if you don't call him, you won't be there when he and I meet for a drink."

"You're meeting Andrew?" The conversation's sudden change of direction threw me off. I wasn't sure what to make of this.

"Well, none of your other brothers speak to me. He called me and said he's got something important to tell us and you won't return his calls."

"He just wants to yell at me. If you meet him alone he'll yell at you."

"That's not what it sounded like. Anyway I'll take that chance. I'm meeting him in the Village, at a place called David Kim's."

"You have no right," I told him, "to be more tolerant of my brothers than I am."

"I'm not. But somebody had to call the poor guy."

"Don't lecture me," I said, annoyed that he'd said that and annoyed that he was right. "I'm calling him right now."

I hung up, fished out another quarter, and called Andrew.

Tony D'Angelo answered the phone. In conversations with my mother, for the last six years Tony has been referred to by me and my brothers as Andrew's roommate.

Tony pounced on me as soon as I said hi. "Oh ho!" he said. "It's Little Sister, in Big Trouble. Boy, have you got the Emperor in a snit. You want to talk to him, finally?"

"Is he really mad, Tony?"

"Oh, no. He's not mad, Lydia. He's just making my life a total misery because it's Tuesday. I banished him to the darkroom and told him not to emerge until he could be civil. That was hours ago. He hasn't been seen since."

"Well, I don't want to interrupt him if he's working . . ."

"Honey, he's only working because he's not fit company for man nor beast. Of which you are the cause. Speak to him."

Before I could say anything, Tony put me on hold. I waited, my blood racing with leftover anger, plus impatience and guilt. The guilt made me more angry. Who was Andrew to make me feel guilty? Just because he was my favorite brother, that didn't give him the right to tell me what to do with my life. I'm working at the career I chose, the career I love. It gives me satisfaction and variety and excitement and who asked Andrew anyway? Danger's a part of it sometimes, but that's my choice. If I don't have any problem with that, my brothers shouldn't either. Or my mother. Or anybody else who thinks it's their job to take care of me and look after me and protect me, when actually—

"He's not here," Tony announced.

"Oh." I deflated.

"He left me a note. He went to see your partner. He's meeting him at David Kim's, on Bank Street."

"I know where that is. Thanks, Tony."

"Lydia? Are you okay? I heard what happened this morning."

"I'm fine, Tony."

"Good. Be careful, okay?"

"Yes," I said, resigned. "I will."

I took the subway, which Mrs. Eleanor Talmadge Ryan probably didn't even know stopped four blocks from her house. I fumed downtown and across town and came out on Fourteenth Street, on the West Side.

The night had turned chilly, as early spring nights often do, just to remind you to be grateful that they aren't winter nights. Even in the chill, people who'd come out earlier in the evening were reluctant now to leave their stoops and street corners and domino games to go back to the apartments they'd been cooped up in all winter. Skateboarders slalomed down the sidewalk between young lovers with their arms around each other and groups of middle-aged men in animated conversation. I skittered to the side to avoid a child charging by on a tricycle, and then to avoid the older brother chasing her.

Older brothers, I thought. Hmmph.

Below Fourteenth Street I turned off of Eighth Avenue onto the quieter streets of the Village, and went over in my mind my conversation with Mrs. Ryan. When I'd recounted it to Bill I'd gotten the nagging feeling that something wasn't right. I wasn't sure what was bothering me: something she'd said. The way she'd said something. The way she'd looked at me. Something about that conversation was setting off a little bell in my head.

I try to listen to those little bells when I get them. That's P.I. instinct, and that's how it develops: by letting your hunches float to the surface, not squashing them just because they're not logical or rational. Hunches aren't based on anything mystical or weird; they're based on experience, just not always consciously. They're sometimes wrong, but they're always, I've found, worth exploring.

However, sometimes listening to those little bells can keep you from hearing the clanging alarm being set off by the situation you're in right now.

A smashing blow from behind to the side of my head sent me staggering against a wall of rough bricks. Pain and confusion clouded my sight, but I spun myself around to face where the blow had come from. When something moved, I ducked, grabbed at it, pushed it away. That turned out to be right: the thing was a leg, lifted to throw a kick. When I pushed, the guy attached to it lost his balance and thumped to the concrete.

He was dressed all in black, his face hidden by a soft, featureless ninja mask. He rolled smoothly to his feet as I steadied myself on mine. I tried to break away from the trap I was in, backed against the wall, but he stepped in sharply and threw a punch at my head. I blocked it, front-kicked his kneecap, and shot the heel of my palm into his masked face. His head snapped backward. I tried another punch, but he yanked my arm forward as he stepped to the side. Throwing his hip into me, he flipped me as neatly to the pavement as if this were Sensei Chung's Saturday morning black belt class.

I rolled to duck the kick I knew was coming next. It came; then was my chance, while he was off-balance, pulling his leg back. Without wasting time trying to get up, I pounded my fist onto the knee I'd kicked before. Then I dug my thumbs into the Achilles tendon behind that ankle and thrust up. He started to topple, I rolled away, and then we were both on the ground.

He sprang to his feet before I could, but he didn't attack again. "Genna Jing," he spat, in a loud harsh whisper. "Stay away from that, bitch. Or I'll be back." He turned and ran, his feet pounding hollowly, swiftly, down the middle of the cobblestoned street.

I struggled to my feet and charged after him, but by the time I got to the corner he was gone. He might be hiding in a doorway, right here, close; or he might be running still, in any direction, laughing at the thought of me standing panting and sweating on deserted Village cobblestones under a sickly yellow streetlight.

David Kim's—or, more properly, David *L.* Kim's, because the "L" was what you saw glowing in red neon script between the other two much more dignified words on the sign outside—was the downtown crowd's newest "in" restaurant, a Korean supper club with food as hot as the place itself. Andrew, naturally, had discovered it just before everyone else, and had become a regular as soon as he'd tasted the *kim chee*.

When I got there, the place was crowded, and the lighting, from tiny, high-intensity spots that picked out the single flower in its vase in the center of each table, was dim. Score one for me, I thought. I had put myself back together quickly in the restroom of a diner, and now, though I could still feel the fight, the only place anyone could see it was the bruise on my cheekbone from where I'd hit the wall. And if the lighting was dim enough, maybe no one would notice that.

I waited at the entrance's etched glass screen and surveyed the room. The air smelled lusciously of roasting meat, fiery pickled vegetables, complex casseroles in covered bowls. Glasses clinked at the bar and conversation hummed. Surprisingly, for a tremendously trendy place like David Kim's, the bar TV was carrying a basketball game. Not surprisingly, the sound was off.

By the time the handsome David L. Kim himself came smiling over to seat me, I'd spotted Bill at a table by the bar. He was alone; Andrew must not have made it yet. Score another one for me.

"I'm with him," I said, pointing to Bill. Maybe I'd have time to get Bill's take on what had just happened, not to mention time to bring my heartbeat and sweat production down to normal, before I had to deal with Andrew.

David Kim kept smiling and picked up a menu, the better to guide me to Bill's table. Then, "So am I," said a familiar voice behind me. I turned; Andrew had just walked through the door.

Score one for him.

As Andrew and I exchanged wary looks, David Kim looked from one of us to the other and beamed more broadly.

"Lucky him," he said.

Bill stood when we approached. He can't help that; it's an old southern habit. He didn't kiss me, though, probably because of Andrew. Bill's met all my brothers, and my mother, too, and he and Andrew actually seem to like each other, in a tentative sort of way. They share a love for jazz, especially piano and bass late at night in smoky bars. Tony and I don't know anything about it, but the four of us have gone together once or twice to hear some performer who Bill and Andrew have both been excited about. Bill's not really social, but I think this is part of a campaign to make himself more acceptable to my family.

It will never work.

Andrew and Bill shook hands, and we all sat down. The owner asked for drink orders, and we got that little bit of business out of the way. Then we were by ourselves. I tried to unobtrusively deep-breathe

71

and do whatever else I could think of to blunt the adrenaline edge Mr. Ninja Mask had left me with.

Bill already had a drink, something amber and half-finished in a short wide glass. "You two want me to referee?" he offered. "Or is this full-contact, no holds barred?"

"It's not like that," Andrew said testily.

"Tell Lydia," Bill suggested.

Andrew faced me. "Why the hell have you been avoiding me all day?" he demanded.

My resolve to be reasonable evaporated in an adrenaline spurt. "Because of this," I shot back.

"Because of what?"

"Because I wasn't interested in you yelling at me like this!"

"I wouldn't be yelling at you if you hadn't been avoiding me!"

"Yes, you would."

"For what?"

"Getting shot at!"

"Well, don't you think that was pretty stupid?"

"How was I supposed to know that was going to happen?"

"I thought you guys thought about things like that. You, too," he jumped on Bill. "You're the one who's supposed to be so experienced. What the hell were you thinking?"

"You're right," Bill said calmly.

"You're wrong!" I snapped.

"She could've been killed," Andrew said to Bill, ignoring me.

"It's not his fault," I protested.

"You're right," Bill said.

Andrew and I both stopped, confused. "Who's right?" I demanded.

The waiter came with Perrier for Andrew and orange juice for me. I clamped onto my straw and tried not to gulp the whole thing all at once.

"Everybody's right," Bill said, when the waiter left. "I should have been more awake this morning and I've been kicking myself since." He lit a cigarette as he said that, and looked at Andrew but not at me.

"I'm the one who should have thought of it," I insisted. "My client, my setup."

"But it might not have mattered," Bill went on. "Just because you're looking for trouble doesn't mean you know where it's coming from. It might have happened the same way anyway."

Andrew and I both drank our drinks. We looked at each other suspiciously, the way we used to as kids when we wanted to get back to playing but neither of us was willing to take the blame for whatever fight we'd been having.

"Listen," Bill said. "You two aren't going to settle this tonight. Isn't there some other reason we're here?"

He leaned back in his chair, sipping his drink and waiting for Andrew, as though Andrew were just a person and not a brother of mine.

I tried to do the same, to act objective and professional. I sipped my drink and leaned back in my chair, too.

"I don't know," Andrew said, still belligerent. "I'm not sure I should tell you about it. You'll probably just get in more trouble."

By "you," he clearly didn't mean Bill. I felt my cheeks redden. Bill shot me a look. I closed my mouth, which had opened automatically. Bill said to Andrew, "But you called. You had a reason for wanting to tell us whatever it is. Is that reason still good?"

Andrew nodded reluctantly. He waited a little, while the sounds of trendy, probably easier conversations drifted under the tiny spotlights.

"Genna's a good friend of mine," he finally said. "I wanted to help her." He looked at me, and he looked sorry about something. "When she asked about you, I thought she just wanted something looked into, some investor or some deal to make sure it was legit. It seemed like that would be a nice safe case for you, something that would keep you out of trouble for a while."

I reddened again. I kept my eyes off Bill, in case he was shooting me another look, but I kept my mouth closed. Andrew went on, "When she told us last night what the problem was, I couldn't believe she just wanted to pay the money. But family business . . . well, who knows what's going on? I don't like to get involved in other people's."

I could relate to that. Chin family business is complicated enough for anyone.

But I didn't know this was family business.

"And you said it wouldn't be dangerous," he added, to me. "And I believed you."

Andrew rested his large dark eyes on mine. His belligerence was completely gone, but his eyes weren't twinkling. My brother was very serious.

I tried to match his openness. "It's what I thought," I said, not apologizing, but not hostile either. "Sometimes I'm wrong."

He took a breath. "The point is, Lyd, I don't want you in the middle of some other family's blood feud."

"What do you mean?" I asked him, leaving aside for the moment the question of what he wanted and who cared. "What blood feud?"

"The Jings'," he told me. "Genna and her sister. That's who stole the sketches. Her sister Dawn."

"Dawn?" I peered at my brother through the half-light of David L. Kim's. "Genna has a sister?"

He nodded. "Eight years younger. Genna doesn't talk about her. I don't think she likes her. But it's complicated."

"It usually is," Bill said dryly. He asked, "What makes you think it was Dawn?"

"Genna's given her money before. I thought that stopped a while ago—I'd heard Dawn was finally making a living—but I guess I was wrong."

"Just because you give your sister money—" I began.

"There's always been trouble between them. I don't even think they see each other anymore. Dawn could easily have gotten desperate enough to do this."

"How come you know so much?"

"What are you getting defensive about?"

"I'm not defensive! I just want to know how you know all this about Genna's sister."

"She's in the business," Andrew told me. "She's a model."

Before I could ask my next question, the waiter appeared to check on our drinks. I suddenly realized I was starving. I ordered another orange juice and a casserole. I don't usually eat big dinners, but I wanted this one, now. Bill's eyebrows raised slightly, but I ignored him. Neither of them ordered anything except another drink; it seemed they both had already eaten.

"Now wait," I said to Andrew when we were alone again. "You think Dawn would do this to her own sister? Why?"

"Oh, come on, Lyd! For *money!*"

"And what about the shooting? What would have been the point of that?"

"I don't know." Andrew shook his head. "But whatever the reason for it was, I don't want you involved."

I ignored what he wanted, but I also passed over the chance to tell him to go fry ice. "She would do that?" I asked, sticking to the case. "This could ruin Genna's whole career. Her sister would do that?"

Andrew just shrugged. I looked at Bill. His eyes met mine, but I wasn't sure what was in them.

Bill spoke to Andrew. "Are you telling us Genna thinks this too? That Dawn stole her sketches?"

"I'm sure she does."

"Well," I said, "that would explain one thing: why she's able to focus on her work while she waits for the next phone call."

"Sure," Andrew agreed. "Because she may be furious, but she's not really frightened."

"But she hasn't talked to you about it?"

"No."

"And why didn't she tell us?"

Andrew sighed. "Because it's her *sister.*" The way he said it, you'd think there wasn't a sibling in the country, no matter what dirt was done to them, who'd rat on the sibling who'd done it.

Bill looked at me, and I at him. "There's a problem with that theory," I told Andrew.

"What's that?"

"Genna's already fingered someone else."

Andrew paused for a beat. "What do you mean, fingered someone else?"

"She called me this afternoon, and said she thought a guy named Wayne Lewis was behind it."

Andrew frowned. "Wayne Lewis? The show producer?"

"That's what she said."

He shook his head. "No way."

"Why not?" I asked.

"Why would he?"

"For money? That's what you said about Dawn."

"For fifty thousand dollars? Talk about ruining careers: that's a big risk to take for fifty thousand dollars."

"For Dawn, too."

"She doesn't have a career to ruin. She probably doesn't even have a credit rating."

"He may have some sudden need for cash," I said.

"I think Genna's blowing smoke, you guys," said Andrew. "She was afraid you'd catch onto Dawn. That may have been my fault. I told her getting shot at and losing her money would make you so mad you'd never give up now. She probably told you she thought Lewis had done it to throw you off."

I exchanged another look with Bill. "Maybe," I said. "But there's another problem, too."

"What?" Andrew asked.

"He's dead."

"What?" Andrew looked quickly to Bill, then back to me. "Who's dead?"

The waiter, as though waiting for the moment of maximum impact, appeared right then with their drinks and my dinner. Bill had to light a cigarette and Andrew had to bite his tongue to get them through the placing of the dish and the opening of the cover and the ceremonial breaking of the yolk of the egg that was baked on top of the meat and the rice.

Finally the waiter left. Andrew leaned forward. *"Who's dead?"*

I swallowed and said, "Wayne Lewis."

"What do you mean, he's dead?"

"Someone killed him this afternoon. Before we had a chance to talk to him."

"Killed him?" Andrew shouted. People at the surrounding ta-

76

bles turned to look. Andrew dropped his voice. "My God, Lydia, what's the matter with you?"

"With *me*? What do you mean, with me?"

"You didn't report this to the police? You're still involved? People are getting shot at and killed and you think nothing can ever happen to you?"

"The police were there!" I threw down my fork. "You have no idea what you're talking about!"

"Why didn't you tell me about this when I first came in?"

"Why should I have? I didn't know why you were here, and I didn't know you knew him."

"And you knew how I'd feel about your still working on a case where someone had been murdered."

"As a matter of fact," I said hotly, "Genna fired us."

Andrew stared at me, narrowing his eyes. "You're telling me you're not involved anymore? I don't believe you."

I flushed in anger. That had been what I was implying, though it wasn't true; but I'd hoped it would get him to stop. But Andrew's known me too long. And I hate being caught in a lie. "No, I'm telling you that what I do is my business, and I'm doing it the best way I know how, and I want to be left alone to do it!"

"You think—"

"You have no idea what I think! All of you just go along making assumptions about me and what I'm doing—"

"Well, someone has to think for you, since you obviously aren't thinking for yourself! And neither are your so-called friends." He turned angrily to Bill.

"Leave Bill out of this," I snapped, before Bill could say anything.

"I don't believe it!" Andrew slammed his palms onto the table. "You want me to just stand around and watch while you get yourself killed, without even opening my mouth?" He stopped and stared at me angrily, suddenly out of words.

I met his eyes. "No," I said. "I want you to let me live the life I choose."

"This life is crazy, Lydia!"

"But it's mine."

He shook his head. "I don't know." He pushed away from the table and stood up. "I don't know."

My brother turned and left.

I watched Andrew stalk out of the restaurant. Then I stood, threw my napkin on my chair, and pushed my way between the tables to the ladies' room downstairs. It had a mosaic tile floor and a vase of flowers and a silver-rimmed mirror in which I could watch the fiery color recede from my cheeks and my jaw muscles unclench.

I rinsed my face and neck, wincing as I touched the bruise I'd forgotten. Then I went back upstairs to my partner and my dinner.

"Don't say anything," I said as I sat back down across from Bill. The waiter must have come by; Andrew's half-finished drink was gone, his place cleared.

"For how long?" Bill asked.

"Until I'm not mad at him anymore."

"Or hell freezes over, whichever comes first."

"Then say whatever you want," I snapped. "But not about him."

"Fair enough." He nodded, as though that really were a reasonable request. "Who socked you?"

I looked at him sharply. "How do you know?"

"You don't eat like that unless you're hurt," he said. "When you ordered a dinner that big I inspected you. You have a bruise on your cheek."

My shoulders drooped. "In a minute," I said. "Okay?"

"Okay."

In the hum of quiet conversations around us, Bill drank his drink and I worked my way through about half my dinner. Finally I felt human again, ready to talk.

I put down my fork and looked at Bill.

"I shouldn't let him get to me like that, should I?"

He shrugged. " 'Should,' " he said. "That really doesn't mean anything when it comes to families."

"What are you saying?"

"Well, look at you. A rich racist on the Upper East Side threatened you; someone mugged you, or something; and you had a fight

78

with your brother. Look which one you're most upset about."

"But that's the point! I have real things in my real life to worry about. Why should I worry about how Andrew makes me feel?"

"I don't know," he said. "But you always will. Who socked you?"

I shrugged helplessly, and shook my head. The headshake was for the fight; the shrug was for Andrew. Bill, I think, knew that.

I told him the story, short as it was, about the fight, the black-masked man, and the cobblestone pavement.

"Would you recognize him, anything about him?" Bill asked, at the end.

"No. Those masks are like hoods; you can't see anything but eyes, and it was too dark to really see those. When he spoke he whispered. I guess it's even possible it wasn't a man, but I think it was."

"Are you okay?" He didn't hover, and I was grateful.

"Yes," I said. I added, "And that's actually a little strange."

"What is?"

"Well, in the end, I was on the ground and he was standing. He was in a good position for a kick or something, and he's obviously trained in some mysterious Oriental martial art." Bill grinned at my sarcasm. "But he didn't do it. He just warned me off Genna Jing, and ran."

"Maybe he hadn't expected you to fight back, and he didn't want any more trouble. Sounds like you were pretty well matched."

"I think we were. It would have been pretty bloody if we'd fought to any kind of finish."

"He'd gotten your attention; maybe that was all he wanted."

"Maybe. But he's going to have to count on me *wanting* to give up the case, because he didn't even try to hurt me so badly I'd *have* to."

"I'm glad."

I stopped, leaned back in my chair, and smiled at him. "So am I. You're a very nice guy, you know."

"No, I'm not. Everybody says so."

"They don't know. Can I buy you a drink?"

"Anytime."

I signaled for the waiter. Bill ordered coffee and I ordered a pot of orange pekoe tea, something uncomplicated and calm. While the waiter cleared away the decimated remains of my dinner and brought the tea and coffee, Bill lit a cigarette. "Did it work?"

"You mean, did he scare me off?" I was amazed that Bill would even ask that; you could hear it in my voice.

He grinned. "I knew it wouldn't."

"Why, because I'm courageous and unfrightenable?" I straightened my shoulders.

"No, because you're willful and disobedient and you hate to be told what to do. Isn't that what your mother always says?"

"Only because I won't stop working with you. Of course, being willful and disobedient, if she suddenly changed her mind about you, I'd drop you like a hot potato."

"Sure you would," Bill said, in tones of confident unbelief.

His sureness irked me.

"Oh?" I queried. "You think you know me all that well?"

He shook his head and said in quite a different voice, "Not well enough."

Feeling my cheeks suddenly hot, I looked into my tea, bronze in a creamy white cup. There's something about Bill, about how he feels about me and what he wants, that makes him take risks sometimes, lets him make himself vulnerable in a way that confuses and upsets me. And frightens me, too: it gives me a power I'm not sure I want.

I swallowed some tea, simple and bracing. Get back to the case, Lydia. Logic and deductive reasoning and work, that'll clear all this messy emotion out of your head.

"Who would want to scare me off the case?" I asked, staring across the room, trying to think.

To my relief—and as I knew he would—Bill took my cue. He put away what just had or hadn't passed between us and went back to work.

"I don't know," he said. "We don't even really know what this case is."

"It's a theft," I said. "Extortion. And a murder."

"Is it? Maybe the murder's not involved. That's what John Ryan said. Maybe, based on what Andrew said, it's true."

"That Dawn stole the sketches? And Genna put us onto Wayne

Lewis to throw us off Dawn? And Wayne just coincidentally happened to be dead when we went to see him?"

"I don't like that, either," Bill admitted. "But don't you think we should talk to Dawn?"

"I certainly do. I wonder where we find her?"

"Well," he said, grinning, "you could call Andrew and ask."

"And you could go jump in the lake. But I do have another idea."

"What?"

"Andi Shechter. And Francie Whatever-her-name-is. They might know how to track her down, if she's really a model."

"And she must really be a model, because your Honorable Elder Brother said so."

"You tread on thin ice sometimes, white man." I stood up to leave, suddenly weary, feeling the soreness in my muscles from the fight.

"You're going to walk out and stick me with the bill?"

"Your kind owns the world. Pay the bills."

I did walk out. It was close to eleven; it had been a very long day. On Bank Street I found a cab, and it wasn't until I was halfway home in it that it occurred to me Bill had not pointed out that I'd offered to buy him a drink.

EIGHT

I woke about nine the next morning, bright sunlight streaming into the room I've always lived in. On my first birthday my parents moved me out of their bedroom into this one, a room of my own. Andrew and Tim, who had shared this room until then, got piled in with Ted and Elliot across the hall. My brothers were always jealous of my space; I was jealous of their illicit late-night laughter, their sharing clothes and their being able to wake from a scary dream and have other people breathing peacefully right next to them.

The night before, I'd gotten home too late to do anything besides take a hot bath and go to bed. My mother, who was sitting fully dressed in the living room watching the Cantonese cable channel when I came in, noticed the bruise on my cheek when I bent to kiss her. My mother notices everything.

"Karate class?" she asked me, frowning disapprovingly.

"Umm," I said. Saying it that way wasn't really lying.

"You shouldn't go," my mother started. "Too many rough men at that school."

"Ba-ba wanted me to," I cut her off. That was unfair but accurate, although I'd been eight then, twenty years ago, when my father started my brothers at a Chinatown Kung Fu school and me at a Tae Kwon Do dojo uptown, where they would take girls. It was unfair because one of my mother's favorite weapons is, "Your father would have wanted it." It's a cheap trick to turn that weapon back on her, but I get the chance so rarely that I use it when I can.

"Humph," she sniffed. She tried again. "You should call your brother."

"An Zhong? We just had a drink together."

One-upped twice. This was too much for her. She reached for something else, but not too far; for my mother, finding something to criticize is never a stretch. She put a shocked look on her face. "Ling Wan-ju, you've been drinking?" She sounded scandalized, even in Chinese.

"Orange juice, Ma. Full of vitamin C. I'm going to bed. I'll get the groceries in the morning."

Now it was morning.

My plan was to dress, get the groceries, and see if I could find someone who could help me find Dawn Jing.

It had occurred to me as I was falling asleep the night before that there was one person who could shortcut that search, and that was Genna. I'd toyed with the idea of just giving her a call and repeating what Andrew had said. "Come clean, Genna!" I'd demand. "Who's who and what's what around here?"

What stopped me was the bruise on my cheek, and the soreness in my hip where I'd hit the pavement. Someone was willing to go some distance to chase us off this case. Since I didn't know who or why, maybe the best thing was to let as few people as possible know what I was doing.

That, of course, didn't include Bill. I called him as soon as I was showered, dressed, and breakfasted.

"Still speaking to me?" I asked.

"Till the cows come home. Hold on a minute. Be right with you, Boooie!" he shouted.

"Very funny."

"Are you okay?"

"Sore. As soon as I get up and move I'll be fine."

"Ah, youth. What's your plan?"

"I'm going hunting for Dawn Jing, after I come home with the water spinach."

"Dawn Jing on a bed of water spinach. Sounds irresistible."

"You're in a jolly mood."

"Want to know why?"

"Of course."

"I just got off the phone with Visa, MasterCard, and American Express. I don't think they believed I was mit der Deutsche Bank in Zürich, but I was so Teutonically pushy they gave me rundowns of Genna's accounts anyway."

"Where'd you get her card numbers?"

"Velez got them for me from TRW."

Antonio Velez was a skip-tracer Bill and I often used to hunt up the kind of data that's most easily gotten from computers.

"How come you called them yourself?" I asked. "Why didn't you just let Velez finish it up?"

"I wasn't sure where it would lead, and I wanted to be able to improvise if I had to."

"And because it's fun," I suggested.

"And because it's fun."

It is fun: the exhilaration of convincing someone you're someone you're not, for a particular purpose; the switch of identities, making up one, assuming it totally, then dropping it; the bearing away of the prize by virtue of your own wits, guts, and fast-stepping.

It's exciting, it's a victory, and sometimes, when maybe you should be wondering about whether it's okay to be doing this, you go with the rush and the thrill and leave that uncomfortable idea behind.

"What did you find out?" I asked.

"John Ryan was right. She maxed out her credit to get the ransom money. She pulled about forty-three thousand out of her credit lines on the cards yesterday. The rest she probably had in the bank; I didn't look. And it's a good thing, too."

"What is, that you didn't look at the bank?"

"No, that she maxed out her credit."

"What do you mean?"

"I mean," he said, triumph shining in his voice, "that she wasn't about to get it anywhere else. John Ryan has not a cent."

"*What?*"

"Negative moolah. One-way cash flow. The guy is maxed to his eyebrows on his credit cards and has been for months."

"You checked him out, too?"

"You bet. He's had two credit cards canceled in the last couple of years. His BMW was practically repossessed last summer. His bank account is periodically overdrawn, this being one of those periods. According to Citibank, they only keep him because his mother is such an outstanding customer."

"No kidding," I said slowly. "So John Ryan isn't what he seems to be?"

"Well, he is a chip off the gold-buillion block. But he's not flush."

"Not flush," I said slowly, emphasizing both words, ruminating.

"Not flush," Bill repeated, "right now."

"Right now?" I perked up. "As opposed to when?"

"Those periods when he's not overdrawn."

"When are those?"

"Random. His account gets infusions of cash, six in the last eighteen months."

"From where?"

"I don't know. It comes in as cash, literally. In ten to thirty thousand dollar lumps."

"Cash? Could it be from his mother?"

"Not from the action I've seen in her accounts."

"God, you've been busy."

"She was crappy to you. That puts her high on my hit list."

He said that lightly, as though he didn't mean it, or if he did, it didn't matter much.

But he meant it. And it mattered.

But I didn't want to talk about that, now. "What happens to all this money?" I asked.

"Some of it he uses as a life preserver to beat the wolf from the door."

"I can't believe you mixed a metaphor like that."

"You wouldn't beat a wolf with a life preserver?"

"No. A shark, maybe."

"You'd beat a wolf with a shark?"

"Oh, stop. What does he do with the rest of the cash?"

"Not entirely clear. But, interestingly enough, his account takes a major drop at just about those times Genna's gets an infusion of its own."

"Is this true?"

"Would I lie?"

"A fruitless line of inquiry if I ever heard one. Well, he said he'd given her money; that's not a surprise. What's his situation right now?"

"Bustola."

"Right. You said that, didn't you? But then what about the big scene at Andrew's about Genna getting the ransom money from him?"

"Exactly: what about it?"

"I don't know." I bit my lip in thought. "Is it possible he has some source of funds you didn't find, and he was planning to give her the ransom money from that?"

"Sure it is. I haven't had a chance to rummage through his whole life yet. He could have a lot of stuff I haven't found. But if he did, don't you suppose he would have rescued his credit rating with it?"

"I'd think so. Bill?" I asked, with a thought that I wasn't sure of the end of. "Does his mother make good his overdrafts at the bank?"

"No, according to them."

"Does she know about them?"

"Yes."

So much for that thought. "So what was he trying to do?" I asked. "Impress Genna because he knew she wouldn't take his money, so it was a no-risk way to look like a generous bigshot? But she's taken it before. How could he be that sure?"

"I don't know," Bill said. "I'm never that sure of anything."

"You hide your insecurities well, though."

"Kind of you to say so. Maybe he was trying to impress you and Andrew."

"Why would he want to do that?"

"I don't know," he said again. "Mine not to reason why."

"God, you're almost unbearable when you're cheery. What are you going to do now?"

"I'm on a roll. I think I'll stay on the phone and see what I can find out about the gun that killed Wayne Lewis. I can't lose."

"How do you figure that?"

"If I find out something, that's good. If I don't, I'll get depressed. Then I won't be cheery and you'll like me better."

"You know," I said, sweetly and ambiguously, "I don't think I could like you any better."

I hung up and went out in search of water spinach.

Water spinach, in Chinatown on a bright weekday morning, is not hard to find. Fruit and vegetable sellers weight their sidewalk stands down with shiny oranges and ugly misshapen jackfruit, crowded beside bundles of foot-long beans as thin as a shoelace and surrounded by bunches of deep green leaves, some rounded, some serrated, all glistening with water sprinkled enthusiastically over them by the sharp-eyed merchants and their fresh-off-the-boat assistants.

I was swinging my string bag down Mulberry Street, past the blue crabs and fish displayed on ice in their cardboard boxes—unless it's a dire emergency I don't buy the fish; my mother is convinced I'm going to pick out a spoiled one and poison us all—heading for the newsstand to buy Ma a copy of the *China Post*, when I heard my name.

"Lydia? Lydia Chin!" It was a handsome man, older than me but not by a lot, wearing a smile, his voice full of surprise and delight. I tried to place him; it took a moment, and then I knew who he was.

"Roland Lum?"

"Absolutely!" He grinned. He wore ironed jeans and a pale silk shirt with no tie under a double-breasted gray raw silk jacket. His fine black hair was brushed straight back from his high-cheekboned face. Hands on his hips, he looked me up and down and said, "Boy, I haven't seen you in years. You look great! How's Elliot, and your mom and everyone?"

"They're all fine," I said. "It has been a long time, hasn't it? Elliot's a doctor. An orthopedist at Mt. Sinai. He's married, you know, with two children, a boy and a girl."

"No way! Elliot? Someone finally hooked Chin Ai Liang, the Don Juan of Chinatown?" He lowered his voice confidentially. "Some Shanghai aristocrat? Or a Swedish masseuse?"

"Janie Ling," I said. "From Bayard Street."

Roland Lum threw back his head and laughed. "Oh, Elliot." He shook his head. "Elliot. Well, more power to him. I really should call him, find out how he did it. Hasn't happened for me yet. But that's cool. How about you? Married, kids, anything? God, I can't get over how great you look."

"Not yet," I said. Then: "I heard about your father, Roland. I'm sorry."

He shrugged. "He was old," he said. "He always thought there'd be more for him someday than that stupid factory, but he bugged out before he found it. Look, you have time for a cup of coffee?" He grinned again. "Come on, let me buy you one, catch up on old times."

I checked my watch, although I didn't really need to. None of the fruits or vegetables in my string bag were urgently needed at home, and my search for Dawn Jing could wait another twenty minutes before it began. It was more to give me a brief moment to think, and to keep me from looking too eager.

Because this was one cup of coffee I definitely wanted to have.

Roland Lum, who had only ever been peripherally in my life as a not-particularly-close friend of my six-years-older brother, and had not been thought of by me since then, had reappeared as a name mentioned by a now ex-client and suddenly, the next day, as a grinning face on the street. Chinatown's crowded and small, and you do keep running into people from your past. Sometimes they even offer to buy you a cup of coffee.

Usually it doesn't mean a thing, except when they sandbag you with a request for a donation to your village burial society or an invitation to invest in a can't-miss real estate deal. But my mother, who believes the entire concept of coincidence is a Western idea invented out of abysmal ignorance of the workings of the world, and is also an evil *low faan* scheme to trick the Chinese—that is, that it's something Westerners are simultaneously subtle enough to manufacture and stupid enough to believe—would, throw up her hands in hopeless disgust if I even for a minute entertained the thought that Roland Lum's materialization on Mulberry Street on a sunny Wednesday morning was not, in some way, connected to this case.

Roland and I strolled to the Maria's on Canal Street, discussing our families and the paths everyone had taken over the years. I caught him up on my brothers, and he told me about his brother Henry, who was a surgeon now in California, and his baby sister Megan, an intern with a public television station.

"She expects me to bankroll her when she's ready to produce her first Bruce Willis film," Roland said with a laugh. "From the factory. I'm running it now, you know."

"Yes, I'd heard that," I said. "Do you enjoy it?"

Roland made a face as he held open the door to Maria's for me. "One of the great privileges of being Eldest Son," he said in a voice heavy with irony. "Proves that an MBA from U. of P. can lead straight to s-h-i-t. I told Megan not to hold her breath."

We found a table, which I held down for us while Roland went up to the counter. Maria's is a Hong Kong bakery chain that, in the past few years, has been hedging its bets against the future like almost every business in Hong Kong by opening overseas branches. Being Hong Kong based, Maria's baking is heavily influenced by British taste, and the three New York stores have introduced the butter-creme horn and the jam tart to Chinatown. They serve strong high-quality black tea with milk, the English way, and the lighting is bright and the tables are brass-edged Formica, the Hong Kong way. All three stores are always crowded, almost entirely with Asian faces. White tourists, in search of the Authentic Chinese Experience, just don't know what to make of Maria's.

The strong black tea was what I had, and though I usually take my tea with lemon, I had it with milk because it's good that way here. Roland had coffee, dark and sweet, and though I'd protested that I wasn't hungry, he came back to the table with two forks and a flaky square of custard-filled pastry on the tray between the tea and the coffee.

"So," he said, grinning as he emptied the tray and sat down on a brass-backed cafe chair, "you told me all about the other Chins: now, about *you*. I heard you're a private eye. Is that really true?"

"Yes," I said noncommittally, over my teacup. "How do you know?"

"Oh, I know one of your clients," Roland said, swallowing some coffee. "Or clients-to-be, or something. John Ryan. Genna Jing's significant other? He's a client-to-be of mine, too. Maybe."

"He told you he was my client?"

"He was bitching to me a day or two ago, about someone trying to extort money from Genna. He said he wanted to hire a private eye to stop it. He asked if I knew you. You know the way the *low faan* always think we all know each other?"

I didn't point out to Roland that we did know each other. "What did you say?"

He winked. "I said of course I knew you. I said you were the best, that you had a tremendous reputation in Chinatown and he'd be lucky to get you. I figured that was the least I could do for old Elliot. Did it work? Did he hire you?"

"We talked," I said. "It didn't go very far."

"Damn," he said. "Too bad. Might have been a good gig for you. Well, I tried. What was it about?"

I lifted my eyebrows. "You can't really expect me to answer that."

"Why not?" He stopped with his fork halfway into the pastry. Flakes of dough splintered onto the plate.

"Because that's where the 'private' in 'private investigator' comes from."

"But this is just John Ryan," Roland protested. "It's not like it's international intrigue or anything. Or is it?" He grinned wickedly. "Genna Jing is smuggling illegal aliens! Right? No: drugs. Heroin, rolled up in bolts of Chinese silk. I'm right, Lydia, I know I am. At least I'm on the right track, aren't I? Come on, tell!"

I just shook my head, smiling.

Roland scooped out another forkful of custard filling. "Hey, try some of this. It's great. You're not going to tell me, huh?"

"No." I picked up my own fork and tried the pastry. The dough was light and the custard was lemony and sweet.

"Damn. Well, I didn't really want to know anyway. I was just testing to see if you really kept things private." Roland's grin let us both know that wasn't true. He stuck his fork back into the pastry. "Well, I just hope whatever his problem is, Ryan's not trying to deal with it himself."

"Why not?"

"The guy's nuts."

"He is?" I licked off some lemon filling and put my fork back on the plate.

"Off the wall."

"What do you mean?"

"You know. He's a rich white guy who thinks the world belongs to him. If he doesn't get his way, he gets a little crazed."

"I guess I saw some of that," I said, thinking back to John's reaction to Genna's saying she'd already borrowed the ransom money.

"Yeah?" Roland dug into the dwindling pastry once more. "Well, that's what's been keeping me from signing on with them. They've been trying to talk me into producing their fall line."

"Genna said you'd already signed on to do it, and then changed your mind."

"Oh, she told you that, huh? Well, I got a great offer I couldn't turn down. But it was a one-time."

"So you might do their line after all?"

"It's a hard call. This would be a good time to hook up with them. If she makes it big and they're an account of mine, I have steady work all six seasons. Better than having to go out and hustle." Having finished the lion's share of the pastry, Roland leaned back in his chair, crossing his ankle over his knee. "But I don't know," he said. He pulled a pack of Marlboros from his pocket, drew one out, flipped the pack onto the table. "The guy's a pain," he said, lighting up. "Might be more trouble than he's worth. And she's a little nuts, too. 'Mandarin Plaid.' What the hell does that mean? I have plenty of accounts, anyway. You want a cig?"

"No, thanks."

"You don't smoke, huh? You don't drink either, isn't that what I remember? God, you probably don't have any vices at all. You still do Tae Kwon Do, practice at six in the morning, all that?"

"Not at six in the morning."

"You used to. In junior high. You used to get up and work out in the morning before school. Elliot would tell me about it. All your brothers had quit martial arts, and you were still going. Like the Eveready rabbit."

"They were studying Kung Fu. Maybe it wasn't as much fun," I said modestly. I was actually surprised to hear that my brothers had even noticed what their little squirt sister was doing, back in those days.

"Or maybe they're just not as tough as you," Roland grinned. He gathered up the Marlboros and the matches. "Listen, this's been great, but I've got to get back to the factory. I have to keep showing my face up there, keep the ladies on their toes. Otherwise they stop working and sit around scheming to get me hooked up with their daughters." He winked again. "I'll give you a call, okay? And tell Elliot congrats on the wife and kids and all. I'll call him, too. And if I ever need a private eye, you're first on my list."

"Thanks," I said.

Back out on Canal Street, Roland gave me a quick kiss on the cheek and another wink. Then he turned and walked away. I watched him striding down the sidewalk, snapping his fingers, until he turned into the building, two blocks down, where his father's factory was.

I took the fruit and vegetables home to my mother.

As I unpacked the string bag and she scanned the front page of the *China Post*, my mother asked me nonchalantly, "How is Roland Lum?"

"Roland Lum?" I repeated, instantly suspicious. "How do you know I saw Roland Lum?"

"Oh, Mrs. Chan called to ask for my recipe for salt-baked shrimp. She told me she happened to see you and Roland having coffee at Maria's on Canal Street. I wish I'd known you were going there. I'd have asked you to bring me some almond cookies, to put in the freezer in case your brothers come."

None of my brothers likes Maria's almond cookies. I don't either. My mother could live on them.

"I didn't know I was going there," I said, trying to keep the annoyance out of my voice. "And since when do you give your recipes to Mrs. Chan?"

"Of course I didn't give it to her. I told her I was too old to remember it and I would have to find it where it's written down."

"Was she devastated?"

"Devastated? Over a recipe? Of course not. She seemed not to mind at all."

"She would've minded if she'd been calling for the recipe," I muttered, dumping the tofu from its plastic bag into the container in the fridge.

"Ling Wan-ju, did you say something?" My mother looked up innocently from the newspaper.

"No, Ma." I headed for my room.

"When you see Roland Lum again," my mother called after me, "tell him to give his mother my regards."

"I don't know when I'll see him again," I called back.

"When he calls, of course," my mother said, mostly to herself, in a satisfied tone. "When he calls you."

The next call, however, was not from Roland to me, but from me to Bill.

"Lo, the Mighty Hunter," he said. "I like a culture where the women provide. Did you bring down vast quantities of water spinach?"

"Herds. I just brought it triumphantly home. But I had the strangest encounter."

"At home? With your mother?"

"That, too. But no, that's not what I mean. Guess who I ran into on the street?"

Bill paused briefly in thought. "Dawn Jing?"

"A reasonable answer, but wrong. Roland Lum."

"Roland Lum?"

"The guy who owns the factory John and Genna are negotiating with."

"Oh, right. But you know him."

"Elliot used to."

"And his factory's in Chinatown."

"Yes."

"So why is running into him strange?"

"Well, for one thing, I haven't seen him in years, so it's a little odd to run into him right now, when his name just came up yesterday. For another, *he* stopped *me* on the street, took me out for coffee, chatted and winked, and then abruptly left."

"I don't like him winking at you, but I'll let it slide. What did he chat about?"

"That's the point. Once we got past the family part, he brought up John and Genna. He tried to get me to let him in on what the case was. Then he told me in three or four nonsubtle ways that John is a loose-cannon type, a guy who goes off half-cocked and messes things up if he doesn't get his way."

"That doesn't come as news," Bill said. "But I don't get why he brought it up in the first place. How did he know you knew John?"

"Apparently John sort of used Roland as a reference for me. He asked him if he knew me, and what he thought of me. Roland can't possibly remember me except as a wild teenager, but he says he gave me a glowing reference, on the principle of Chinese solidarity. It annoyed me."

"I wish *I* remembered you as a wild teenager. At least I'd have my memories. Chinese solidarity annoys you?"

"People doing me patronizing favors annoys me."

"Sounds like he might have been just trying to help."

"Maybe," I said grudgingly.

"How did he react when you wouldn't tell him about the case?"

"How do you know I didn't?"

"Do I really have to answer that?"

Alone in my room, I smiled. "No, sorry; it was just a reflex." I thought back to the bright fluorescent lights of Maria's. "He pushed a little, then he gave up."

"Did he give up because he really didn't care all that much, or because he knew it was useless no matter how much he cared?"

"That's an interesting question," I said. In my mind I saw Roland's grin, the flicking ash of his cigarette. "I'm not sure. Both. Neither. Something in between."

"It's the casual attitude toward specificity in the Chinese character that makes you people so intriguing."

"A rigid hang-up on specificity is what makes Westerners narrow-minded physical determinists," I pointed out haughtily. "A way of thinking, I might add, that is leading this planet straight into disaster."

"And which the entire non-Western world is hell-bent on imitating," Bill said.

"Only because of the short-term gains."

"Which this line of conversation is very deficient in. Let me ask this about Roland Lum's short-term gains: what do you think he wanted and what do you think he got?"

"You only want to drop that conversation because you were losing," I said. "What did Roland want? Either to find out what the case was about, and if that's it he got nothing; or to warn me about John. If that was it he succeeded, at least in getting his opinion across."

"Why would he want to do that?"

"Warn me? Proprietary interest. He was a friend of my brother's. He also seems like a guy who likes to be on the inside. If he really thinks John's a nutcase, Roland struck me as the kind of guy who'd want to impart his superior wisdom rather than letting me make my own mistakes."

"Then maybe the whole thing wasn't so strange. It was just what you thought it was: a planned encounter, for a reason."

"I don't know," I said doubtfully. "It just seemed to me there was something else going on."

"Like what?"

"I'm not sure. Don't start with that specificity stuff again," I warned.

"I never try the same line twice on a woman. Is it possible Roland was just looking after you?"

"Because he used to know me?"

"Uh-huh. Maybe he saw you there on the street and was overcome with one of those urges to protect you that gets you so steamed."

"Maybe," I sighed. "Why do people get those urges? Do I seem that incompetent and helpless and useless to everybody?"

"That," Bill said. "And you're short."

NINE

After I hung up on Bill I looked in the Manhattan phone book, came up empty, and then made some more calls, to directory assistance in the four boroughs I didn't have phone books for. After they'd all told me they didn't have any such listing I tried the Manhattan operator, too, in case the number was new, but she didn't have a listing for a Dawn Jing either.

I expanded my search to Jersey City, Hoboken, and other places where hopefuls take first apartments, within view of New York, watching the lights across the river and waiting impatiently for their chance to see the view from the other side of the looking glass.

No luck anywhere.

There were all sorts of simple explanations for this. Dawn Jing could have a roommate and the phone could be in the roommate's name. Dawn Jing could have taken over an illegal sublease and the phone could still be in the real tenant's name. Dawn Jing could be using an alias, some kind of professional name. All sorts of explanations, but a fat lot of good any of them did me.

There was nothing to do but to call Oak Park.

There weren't a lot of Jings in Oak Park, Illinois; in fact directory assistance could only come up with one. An H. P., on Elmwood Avenue. I sat for a few minutes, looking at without really seeing the blue sky and black rooftops out my window, until something Andrew had said the night before came back to me. Serve him right, I thought, if he's my inspiration. Filling in the details until I had a story that could work, I called H. P. Jing.

The phone was answered on the third ring by a woman.

"Good morning," I said pleasantly. "May I speak to Mrs. Jing?"

"This is Mrs. Jing." The woman's voice was reserved and held a slight Chinese accent. "Who is calling?"

"My name is Angela Fowler." I made myself sound apologetic and ethnically neutral. "I'm sorry to bother you. I'm with the credit department at Saks Fifth Avenue in New York. We have a little mix-up I hope you can help us with."

"I don't believe I have a charge account at Saks," she said, warming up not at all.

"No, the mix-up isn't in your account," I said quickly and, I hoped, reassuringly. I didn't want her thinking this was some kind of credit scam and hanging up on me. "It's your daughter, I believe? Dawn Jing?"

"Oh?" The mention of her daughter's name did not make her throw her arms open and welcome me. "What is this about?"

"It's a small thing," I assured her. "Her revolving credit account is unpaid for the last two months."

"Yes? And what has this got to do with me?" Mrs. Jing's tone had gone from reserved to guarded.

"I'm sure it's only an oversight," I went on. "There's not a great deal of money involved, and I'm sure Ms. Jing has other things on her mind. It's just that it's my responsibility to contact our customers in these situations. Before a problem develops with their credit ratings. No one wants that to happen."

"And please tell me why you're calling me? You must know that Dawn doesn't live here." My subtly implicit reassurances and threats seemed to be bouncing off Mrs. Jing like rain off a car hood. Careful, Lydia, I warned myself, or you'll lose her.

"It's just that when I tried to call your daughter, the telephone number she'd given on her credit application had been disconnected. Do you have her new number?"

"How did you find me?"

"She listed your home on her credit application as a former residence."

"I see." A depth and resonance I heard in her tone made me suddenly want to ask, What? What do you see? Tell me about your daughter, both your daughters; would one of them truly do something like this to the other?

But that wouldn't do, and I knew it.

"I don't know that I should help you," Mrs. Jing said. "I don't want to be responsible for creditors harassing my daughter."

"I understand that, Mrs. Jing. On the other hand, she's probably forgotten all about this bill, and she'll thank you for helping out before a problem develops."

"I suppose that's possible. What number was it that she gave you?"

I made up a ten-digit New York phone number and gave it to her for an answer.

"I'm not familiar with that number," she said. "But Dawn is hard to keep up with. She travels often, for her career. If I need to get in touch with her, I usually call my other daughter." She carefully did not, I noticed, give me her other daughter's name. "She's much less trouble to find. I'll call her and tell her to suggest to Dawn that she call you at Saks. Is that satisfactory?"

It was not satisfactory, but it was clearly her best offer. I thanked her and hung up, assuring her, one final time, that this was nothing serious.

And then I sat, staring without seeing out the window once again.

Genna was much less trouble to find. I was willing to bet she was much less trouble overall. Not a good Chinese daughter, Dawn, from the sound of it, the sound of her mother's voice. I wasn't much of a good Chinese daughter, either. Would my mother's voice sound like that someday, guarded, angry, but not surprised at my failings? Not indulgent, not impatient, but finally disappointed and cold?

Not a profitable line of inquiry, Lydia, I told myself firmly. I reeled myself in and made another call, to *Vogue*.

"Simone Sinclair, please," I asked the operator, using a French accent. I'd gotten *Vogue*'s phone number and the list of assistant editors, from which I'd picked Simone Sinclair, from the masthead on the copy I'd bought while I was out. This was my fallback scheme for finding Dawn.

Three rings, and then, "Simone Sinclair," said a musical young voice.

"Bonjour," I said. "My name is Marie Leclerq. I'm sorry to trouble you, but I represent Botanica Nature. You have heard of us perhaps? Well, no matter. We are preparing to introduce our newest scent, Au Revoir, to the American market. We are planning parties, advertisements—including those wonderful scented strips in the magazines you Americans are so clever at—oh, so many things. My marketing director believes he has found the perfect models to represent Au Revoir, but alas, I do not know how to reach them. This is my responsibility, and I dislike to disappoint. I thought perhaps that you would be in a position to help me . . . ?"

"I'd be glad to try," said Simone Sinclair, responding, as I'd hoped, to a combination of my hint of underlying desperation and the suggestion of a possible advertising campaign in her magazine. Then she added eagerly, "D'où venez-vous? Êtes-vous Parisienne?"

My actual French consists of three years in high school, and high school was a long time ago. The meaning of what she'd just said—Where are you from? Are you from Paris?—I could just about make out, but there was no possible way I could hold up my end of a French conversation.

"Oh, no, no, no," I scolded. "I am living in America now; I must improve my English, which is sad and weak. I am from Paris, from the fourth Arrondissement," I added. "The rue des Chinois, do you know it?"

"No," she said. "I've only been there twice. But my mother's French."

"I suspected, from your lovely name," I told her.

"Well, I'll try to help," she said, sounding pleased. "Who are you looking for?"

"Dawn Jing," I said. "And Andi Shechter."

"Oh, I know Andi Shechter. Let me look her up." I heard the click of computer keys. "Who was the other?"

"Dawn Jing," I repeated, and then, because it's a hard name to make clear in a bad French accent, I spelled it for her.

"I've never heard of her. Here's Andi Shechter. She's with Snap, Inc. That's her agency. You can contact her there. But . . ." She let her voice trail off.

"But, it is what?" I asked.

"Well, there's a note in the file. Maybe I'm not supposed to tell people. But then why would it be here?"

"A note?"

"I don't want to get her in trouble."

"No, no, do not worry. Only, if I know a problem, perhaps I can find a way to help to, as you Americans say, work around it?"

As I hoped, the word *work* gave her the push she needed.

"Probably it's not a big deal anyway," she confided. "It just says she was late to her last two shoots. It says 'unreliable and uncooperative.' But probably she was just having a bad day."

Uh-huh, I thought. Two of them. "Oh, I agree, I doubt if this has any meaning. My director, I am sure, will want to speak with her in any case."

"Good." Simone Sinclair sounded relieved not to have ruined Andi Shechter's chances at becoming the face of a new French fragrance. "Let me give you the phone number." I wrote it down as she did. "The other one, Dawn Jing, she's not in the computer," she said apologetically. "That doesn't mean anything, except that we haven't used her in a spread. I could ask around for you," she offered.

"No, please do not trouble yourself. I will make other attempts. If still nothing results, I may call you again?"

"Oh, absolutely."

"Merci."

"De rien," Simone Sinclair said, her voice smiling.

I called Snap, Inc. I asked to be put in touch with Andi Shechter, but didn't tell them why.

"I can't give you her number," the receptionist said, popping her gum. I bet her mother hated that. "I can take yours and see if she wants to call you."

"That would be fine," I said, keeping the French accent going. I gave her Marie Leclerq's number and told her Marie Leclerq would be leaving within a half-hour. Then I asked for Dawn Jing.

"Who?"

"Dawn Jing, is she not with your agency?"

"I don't think so, unless she's really new." A short silence, then, "No, she's not one of ours."

I hadn't thought so, but it was worth a try. I thanked her, told her I'd wait for Andi Shechter's call, and hung up. I turned off my answering machine, so if I were in the other end of the apartment, Andi Shechter wouldn't be faced with Chin Investigative Services answering calls in Chinese and English. Then I dumped my bureau drawers out onto the bed.

There's a lot of waiting around in this profession, and you learn to do mindless constructive things while you're waiting. At my office I shuffle paperwork. At home I organize.

My mother passed my door as I was putting T-shirts I no longer wore in a shopping bag to take to Goodwill.

"Ling Wan-ju, what are you doing?"

"Waiting for a phone call, Ma."

She smiled a small, knowing smile. "He won't call this soon, silly girl."

I looked at her blankly. "Who won't?"

" 'Who won't?' " she repeated teasingly. "You don't need to pretend with your mother, you know."

"Ma, I don't know what you're talking about."

"No, of course not." She smiled again. "But I'm glad to see you taking an interest in your wardrobe. That's important to people in the clothing business."

She continued down the hall, humming to herself.

I stared after her, dumbfounded. It's too bad, I thought, that they don't give prizes for that, because if they did, she'd be a Lifetime Grandmaster.

The ringing of the phone brought me out of my mother's world and back to reality. I grabbed it, and, reactivating the French accent, said, "Allo?"

"Marie Leclerq, please. This is Andi Shechter."

"Ah, yes, Miss Shechter. This is Marie. So good of you to call. There is something I am hoping you can help me with."

"Yeah, sure. What's that?" Impatience cut her words short, a jumpiness I wasn't sure of the source of. But I wouldn't have classified it as uncooperativeness.

"My firm, Botanica Nature, would like to contact a young American model. I do not know where to find her. I thought perhaps you might know her: Mademoiselle Dawn Jing."

"Oh." I could hear her disappointment. "I thought you were calling because you wanted *me.*"

"I am so sorry," I said. "For myself, your look is ideal for our product. But my creative director has discovered a photograph of Dawn Jing, and he very much likes to find her."

"What makes you think I know her?"

"I do not know so very many American models, nor where to look for them," I said soothingly. Nor do I know, Mademoiselle Andi Shechter, what you and Monsieur John Ryan were discussing last night at Donna's. Is it that you could enlighten me, please? No, Lydia, back to the business at hand. "Someone has told me, Andi Shechter knows many people, especially models up-and-coming."

"Oh, yeah, I know everyone," Andi said bitterly. "I know Dawn. But if you're looking for up-and-coming, you're not in the ballpark."

"Ballpark?" I said uncomprehendingly. "It is scent we create, not sportswear. Is it that you can tell me how to find her, yes?"

"You're making a mistake," she said. "There are other Asian girls you'd be better off with, if that's what you're looking for."

"I am sure you are correct," I told her politely. "It is not myself, but our creative director who has, how do you say it, this bee in his hat. If Miss Jing does not suit, he will look at others, but he first must remove this idea from his system. I am sure you understand."

"Yeah," she said. "Someone gets a girl stuck in his head and the rest of us don't exist. That must be an *old* picture of her he's working from."

"Oh? Why is that, please?"

"You'll see. In fact, I didn't even think she was in the business anymore."

"Miss Jing no longer models?"

"Oh, hell," Andi said. "What do I know? Maybe she got lucky and the laugh's on the rest of us. Maybe you're her ship and it finally came in."

"I arrived by airplane," I corrected her. "To Kennedy, such a busy airport. Do you have her telephone number?" The professional jealousy I was hearing, if that's what it was, was getting on my nerves, along with my own accent.

"Oh, if you insist. I guess the sooner you find her and your creative director gets over her the sooner some other girl gets a job, right?"

"Oui, I believe so," I said kindly.

"Then call Everest models," Andi said cooperatively, although I thought I also heard a sneer. "The Peak of Perfection. Last I heard, she's with them."

TEN

Everest Models. Well, Ed Everest had told me, as he was touching my hair, that he handled exotics. I guess being brought up in Oak Park didn't disqualify Dawn Jing.

On the phone with Everest Models, I used the same French name and French accent that had been proving so successful today. I explained about Botanica Nature and asked if they could put me in touch with Dawn Jing.

Then my streak was over.

"I'm sorry, we have no client by that name," a thin-voiced receptionist said with an air of bored finality.

"Oh, but I was told—"

102

"I can't help what you were told. We don't have a client by that name."

"Oh," I said. "Quel dommage. May I speak to Mr. Everest, in this case?"

She put me through to Ed Everest, who answered the phone heartily. Laying the French accent on thick, just in case he remembered Mishika Yamamoto, I told him what I'd asked the receptionist and what she'd told me.

"No, that's true," he agreed, sounding regretful. "I don't know the name. Dawn Jing? No, not a client of ours. Sorry."

"Perhaps," I said, "it is possible she is using another name?"

"She could be. But she's still not with us. I'm really low on Asians right now, and the two girls I do have, I know pretty well. One's Burmese and the other's just off the boat from Japan. And they're both booked heavily for the next month or so," he added. "So there's really nothing I can do to help you. Why don't you try Asian Faces? They specialize in Oriental girls. You could probably find what you're looking for there."

"Oh, there are agencies which specialize?"

"Sure. Asian Faces, or Chinoiserie. Give them a call."

"Merci, monsieur."

"No problem. Happy to help."

I hung up the phone and sat tapping the receiver thoughtfully. Then I packed up the T-shirts for Goodwill, closed my now neat-and-beautiful bureau drawers—I gave them a week like that, at the outside—and surveyed my closet critically.

I couldn't do a cropped top and tight black pants, but blue jeans, a crisp white shirt, and black boots had some currency on the street right now.

Besides, Mishika Yamamoto wasn't supposed to know what she was doing.

I fluffed up my hair and moussed it, then examined myself in the bathroom mirror. If you measured to the absolute tip of the highest-standing hair, I could pass for five-foot-three. I clipped on big red round earrings, and even, since I was home where the supplies were, painted my lips with a purply, eggplant lipstick and smoothed out the color on my face with a bronze base that, oh by the way, covered up the bruise on my cheek.

I put a black leather belt with a silver buckle through the loops on my jeans and a carved cinnabar necklace around my neck and stepped back to admire the effect in the full-length mirror on my closet door. Then I called Bill.

"You should see me," I said.

"Why?"

"I'm in disguise."

"Dressed as Santa Claus?"

"Hardly." I told him about my search for Dawn Jing and the dead end I'd run into.

"Maybe Andi was lying," he said.

"Why would she lie? If she didn't want me to find Dawn for some reason, she could just say she didn't know her. Telling me she's with an agency she's not with is a lie that can't go very far."

"True. Maybe she was just wrong. Or maybe Dawn Jing used to be with Everest and she's moved on."

"She sounded awfully sure," I said. "But even if she was wrong, there's something strange about Ed Everest."

"What's that?"

"Well, for one thing, if Dawn used to be with him he'd know her. He said he'd never heard of her. And also, he told me his Asian models were all booked. For the next month. He didn't ask me my schedule, or what kind of a deal it was. Maybe it would be worth canceling someone's booking for. In fact, he didn't even try to find out whether I really needed an Asian model, or if he could sell me someone else. Is that how it works in this industry?"

"I don't know the industry," Bill said. "But you're right, it sounds peculiar."

"And there's something else about him."

"What?"

"I don't know. But Andi and Francie brought his name up when they heard about Wayne Lewis's death."

"You told me. So what are you going to do?"

"I'm going to go up there. After all, Ed invited Mishika. I'm going to go see what I can see."

"Well," Bill said, "it's what I would do, in your position. But keep in touch. I don't want to have to worry."

"If you start worrying, like the rest of them—"

"I won't worry like the rest of them. I'll worry in my own special way. It will be unique, idiosyncratic, and probably quite embarrassing. I think you owe it to me to save me from myself."

"There's no one," I told him, fiddling with my cinnabar necklace, "that I'd rather save anyone from."

I called the cold-fish receptionist at Everest Models again, using a breathier, unaccented voice and told her Mr. Everest had asked Mishika Yamamoto to come see him. We set it up for forty minutes from now and I was on my way.

Everest Models was up in Genna's and Andrew's neighborhood, Chelsea, on Twenty-second Street in a converted loft building. A bold white-on-black graphic of a double mountain peak was the first thing that grabbed your eye when you got off at the fourth floor elevator lobby. I knocked timidly, then opened the door and went in.

The receptionist had a knife-sharp nose and a suspicious look in her eyes. The look didn't change when I told her who I was.

"Sit down," she ordered, and spoke over the phone on her desk, presumably to Ed Everest. She ignored me totally after that, but since she hadn't told me to go get lost, I figured I should wait.

The chairs in the small waiting area were black leather, the walls stark white. A dozen photographs of young women were all the decoration there was. Some of the women were Asian, some black, some with the sultry eyes and thick dark hair of the Middle East. All were gazing seductively into the camera. One, wearing a fog of flowing chiffon, embraced a brightly decorated column on a Shinto shrine. Another, wearing shockingly little, lay sprawled on a Turkish carpet.

All of them were showing more smooth-skinned thigh, arching back, and bare shoulder than Mishika Yamamoto was comfortable with.

The glass-and-brass coffee table was weighted down with books of more glossy photos. I was flipping through the second of them when a door swung open across the room.

105

"Mishika! Sweetheart!" A beaming Ed Everest blew like a wind into the room. "Great to see you. Come on in. Irene, hold my calls." He took my arm and swept me past Irene the receptionist and through the door he'd come from. As the door closed behind us, I saw something I read as disgust in Irene's eyes, but I didn't know who it was for.

"So, Mishika." Ed Everest rounded his desk, plopped down behind it, and waved me to a leather-and-chrome chair. He wore pleated dark navy pants and a shirt the color of cocktail olives. His navy tie had blobby red accents like the pimientos they stuff those olives with. He smiled at me broadly, exposing a solid set of gleaming, capped teeth. "Take off your jacket, hang it over there. Sit, sit. Glad you came up, sweetheart. Shows you're serious, take advantage of opportunity. I like that. It's key in this business. Now, what've you done?"

I slipped my jacket, one of Ted's old tweeds with the sleeves rolled up, onto a hook, and sat demurely on the chair opposite Ed Everest. "Well, back home—"

"Where's home?"

"San Francisco."

"Good. A city girl. Knows the score. Born here, Mishika? U.S.A., I mean?"

"Yes, I—"

"Great." He cut me off again. "Now, you don't have a book, right?"

"That's true, but—"

"No problem, sweetheart, no problem. Just means whatever you did back home isn't worth much. Clients want to see it, Mishika." He grinned wolfishly. "We'll set you up. Send you to my guy, he's a genius. We'll get you head shots, full-length—we'll make a book. No problem."

"How much will that cost?" I asked, trying to look as though I was trying not to look worried.

"Runs close to a grand," Ed said. "You have it?"

"Oh, I don't think—"

"Don't worry, sweetheart. Most of the girls don't. I'll front it." His grin broadened. "Well, come on, don't look so surprised. I'm investing in you. Mishika, my little gold mine. That's how it works. I do for you, you do for me. How can I make my fortune on your fabulous career if you don't get started? Stand up, honey, turn around." He circled his hand, stirring the air.

I stood and slowly turned.

"Good, good," he said. "Terrific. I'm getting ideas already. Listen, can we talk about your hair for a minute?"

My hand went to my head. "My hair?"

"It's all wrong. You're a smart girl, you see the other girls. You have a great head, Mishika, I told you that. I want to *see* it. Clients'll love it. *Love* it! You know Tulipe? Sixty-fifth, near Madison? Tell them it's for Ed. I'll have Irene call."

I blushed. "Tulipe? I can't—"

"Afford it? Get with the program, Mishika. It's on Ed. You can owe me. And makeup. Go down to Mac, get what you need. If you don't know what you need, get them to show you." He stood and came around the desk. Taking both my hands, he smiled. His blue eyes, fixed on mine, seemed to be filled with excitement, a promise of adventure ahead, wonderful things waiting to happen to me. The smile remained, but his voice, when he spoke, was serious. "Mishika. Bottom line. You walk around looking like that, nobody'll ever look twice. You do what Ed tells you, you'll make it. I take you around, introduce you to the people who can help. All you have to do is be nice and be *gorgeous*. Simple as that. Get it?"

Looking into his eyes, I nodded to show that I'd gotten it.

"Good," he said. "Good." His smile blossomed into a joyful grin, as though the adventure had already begun. "I knew it, Mishika. I knew you had it."

Then he dropped my hands and checked the Rolex on his wrist. "I'm sorry, doll. I have things to do, people to take care of. You know? Look, you get started. Hair, makeup, get yourself some clothes if you need them. Leave Irene your info, where to get in touch. You have a beeper or a cellphone?"

"No . . ."

"Phone's better. Get one. *Communicado*, baby. It's key. See if you can get to Tulipe this morning. Irene can get you in. We'll talk in a day or two, get the book done after the hair and makeup thing. Okay, sweetheart?" He beamed at me.

"Thank you," I began.

"Oh, no. No problem. I'm doing this as much for me as you, doll. You're going to make me rich, Mishika, I can see it. I can just tell." He put his hand on the small of my back, grabbed my jacket off the hook, and ushered me out the door. "Good-bye, hon." He dropped his hand lower, cupping my rear, and copped a quick feel. I slid uncomfortably away. He smiled down at me. "Later," he said.

Ed Everest closed the door behind me. I smiled at Irene the receptionist, but the look she gave me over her typewriter had changed from disgust to contempt.

ELEVEN

I came out of the subway half an hour later on the Upper East Side. The wind had picked up, and it tossed my hair around as I marched down the sidewalk in the bright sunlight. I brushed my blowing bangs off my face, wondering if I'd miss having hair that could touch the top of my collar. But I'd been wearing my hair this same way for a while now. And I was due for a cut anyway. Even my mother had noticed.

Not that my mother was going to love this. My mother considered any haircut that left you without something long enough to braid to be a man's cut and therefore hopelessly unattractive. Tulipe, on the other hand, was the envelope-pusher in this season's supershort women's styles.

The great thing about hair, though, is that it always grows back.

I'd discussed this cut with my conscience all the way up on the train. This was a $150 haircut, something I never in a million years would have spent this kind of money on even if I had it. The prosecution argued that, since I had no intention of ever modeling for Ed Everest, it was some sort of larceny to take advantage of his largesse. The defense, however, maintained that it could be a useful step in my search for Dawn Jing, even if its only use was to keep Ed from suspecting my motives in coming to him.

The defense further pointed out that Ed had, uninvited, squeezed my behind. Most men who do that to you get away with it; the worst you can do to them is glare. It would be justice, the defense's summation held, to make one really pay.

The defense rested. Deliberations were brief and the verdict was unanimous.

Tulipe was in a limestone-fronted townhouse a few buildings in from the corner on a residential street. It had an elegant gray-and-cream sign outside and an elegant gray-and-cream waiting room inside. Crimson tulips bloomed happily in the tiny front garden; they had those inside, too. I wondered what they did in the other three seasons.

The waiting room was empty when I opened the heavy wood door. I gave my name to the receptionist, a bony woman with arched eyebrows and a sort of fade cut, shaved on the sides and about half an inch long on top. I'd have to make sure they didn't give me one of those; it would be beyond my mother's ability to cope.

"Mishika?" She sounded dubious, and consulted a large appointment ledger. "Oh, yes, right. Irene called about you." Her accent was British, her long nails deep dark red. Her tone implied that, against her expectations, I'd passed the first test—being in her book—but I shouldn't let it go to my head. "Robert will take you as soon as he's ready." She nodded languidly toward a gray leather sofa and went back to the fashion magazine she'd been thumbing through. I could smell the heavy sweetness of the perfumed advertising strips from where I stood.

"Thank you," I said, giving her Mishika's timid smile. "I'm surprised I was able to get an appointment so fast."

"I should say." She didn't look up. "Robert is always booked weeks in advance."

"But I was lucky enough to catch him just when he had an opening?"

Now she did look up. "Certainly not. Robert never has an opening. But as it happens we have an arrangement with Everest Models."

"An arrangement?"

Although I was clearly interfering with her study project on popular culture, she took a breath and explained the situation. "Mr. Everest sends all his models here. He's an excellent client, so we try to accommodate him."

"He does? Do all the agencies do that? I'm new," I explained shyly. "So I don't really know how it works."

"Pay for their girls' cuts, do you mean? No, not actually." Her eyes narrowed, the better to focus on someone so new she didn't know salon protocol.

"I'm so glad Mr. Everest wants me," I confided. "I'm so excited about being a model. And I never could have afforded this by myself."

"Yes, I suppose that's true," she said, going back to her magazine.

"The other girls he sends," I went on chattering, "what are they like?"

She looked up briefly from the perfumed pages. "You'll fit right in." She turned to an article on Glorious Cashmere and began to read.

"I will? Oh, I'm so glad! How will I? What kind of girls are they?"

She paused before she answered this time, the way my third-grade teacher used to do, which was how I knew to stop asking questions or I'd be staying after school.

"The Everest girls," the receptionist told me, "are all rather quirky."

"Quirky? Quirky how?"

She seemed to search briefly for the right words. "Mr. Everest seems to have a generous concept of a girl's potential. But then, it is his agency, so perhaps he's correct. Although," she added, flipping magazine pages again, "I haven't yet seen any of the Everest girls in a major spread."

I decided to ignore the unmistakable notion that I'd just been insulted. "You haven't?" I made my voice sound disappointed. "The Everest Agency doesn't have any famous models?"

She smiled for the first time, a thin smile. "I'm quite sure you'll be the first."

"Do you think so? You don't think I'm quirky?"

"Possibly that was a poor word choice." The thin smile continued. "In your case, it's only that, for a model, you're rather short."

It was a great haircut.

Robert, owner and resident genius at Tulipe, was an elfin man with pointed chin, sharp nose, and a widow's peak in his own short dark hair. He wore a ruby stud in his left ear, like my brother Andrew's, and three gold hoops in his right, which Andrew doesn't have. He zipped around me, peering intently into my face from in front, then in the mirror, combing my wet hair forward, back, to one side, to the other side. Three other women in three other soft gray smocks occupied the remaining chairs in the small, square salon. They were each being well-fussed-over by their hairdressers, but I was the one in the seat of honor just inside the door, where a large bowl of crimson tulips on the counter was doubled by its mirrored image.

"No scalp showing," I told Robert, speaking to the mirror.

He scrunched his lips together and furrowed his reflected brow. "Are you sure? We could shave it. The Sinead O'Connor thing. No, you're right. That look's old. Let's do this." He fastened most of my hair to the top of my head with bright red plastic clips and began to snip, comb, snip what wasn't clipped. I felt a pang of fear as I saw locks of hair longer than I thought I had flying from his scissors, but after the fourth or fifth snip it was too late to worry about it, so I decided to relax.

"This is wonderful," Robert enthused, scissors and comb motionless while he spoke. "This thick Asian hair, and such a great head. God, this'll be fabulous." When his words stopped, his hands started up, combing and snipping.

"Do you do many Asians?" I asked.

"Lots and lots." He stopped again and smiled in the mirror. Artists apparently can't work and talk at the same time. "Don't worry."

"I'm not worried," I said. "I'm sure it will be wonderful. I'm really asking because a friend of mine got a great cut, and I'm wondering if she came here for it."

"If it's great, she probably did. What's her name?"

"Dawn Jing."

"Dawn Jing, Dawn Jing, Dawn Jing," Robert mulled, snipping and combing. He unfastened some clips, rearranged others. "I don't know. But I have a terrible memory for names. Describe her."

That was something I couldn't do, never having seen even a picture of Dawn. But I had an inspiration. I described Genna.

"Hmmm," Robert hummed, working on the back of my head. Pausing, he said, "Sounds familiar. But I don't know. I'm not saying you all look alike," he caught my reflection's eye, "but truly, it's like saying 'tall, blue-eyed, and blond.' It could mean so many people." He went back to comb and scissors, frowning in concentration.

"She has really beautiful hair," I pressed on. "Fine and straight and very shiny. And perfect pale skin. And tiny ears."

"Tiny ears," Robert mused, but got distracted by his work again.

"You know who she sounds like?" The question came from the hairdresser at the station next to Robert's, a round-cheeked woman twisting her client's golden hair over thick ridged rods, for a perm. "That little one," she said. "She came twice. You did her, Robert. And we all said how funny it was that someone who looked so delicate was like that?"

"Like what?" I asked.

"Oh, I remember!" Robert declared. He waved his comb and scissors. "That one! Right! What a sensational head! But that wasn't her name."

"It wasn't?" I asked. "But maybe it was her anyway, using some kind of professional name or something. What was she like?"

Robert stared into his own eyes in the mirror. "Ruby," he said. "Jade, starlight . . . Pearl! Pearl Moon! Wasn't that it, Mattie? Pearl Moon, wasn't that her name?"

Mattie, her tongue poking out in concentration, nodded without looking up from her rods.

"Could that be your friend?" Robert asked me. "Does she ever use that name?" He started to work again, now on the crown of my head.

"I don't know," I said. "You said it was funny, what she was like. What was she like?"

"Tough," he said, stopping again, this time to catch my eye.

112

"No, not tough. That makes her sound like something you couldn't chew. This one was something you'd break your teeth on if you even tried to bite. And you wouldn't make a mark on her." He shook his head and went back to work, taking the last clip from my hair. "Sharp and beautiful," he said, pausing in the mirror one more time. "Not like a pearl, really. More like a diamond."

TWELVE

It took six rings before Bill answered the phone.

The fact that his service didn't pick up meant he was there; the fact that it rang so long meant he was probably at the piano. He hates to stop when he's practicing, and playing the piano is one of the few things that makes him feel really good.

He doesn't think I know that about him, but I do.

After the sixth ring I felt so guilty about interrupting him that I started to hang up, but just before I let go of the receiver I heard his voice.

"Smith."

I yanked the receiver back. "It's me," I said. "Have lunch with me."

"Anywhere, anytime. Are you still in disguise, with lipstick?"

"Purply lipstick, and eyeliner, too. And something else, but it's not a disguise."

"You're being cryptic."

"It's new. You'll love it."

"I never know when you say that if it's good or bad."

"Me, either."

"I'll take a cab. Where are we eating?"

"In the Village," I said. "Graziella's. On Greenwich, across from the bookstore." I added, "I'm buying."

"Great. Why?"

"To even the score between us."

"Won't work."

"Why not?"

"Because you're always racking up new debt."

"Have I recently?"

"Uh-huh."

"What?"

"I'll tell you about it over lunch."

We hung up and headed for lunch, me taking the subway from the Upper East Side—although along with my snazzy new haircut I felt Ed Everest really should have ordered me a limousine—and Bill taking a cab, or so he claimed, up from downtown.

The haircut was the shortest I'd ever had. It radiated out from my crown, coming forward to form a row of pointy bangs high on my forehead and little points in front of my ears. At the nape of my neck was another, softer row of little points. You couldn't exactly see my naked scalp, but you couldn't have found a hair on my head longer than three quarters of an inch.

I looked at my reflection in all the shop windows on the way to the subway and was surprised every time.

As I trotted down the subway steps I heard the sounds of drumming. On the platform, a muscular black percussionist tapped, beat, and pounded three upturned plastic tubs, a wooden box, the concrete in front, the steel shutter behind, and anything else he could reach. He looked sweaty and breathless, with popping eyes, as though the warp-speed movement of his arms and hands had gotten away from him. But the exhilarating satisfaction I felt as I followed the sounds told me this man was a master, in complete control. The illusion of spin-out desperation was thrown in just to thrill the audience. I stood completely enthralled until my train pulled in. Then I dropped a dollar in his box and scrambled aboard as the doors began to close. I caught sight of myself in the train's window and ran my hand over my head, still surprised.

I thought hard all the way downtown. I didn't like what I was thinking, but it got more and more difficult to convince myself I was wrong.

I was buttering a piece of fresh, hot bread when Bill came into Graziella's.

"Oh," he said, pulling out a chair and sitting down without taking his eyes off me. "Wow."

"What do you think?"

"Wow."

"You said that."

"It's the only word I can think of."

"That means you like it?"

"It's inspired. In fact, it's inspirational. It inspires me—"

"Don't tell me."

"What made you do it?"

"Duty."

"To your public? To the goddess of beauty? Who is the Chinese goddess of beauty, anyway?"

"We don't divide them up that way. And in this case, it was my duty to our client."

"We don't have a client."

"We did. Once a client, always a client." I told Bill about my visit to Everest Models.

"So, see," I finished up, "I had to get the haircut so Ed Everest wouldn't suspect we were on to him."

"Ah." He nodded gravely, looking impressed with what I'd said. "Extremely clever. Except for one detail."

"What's that?"

"We're not on to him."

"Ah ha." I bit into my buttered bread. "That's where you're wrong."

The waiter, a short, swift man in a black vest and red bow tie, skidded to a stop beside our table at that moment and recited the specials for us. We ordered linguine with white clam sauce for Bill and spinach ravioli for me. Then Bill asked his question again.

"Are we on to Ed Everest?"

"I'm not pretty, you know," I answered him.

"No," he agreed. "You're gorgeous. Amazing. Sensational. Spectac—"

"Oh, leave it alone," I demanded. "My nose is too big. My eyelashes don't exist. My skin is dark and my shoulders are wide. I'm a peasant girl from Guangdong. All my ancestors are peasants."

"So peasants are beautiful."

"Will you stop? Chinese people have standards of beauty like anybody else!"

"And . . . ?"

"And I don't meet them."

"Okay," Bill said, although I could see he didn't think it was okay at all. "Where is this going?"

"Ed Everest wants me to be a model."

"Ed Everest," Bill said, "is a model's agent. If you're a model, he makes money."

"No, he doesn't. He won't make any money off a wannabe-model who looks like me."

"Well, admitting for the sake of argument that you're right—and I can see I could be in trouble here either way—you obviously think he's up to something. Any idea what?"

"He told me I needed a set of photographs. A book, they call it. He said he'd send me to his photographer to get them done."

"Oh," Bill said. "I begin to get it. How much was that going to cost you?"

"No, that's what I thought, too. But he said he was going to pay for it. As an investment in me. He said when I was rich I could pay him back."

"Is it just possible he knows more about your modeling potential than you do? No, I guess not," he said, catching sight of my sour expression.

"He said he didn't know Dawn Jing," I said. "But Andi Shechter said he did. And Robert, the genius who cut my hair, also cut the hair of a Chinese woman who sounded like my description of Genna to him. A woman sent by Ed Everest."

"You described Genna to him?"

"Well, I've never seen Dawn."

"Quick thinking."

"But he said that wasn't the name she was using."

"Not Dawn Jing?"

"Right. She's calling herself Pearl Moon."

116

Bill frowned slightly, without comment.

"Think of it this way," I said. "Suppose, instead of being a sensitive, empathetic, postfeminist New Man, you were a regular guy."

"Your thesis is flawed."

"Never mind. You take a woman to dinner, to the theater, for drinks afterward. You buy her flowers and perfume. What do you think?"

"Me, Mr. New Man, or the Regular Guy?"

"The Regular Guy."

"She owes me."

"Men," I told him, "are only interested in one thing. That's what you mean by 'owe.'"

"The first part of that statement is false. But the second is true."

"Ed Everest is going to do my book. He told me to get makeup and clothes if I needed them. He already paid for my haircut. I owe him. In Chinese tradition," I said, "the moon represents the female principle. And the pearl stands for the fulfillment of desire. She owes him, too."

The waiter came speeding from the kitchen, bringing our pasta. The scents of garlic, clams, and oregano swirled around our table.

"Ed Everest," Bill said to me, when the waiter left, "can't be going through all this just to get laid."

"No," I agreed. "There are too many wannabes out there. He doesn't have to spend like this. All he'd have to do is tell them he heads an agency. They'd fall at his feet." I edged my fork into my ravioli, plump little pockets shiny with sauce. "The receptionist at La Tulipe told me none of the Everest girls is famous. She also said we're all quirky."

"What does that mean?"

"I bet it means they're all like me. Women who have no chance of ever being models. Dreams, but no chance."

"Genna Jing wanted you to model."

I stopped and considered that. "She was at least half kidding. And with her it was *because* I walk like a truck driver, not in spite of it."

"There may be other truck driver lovers out there."

"Not enough. Think about it. Who do you see in the magazines?

117

Whose pictures go by on the sides of buses? Those women weigh ninety-two pounds and they have cheekbones you could ski-jump off of. Plus they're fifteen. And maybe there's one Asian a season. Maybe. No." I scooped up some more ravioli. "No legitimate agent would waste his time on me."

"Does that bother you?"

The question caught me completely off guard. "What?"

"Does it bother you?"

I looked at him, but I wasn't seeing him. I was seeing all the girls in my high school: the popular ones with their flat hips and flawless skin, and their secret, dead-on instincts about eyeliner, about haircuts and hem lengths; and the other ones, chubby or with thick glasses or who wore the clothes their mothers bought them. They were the ones who hesitated with their trays in the cafeteria, looking for someone who wouldn't mind sitting with them; the ones who didn't come to the Saturday night dances or, if their mothers made them, spent the whole night standing miserably alone against the wall.

And I was seeing myself, somewhere between the two groups, fraudulently passing on the fringes of the one, desperately, guiltily grateful not to be in the other.

"That's not the point," I said. "I don't want to talk about that."

We were both silent. I don't know what Bill was thinking; I was thinking about things I'd wanted, really wanted, in my life, and what desperate, dumb things I'd done sometimes to get them.

"These women all owe Ed Everest," I finally said. "But I'll bet he's not the one who collects."

Bill nodded. "A new angle on an old game."

"Doesn't it look like it?" I asked. "Ed Everest takes women who'd give anything to be models, women nobody else will touch. He lays it on thick. 'You can make it, baby, but only if you want it really, really badly, and do what Ed says.' You should have heard him, Bill. He almost made *me* believe it."

"Then he spends money on you, enough so that he has leverage."

"And he still has your dreams for leverage, anyway," I said.

"And then he takes you places, introduces you to people. To men," Bill said. "Some of those men, he tells you, are very important in the industry. He suggests you be nice to them. *Very* nice to them."

"Then you find that men are calling the agency especially to request that you come be nice to them. You're not sure you want to do it this way, but Ed says, 'Don't you want to make it, baby? This is how the game is played. And besides, Ed has a tidy little investment in you, sweetheart. You just go along, that's a good girl. I do for you, you do for me.' "

"And before the girls know how it happened, they're hookers and Ed's pimping them any way he can."

"Damn!" I growled. "Damn him! Can we get him, Bill? Do you think we can shut him down?"

"Get enough on him to bring the cops in, you mean?"

"That's just what I mean. I know—we'll give it to your friend Krch. That'll put him in a good mood."

"I don't think so, unless he can prove I was masterminding it." Bill sat back and reached for a cigarette. Then he looked around at the size of the restaurant and the No Smoking signs on all four walls. He slipped the pack back in his shirt.

"Better for you anyway," I said.

"But not as good for you. I'm not sure I can concentrate anymore without a smoke."

"I'll be through in a minute. We can go pollute the air in the outside world. But Bill, listen. This would explain about Dawn, wouldn't it?"

"Explain why she might be desperate enough to try to extort money from her sister? I think so."

"To get out of this life. And it would explain why Ed Everest said he'd never heard of her, when I was Marie Leclerq. The last thing Ed needs is some legit operation looking for one of his models. Because he doesn't really have any models. He just has hookers."

I choked a little bit on that last word. It surprised me; hookers aren't news to me. I know some I go to as sources; I've worked on cases involving others. But I kept seeing Genna—her elegance, her practicality, her determination—and wondering what it was in Dawn that had kept her dream so desperately alive but made it impossible for her to find a way to make it come true.

"I want to find her, Bill," I said. "If she stole Genna's sketches because she needs money to get out of this, then I want to find her and get her out of the way before we bring the cops in."

Bill nodded. "If that's what you want," he said, "then there's something you should know before we go any further."

There was something in his tone that made me think I wasn't going to like this. "What's that?"

"Remember I said on the phone I'd dug up something? Well, it ties the murder of Wayne Lewis to whoever stole the sketches."

"It does? How?"

"Lewis was killed by the gun that shot at you."

THIRTEEN

I'm calling Andrew." I dropped my napkin on the table and pushed back my chair.

"You're going to tell him about this?" Bill asked.

He had run down for me how he'd found out about the gun, and which of his NYPD sources he was in debt to over it. The route had been devious and he owed more than one favor now, because he hadn't wanted to do the obvious thing: suggest to some friendly detective that the two ballistics reports be compared. The NYPD doesn't do that automatically: only if they think there's a real reason for it, like two crimes with similar MOs, and even then someone has to notice the resemblance. That usually happens if the crimes are committed in the same precinct, and especially if one detective happens to catch both cases.

These cases, though, were very different: a shooting in Madison Square Park where no one was hurt, and a homicide in Greenwich Village. And no friendly detectives. The NYPD had no reason to connect the cases as things stood, and Bill had wanted to keep it that way, because if they made the connection, the road from Wayne Lewis to Genna Jing would not be long.

Especially if he and I stood like signposts on it.

"So I cashed in three or four chips," he said, "and I got copies of both reports without having to tell anyone why. I compared them myself."

"I didn't know you knew how to do that."

He raised his eyebrows. "Ever seen a ballistics report?"

"No," I admitted.

"It's just a list. Bore, groove, riflings. Accessible even unto such a one as I."

"And these two were the same?"

"Close enough for jazz. .44 IMI Samson cartridges."

"Does that mean something special?"

"Israeli-made. Unusual on the street. Not cheap. Made for the Desert Eagle, which is a good gun, by the way. High accuracy, low recoil. Maybe a little flashy, but it's not cheap either."

"Does this mean the shooter used a Desert Eagle?"

"No, but it means he's a high-end shopper."

"Or she is," I said glumly.

Which was when I decided to call Andrew.

"He may know where to find her," I said, standing. "Dawn. I'm not going to tell him why. I'm just going to tell him he has to help us."

Bill said nothing, just watched me as I wormed my way between tables to the back of the restaurant, where the phone was. He was probably wondering what made me think Andrew would help us just because I told him he had to.

It was a very good question.

"You're crazy," Andrew said, curt with impatience. Getting him on the phone had been easy; asking him to help me out and then listening to his answer was turning out to be harder. "No way."

"Andrew—"

"Lyd—"

"Listen to me!"

"Why? Last time I listened you talked me into letting you do something that almost got you killed."

121

"*Letting* me?" Anger surged in me. "How exactly were you going to stop me?"

"I don't know. But someone obviously has to stop you, since you don't have the sense to stop yourself."

"Oh, as opposed to all my big, smart older brothers, right? God, Andrew, I hate it when you do this!"

"Do what?"

"Follow the party line. You're the only one I can count on, and then you start with this same stuff. Come on," I said, half-pleading, "I don't want to fight with you this way."

"I don't want to fight with you, either, Lyd." Andrew's voice dropped, as though he wasn't quite sure even he wanted to hear what he was about to say. "But you scared me. I don't want you to get killed."

"I scared you?" A little light bulb suddenly went on for me. "Andrew? You're mad because you're scared?"

"Lyd . . ." Andrew paused. I gave him room. "When you started doing this," he went on, slowly, "this detective stuff, I was the one who encouraged you. Now I'm not so sure that was a good idea. I didn't want to be like Tim and Ted. But maybe they were right."

"Andrew!" I said in a shocked voice. "Tim and Ted are *never* right."

"Well, there's that," he admitted. "But they worry about you because you're their little sister. And you're my little sister, too."

"And you're my big brother, and I worry about you. Like the time you and Tony went camping in Montana, and I was sure you were going to get eaten by bears. But I didn't tell you not to go."

"That wasn't very likely, those bears."

"But it was possible. It's not likely that I'm going to get killed, either. But if I do—"

"Don't say that."

"—If I *do*, I'll get killed doing what I wanted to do. How many people can say that? This is what I want to do, Andrew. This makes me happy. Don't you want me to be happy?"

"I want you to be alive."

"Well, let's make a deal. I'll do what makes me happy, for me, and I'll do my very best to stay alive, for you. And you can go camping anytime you want," I added.

"Lyd—"

"Okay, good. It's a deal. Now listen: speaking of worrying about little sisters . . ."

"No."

"Andrew, come on, this is important. I think Dawn's mixed up in something bad. Genna's trying to protect her even from us knowing about her, but that's only making it worse. If we find her, we may be able to help." That is, I added silently, if she didn't actually kill Wayne Lewis.

"Mixed up in what?" Andrew's voice was curious.

"I can't tell you. Bad things."

"Worse than stealing her sister's sketches and shooting at you?"

"Yes. But that doesn't mean she's dangerous," I threw in quickly. "It could mean she's in danger."

"Oh, good. And if I help you find her, you could be in danger, too."

"Maybe not. After I talk to Dawn I might be out of this case."

"I thought you'd been fired already."

"But you knew that didn't mean I'd quit."

"And if I helped you find Dawn, you would?"

"Maybe."

"Maybe?"

"That's the best I can do."

There was a long pause. "Lydia—"

"Don't start from the beginning, Andrew. Yes or no?"

I heard his breath sigh out. "Well, it doesn't matter. I don't know where to look for her anyway."

I was momentarily speechless. "You mean we went through all that and you can't even help?"

"Serves you right. No, really, Lyd, I don't know. Genna's my friend. I never even met Dawn."

"I thought you knew everybody."

"Not Dawn Jing."

It was my turn to sigh. "I want to find her, Andrew. Genna must

123

be really worried about her or she wouldn't have tried to steer us away from her. Don't you know anything that might help?"

"Not that I can think of."

"Damn. I—oh!"

"Oh what?"

"Oh she's using a different name now. Did you know that?"

"No. How do you know?"

"Someone told me. I think it's her. Maybe it's a wild goose chase—it could be someone else entirely. But I think not. Pearl Moon: does that mean anything to you?"

"Lydia, are you serious?" Andrew sounded as though I'd told him I'd just grown a second head. "Pearl Moon? She's Dawn Jing?"

"You know her?"

"She's Dawn Jing?" he repeated.

"Why?"

"My god."

"What, Andrew? Can you find her?"

"Pearl Moon, probably. She's really Dawn Jing?"

"I don't know. I think so. Why is that so weird?"

"You'll see."

"Do you have her number, or do you know where she lives?"

"No. But there's a club I've seen her at a couple of times, late at night."

"Where?"

"Oh, no, forget that. I'll take you."

"No."

"You don't know her," he said reasonably. "You'd need someone to point her out."

I still said, "No."

"Then no."

I could see what this was: a childhood game of did-not/did-too, in another dialect. I never liked that game; it always seemed like a dead-end to me. But whenever Andrew started it, I used to play him to a draw, just to prove I could.

But proving something to Andrew was not the point right now. Besides, I had the feeling I'd already won.

"All right," I said. "All right all right all right."

"Good. Come here tonight, about ten o'clock. We'll go from here."

"Of course. Anything you say, third brother. And thanks."

"Oh, sure," he sighed. "Anytime I can help my little sister put her life on the line. Just do me a favor, okay? If you do get killed and you come back and haunt us all, just please don't tell Ma I helped?"

"Deal," I said.

I found Bill on the sidewalk outside the restaurant, finishing a cigarette.

"You paid the check," I accused.

He shrugged. "I'm getting used to it."

We fell into step together, walking west.

"I'm exhausted," I told him.

"Andrew wore you out?"

"Andrew, and this whole case. I hope we find Dawn and I hope she had nothing to do with the murder, and I hope whoever killed Wayne and shot at me in the park is easy for the cops to find and they take up Ed while they're at it and we can forget this whole thing."

"It's nice to know your hopes and dreams," Bill said.

"He was scared," I said. "Andrew."

"Scared?"

"That I'd get killed. That's why he was so mad. He was worried about me."

"That's good, isn't it?"

"Is it?" I watched the new green leaves wiggling against the blue sky. "I suppose it is. I suppose it's good to have someone worried about you. But all they ever do, my family, is try to put a fence around me."

"To keep you safe inside."

"I guess. But I don't want to be inside."

"Or safe."

I looked up sharply. "What?"

"The fence is only half the problem," he said. "Isn't it?"

I stopped on the sidewalk. Bill stopped, too. His face was half bright with the afternoon light, and half in shadow. I felt the sun's warmth on my side and knew mine was that way, too.

I started forward again, briskly, over the old slate sidewalks and

125

past the brick-fronted houses of the West Village. Bill caught up and fell into step beside me, his long legs giving him a pace that was easier, but no faster, than mine.

We were silent beside each other until we were within a block of Wayne Lewis's apartment on the tree-lined street where the sidewalks were mottled with shadow and golden sunlight.

"How are we going in?" Bill asked.

Our plan was to talk to Wayne Lewis's neighbors, to get some sense of who he'd been, what his life was like, what he'd done to get himself killed. Until Bill had told me about the gun, I'd harbored the faint hope that this might be just an academic exercise. Now that hope was gone. Neither of us had any real idea what we were looking for, but when we left the restaurant we headed west as surely as the setting sun.

I thought about Bill's question. What he was asking was what game we were going to play, what identities we were going to take on. What we were going to pull, this time. My case, my choice, though if I chose something he thought wouldn't work or was too weird, I'd have to convince him.

I came to a decision. "We'll go in straight," I said. "You and me. Private investigators."

Bill's eyebrows rose a little. "You're kidding."

"We shouldn't? Why not?"

"No reason. It's probably what I'd do. But you never go in straight."

"This time," I said. "I'm confused enough. And I'm tired."

We stood for a few moments in front of the building where Wayne Lewis had lived, the building where he'd died. Four stories, red brick, just like three to the west and two to the east of it. The windows had pretty French-blue shutters; the tall ones on the parlor floor had window boxes, too. Lewis's, on the ground floor, had bars.

His French-blue door was highlighted with yellow crime scene tape.

"Where to?" Bill asked.

"Upstairs neighbor," I said, and so we started there.

As it turned out, we ended there, too.

The neighbor on the first floor was a Mrs. Edith Lattimer. We rang her bell and waited.

A dog started yapping immediately. Along with the sound of a door being unbolted we could hear a voice, shushing the dog: "All right, Bobo. Now you be quiet."

The building's front door opened. A chunky woman with short gray hair organized into waves narrowed watery blue eyes at me and Bill. "Yes?"

"Mrs. Lattimer? I'm Lydia Chin," I told her, smiling reassuringly. "This is Bill Smith. We're investigating—"

"It's about time. Come this way." She turned back into the building.

Bill and I exchanged looks. "Ma'am?" he asked.

"It's been at least twenty minutes since I called," she complained over her shoulder, opening the door to her apartment and leading us through. Her voice had the gravelly depth of alcohol. "I thought I was going to have to call again. I had to when I heard the shots, you know."

"The shots?" I asked, following her.

"Yesterday. When Mr. Lewis was killed. Didn't they tell you that when they sent you, that I was the one who called yesterday, too?" She glared at us. "Nobody's really in charge, are they? Nobody really cares. You'd think after yesterday, the police might show more interest. But it's just the same as always. I'm not surprised. This whole neighborhood is going to hell. It wasn't like this years ago, you know. It was safe and friendly. And clean. Now it's filthy. You knew who your neighbors were then, not these damn yuppies moving in and out like a revolving door, with their damn music."

As we passed through the kitchen, she plucked a half-empty glass of clear liquid from the counter. "You knew who your cop on the beat was, too. I don't suppose either of you ever walked a beat. Cops don't do that anymore. You just ride around in cars, while all sorts of things happen on the streets." She stopped to glare at us again, but not to let us answer. A small poodle bounced around our feet, sniffing and panting. "That's his dog, you know," she told us, making it sound like an indictment. "The police just left him here yesterday. Just walked away and left him. You'd think they'd be more concerned, but why should they? Nobody gives a damn about people, why should anyone care about a dog? Poor Bobo." She pulled open a door in the back wall. The poodle charged out onto the wooden deck. Mrs. Lattimer followed, leaving the door open.

Bill stepped aside to let me go before him. "It's a lot to ask, for me to start taking care of a dog, with everything else," Mrs. Lattimer was saying, "but you don't see anyone else offering to take him. Poor Bobo. Well, there it is."

She waved the glass in her hand at the garden below. Stairs curved down from the deck we were on to a small flagstone terrace that met an area of hard-looking soil, scattered crocuses, and pots bristling with the straw remains of last fall's chrysanthemums.

"He never gardened, you know," Mrs. Lattimer said. She sipped from her glass. "I do it all. It's too much for me, by myself, but no one else cares. Well, go on. You don't expect me to go in there with you?"

The dog had run down the steps and was scurrying around the garden. "I don't know anything about it," Mrs. Lattimer said, her voice taking on a defensive tone. "Just that the tape is broken. It must have happened last night. The police didn't turn his alarm on when they left, you know. Not a bit worried, even though someone could have broken into the building and murdered us all in our beds." She finished what was in her glass. "I probably shouldn't even have called. I knew it would only be trouble for me. But someone has to do what's right. I only saw it because I was in the garden this morning looking at the mess the damn squirrels made digging up the tulips. But they weren't blooming anyway. They froze two weeks ago, when it got so cold."

"Thank you, Mrs. Lattimer," I said, stepping efficiently past her and starting down the wooden steps. "The city needs more public-spirited citizens like you. Smith?" I turned back to Bill.

"I'm on my way," he responded.

FOURTEEN

At the bottom of the curved steps, under the deck, was the door into Wayne Lewis's garden apartment. It was closed, but the yellow crime scene tape on it was broken.

I extracted a pair of photographer's thin white cotton gloves from my bag, inordinately pleased with myself for having put them in there that morning. I hate to carry a handbag; with me, it's generally a briefcase, a satchel big enough for me to sit in, or nothing. But the handbag had been part of the disguise for Ed Everest, and I'd stuffed the gloves in it along with my wallet and sunglasses as I was dashing out of the house because you never know.

Gloves on, I tried the door.

It opened.

It opened because the lock, having obviously been jimmied, wasn't going to work again.

Scratch marks and gouges all up and down the door frame testified to the hard work someone had done, probably with a tire iron, to get into Lewis's place. As the door swung open in my hand, I looked at Bill. He shrugged. We went in.

I closed the door behind us.

"Why is it," Bill asked, "that when I'm with you, we can't even go in straight when we're going in straight?"

"Don't tell me *you* would have resisted a chance like this handed to you on a silver platter," I retorted. "Now, come on, we probably don't have much time."

"No," he said, "Which may be just as well, since for sure we don't know why we're here."

"What I want to know is why the last guy was here. The guy who broke the tape."

"Maybe he came to adopt the dog. Poor Bobo."

I gave Bill the evil eye when he said that, but he wasn't looking at me. He was standing still, hands in his pockets, gazing around the apartment, moving his eyes slowly over everything.

That's how Bill works, and I try to learn these things from him, because I'm the type who charges in, not actually without thinking, but sometimes without thinking really hard. I like to stir things up and see what's at the bottom of the pot. Bill would rather sniff the steam and read the recipe first.

We surveyed the apartment. We could see the whole place from here. The kitchen, where we were standing, was ended by a counter; beyond that was a living room whose hardwood floor, covered partly by a Southwest-looking rug, stretched to the front windows. A double bed was carried on a loft built against the wall, with a desk tucked under it.

It was the floor near the Southwest rug that had the chalk outline of Wayne Lewis's body.

"The police have been over this place, you know," Bill said, still not moving, still looking.

"I know. But someone thought it was worth breaking into anyhow."

"That doesn't mean they found what they came for."

"Just a quick look," I said.

"Sure," said Bill. "Before the real police come."

I wasn't so sure they would. "She said she had to call them twice when she heard shots. How fast do you think they'll come just because the tape is broken?"

"Fast enough," Bill said, "to dig our graves. Three minutes, then we're gone."

"Okay."

I looked around again. We'd come to learn something about Wayne Lewis, and I'd learned one thing already: he'd been a very neat man. Possibly obsessively, though that was judgmental and who asked me?

I could see obvious evidence of cop activity: papers piled sloppily, drawers not quite closed, closet doors ajar—though any of that might also be evidence of whoever had broken in here last night. But under that, the true Wayne Lewis shone through. A spice shelf, bottles organized by size. Books in the bookcase alphabetically by author, and within author by title. Plants on the windowsill in identical green glazed pots. A matched and extensive set of enameled cookware hanging from perfectly spaced hooks above the kitchen counter.

I was willing to bet that there wasn't a drop of spilt milk on any refrigerator shelf, and that the sheets in the closet were ironed.

"A lot of electronics," I said to Bill, pointing to the sleek black stereo recessed in the wall, the TV with built-in VCR on a swivel shelf, the digital readout on the microwave. The stove had as many dials and buttons as the dashboard of Bill's car. A blank computer monitor and keyboard stood to technological attention on Lewis's desk.

"Mmmhmm," Bill said, looking over the computer. "Do you think you can work that?"

"Sure," I answered, glancing apprehensively at the thing. I have a little laptop, which I haul back and forth between home and office, and which I adore, but I think I treat it a little too much like a person: people are reputed to only use a tenth of their brain power, and that's about how much I use of my computer's.

"Of course, the police will have checked it out already," he said.

"Of course. But they weren't looking for what we're looking for," I answered, heading across the room.

"Which is what?"

"Who knows?"

I switched the machine on and waited for the menu to come up. When it did, I scanned the directories available. Bill still hadn't moved.

"Anything interesting?" he asked.

"It's hard to say." I switched into some random directories and opened some random files. "These all have to do with his work. There's not that much here. A memo about shoes, a letter to a lighting designer . . . I don't know. There might be something helpful, but I'd have to look at it awhile before I could know."

"Download it onto a disk and take it with you."

I had just decided to do that. I picked up a box marked "blank" and slipped a disk into the floppy drive. "I'm impressed you know 'download,' " I told Bill. I searched the disk to make sure it really was blank, then copied Lewis's files and the directories they were in.

"Jargon's easy," Bill said. "Comedy's hard." He crossed the room to the desk where I was, but he didn't look at the computer screen. He crouched, took a handkerchief from his pocket, and with it pulled a briefcase from under the desk.

It was a fine, square-cornered leather one, no scratches anywhere. Bill clicked it open. Inside, it was leather also, with special places to put pens, calculators, business cards, and yellow legal pads. It had one of those, but nothing was written on it.

"In the computer," Bill asked, contemplating the inside of the briefcase, "is there some kind of appointment calendar? A datebook, that kind of thing?"

"I don't think so." I went back to the directories. "I don't see anything called that, and the only program he's got here is a word processing one."

"That means something?"

"Well, it's not what you'd use for keeping appointments. You know, I really think you should take a computer course, so at least you'd know as much as the average ten-year-old."

"All comparisons are invidious." Bill pulled open some desk drawers, closed them, and made his way around the counter back to the kitchen again. He opened drawers and cabinets. "Hah," he finally said, standing with an accordion file in his hand. He began flipping through it.

"What's that?" I asked.

"Don't you have one of these? A place where you keep all your warranties and manuals and instruction booklets?"

"My mother puts them in a shoebox, but I haven't seen the shoebox in years. She figures that since they're written in English and she doesn't speak English, they don't mean anything." I pointed to the file he held. "That one's all alphabetized. Is yours like that?"

"Of course."

"Amazing."

"Must be a man thing."

"I thought men never read manuals."

"We never do. But we keep them all."

"What are you looking for?"

132

He pulled a small booklet from the folder. "This." Leafing through it, he asked me, "Do you have a datebook?"

"Of course I do," I said. "How else would I remember my second cousins' wedding anniversaries?"

"I don't have second cousins. But I scribble things on scraps of paper and stick them in my pockets. And I have a wall calendar I write important things on. Your birthday, for example."

"You have to write that down or you'd forget it?"

"I have to write it down to restrict it to one day. Otherwise I'd be celebrating it every day of the year."

"Nice recovery."

"Look in there." Bill pointed at the open briefcase.

I followed his finger. "What am I looking at?"

He gestured the booklet at the briefcase. "Pens. Pencils. Business cards. Reading glasses. Everything tucked into its place. But no datebook. No desk calendar. No wall calendar with birthdays written on."

I stared into the briefcase, then at him. "You're a genius."

"No—what do you nerds say, hard copy?—implies to me some electronic device to do what scraps of paper were made for. If it's not on the computer it must be somewhere else." He held up the booklet for me to see. "The Fushida Model CS1936 Electronic Wizard Pocket Time Manager with Calculator, Clock, Calendar, and Address Keeper."

"You're a genius," I said again.

"I could be wrong."

"So could I, about your being a genius. But I don't think so. I think you're right: that's what's missing."

Bill consulted the booklet. "There's a pocket in there next to the glasses about two and a half inches wide," he said. "That's just about the size of this thing."

"He'd have to have one," I said. "Especially if he worked freelance. To keep track of everything."

"Especially," Bill added, "a guy as compulsive as this."

"You think so, too?"

He gave me a look that I felt free to interpret any way I wanted to.

133

"I have another question," I said.

"Me too. What are we going to do about *that?*" Bill nodded toward the front window. I swiveled my head, then crossed the room quickly to get a better look.

A Sixth Precinct car was double-parking in front of the house.

Bill slipped the instruction booklet for the Electronic Pocket Wizard into his jacket and shut the folder in the cabinet he'd taken it from. I closed Lewis's briefcase, slipped it back under the desk, and turned off the computer. Over our heads we heard the sound of the doorbell and the scrabbling and yapping of Bobo the dog.

We looked at each other and at the back door as footsteps creaked above.

Then, two minds with but a single thought, we both sped toward the front.

My first fearful thought was that this was the kind of door that you needed a key to get out of, as well as in. I'd started from closer, so I reached it first. I turned the two thumb latches, crossed my mental fingers, and pulled the door.

It opened.

Bill right behind me, I ducked the crime scene tape and found myself under the front stoop. It smelled damp and stony. Silently, Bill pulled the door shut.

I waited, listened, then chanced a peek at the street.

The police car was empty; both cops must have gone up to see Mrs. Lattimer. I wondered if seeing Mrs. Lattimer was, in this precinct, a well-known two-cop job.

"Let's go," Bill suggested succinctly.

We went. Up the stairs, down the block, walking at a healthy pace but not running, because people notice you if you run.

"You think she remembered our names?" I asked Bill as we rounded the corner and headed north, against the traffic. In the Village, it's possible to get all the way to the subway on one-way streets so narrow that police cars would get stuck if they headed down them the wrong way.

"Yours, maybe," Bill grinned. Without breaking stride, he lit a cigarette. "Mine's too hard."

e made the Eighth Avenue subway without anyone following us, arresting us, or lifting our licenses. The local rolled into the station first, and we jumped on it. Once headed downtown, I relaxed.

"You have awfully long legs," I said, plopping down on a seat next to Bill, catching my breath.

"They actually get longer when I'm with short people in a hurry," he said, stretching out those very legs in the near-empty car. "It's a scientific fact."

"Science is amazing. It brings us facts like that, and electronic datebooks that are also address books. You know, the police may have it."

Bill shook his head. "They'd have taken the instructions."

"Maybe they couldn't find them."

He lifted one eyebrow at me. "Any man could have found them."

I lifted both eyebrows back and stuck my tongue out besides. "Well, maybe they didn't look. Maybe they thought they'd get a set from Fushida."

"That would take a few days. Why wait?"

"But why not take the thing?"

"They probably didn't look closely at it. They probably thought it was a calculator or something."

I thought for a minute. "Okay, suppose I buy that. Why do you guess someone cared enough about it to risk breaking in to steal it?"

Bill slipped his hands into his pockets as the train rocketed on. "Because there's something in it someone wanted."

"And I called you a genius. Can't you get any closer?"

Bill frowned. "The crystal is growing cloudy. The connection is failing. If you bought me a drink I might get smarter."

"That never works. But I do owe you one, don't I?"

"You bet you do."

"Well, can we save it for later, when we meet Andrew? I sort of want to go through these files now." I patted my bag, where Lewis's disk was.

"All work," Bill grumbled, pushing to his feet as the train rolled into the Spring Street station. "That's what they said about you. That Lydia Chin, they told me, she's no fun. I should've listened. Does nothing but work, work, work, they said, never even buys a guy a drink . . ." He was still muttering to himself as he left the train.

"I'll phone you," I called through the closing doors. Bill and the lighted platform disappeared quickly as the train plunged into the darkness of the tunnel, carrying me toward Canal Street and home.

Home was where my laptop was at the moment, so home was where I went. The late-afternoon sidewalks of Chinatown were crammed with people: new immigrants with bad teeth and wary eyes, looking over one shoulder for the authorities and the other for the main chance; prosperous businessmen from Hong Kong and Taiwan, striding through the streets in three-piece suits, cheerfully considering buildings for investment the way you'd chose among bracelets in a jewelry store; sidewalk vendors, selling knockoff watches and fake Chanel scarves next to jade pendants and tiny clay figures of fat, contented fishermen. The soft spring breeze did nothing for the odors of oranges and frying scallion cakes and fish in piles in cardboard boxes except to mix them all together.

I sidestepped people, fish, and a Chinese chess game that, judging from the intensity of the spectators, had quite a lot of money riding on it, and arrived at my own front door. Up the four flights, through the door with the four identical locks—this week, only the first and third were locked, based on my mother's theory that if you leave half your locks unlocked, a lock-picking thief will drive himself crazy locking some as he unlocks others—and into the tiny vestibule where I kicked off my shoes, pulled on my embroidered slippers, and looked up to find my mother staring at me.

"Ling Wan-ju!" she breathed in horror. "What happened to your head?"

It took me a second to realize what she meant. I straightened to face her. "Come on, Ma," I said. "This is the latest thing going. All the models wear their hair like this."

"They do?" She sounded as astonished as she would have if I'd told her all the models were actually men. "Why?"

"Men love it," I said, putting words to her deep, unspoken—or, more precisely, not-yet-spoken—fears. "And don't worry," I added, to reassure her that I was not permanently disabled, "it'll grow back."

She stared, then shook her head sharply, as though to force herself back to reality from a bad dream. My head and I were still there, however, so she said, "Well, I suppose until then you can wear a hat."

"Oh, come on," I said. "You'll get used to it, Ma. You'll learn to love it."

She frowned at me, as though I'd already spoiled her plans for something. I headed for my room, when from behind me she spoke again. "He called," she said.

I turned to face her. She was still frowning. "Who?" I asked.

"Who?" she repeated with a wave of her hand. "I hope you don't act this foolish around him. He's very clever, you know. He has a good degree, an MBA."

As opposed to yours, Lydia: sociology with an emphasis on criminal justice. Useless, unless I wanted to be criminal, about which my mother by her own admission had suspicions, given the quality of the people I knew.

But who did I know with an MBA?

Suddenly a light dawned, though it was a strange light, an odd quality to it casting weird shadows. "Roland Lum?" I tried.

"Of course. Who else would be calling you? You chased Paul Kao away; don't make the same mistake again. I hope Roland Lum likes short haircuts. Now go call him back. Don't keep him waiting."

Paul Kao was a friend of Andrew's I had dated briefly a few months ago. My mother had high hopes for him; he was educated, cultured, handsome, and very polite to his elders, especially her. Like a lot of men who claim to be fascinated with my profession at the be-

ginning, though, the reality of it—unpredictable hours and pre-
dictable trouble—got to him, and we called it quits in a friendly way.
I missed him a little, then got over it.

My mother hasn't.

The only way to avoid a replay of the Paul Kao argument, I
could see, would be to go do what she was telling me to do. That, cou-
pled with the fact that my own curiosity was killing me, made my
choice clear, and I went and did it.

My mother gave me both Roland's home and factory numbers.
It wasn't very late, so I tried the factory first.

The phone was answered on the second ring by a sort of pan-
lingual, "Yah?"

I asked, in English, for Roland. The phone clattered in my ear
and I heard a shout. While I waited for something else to happen, I
listened to whines and screeches and clanks just like the ones that had
been part of my childhood, the sounds of the long hours and sometimes backbreaking, sometimes numbingly dull work it takes to put
together a shirt or a skirt that will end up in the Goodwill bag a year
later.

"Hello!" It was Roland's voice, the greeting not a question but
an emphatic statement, delivered in a half-shout over the noises of
the machinery.

"Roland? It's Lydia. My mom said you called?" It suddenly
flashed into my mind that it was actually possible he hadn't called; that
it was within the bounds of believability that this was a sly match-
making trick of my mother's.

But not so. "Lydia!" Roland yelled back. "I sure did. You home?"

"Yes, why?"

"Can you meet me? I have—well, sort of a problem, and I
thought, boy, Lydia's the one I need! And I'll bet she could use the
work, too! What do you say? Can you?"

"Meet you when? What sort of a problem?"

"Anytime. How about now? I'll tell you about it when I see you."

"Well . . ." I glanced over at the clock. "I'm meeting someone
at ten, and there was something I wanted to do before that—"

"Great! You do that, and I'll finish up here, and then I'll buy you dinner. Eight o'clock, Tai Hong Lau? A buddy of mine's a chef there. He'll take good care of us."

From just beyond my bedroom door I heard the floorboards squeak as my mother shifted her position in the hallway. "Okay, Roland," I said. "That sounds good. See you later."

"Terrific! See you."

We hung up. I went out to the hallway where my mother was straightening the pictures on the wall.

"Why do you bother to eavesdrop?" I asked her. "We were speaking English."

"I don't know what you mean," she huffed, dusting the top of a picture frame. "Although it's a shame that you children forget all your Chinese. Mrs. Chan says Roland Lum can't even talk to the ladies in his shop now, except to give them orders. None of you children can even speak to your own relatives anymore."

"Roland's ladies are probably all Fujianese by now, so even if his Cantonese were perfect, he wouldn't be able to speak to them. And I'm speaking to you right now, Ma," I said, although the obvious never scored any points with my mother. "Anyway, I won't be home for dinner."

"Oh?" She was a study in lack of interest. "Do you have plans?"

Might as well give her a sweep. "I'm having dinner with Roland Lum," I told her. "And afterwards I'm going to have a drink with An Zhong."

I disappeared into the bathroom, leaving my mother in the hallway, dumbstruck at her incredible good fortune.

I took a shower; then, wrapped in my yellow silk robe, I sat down on my bed with the laptop and Wayne Lewis's disk. I went through things methodically, trying to be like Bill, or like he'd be if he had any clue how to use a computer. I opened directories and then files, scanned them, opened the next ones, and scanned them, too. It was a bust. Or, at least, if there was anything on it that was useful to me, I didn't recognize it. Most of it was letters or lists: lists of models; of music organized by designer and year; of themes—the seaside, angels, ladies who lunch—also organized by designer and year. Probably so his clients wouldn't repeat themselves, or each other. On the models list I found Andi Shechter's name and number, which would have been useful this morning and which I wrote down in my address book, but the fact that she was there wasn't necessarily surprising, and I didn't find anybody else I recognized. I didn't find Dawn Jing.

The letters, as business letters tend to be, were dull. Let's get together when you're in New York; we'll need forty more yards of green canvas; all the high-heeled sneakers were defective and not only is my client not going to pay for them, you'll be lucky if we don't sue you. They reminded me why I hate my own paperwork. I finally gave up. I tucked the laptop in its case and the disk in among my own disks, and got dressed for dinner.

As I stared into my closet I was a little sorry Andrew hadn't told me what kind of a club it was that Dawn Jing haunted. In New York there are as many acceptable looks as there are places to wear them, and it's a large number. Not that I could cover all of those from my closet. Most people's clothing, including mine, tends to stick within stylistic limits. People wear things they like and feel good in, things that identify them with the sub-tribe they want to be part of. You generally don't find people with a closet full of Dior suits also owning a bureau packed with bulky Guatemalan sweaters. It's all a matter of who you're claiming to be.

Because of my profession, though, my clothing vocabulary is larger than most people's. It's not really a question of disguise, more of acceptability, ease of movement from one world into others. If you look wrong you're instantly noticed, and, quite properly, distrusted: you're not a member of the tribe. In my job, getting past people is a major preoccupation. Dressing for Success means something specific to a P.I.

So I took from my closet a midnight-blue silk vest and a pair of black silk pants tailored like jeans, with pockets and everything. I added a pair of black heels I'd paid a lot of money for because they look classy but I can walk in them. I stuck my little .22 in a holster in the back of my waistband. The vest would cover it there, and it wouldn't show if I sat up straight. Maybe I should tell my mother that carrying a gun was good for my posture. I put on some gold bangles and a thin gold chain around my neck. I started to brush my hair and had to laugh at myself.

I checked the mirror. Not bad. The silk jeans made the look slightly trashy, which was probably good for just about any place I'd find myself tonight.

And Roland Lum would probably appreciate that, too.

I wasn't sure how to take Roland, or what to make of his calling me today. My first instinct was to go up in his face, subtly, of course, but in a way that would make sure he knew that Lydia Chin didn't need his help, not his warnings about other clients being nuts or the work he thought I could use.

On the other hand, it was possible that my annoyance with him was my problem, and Roland was just a brash, pushy old friend of the family.

I collected keys and cash into a black silk handbag the size of a postage stamp, and called Bill.

"Oh?" he said, after I'd announced myself. "To what do I owe this honor?"

"I was thinking about pushy men. Besides, I said I'd call."

"You said you'd call," he echoed. "Hah. You said you'd buy me a drink. You said you loved me madly."

"Good try, but forget it. I'm having dinner with Roland Lum."

Bill was briefly silent. "How did that come about?"

"My mother lit incense. Roland says he has a case for us."

"A case? What kind of case?"

"I don't know."

"Is that a good idea?"

"What? Taking another case in the middle of this one, or taking a case from Roland Lum?"

"Both."

"I don't know."

"Gee," he said, "there's so much you don't know. Maybe I could teach you. Maybe I could—"

"Maybe you could meet me at Andrew's at ten, looking cutting-edge."

"Maybe I could fly to the moon. What the hell do they wear on the cutting edge?"

"Forget it. Just wear black. You know which one is black?"

"Sure. The one you look so gorgeous in. Though come to think of it, that doesn't narrow it down very far, does it?"

"You're getting on my nerves."

"I'll take anything I can get on. Andrew's, at ten. Black," he said, and for the first time in recorded history, he hung up on me.

I put on a black velvet hat, took my black-and-red silk baseball-style jacket from the hall closet, called good-bye to my mother, and slipped out the apartment door. That didn't work; she poked her head out as soon as the door closed.

"What are you wearing?" she asked suspiciously.

I climbed back up the two stairs I'd made it down and posed for her on the landing.

She pursed her lips at my outfit. "I'm glad to see you're wearing a hat," she said. "Even that one."

"Thank you."

"But you should be wearing a skirt, not trousers."

"Pants are very in."

"In," she scoffed. "What difference does 'in' make? 'In' doesn't make you attractive. A skirt will make a man look at you."

"Beauty's in the eye of the beholder, Ma," I said, although I got the uncomfortable feeling it didn't sound nearly as convincing in Chinese.

Certainly not convincing to my mother. Her look was incredulous. "What sort of nonsense is that? Is that something you heard from Crooked Face?" My mother steadfastly refuses to learn Bill's name. "Some things are beautiful and some aren't," she snorted. "The same as right and wrong. Any man who thinks you look good that way . . ."

She pulled her head in and shut the door, bringing the rest of the sentence with her. I gathered, though, that it had something to do with undesirable sons-in-law. As I headed down the stairs, I heard her decisively locking our first and third locks.

Tai Hong Lau was a few blocks over, on Elizabeth Street. I walked there, through streets that were beginning to quiet down now, as the sidewalk vendors and vegetable sellers packed up and went home to eat their rice and catch a few hours sleep in rooms they shared with five or six other newly arrived men. Tomorrow morning they'd be up before dawn again, bringing out their merchandise, getting a jump on another day in the Beautiful Country.

I reached Tai Hong Lau at five to eight. It's one of Chinatown's new, upscale restaurants: tables draped in white tablecloths and set with fine china, standing a discreet distance from each other in a plant-and-mirror lined, marble-floored room. The waiters wear crisp white shirts and black pants, and the cooks, who are called chefs at Tai Hong Lau, experiment with the use of shockingly foreign ingredients like mayonnaise. The price is high, for Chinatown, but dinner for two plus cappuccino afterward a few blocks north in Little Italy still costs less than dinner for one in a white-tablecloth restaurant uptown. That way a guy like Roland can impress his date without really putting a dent in his bankbook.

Thinking that made me wonder, as I entered the restaurant, whether Roland thought of this as a date, or if my mother was the only one making that assumption.

The business-suited manager smiled a professional smile when I gave him Roland's name. He showed me to a table up a few steps in the back part of the restaurant, left two menus, and hurried back to his station at the front to smile professionally at someone else. A waiter came over and asked what I wanted to drink. I sipped the seltzer he brought me, watched the diners and waiters move sedately around the room, and waited for Roland.

I grew up in Chinatown restaurants: my father was a cook, and though he died when I was thirteen, I remember at least five different places he worked in. Relatives of mine own, work in, or have worked at some time in probably half the eateries in the neighborhood. But they're the old-style restaurants and noodle joints, the ones with Formica tables and stainless steel teapots, thick plates, and rushing, harried waiters. I didn't know anyone at Tai Hong Lau.

Roland, of course, was a little different. As far as Chinatown has a high society, he grew up in it; as far as there's a right side of the tracks here, he was from it. There weren't restaurants like Tai Hong Lau when Roland and I were growing up, but I wasn't surprised that Roland had made friends with a chef in a place like this as soon as there was a place like this.

And speaking of Roland, he was late. I sipped my soda and tried to keep my foot from bouncing impatiently up and down. I was curious about Roland's problem, and why I was the person to solve it. And I don't like to be kept waiting.

Fifteen minutes later, when I was on my second seltzer, Roland pushed through the glass doors and cut easily to the front of the short waiting line that had formed since I came in. One hand in the pocket of a soft-fabric navy suit, he spoke some old-buddy words to the manager and was pointed in my direction. He grinned up at me; then he hustled through the restaurant, taking the steps in one bound, and came to a stop at my table.

"God," he said, still standing, his grin spreading. "You look fantastic. Your hair wasn't like that this morning, was it?"

"Hi, Roland," I said. "Imagine meeting you here. Hey, why don't you sit down?"

If there was any irony in my voice, he missed it completely. Maybe I'd have to work on irony. He pulled out the opposite chair and sat, signaling the waiter.

"I'll have a Heineken," Roland said, in Cantonese. "And bring the lady another of whatever she's having. And tell Lee Yu Sing in the kitchen that Roland's here. He knows what to do."

The waiter smiled and took our menus away. I gave Roland a quizzical look. "You ordered already?"

"I called Yu Sing before and asked what's good. He's got some great fresh perch and some huge oysters, so I told him full speed ahead. That's okay, isn't it?" His face said that the idea that perch and oysters might not be okay with me was absolutely brand-new to him. "You like oysters?"

"I love them," I said truthfully. There had been a sizzling four-spice chicken dish on the menu that I'd been interested in, but I guessed I'd try that next time I came.

"So." Roland leaned back in his chair. "Sorry I was late. On the phone with my brother. He wants a loan." Roland made a face. "I'm going to give it to him, but not as big as he says he needs. We had to talk, I had to cut him down. He was disgustingly grateful anyway. You don't fawn on your brothers, I'll bet."

"Never."

"Good. It's really a drag, let me tell you. Hey, did I mention you look terrific? The haircut is great. You didn't get it just for me, did you?"

"Sorry. I got it before I even knew you called."

"Well, it's great. Makes you look more feminine than this morning. You're going out after this, right? Some hot date in a cool spot?"

"I'm going to a club with my brother," I told him. If that news either relieved or disappointed him, I couldn't tell.

"Old Elliot?" he asked.

"No, Andrew."

"Andrew. How is Andrew?" Roland's voice took on a tone of knowledgeable insinuation. "Is he still . . . single?"

"Just like me," I answered.

"Well, maybe not *just* like you," Roland grinned.

Luckily I didn't have to say anything then, because the waiter came over with Roland's beer. He started to pour it, but Roland's face changed in an instant, flashing into anger. "Heineken!" he barked at the waiter, who looked in surprise at the bottle of Chinese beer in his hand. "Not this shit! Why don't you listen? What the hell's the matter with you?" The waiter's face darkened, too, and he might have said something, but the manager was at our side, apologizing, steering the waiter away, assuring Roland everything was being taken care of.

Roland watched them walk away. Then his face changed instantly again, from hard back to breezily cheerful. "God," he grinned, shaking his head, switching back to English. "Some people, huh?"

Yes, I thought, that's true. Some people.

A different waiter came over with the right beer, and another seltzer for me. Roland took the bottle from him and poured it himself, carefully down the side of the glass, to avoid making a head. Bill, I remembered, likes a head on his beer.

Before Roland was finished pouring, the new waiter was back, presenting with a discreet flourish a platter of sizzling oysters in a garlic and scallion sauce. Well, at least I'd gotten something sizzling.

"Hey, not bad for starters, huh?" Roland asked, beaming at the oysters as though he'd made them himself. He dished some out for me and then took some. I tasted them. They were wonderful, something bitter in the sauce setting off the richness of the oysters perfectly.

"You know, I really can't believe my luck," Roland said, after he'd eaten half his plate of oysters and washed them down with beer. "I run into you this morning, I need some help this afternoon, and bam! you're having dinner with me tonight. What a world." He shook his head in delighted bafflement. "So what do you think? You picked up any new clients today, or can you take my case?"

"No new clients," I answered. "What's the case?"

"The case," he said. "The case. It's a missing person."

"Who's missing?"

"A girl who works for me. Peng Hui Liang. At the factory."

"How long has she been missing?"

"Since yesterday."

"That's not very long," I said. "Are you sure she didn't just give herself a few days off?"

"They don't do that," Roland answered, scooping some more oysters onto his plate, leaving the spoon handle pointed in my direction. "They don't even take the ones I give them. They're too afraid they'll come back and find someone else at their machines."

"Would they?"

"What?"

"Find someone else."

"Well, I have to meet my orders." Roland defended himself and his hiring practices with a smile. "I don't have much margin. I can't sit around short-staffed with empty machines."

"So then why do you care?"

"About what?"

"Peng Hui Liang. If she's been missing since yesterday, you must have already replaced her."

"Well, but that doesn't mean I'm not worried about her."

"Do you worry about all your workers if they don't come in?"

"Sure. Anyone doesn't come in, I call her to make sure she's okay. And to make sure she still wants the job."

"And you called Peng Hui Liang?"

146

He nodded. "They said she didn't live there, whoever answered the phone. That happens."

That happens mostly for one reason. "Is she illegal?"

Roland gave me a shrug and a half-smile.

"So maybe she's been picked up by Immigration."

"I thought of that. I checked. I have a buddy over there."

A buddy. What Roland probably had at INS was what every factory owner dreams of and many of them have: a bagman, someone he could pay not to notice that the people sitting behind his machines for ten hours a day at four dollars an hour six days a week were what are politically correctly called "undocumented workers."

"Under a different name?" I suggested.

"I showed him a picture. Not there."

"What do you think happened to her?"

"I don't know."

"And why do you want to know?"

Roland's face was innocent. "I told you, I'm worried about her."

"Why?"

"Because she's missing," he said, with a look that said he didn't understand what my problem was.

"Hiring a P.I. to look for a worker who didn't show up for work shows an impressive level of concern from an employer. Do you do it often?"

Roland let out an exasperated sigh. "Lydia, I'm offering you a paying job. Do you want it or not?"

"I want to know why you want to find this woman."

Roland pursed his lips and tapped his chopsticks on the table, looking like he was trying to decide whether to answer me. He bought a little time for free, because just then the waiter brought the fish. It was a whole perch, steamed and glistening in a ginger-scallion sauce, topped with delicate strands of carrot, red pepper, and bean thread. With it came a platter of watercress sauteed with garlic, and a large covered bowl of fragrant rice.

"That's beautiful," I said.

Roland said, "I told you Yu Sing knows what he's doing," and began to expertly debone and serve the perch.

I didn't interrupt; there was no point in getting bones in my fish in order to win a point. When the perch and the watercress and the rice were all sitting in splendid readiness on my plate, however, I started up again.

"Why do you want to find her?" I asked. As I waited for his answer, I lifted some perch on my chopsticks and gave it a try. It was perfect, firm and moist, the ginger piquant and the scallions crunchy.

Roland moved his shoulders casually. "She's alone here," he said. "She hasn't got anyone, and now the people at her phone number are saying they don't know her. I don't like it."

"And I don't believe it."

Roland's cheeks flushed red. "What don't you believe?"

"The concerned-boss routine. Illegals disappear all the time, for all sorts of reasons. Maybe she got a better job. Maybe she got married. Maybe she went back to China. No one who didn't have a personal relationship with her would be losing any sleep over it."

Roland looked at me for a long time, drumming his chopsticks lightly against his glass. Then he dropped his eyes to his plate and dug back into his perch. He finished the piece in front of him before he looked at me or spoke again.

"Still the toughest little thing in town," he said, one corner of his mouth turning up ruefully. "You're going to make me say it, aren't you?"

"I don't know what it is," I answered. "But you need to tell me before I decide whether to take the case."

"You don't know what it is," he repeated sarcastically. "Like I'd really believe someone like you wouldn't have figured it out. Okay, if that's what you want, I'll say it. We had a thing going on. I think she ran away because of me."

I gave myself some more rice and considered this. "Why would she do that, if you had a thing going on?"

"Maybe one of us thought more was going on than the other one did."

"Which one were you?"

"Guess."

"What are you telling me? You came on to her and she ran away?"

148

"Not like that. We did have a thing, saw each other a few times, you know. Not that it was serious or anything. I mean, not really. But, you know . . ."

"I don't know."

He looked at me over a hard smile. "My God, you're really something, aren't you? Lydia, for god's sake. She's pregnant with my kid."

Sixteen

I called Bill from the phone outside the ladies' room at Tai Hong Lau. All I got was his service. I didn't leave a message; there wasn't any point. I'd wanted to bring him up to date on Roland's troubles before we met at Andrew's, but it could wait. I grabbed a cab and headed for Chelsea.

I'd told Roland I'd do it. I'd gotten from him the phone number where they said they didn't know Peng Hui Liang, the photograph he'd shown to his buddy at the INS, and instructions.

"Don't let her know I'm looking for her, okay? It'll only make it worse. I just want to know that she's okay and she hasn't done anything stupid."

"What's stupid?"

"Lydia, come on."

"You mean you want to make sure she hasn't had an abortion? Or you want to make sure she gets one?"

Roland didn't answer that. He finished his fish, his watercress, his rice—I was already done—and waved the waiter over to take the plates. Then he poured out the rest of his beer and drank that. Leaning back in his chair, he lit a Marlboro and flipped the pack onto the table.

"You know, Lydia, I sort of admire your approach. I'm a pretty direct guy myself. Don't care much what people think. If it's what I mean, I say it. Same for you, huh?"

"Sort of."

"Thing is, I'm not sure how far it'll get you in your business. People who hire private eyes might want a little more discretion. I don't know. Maybe I'm wrong." Cigarette dangling from his lip, he signaled the waiter with an American Express Gold Card. "You just find Hui Liang for me. Discreetly. Then we'll talk."

Now, in the cab on the way uptown, I was thinking about searching for people. What a strange relationship it put you in, this circling closer to someone who, in Peng Hui Liang's case, didn't want to be found; in Dawn Jing's, didn't know anyone was looking. It was like a split-screen movie image, where the actors on one side of the screen didn't know about the actors on the other, where everyone just went about their business but the audience could see the connections and sense what was coming.

Of course, the metaphor wasn't quite right, because I was both actor and audience, about to reach out from my side of the screen, about to step across to the other set of images.

Bill was at Andrew's when I got there. I don't know what their conversation had been, but when Andrew met me at the elevator that opened into the loft, he seemed in a much better mood than I'd been prepared for.

"Nice outfit," he smiled, leading me into the living area, where I'd met Genna Jing and John Ryan two nights before. "What if I told you we were going to a grunge bar?"

I frowned. "We're not, are we?" Grunge, which depends heavily on flannel and torn denim, was one of the New York scenes this outfit would not cover.

"No."

"Then if you told me that, I'd know you were lying. Hi," I said to Bill, who'd been scrutinizing one of Andrew's photographs on the wall when I came in, but was now scrutinizing me.

"Hi. Nice outfit."

"You, too. Good color choice."

Per instructions, Bill was wearing black jeans and a black T-shirt. The tail of the big blue snake tattooed on his left arm was visible below

150

the shirt sleeve. That alone would probably get us into any club in New York.

Bill pulled a pair of small round sunglasses from his T-shirt pocket. He slipped them on and I had to grin. It was very Hollywood.

"Cutting edge," I said approvingly.

Andrew was in black slacks, too, but with a black-buttoned white shirt fastened all the way up to the neck, no tie or jacket. His hair was combed straight back, his usual way. The ruby stud winked from his left ear. My brother, I mentioned to myself again with the slight surprise I always feel when I notice it, is a very handsome man.

Tony waved a languid hand from where he was settled on the sofa. "The princess of private investigation," he greeted me. "The queen of questioning, the duchess of detection. 'Lo."

" 'Lo." I went over and gave him a kiss on the cheek. Tony's handsome, too, with short sandy hair. He's as tall as Bill, and his muscles are well-defined because he works out at the gym. Bill's muscles aren't as sculpted-looking, but I have no question who'd win if the two of them ever had any reason to go up against each other. Bill likes to keep his strengths hidden, but they're there.

"Lydia," Tony ordered, staring closely at me, "remove your hat."

"Okay," I said. "But I want you guys to maintain a certain degree of cool."

I took the hat off.

Andrew breathed, "Wow," but quietly. Bill grinned. To his credit, probably because he'd already seen the haircut, he didn't whistle.

Tony did.

"You," I pointed at Tony, "lose. So what do you think, you guys? You like it?"

"It's perfect," Andrew said.

"It's fabulous," Tony agreed.

I raised an eyebrow at Bill. "Don't tell me you have nothing to say."

"Oh, no," he answered. "I have plenty to say. But I think it's better said in private. Where I can whisper in your shell-like ears, which I can now see. Where I can—"

"Well, I don't know where that would be," I overrode him. "But I doubt if it's where we're going tonight. And by the way, where is that?" I turned to Andrew. "And shouldn't we be going?"

"We're going to a club called Quiver," Andrew told me. "Not far from here. We can leave whenever. The action doesn't start there until late."

"When does Pearl Moon get there?"

"The couple of times I've seen her there, she's come in around eleven."

"Then let's go," I said. "The thought of missing her is making me antsy. Besides, I need to put my hat back on. My head's getting cold."

Bill, picking his black leather jacket up off the sofa, opened his mouth. I shot him a look. He had been about, I could tell, to offer to keep me warm.

Quiver was a hot, happening club near Union Square. That meant it cost us $15 apiece to get in, and we might not have been admitted, even so, except that the bouncer waved us to the front of the line as soon as he saw Andrew.

"Hey, man," they greeted each other, with the shoulder-level handclasp that men in the in crowd use to differentiate themselves from the rest of us. Then we were ushered through the door, on which was painted a fat, lascivious cupid reaching for an arrow to fit on his bow. Oh, I thought, *that* kind of quiver. Cupid had sunglasses and a cigar. We were invited to pay our money to a bored-looking young woman on a high stool, and permitted down the stairs and into the sanctuary.

The club was in the basement. The pounding music we'd felt at the top of the stairs was a physical presence here, a thumping and howling that worked in partnership with the strobing colored lights, the swirling cigarette smoke, and the two huge video screens at the ends of the cavernous room to provide the decor, ambiance, dance music, and excuse not to make conversation all at once. Smoke-blurred people stood around the edge of the dance floor, or, on the floor itself, swayed and twisted, moved apart, or held each other close.

Bill and I looked at each other, but neither of us tried to say anything. There wouldn't have been any point. Andrew grinned and motioned us to follow him. We did, working our way through the crowd to an archway in a side wall. It lead to a short corridor, another archway, another corridor. With each thick wall we passed, the music diminished. At the end of the second corridor, a final archway opened into a midsized room, high-ceilinged but not huge. The music here was provided by a live band at a loud but listenable level, and there were tables, chairs, banquettes, and a bar.

Andrew, Bill, and I settled at a table away from the band while Tony went to the bar to get drinks. "This is the 'A' room," Andrew said, leaning forward across the table. "The front room is mostly for the bridge-and-tunnel crowd, unless there's a hot group playing there. They like the scene, the lights, and everything."

"So when cool people come to Quiver, this is where they come?" I asked.

"You're here," Andrew said, as though that was the answer to my question.

Tony came back with the drinks. Bill lit a cigarette, we all leaned back, listened to the band, and watched.

The band was pretty good, especially the drummer. He was the total opposite of the wild man I'd seen in the subway. This one seemed almost catatonic, a tall thin kid who stared straight ahead, never seeming to look at his drums or anything else. But he was always completely on top of the music, always giving the singer or the guitarists exactly what they needed, and his solo was terrific.

While we waited in hopes of Dawn Jing, I checked out the other people who knew about the 'A' room. The place was full but not crowded, nothing like the crush in the big, main club. The women mostly wore short, tight skirts, black hose, and high, thick-heeled shoes, although I was not the only one in pants. I made a note to tell my mother that. The men wore black or white shirts, some with jackets with casually rolled-up sleeves, and as far as I was concerned, an overrepresentation of cowboy boots.

The band finished a set, took a break, started another set. We made not very much conversation, and we each had another drink. I wanted to tell Bill about my dinner with Roland, and from a look he'd

153

given me as we were leaving Andrew's, I could tell he wanted to know, but I didn't want to do it with Andrew and Tony around. Besides, although what we were getting from the band in here was loud music and not the thumping, over-the-top noise they had in the other room, it was still of a level that would have made it difficult for me to convey any of the subtleties of the tale.

In the middle of the second set, I had to go to the bathroom. I made Andrew promise he'd throw a net over Pearl Moon if she came in while I was away, and I headed for the corridors and archways, following his directions.

The room was a white-tiled grotto smelling of perfumed soap. I did what I had to do in a hot pink stall with huge paintings of the cigar-smoking cupid on both sides of the door. You could have called them twice life-size, except who knows how big cupids really are? I finished, pulled open cupid's door to go wash my hands and get back to the band, and found Dawn Jing leaning on the tiled wall, arms crossed, waiting for me.

It had to be her. She wore a tight, skimpy black velvet dress with rhinestone straps, showing off the small, pale yellow moon and blue clouds tattooed on her left shoulder. She had Genna's features, but with tiny differences of proportion and emphasis that amounted to this: where Genna was beautiful, Dawn was stunning.

She wore expert makeup and a haircut as short as mine. No, shorter, and with a harder edge. I felt the same edge when I looked into her dark eyes. Her brown-toned lips were not smiling.

"You're new," she said to me.

I was surprised, and tempted to say, I thought the haircut would take care of that. But what I said was, "Are you Pearl Moon?"

"You're with Ed Everest?" she asked, ignoring my question in favor of her own. "I can tell from the haircut."

I nodded. Ed Everest, who'd said he'd never heard of Dawn Jing. I wasn't sure what we were doing, but Ed's name bouncing around in the tiled room made me decide to follow this path a little ways. "Mishika," I told her.

"Ed should know better," she snorted. "Sending girls here." She pushed off the wall and took a step toward me. "This place is off limits to Ed, honey. Scram."

"Ed didn't send me. I'm here with friends."

She blew air out from her nose in a rude sound. "First of all, news flash: johns are not your friends. I've had my eye on you for about half an hour, honey. Between you and me, two of the guys you're with aren't even straight. Rookie mistake. Don't make it too often or Ed'll get pissed. But that's your problem. Ed's girls don't work this club, Mishika. They didn't before, and they don't now. Ed should have told you, and it's just like him not to, because that's the kind of worm he is. But Pearl's telling you. Get lost."

"I'm not working."

"Oh! Oh, please." She rolled her eyes. "Okay, you're just showing some folks a good time. Buyers, right? From out of town? I'll bet the big one's looking for catalog models. Has a chain of stores in the Midwest? That's always good for a few hot nights. What about the queers—business associates he couldn't shake?" Then a thought seemed to hit her and brought a sharp smile. "Or is Ed running boys now, too? You and that Asian boy work as a team? Good old Ed. Kinky bastard." The smile faded like sunlight on a cloudy day. "Look, honey. I know what Ed's thinking. He's thinking without Wayne I can't hold the territory. That's bullshit and you can tell him I said so."

"You worked with Wayne?" I hoped I didn't sound as surprised as I actually was. "He was your—partner?" The other word I'd been about to use wasn't such a nice one, and I swallowed it.

"Ed didn't tell you that either, hmm? Ed's a shit, honey. You'll figure that out for yourself. Wayne and I helped each other. But not so much I can't get along without him. Only, one thing: you can tell Ed that what he used to come to Wayne for he can find somewhere else. I'm not picking up that part of the business."

"What was that?" I asked. "That Ed came to Wayne for?"

"Ed knows. If you don't, you don't have to. Now I have to take a pee. You and your 'friends' be gone when I come out."

"Actually," I said, "I came to this club especially to find you."

She stopped in the act of entering one of the cupid booths. "Oh? And why was that?" She turned and looked me up and down. "Ready to leave Ed so soon? Good instincts; you'll never make a nickel with him. But some of the johns are okay. You can take home some nice perks. That guy you're with doesn't look half bad. See if

155

you can hit him up for a good pair of shoes or a bag or something."
She shook her head. "I don't know if I'm ready to take any talent off
Ed right now, Mishika."

"My name's not Mishika," I said.

"And mine's not Pearl. So what?"

"I'm Lydia Chin," I said. "And you're Dawn Jing. I'm here because of your sister."

She let her hand drop from the stall door. "Genna?" she said,
making no attempt to deny her identity. "What's that supposed to
mean—because of her?"

This conversation so far hadn't gone at all the way I'd expected
it to, and I could see it wasn't changing now. I kept on anyway.

"She has a problem. I wanted to talk to you about it."

"Genna has lots of problems. I'm never the one she wants to talk
to about them."

"She doesn't. I do."

"And remind again just who you are?"

"Lydia Chin," I said.

That didn't seem to be exactly what she wanted, but I wasn't
ready to give her any more yet.

"And the problem is—?"

"Stolen sketches," I said.

"Stolen—why, you enterprising little bitch." Her tone was full
of wonder and admiration; it took me a moment to get past it to her
words. When I did, they didn't make a lot of sense to me. "Maybe I
ought to reconsider helping you leave Ed," she said thoughtfully. "We
might work well together. But meanwhile—" She took a sharp step
forward, caught my shoulders, and jammed me back against the sink.
Face up close to mine, she snarled, "You made one big mistake,
honey. Don't make it worse!"

Twenty years of Tae Kwon Do wanted to chop into her ribs,
then throw her over my hip to the cold, tiled floor as she crumbled.
But I didn't. She had me pinned but she wasn't hurting me, and I
didn't want to hurt her.

I also wanted to know what was going on here.

"Let me go," I demanded.

Her response was to push me harder against the wet porcelain

156

sink. I felt a damp puddle seep through my vest. "I don't know how you knew," she growled, "but you've got some balls coming to me. I suggest—"

Loud music flooded the room as two young women, one black, one white, both thin and bony, came laughing through the door. Dawn yanked herself back away from me. One of the bony women entered a stall and the other leaned over the sink to inspect her makeup.

Dawn shot a look at the woman at the mirror, then back to me. "In the hall." She pushed through the door, leaving it to swing behind her.

I washed my hands, repaired my own lipstick, straightened my vest and followed her out of the ladies' room, glad to get away from the scented soap. Her eyes were burning where she waited for me in the arched corridor. She had lit a cigarette; it stayed between her lips as she talked. She squinted an eye against the smoke.

"I think you have this wrong," I said.

"No, rookie, *you* have it wrong. Stealing Genna's sketches was shitty. Letting someone grab the money from you was stupid. Oh, yeah, I heard what happened in the park. Someone came and snatched it after those idiot P.I.s dropped it off, before you could get near it, right? Well, too bad, kiddo. That's your problem. But coming to me, here, for more money—shit, that's dangerous, honey."

The menace in her voice made that believable, but I wasn't focused on that right now.

"You think I stole the sketches?" I asked.

"Of *course* not," she assured me, with a broad wave of her hand. "And you're not a hooker, either, are you? You're the Queen of fucking Sheba. What you really are, Mishika or Lydia or whatever, is too stupid to live. Go back home, honey. New York'll eat you alive."

"If you didn't take them, how do you even know about the sketches?"

"If I didn't—? What's that supposed to mean? And how do *you* know where the money comes from?"

She glared at me, I stared at her, and I almost had to laugh. Here we were, two short Chinese women in silk and velvet and fabulous haircuts, facing off in a hallway to the pounding of a rock band, tension between us so thick you could slice it and make sandwiches, and both of us so confused that there might be nothing to do at this point but tell the truth.

"I'm a private investigator," I said. "I don't know anything about the money. I came looking for you because I thought you stole the sketches."

The angry set of her shoulders didn't change, but she blinked. "You're a—You thought—Wait. I . . . Who *are* you?"

"Lydia Chin," I repeated patiently. "I'm a private investigator. The men I'm with, one's my partner. The Chinese one is my brother. Maybe you should come have a drink with us. I think we need to talk."

SEVENTEEN

It was practically worth having been shoved back against a cold wet sink to see the expression on Andrew's face when I came back to the table with Dawn Jing in tow. Bill stood when he saw us approach; Andrew and Tony, a little belatedly, did the same. Andrew looked in confusion from Dawn to me, and Tony looked the same way from me to Andrew. Only Bill looked unperturbed as we shuffled the chairs around and sat.

The fact that Bill was saying nothing was probably what kept Andrew and Tony from blurting out the questions on their faces. With Bill it was because he didn't know what the gag was and was waiting for a cue from me. But there was no gag. I hadn't gone in straight with Dawn Jing, but she and I had come out that way.

"This is Dawn Jing, everybody," I said. "Sometimes known as Pearl Moon. My partner, Bill Smith," I said to Dawn, pointing as I went. "Andrew Chin. Tony D'Angelo." They all shook Dawn's hand.

Up on the stage, the band finished a number with a screech of guitars and a crash of drums, and prepared to take a break.

"So," Dawn said, turning back to me. "What's going on? I don't have all night. I need to make a living. My date's waiting."

Andrew, it seemed to me, blushed. No one else reacted.

"I want to talk about the stolen sketches," I said. "We came to find you because we thought you stole them."

"Why the hell would you think that?"

"You and Genna have had trouble before."

"Oh, not really what you'd call 'trouble,' " she said sarcastically. Music from an unidentifiable rock album started up with a howl, as the DJ started mixing cuts to fill the silence left by the band. Dawn raised her voice, not quite a shout. "She just pretends I don't exist. I changed my name to make it easier for her."

"To make it easier for her to pretend you don't exist?"

She shrugged. "I thought if she could deny it in public, maybe she'd admit it in private. But that's none of your business," she added suddenly. "Aren't you people going to at least offer me a drink?"

Her eyes swept the table and settled on Tony. "Martini," she said. "Two olives, no onion."

Tony glanced at Andrew and realized he was elected. He rose and went off to the bar to get Dawn's drink.

"But," I said, for the benefit of Andrew and Bill, "before I got the chance to accuse Dawn of stealing the sketches, she accused me. She thought I was here to shake her down."

Bill pulled a cigarette out of the pack in his pocket. Before he'd gotten his match lit, Dawn had snapped a Virginia Slim out of her purse and was holding it airily in front of her. Bill reached over with the match; Dawn put her hand gently on his to guide it to the right place on her cigarette. I guess it's easy to miss the right place if you don't have help. She smiled her thanks into his eyes.

"All right," Bill said, his hands back on his own side of the table again, "I'll bite. Why would you try to shake Dawn down over Genna's sketches?"

The question was addressed to me, but he was looking at Dawn. She held his eyes for a moment, then leaned back in her chair and blew out a puff of smoke. "Who are you guys working for?"

"Genna hired us," I said. "To make the payoff."

159

A light came into Dawn's eyes. "That was you? The idiots in the park?" She met Bill's look again with a scornful smile. He gave her back a c'est-la-vie one.

"Unforeseen circumstances," I said.

"Oh, don't sweat it, honey," she told me, streaming out smoke. "If someone shot at me over someone else's money, I'd hide *my* butt under a rock until it was over."

Tony returned, martini in hand. Two olives, no onion. He'd brought a fresh bourbon for Bill, and a Budweiser for himself. Andrew and I were still nursing the last round of mineral water.

Dawn raised her glass to Bill before she drank.

"Wait," Andrew said. "Wait. If you didn't steal the sketches—and how do we know she didn't, Lydia? —and if you didn't, how do you know what's going on? I thought we were the only people besides Genna and John who knew about this."

"Big shot," Dawn murmured to her cigarette. Andrew flushed.

"But it's a good question," I said. "John and Genna insisted we keep this quiet. It doesn't sound to me like you and Genna are particularly close." That got me a roll of the eyes. "How *do* you know?"

Dawn tapped her cigarette into a pink cupid ashtray. "The people who made the payoff—" she gave Bill the contemptuous look again "—and lost the money, were fired. So you don't work for Genna anymore." She turned her hard eyes on me again. "Why are you here?"

"This case has gotten complicated," I answered. "And dangerous. If you stole the sketches, we need to talk to you."

"And if I didn't?"

"We still need to know how you're connected."

"Why? How come you still give a damn, if you were fired?"

"Someone shot at me. That gives me an interest. And I don't like to be fired."

Dawn gave me a long, silent look. I met it. Something passed between us, I thought, of recognition, and of acknowledgment. She tamped out her cigarette and spoke. "And I don't like to be accused of things I didn't do. Whose stupid idea was it that I stole the sketches?"

"Mine," Bill said.

Andrew, who had been about to speak, covered himself with a pull on his Perrier.

Dawn looked at Bill, and gave a brief snort. "That figures. What did Genna say?"

"We didn't talk to her about it," I said. "But I think the thought may have crossed her mind, too. Or I thought so, until you started talking about the money and where it comes from. I want to hear about that."

"And I want to hear about why you think Genna thinks I stole the fucking sketches."

"Deal?" I suggested.

"Maybe. What did you mean when you said *dangerous?*"

"People are shooting. Killing. Wayne Lewis is dead."

"Wayne?" A vertical line marred her perfect porcelain brow. "What does Wayne have to do with it?"

"We think he might have been the thief."

"Wayne?" She stared at me. "You're crazy. Everybody in the industry knows Wayne. Knew him. Shit." She sipped some martini. I thought I saw a shudder run through her, but maybe she was cold. "Who would he have sold them to? And why bother? He wasn't hard up. He had other fish to fry. Whose dumb idea was that? Yours, again?" She threw a look at Bill. He smiled back, and shrugged.

"Genna's," I said.

"Genna's?" Dawn looked swiftly at me. "She told you that?"

"Not at first," I said. "First she said she couldn't think who might have done it, and just wanted the payoff made. Then later she called me, when John wasn't there. She said she thought it was Wayne but John didn't. We went to check him out and he was dead."

Dawn shifted in her chair, sliding her thumb along one of her rhinestone straps to adjust it. "Wayne," she said dismissively, "was a dumb idea. Just about as dumb as Wayne was, so I guess it's justice."

"Someone killed him."

"Someone kills everybody, sooner or later." She shrugged. "Or some thing. Or some time."

I wasn't having any of her Hallmark-card-in-a-cracked-mirror philosophy. "Why would someone do that, if he weren't involved in this?"

"Because he was involved in other shit! God, most of us can do more than one thing at a time." She rolled her eyes again, this time at Bill, about me.

"You worked with him."

"Oh, what? And that means I killed him?" Her retort was impatient but not surprised, or, it seemed to me, insulted.

"You don't seem very upset that he's dead."

She gave me a cold smile. "Have you met anyone who was?"

"Did you kill him?" I asked the question without a change in the straightforward tone I'd been trying to use for this whole conversation, but I held my breath for the answer.

"Oh, shit," she said. "Of course I didn't. Why the hell would I? He was dumb, but he was mean. That was the combination I needed."

"For what?"

"For what do you think?"

"Protection?"

"No, honey." She sounded resigned, the graduate student forced to deal with the know-it-all freshman in Life 101. "In my business you work alone. When there's trouble, you take care of it yourself or you find other work. I don't need anyone to protect me." She crossed one leg over the other. Her skirt rode even further up her thigh.

"Then what?"

"What the hell made my life your business?" she snapped.

"The police," I answered calmly, "are interested in the murder of Wayne Lewis."

"So?"

"They must not know you were connected with him, or they'd be all over you already. But they could find out. Then they might get interested in you, whether you had anything to do with his death or not."

"You'd call the police on me? I'm your client's sister."

"We were fired, as you pointed out. We don't have a client."

"Shit."

"Am I right thinking a police investigation would be a problem?"

She sighed. "Depends. It could be a real pain in the ass."

"Then maybe answering my questions could be less of a pain in the ass."

162

Bill raised an eyebrow. I never use that kind of language.

"Maybe," Dawn conceded, grudgingly. "What the hell is it you want to know?"

"Your relationship with Wayne."

"That asshole." She took another cigarette from her purse. Bill had a match out before her purse clicked shut. "He was the gate-keeper."

"What does that mean?"

"I'm not so easy to find," she said. No kidding, I thought to my-self. "I keep it that way on purpose. You wanted me, you called Wayne. He weeded out some of the real lunatics and losers." Oh, I thought to myself some more. So he was protecting you in a way, wasn't he? "I paid him," she said, as though I'd spoken out loud. "It wasn't the usual arrangement, where some pimp takes it all and gives you nick-els and dimes. He kept the books, fielded the calls, and I paid him."

"Books?"

"Who likes what, that kind of thing. None of them are that damn original that it sticks in your mind, honey." She took a long draw on her cigarette. "Wayne also was mean enough that when he did negotiations, they stuck. It was just too much trouble to have him screaming at you over the phone."

"Negotiations? Like with Ed?"

She gave me a nod. "Yeah. Like with Ed."

"That's why Ed's girls don't work this club?"

"That's exactly why. I like to bring my dates here. My dates are into me being Chinese." She threw Bill a pointed look. "Ed's girls are all exotics," she went on. "They're also a bunch of cheap hookers. They're way below me on the food chain. I don't like them strutting their pathetic stuff in front of my dates."

"Didn't you used to work for Ed?"

Dawn bristled. "What makes you think that?"

"Andi Shechter said you were with Everest Models."

"Oh, God. Andi. What the hell made you ask her?"

"I asked a lot of people. I told you, I was looking for you."

"Genna?" Surprisingly, she sounded worried.

"No. I don't think she knows we know you exist. Did you work for Ed?"

She let out a breath. "Yeah, years ago. For a little while, I actually wanted to be a model." She smiled. "No, that's not true. I never really did. I just wanted to be doing something like what Genna did. I thought she'd like me better. I spent years, boys and girls, trying to prove something to Genna. Then I just gave up." She looked around the table at us. "I guess you could say Ed gave me my start in this business. And I found out two things. One, that I liked it. Two, that Ed was dead weight. I ditched him and went into business for myself." She tamped out her cigarette. "So that's enough about my life," she said. "Now you tell me why you thought I stole Genna's sketches."

Fair's fair; I answered that. "You aren't the only person who thought Wayne was a dumb idea. So it occurred to us that, if Wayne really weren't involved, he might be a red herring. Genna might be deliberately steering us away from someone. We thought that might be you."

"And just why the hell would she do that?"

"To protect you." That came, quietly, from Bill.

Dawn stared at Bill while the music howled to a crescendo. As the DJ edged one track into another, she smiled and shook her head.

"To protect me," she repeated, then chuckled, still shaking her head, as though Bill had said something really funny. "It's a good thing Genna fired you people. You're clueless." She lifted the tiny arrow stuck through her olives and with a delicate tongue licked martini from them. "If Genna really was protecting anybody," she said, redunking the olives, "I guarantee you it was herself."

"From what?" I asked.

She smiled, licking the olives again. "From the rest of the world, and especially John, finding out about me. Finding out that Genna Jing's sister is a whore."

Andrew flinched. Dawn caught that. "Oh, I'm sorry," she said solicitously. "Are you sensitive, too, like Genna? Not a whore. That's a bad word. An escort. A worker in the sex industry. I heard that one the other day. Like it?" She flashed a radiant grin at Bill. "A whore," she announced. "The best goddamn whore in New York."

Bill grinned back. Her smile grew, if anything, wider, and she threw back the rest of her drink. "I have to get to work, boys and girls.

164

It's been a pleasure." She pressed out her cigarette and started to collect herself.

"Wait," I said. "We had a deal. We'd tell you about Genna, you'd tell us about the money."

"Oh, the money?" Dawn's eyes widened innocently. "Well, the money's the funny part. Genna's so completely paranoid that John will find out about me and dump her that I had to change my goddamn name. And all this time, who do you think's been bankrolling John?"

Eighteen

I don't get it," Bill said.

"No," Dawn answered Bill, "you wouldn't."

The M room at Quiver was shoulder-to-shoulder crowded now, short tight dresses and spikey heels swaying next to T-shirts, jeans, and silk jackets. And cowboy boots. People stood pressed together under the smoke that spiraled through the spotlights, watching the band mill around on the bandstand again and begin tuning up.

I didn't believe Bill. I could see in his eyes that he got it. But just like me, he probably wanted to hear it from her.

Dawn turned to me. "Do you have brothers or sisters? Oh, yeah, him." She nodded in Andrew's direction. "Any more?"

"Three more," I said.

"Do they like you?"

"Yes," Andrew said, cutting my answer off.

Bill and Tony both smiled, and hid their smiles in their drinks.

"That's nice," Dawn said. "What if they didn't?"

"They'd still be my brothers," I said.

"And what if one of them wanted something all his life, wanted it so badly it was eating him up, and when he got close to it you could help? But he didn't want your help because he didn't like you?"

165

"I don't know," I said.

She gave me a look that said she thought I did know.

"Genna's had crappy luck lately," Dawn said. "At just the wrong time. She had a factory lined up and they backed out on her. One of her suppliers is suddenly out of stock on buttons they promised her. She designed a whole damn dress around those buttons. Even that asshole Wayne dropped her as soon as he got a better offer. It's a bad time and she needs cash. She doesn't like me so she won't take mine."

I asked, "You have that kind of money?"

She flashed me a grin. "You know what they say, honey: do what you love; the money will follow."

Feedback shrieked from one of the loudspeakers. Dawn waited until the band had wrestled their equipment back under control.

"Genna doesn't want to take John's money, either," she said. "But she's desperate, so she will. She treats it like he's making an investment. It's how she pretends she doesn't need anyone."

She looked at me. I didn't look at Andrew.

"The trouble is, John hasn't got any money."

Bill and I exchanged looks. "We sort of knew that," I said. "No ready cash, anyway."

"No money," Dawn repeated. "Nothing. One building, a real dump. He showed it to me. He bought it to fix it up for him and Genna, just before his mother cut him off. Sweet guy, but not a thinker. Like most sweet guys."

That remark was directed, with a superior smile, to Bill. I could have told her Bill wasn't a particularly sweet guy, but she didn't ask me.

"His mother?" I said. Dawn looked back to me. "She was supporting him?"

"Not exactly. His father left him a trust, administered by her. She doesn't have to give him money out of it if she doesn't feel like it."

"But it's his?"

"For what that's worth."

I wasn't surprised, but I was a little appalled; John Ryan was older than I was. "He could get a job," I suggested.

Dawn shook her head. "He works for Genna. Fifteen hours a

day, seven days a week, just like her. She couldn't afford to pay some-one to do what he does, and he's good at it. When he started, he had money. His mother hadn't caught on yet that Genna wasn't a wasp from Newport."

"So you give John money, and he gives it to Genna, and she thinks it's his?"

Dawn nodded. "And what she doesn't know won't hurt her. Now explain it to Sinbad over here." She slung her purse over her shoulder. "You guys have been enough trouble for one night. See you around."

"How did you meet John?"

"How do you meet guys in this business?" she threw back, im-patiently. "Everyone's a friend of a friend. I really don't remember. I never dated him, if that's what you're worried about." She stopped and gave me a hard look. "Genna has no idea we know each other. I'd like to keep it like that."

"That's how you knew what happened? About the stolen sketches, and in the park?"

She shrugged her rhinestone-strapped shoulders. "John needed the ransom money. He had to get it somewhere."

"One more thing," I said.

"Oh, really?"

"What was the relationship between Ed Everest and Wayne Lewis? That Ed came to Wayne for?"

"Ed went to Wayne for lots of things. Wayne and I run—ran—a much higher-class operation than Ed does."

"That's no answer."

"Wasn't much of a question. Oh, all right," she said, probably in answer to the flash of annoyance on my face. "Wayne didn't think I knew, but he was selling names to Ed."

"Names?"

"Yeah, sweetie, names. Johns. Creeps and losers who wanted me that I didn't want to deal with anymore. For a price, Ed bought their names and numbers and pimped—" with a glance at Andrew and a small smile, she amended her words "—and introduced them to his girls."

She stood. Bill pushed back his chair and stood, too, which

made Andrew and Tony rise. I was the only one sitting. Dawn looked down at me.

"I didn't steal the fucking sketches. If you find out who did, let me know. Otherwise, have a nice life. And don't forget what I said about the shoes. A really hot pair." She tilted her head in Bill's direction, so I'd know what she was talking about. Then she walked away.

Bill, without a word to us, gave her a moment, then turned and followed her as she melted into the crowd. I stayed where I was. Andrew turned to me, looking a little dazed.

"I thought she was a model," he said weakly.

"Jesus H. Christ," said Tony, staring after Dawn. I was surprised to hear from him. Tony hadn't said a word in the last half hour. Tony knows all my brothers, and he's met my mother once, briefly in a crowd at our apartment last Chinese New Year. Andrew had brought him so that Tony could get a look at our whole family and understand better why Andrew's still in the closet as far as Chinatown's concerned. When Tony's with more than one Chin, he ends up silent a lot. Maybe he thinks it's safer that way.

"You thought Dawn Jing was a model," I said to Andrew. "What about Pearl Moon?"

"No," he said. "No, not her. I knew about her."

"Knew what?"

"Knew that." He gestured in the direction Dawn had gone. "That she was a call girl. That's why I was so blown away when you said they were the same person."

"Why?"

"Well," he pursed his lips in thought, "I guess I was thinking, for Dawn to steal the sketches and for Genna to be willing to pay her off, Dawn must be a pretty . . . I don't know, pathetic human being. Not a . . . not someone like her."

"Someone pathetic," I said. "A little sister."

Tony stifled a grin.

Andrew said, "Don't start that! That's not what I meant."

"Wrong," I said. "It's just what you meant. But never mind. I can't think in here. As soon as Bill comes back, let's leave."

"Where did Bill go?" Andrew asked.

"To get Dawn's phone number," I said. "So we can find her if we need her again."

"How do you know that?"

I looked at Andrew blandly as the band counted down and crashed into the beginning of a new set. I asked, "Where else would he have gone?"

I was, of course, right about that. Bill was back inside of five minutes. I was glad to see him: the band had cranked up the volume to where even the music itself bounced madly from wall to wall, looking for a way to escape.

Bill dropped himself into his chair again, lit a cigarette, and tossed the matchbook to me.

"Oh," I said, my voice loud but almost lost against the band. "Gee, thanks. This is in case I need a smoke? You've given up leaning across the table?"

"Dawn's number's inside," Bill grinned. "She said if I ever wanted the real thing to just give her a call."

"The real thing?" I demanded. I felt my cheeks getting hot. "Instead of what?"

He made a palms-up gesture of complete innocence. "Just doing my job, ma'am."

"You seem to enjoy your job."

"And she seems to enjoy hers."

"Yes," I said. "She certainly does. Can we get out of here, guys? I think this place is just too cool for me."

We emerged from underground into the night air of Union Square. There we split up.

"What are you going to do now?" Andrew wanted to know, as we stood casting odd shadows under high yellow streetlights.

"I have no idea," I told him.

"Lyd—"

"Not only do I have no idea," I said, "I don't want to hear any of yours."

"I was—"

"Andrew. Darling. Third brother, whose very footsteps I idol-

169

ize and adore. Go home. Don't call us, we'll call you."

So Andrew and Tony headed the few blocks north and west, to their loft, and Bill and I started south, toward his apartment and mine.

The night was hazy, with that cool of early spring that's only a little warmer, but so much softer, than the chill of winter. We walked in silence down nearly deserted University Place. The blocky buildings on our left loomed over mist-draped Washington Square Park across the street. On a night like this, that park, with its bare trees and curving walks and cast-iron streetlights, seems achingly turn-of-the-century to me. I almost think that just by stepping inside the low railing that surrounds it, I'd become part of a world of gaslights and long dresses and the clip-clop of horses' hooves.

But, of course, I wouldn't.

And if I did, I'd probably find I was the chambermaid.

"What's up?" Bill asked, after we'd left the park behind and cut between the unmistakably twentieth-century apartment towers south of it.

"I don't know," I said. "I'm depressed."

"Why?"

"I love that park."

He glanced at me sideways. "That park's not going anywhere."

I stepped up onto the curb. It was a very high curb; for a moment I was only six inches shorter than he was. "Neither are we," I said.

"What do you mean?"

"Oh, Andrew and his bright ideas," I said. "Dawn is Genna's pathetic little sister, Dawn must have stolen the sketches because she's desperate, Genna must be protecting her. And I bought it! That's not Genna and Dawn. That's what Andrew thinks of little sisters. I can't believe I didn't tell him to go soak his head. Look at all the time we've wasted!"

"Are you sure we've wasted it?"

"Of course we have! We spent all day looking for Dawn, and now we found her and guess what? *She* was the red herring all along!"

"You don't think she could have been lying?"

"Oh, sure. She could have been a Martian, too. Green slime with three heads, actually, not a slinky sexpot Chinese call girl at all!"

"Really?" he said. "I didn't notice."

"With a better haircut than mine!"

"Not much better."

"What?" I demanded, turning and blocking his path. "You really think hers is better?"

"No." He smiled. "I don't think anything could be better than you in a new haircut in the middle of the street in the middle of the night."

He reached and, at the back of my head where my hat didn't cover it, he touched my new haircut. At the brush of his fingers, my whole scalp tingled, and my spine, and the tips of my toes.

He looked at me. I looked at the sidewalk. Then I reached for his hand and moved it away, down where hands belonged, in the space between people. I held it in mine. His was warm. Mine was cold.

He shrugged, and smiled again. "Sorry," he said. "I thought . . ."

I shook my head. I knew what he thought. What I didn't know was what I thought.

"*I'm* sorry," I said. "I'm upset. It's not you. It's really not. I just want to walk."

He nodded, and we started forward, still holding hands.

"Let's change the subject," he said, after we'd made our way across the expanse of Houston Street and through the empty blocks of Soho, past gated-up boutiques, grimy-faced tenements, and trendy restaurants where weary waiters were putting the chairs up on the tables.

"We haven't said anything," I pointed out.

"Good. Let's change that."

"To what?"

"To your hot dinner date."

I looked at him swiftly. "It wasn't like that."

"What was it like?" He asked the question casually, with a lightness of tone I couldn't quite buy.

"Roland's a client," I said. "Or he wants to be. That's all."

"That's not what your mother thinks."

I stopped and turned again, letting go of his hand. I drew a breath; he waited. "What's between you and me," I finally said, speaking quietly, searching his eyes, "or isn't, doesn't have to do with my mother."

He was silent, and so was I. A truck grumbled and bounced over the potholes of Canal Street.

"That's not true," I contradicted myself. "It has to do with her, but not because of what she wants or what she tells me to do. Because of who I am and who you are. Where we come from and what we know. It's different, Bill. I can't make it the same."

"It doesn't have to be the same."

"It has to . . . to intersect at some points."

"Doesn't it do that?"

"Others," I said. "More than how we work together, more than how we feel about each other."

"More than how we feel about each other?" His voice was soft. His words were mine, and I was surprised to hear them.

"I—that's not what I meant."

His eyes, also soft, held mine. I felt the tingle again.

"I think it is," he said.

I knew he was going to kiss me. I knew it was a bad idea. I didn't move to stop him.

Maybe other trucks went by; maybe the sun rose and set again; maybe the Martians landed. I wouldn't have known. When we separated, the night was still lit with a sodium-vapor glow and the buildings hadn't changed at all.

I stepped back, not by much, an inch or two. "I just can't," I said.

"You just did."

I shook my head. "Not with you," I said. "With someone else, someone I didn't care so much about, if I felt like this I'd be jumping in a cab to your place, even though I knew it wasn't going to work out. I can't do that with you."

"You don't know it won't work out."

My eyes held his again, trying. "Unless I know it will."

"How will you know that?"

"I don't know."

Bill looked down at his hands. They were empty. "You mean," he said, "if you cared about me less, I'd have a better shot?"

I shrugged foolishly. It sounded dumb, like that, but it was true.

"Well," he said, suddenly grinning, "at least now I can have a plan."

"Plan?"

"To make you love me. I'll just be really obnoxious and make you hate me."

I smiled, grateful that he was making it easy. "That hasn't worked over the last couple of years," I pointed out.

"Oh. Well, that's true. I'll try harder from now on, I promise. Now, tell me about our new client."

We started forward, walking to the end of the block, to the light at Canal. We didn't hold hands. As we walked I described dinner with Roland.

Bill, missing a chance to be obnoxious, didn't comment on the oysters.

At the corner we waited for the light to change. We crossed the street, and I finished my story on the other side.

"What's your take?" Bill asked, turning to walk east.

"You don't have to walk me home." We were much closer to his Tribeca apartment than we were to Chinatown.

"If I don't, I'll have to sit around at my place waiting for you to call when you get there."

"I won't."

"I know. And then I'll worry all night. I won't be able to sleep. My health will deteriorate, I'll get to be a nervous wreck, probably turn psychotic. I'll cause mass havoc and destruction. You'll be responsible for the senseless acts of terror I'll unleash on an unsuspecting world."

"Is this part of your plan to be obnoxious?"

"Is it working?"

"I'd have preferred a crack about the oysters."

"Don't think I didn't think about it."

I gave up and we fell into step together, east toward Chinatown.

"So," he prompted. "Your take on Roland?"

"What about yours?"

"Mine? I've never met the guy."

"I know. But what's your take on the situation?"

"Hmm," he said. "Okay. Two possibilities. One: he's just some guy who heard your name a few days ago after years, then saw you on the street and decided to get back into your life. Then he realized there was something in it for him when his girlfriend disappeared."

"What's the other?"

"That he heard your name a few days ago after years and then planted himself in front of you on the sidewalk for a reason that, since he heard your name from the client in this case, we can assume has something to do with this case."

"That's the idea I can't shake," I said. "Do you think it could be true?"

"I think either one could be true. But I think we'd be nuts not to check it out."

"That's just what I figured! That's why I said I'd take his case."

"How do you want to go about it?"

"This is something I'll have to do alone. No one in that community will talk to you."

He sighed. "Why should they be different from the rest of the civilized world?"

"The way I'm going to start," I went on, thinking out loud, "is the way I'd go about it if this really were the case."

"Meaning, if what Roland said he wanted were what he really wanted?"

"Yes. Which it may be."

Bill lit a cigarette noncommittally. "Well," he said, "there are a few things I can profitably do on the other case, in the meantime."

"Like look into Dawn's finances?"

"That's one. I'd like to be able to either verify her story, or torpedo it."

"Be my guest. Let me know."

We turned onto Mulberry and walked down it, quiet together. Funny, I thought. The buildings here are as old, older, than Washington Square Park, but the soft mist haloing the streetlights in Chinatown didn't make me think of anything further back than my own childhood, than the nights when, sleepy and full, I'd been carried up the stairs by my father after a cousin's wedding banquet or a village association feast; the nights, later, after a date or a party when I'd walked home down these echoing empty sidewalks, escorted by the guy I'd gone out with or by one of my brothers—or, some uncomfortable times, by both—to the old brick building on Mosco Street. And then up the three flights of stairs to the apartment where my mother was inevitably awake, waiting.

Which I'd have given good odds she was right now.

"Bill?" I said, as we neared my door. "What did you think of Dawn?"

He took a moment before he answered. "Would it bother you if I said I liked her?"

"No." I shook my head. "I just . . . I can't believe she can do what she does, and like herself."

He zipped up his jacket; the night had turned colder. He asked, "How many people do?"

I didn't like the question. I didn't answer it.

"The dress she was wearing?" I said, as I turned the key in the lock. "It was a Genna Jing." I gave his hand a goodnight squeeze, and went home.

Nineteen

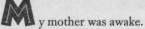y mother was awake.

She was in her nightgown, a pastel-flowered thing of the type my brothers buy her for Mother's Day when they don't have any good ideas. To her credit, she had the grace to try to look as though she'd been asleep and had just happened to get up for a midnight snack as I walked in the door. I didn't believe it, but I appreciated the effort.

"Well, you're home," she said, as I slipped off my black heels in the entryway and pulled on my embroidered slippers. "How is your brother?"

I appreciated that, too, that she asked the proper, family-oriented question first, before the one I knew she'd stayed awake to ask.

"Fine, Ma," I said. I considered saying a quick goodnight and heading straight to bed, but that would be too mean. I joined her in browsing at the open fridge door.

As soon as I got there, of course, my mother found what she wanted—a Saran-wrap-covered bowl of mango pudding—and closed the door. "You children always let the cold out," she scolded me. I gave up on the thought of leftover soy sauce chicken and reached for a banana from the fruit bowl on the table.

After downing two quivering lumps of pudding, my mother finally spoke again.

"Oh," she said offhandedly, looking with great interest at the glistening orange stuff in her bowl, "and how is Roland Lum?"

Ah, we'd come to the point. Once we'd gotten through this, I could go to bed.

"He's fine," was my opening gambit.

"Did you send my regards to his mother?"

"Of course," I said, though I was pretty sure I hadn't. If Roland was a good Chinese son, he'd convey my mother's greetings to his mother the next time he saw her, safe in the assumption that I was meant to tell him to do that and forgot. If he wasn't, he wouldn't, even if I'd remembered.

"And his business is going well?" my mother asked politely.

"It seems to be," I answered.

"Oh, didn't you talk much about business?"

Uh oh, I thought, red flag. "Actually, no. The truth is, Ma, he wants to hire me."

I'd thought this idea would put a damper on her enthusiasm, but my mother is a woman of eternal hope.

She smiled, swallowing the last of the pudding. "Hire you," she repeated. "Ling Wan-ju, you must learn not to be so difficult."

"Me?" I said, aggrieved. "I wasn't difficult. I agreed. I took his case."

"His case." She kept smiling, and she made it sound as if I'd said "his ticket to the moon." "If Roland Lum thinks that to keep seeing you he has to make up a case and hire you, you must have been very difficult. You're lucky he's so persistent."

I carefully peeled the last of my banana while I contemplated the wonders of the human mind. "Okay, Ma," I said, finishing the banana and dropping the peel in the trash. "I'll work on it."

I kissed her and went to bed. She shuffled down the hall in her nightgown and slippers, humming to herself. I could have made an effort to convince her that, whatever Roland was up to, it wasn't an elaborate subterfuge for the purpose of spending time with me; but with my mother, especially on this topic, there's not much point in offering her truth or reality if they conflict in any way with what she already knows.

In the morning while I showered, I formulated a plan.

The first part of it had nothing to do with either case, and I'd actually formulated it the night before: it was to go up to the dojo and take the early-morning advanced form class. A little more sleep would have been nice, too, I thought as the alarm poked its annoying electronic beep into a mist-draped dream that faded immediately away. But I was feeling smoke-filled and slow from my late, frustrating night among Manhattan's in crowd. I was also still mad at myself over the streetfight two days ago that maybe I didn't actually lose, but I couldn't have been said to have won. And I was still mad at Andrew for making the assumption that little sisters were by nature pathetic, and at myself for making the assumption that big brothers were bound to be right.

Class helped. Practicing form, repeating the traditional moves in their prescribed combinations, again, again, again, with no involvement with anyone else, nothing but the relentless, exhausting effort to perfect yourself: that helped. By the end of class I wasn't anything near perfected, but I was sweaty and my mind was sharp. I waited my turn for the tiny shower, bowing to the higher ranks who went before me and the lower ones who waited until I was through. By the time I was dressed—a three-minute operation here; you didn't take up any time or space you didn't need—my hair, I noticed, was dry.

Back out on the sunny street it was still early. Bill can say what he wants about the pleasures of late-night jazz joints and darkened bedrooms where you can burrow under your blankets and sleep until

177

noon. If you ask me, there's nothing like the clean morning air and a day whose promises are all still ahead.

I stopped for a cup of tea and some raisin toast at a cafe halfway back to Chinatown. While my tea was steeping I called the number Roland had given me, the number where they claimed not to know Peng Hui Liang. It took eleven rings to get someone to the phone. That would make sense if this number were an immigrant rooming house, some tenement's divided basement where a dozen invisible illegals slept on mattresses in rooms without windows, all sharing a single filthy toilet at one end of the hall and a grease-covered hot plate at the other.

The young man who finally answered the phone grunted angrily into it, in Cantonese. "Yes?" he barked. "What do you want?" I'd probably woken him, and I felt bad about that. The new immigrants work too hard, and sleep too little, to have to put up with being annoyed on their few hours off by an ABC like me.

I asked for Peng Hui Liang in my most whispery, apologetic Cantonese. The man on the other end of the phone snarled, in Cantonese considerably less apologetic, that no one of that name lived there. I told him meekly that Hui Liang was my cousin and asked if he could please tell me where she'd gone. He growled that no one of that name had *ever* lived there.

"Please," I said hastily, before he could hang up. "I have a message from her older brother. I promised to deliver it, but I can't find her. What can I tell her brother, if I fail?"

There was a brief silence on the other end of the phone.

"Her cousin?" the man grunted.

"Peng Mei Zhi," I said shyly.

Silence again. Then, "Flu Shing. She's moved. She quit her job. It's a house on Main Street, near a beauty parlor. I don't know the number."

"Does she have a phone?" Pushing your luck, Lydia, I thought.

He thought so, too. "A house on Main Street," he said impatiently. "Near a beauty parlor. That's all I know."

"Does she live with someone? Maybe one of the sewing ladies from her factory?"

"I don't know! She's gone."

178

"Do you know where she works now?" It would be surprising if she'd found another job so soon after leaving Roland's factory, but if she was enterprising it was possible.

"No. Why don't you go out to Flu Shing and bother them?" He added, just a touch more softly, "Good luck finding her. For her big brother."

Then he hung up.

Flu Shing, I thought. That well-known section of New York's largest outer borough, where so many new Chinese immigrants—and Korean and Indian, too—made their first homes in New York.

Flushing. In Queens.

Something was bothering me about that conversation, I realized as I went back to my table, but I wasn't sure what it was. I munched my raisin toast, squeezed lemon into my Irish Breakfast tea—the perfect thing with raisin toast—and watched the rhythm of the streets change, as the nine-to-fivers disappeared into their offices and people on more singular, erratic missions took their places on the sidewalk. The early-morning mist had all burned off and the sun was sharp. It spread a light that was still white, not yet started on the transit through yellow to thick gold to red that marks the day.

When I was finished I headed to the second part of my plan. I could go out to Flushing later, if I had to. But right now I had something else I wanted to try.

In New York, Forty-seventh Street has for years and years been the center of the jewelry trade. It still is, and black-coated Orthodox Jews trading diamonds on a handshake are still a common sight in Midtown. But Canal Street is coming up fast. Some of the gold and the stones that used to go through Amsterdam to Forty-seventh Street now come through Taiwan and end up on Canal, where Taiwanese and, lately, Hong Kong merchant families have set up bright, glass-fronted shops to sell engagement rings and lucky pendants.

The family of my mother's old friend-and-rival Mrs. Chan is one of those. Like my mother, Mrs. Chan sewed in Chinatown sweatshops when she first came to America, and for years after that. That was where they'd met. Also like my mother, Mrs. Chan gradually and grudgingly retired, permitting her children to support her, making only the occasional guest appearance back at Mr. Leng's to help out at times of especially heavy volume. They had to do this, they both insisted with deep sighs, because the new Fujianese girls who come from China now don't know anything at all.

But three years ago Mrs. Chan's husband's cousin from Taiwan opened not one but two jewelry stores, one on either end of the stretch of Canal that runs through Chinatown. Mrs. Chan immediately decided she would be more much useful overseeing operations in one of the stores than teaching a new, exasperatingly young crop of seamstresses the fine points of double-stitching.

Not that Mrs. Chan knows anything about jewelry. But she can be found six days a week in the westernmost of her husband's cousin's stores, on a high stool at the counter where the gold chains are, smiling a silent smile, keeping an eagle eye on everything that happens inside the store and outside up and down Canal Street.

That was how she'd seen me and Roland Lum going into Maria's. And that was why I wanted to talk to her.

The store, Golden Dreams, had just opened for the day when I walked in. The chrome-edged jewelry cases formed a tight U along the sides and back of the narrow, spare space, glittering with bracelets and rings, diamonds and jade and colored gems. The white walls were bare except for two framed scroll paintings, horses in the mist on one, a duck and a drake on the other. Up high in the back, discreetly placed, General Gung, whose heavenly job it is to watch over business enterprises, sat on his red-and-gold altar above his pyramid of oranges and his sticks of incense.

The two young men behind the counters smiled helpfully as I entered. I smiled back, but I had come to see Mrs. Chan. She was seated exactly where I expected to find her, surveying the store and the street from behind the counter where lengths of gold chain were set out on white satin.

In the manner of Chinese women everywhere, Mrs. Chan didn't break into an effusive grin when she saw me, just a small smile, but one that made her chubby cheeks bunch up and her eyes glow.

"Ling Wan-ju," she said. She reached across the counter to take my hands in her small, pudgy ones. "How long it's been since I've seen you! Much too busy to spare a visit to your old auntie, is that it?"

"No, Auntie," I answered, smiling back, speaking Cantonese, as she had. "I know how hard you work here in the store, running Uncle Wen's business for him. I haven't wanted to take up your time."

She nodded, pleased; that was the appropriate response, though she knew it wasn't likely to be true.

"And how is Uncle Wen's business?" I added politely. "The stores seem to be prospering."

"Oh, we're not bankrupt yet," she said with pursed lips, waving away any idea that things were going well. You never know what malevolent spirits, lurking jealously nearby, might overhear a chance remark and in a spiteful moment decide to change your luck. "Winter was very slow, even Christmas. We're hoping things will be better soon."

"I hope so, too," I told her.

She smiled in a knowing way. "Well," she said, "and how are things with you, Ling Wan-ju? I spoke to your mother recently. She said you are doing very well in your field."

Leave it to my mother. What I do for a living is a daily aggravation to her, but let it never cross anyone's mind that I'm anything but the world's biggest success at it.

"I'm fine, thank you, Auntie. Actually, I came this morning to ask you something." We had now been talking long enough that it was not unreasonable of me to get to the point.

"To ask your old auntie something? Well, I'm flattered." She shifted on her stool, sitting a little straighter.

"You see everything from here, Auntie," I said, indicating the store and the street. "You know everything that goes on."

"I see some things," she admitted. "Although I'm so busy in the store I have no time to watch the comings and goings of strangers."

"But when people aren't strangers, sometimes you might notice them," I suggested.

"Sometimes."

I smiled bashfully. "Roland Lum," I said. "He's not a stranger to you."

"Of course not. I've known Roland Lum since he was a baby. And his factory is so close, right over there." She smiled back at me, a sideways, sly smile, as though she knew why I was asking about Roland Lum.

"Well," I said, hesitating, as though I were uncomfortable, "I was wondering about something about him."

Mrs. Chan didn't answer, just waited, her face a composed picture of helpfulness.

"I don't know if you know this," I said to her, "but I've been seeing Roland lately. Just once or twice," I added quickly, so she'd know I wasn't jumping into anything.

"Oh, really? Your mother didn't tell me," she said innocently, as if she hadn't been the one who'd told my mother.

"Well, it was just once or twice," I repeated. "But now I'm wondering . . ." I let the question trail off, as I would if I were embarrassed to be asking it.

"Yes? Don't be shy, Ling Wan-ju. I'm your old auntie."

I smiled gratefully. "Someone told me," I said, "that Roland was seeing someone. Someone he was serious about. A seamstress in his factory, named Peng Hui Liang. I didn't know that when . . . when I started seeing him."

Mrs. Chan's face darkened. "Who told you this? Some gossip-monger."

"I just wanted to know," I said quickly, "what she looks like. If you've seen her, I mean. Is she pretty? I . . . If he's serious about her, then I won't . . . well, you know. Get any more involved with him." I looked down at the counter, not meeting her eyes.

Mrs. Chan clucked her tongue. "Oh, Ling Wan-ju! A seamstress in Roland Lum's factory? Whoever told you that must be someone very jealous."

I looked up. "Jealous?"

"To say something so untrue." Mrs. Chan's face had taken on a scowl of righteous indignation on my behalf.

"It isn't true?" I said.

"Roland Lum," she told me, pointing out to the street, "is always alone when I see him. Coming to the factory, going home. Out during the day, on business. Such a shame, such a handsome man, but always alone."

I thought for a moment, and asked her, "Maybe he sees Peng Hui Liang at night? When you aren't here to see?"

She sniffed, almost offended. "We stay open into the evening.

182

And your uncle Wen often needs me here for some time after closing." Meaning, you can't be seriously suggesting there's anything that goes on on Canal Street that I don't see.

And I wasn't. But this was an unexpected twist. I wanted to cover my bases as completely as I could.

"Maybe he's interested in her," I said, sounding unconvinced. "Maybe he wants to be involved with her, but she just hasn't gone out with him yet."

Mrs. Chan tapped sharply on the counter with her red-lacquered fingernail. "Now you stop this foolishness, Ling Wan-ju. You and Roland Lum are perfect together. The person who told you this nonsense either was trying to upset you, or got hopelessly confused when she heard Roland Lum complaining."

I said, "Complaining?"

"Roland Lum has been complaining to the ladies who work for him for months. Teasing them. Mrs. Wong tells me."

"Teasing them about what?"

"Complaining," she said, "that they do their work so well he can't fire them, which is too bad, because none of the young ones are single and none of the single ones are young. How will he ever find a wife, he asks, if the only women he sees all day are his little sisters and his old aunties?"

TWENTY

So Peng Hui Liang, the soon-to-be mother of Roland Lum's child, didn't work at his factory. Whoever she was, and whatever reason Roland had for wanting me to find her, she wasn't some sweet young Fujianese seamstress he'd been coming on to between the Singers and the steam press, and squiring around Chinatown, not even just down Canal Street to a cheap Chinese-run Bowery hotel. Then who was she, and what was Roland's game?

I contemplated these questions as I walked along Canal Street in the spring breeze, smelling the water scent from the East River. Sometimes, for all your senses are able to tell you, New York might be landlocked. We could be living in a prairie town somewhere, a city on the plains where the land rolls away in all directions, mile after solid, endless mile. And then, other times—bright spring mornings when the smell of water carries on the breeze and the cawing sea gulls race the clouds from west to east—you suddenly know you're clinging to the shores of the continent, wrapped by rivers blending into the sea. At the ragged end of one place and time and the beginning of another.

Who was Peng Hui Liang? And why had she left Chinatown and moved to Flu Shing, to a house on Main Street near a beauty parlor?

I skidded to a stop on the street, creating a three-Chinese pileup. She hadn't.

Over my apologies to the people who'd rear-ended me and theirs to me, I heard in my head my conversation with the man on the other end of the phone number Roland had given me, and I knew what was wrong with it.

It was in Cantonese.

The new immigrants, the ones who live four or five to a tiny basement room waiting to make their fortunes, stick together as all immigrants do. The Fujianese, particularly, are a tight group. Many of the Cantonese who came here in the fifties and sixties, as my parents did, have remained poor; but they live in their own more permanent slums. They don't bunk with the Fujianese.

And they don't speak it, either.

Just as the Fujianese, required by law in the People's Republic to learn Mandarin, and Fujianese-speaking at home, have no reason on earth to speak Cantonese.

Cantonese. The language I was raised on. Me and Roland Lum.

Roland, according to my mother, had had to learn basic Fujianese just to give orders in the factory, because all the new young women—the ones my mother and Mrs. Chan had no patience with—were from Fukien.

Whoever that man on the phone had been, I was willing to bet

184

he hadn't been Peng Hui Liang's roommate. He probably didn't even know her.

If she was even real.

I hurried to the phone on the corner and called Bill. I wanted to tell him what had happened and what I thought it meant. I also wanted to tell him what I was about to do next, and how he could help.

He wasn't there.

I left a frustrated message with his service and hung up, wondering just where he was, and why. He'd said he was going to be checking on Dawn Jing's finances this morning. That was telephone work, the kind you do from home. So why wasn't he home?

I called my own machine, to check my messages in case he'd called to tell me what he was up to, but there weren't any. I hung the phone up more sharply than it deserved and stood staring into the bright blue morning.

Okay, Lydia, you're on your own. Big deal. You like being independent, in the general way of things. The question is, how are you going to pull this off without help?

What I wanted to do was to find out why Roland Lum was paying me to look for a woman who at best wasn't who he said she was. And maybe didn't exist. And why he'd had some Cantonese-speaking juvenile delinquent friend of his try to send me off on a wild-goose chase to Queens.

There were two routes I could see to the answer. I could confront Roland and demand to know, but somehow I had a feeling that that was the more likely dead end. Or I could sneak around behind his back, sniffing into his life, poking around in places he didn't know I was.

The Lydia Chin way.

I walked a ways uptown, into Soho, just to help me think. I window-shopped in art galleries, gourmet coffee stores, and boutiques, I admired a long-sleeved black silk evening dress whose skirt changed abruptly at the wide part of the mannequin's hips into the sheerest lace. I wondered where you'd wear something like that. It made me think of Genna. I decided I needed a cup of tea, so I walked down the block to the Korean deli to pick one up. I threaded my way into the shop past big white buckets of tulips and daffodils.

As I was paying for the tea, my idea hit me.

I hurried outside and zipped across the street to the pay phone. I called Bill again. He was still out. I called my machine, but it didn't know any more than I did. Some partner, I thought. Some employee. Some pal.

So, without advice, encouragement, or backup, I called Roland Lum.

The phone rang a few times; then, behind Roland's loud "Hello!" I heard, as I had before, the factory noises of my childhood.

"Roland? It's Lydia."

"Lydia! Hey, what's up?"

"I have something you might be interested in."

"Yeah?" he said cheerfully. "What?"

"I think I found Peng Hui Liang. But there's a problem."

As I expected, there was a second of silence, a beat and a half Roland missed. Then he bounced right back. "Hey, that's great! But what do you mean, problem?"

"I can't tell you over the phone. I think you should come here."

"God, Lydia, I'm up to my butt in work."

"This is important, Roland."

"Well . . ." he sighed. "Where are you?"

"Uptown. Amsterdam and Ninety-third." I wanted to say, Flu Shing, you rat, but I didn't think I could get him to go all the way out there. And I didn't really care where he went, as long as he left the factory.

"Ninety-third? Does it have to be now?"

"I think it would be a good idea."

"You can't come here?"

"If I could I would." And as soon as you're gone, dearie, I will.

"What's this about?"

"Not over the phone, Roland."

He sighed again. In the background I heard the hiss of the steam press.

"All right. Give me the address."

"Amsterdam and Ninety-third, on the northwest corner. Great Wall. It's a Chinese take-out place." It was, too. I'd eaten General

186

Tso's chicken from there a couple of times, visiting friends on the Upper West Side. The food was good, but the place was remarkably inconvenient to get to from Chinatown.

Up until right now, that had always been a disadvantage.

I gave him ten minutes, just to make absolutely sure our paths didn't cross. During that time I pretended to anyone who cared, including myself, that I was truly interested in shop windows full of cabbage-rose-patterned pantyhose and shoes with wide, high Plexiglas heels.

I figured Roland for a taxi kind of guy. If traffic wasn't a problem, he could make it to Amsterdam and Ninety-third in twenty minutes. I gave him an upper limit of five increasingly ticked-off minutes waiting for me while the impassive-faced counterman at Great Wall, who didn't know me from a hole in the ground, folded dumplings. Then another taxi home, another twenty minutes.

What I had to do at the factory could take less time than that, or more, but forty-five minutes at the outside was the time I had. I only wished I knew what it was I was going there to do.

I was heading into Roland Lum's factory in the same spirit Bill and I had invaded Wayne Lewis's taped-off apartment: because it was there. Physical evidence: this was one of the things I'd learned from Bill, one of the things he'd learned from the police captain uncle he'd lived with. Every crime leaves physical traces. Always, every time. A crime is an aberrant event, a break in routine. It will leave marks behind, something outside the pattern. That's what Bill was looking for, standing so still inside Wayne Lewis's door: the pattern, then the marks. You just have to be able to see them, he says. And then to understand what they mean.

After my ten minutes, I went back to the phone. I dialed the factory number again and held my breath.

It took longer before someone answered this time, and it wasn't Roland. Another man barked a greeting into it, in Cantonese.

Cantonese is what I responded in. "INS!" I told him, urgent warning in my voice. "INS is coming! Inspectors on the way. All the factories on Canal Street. They're here now. At your place in five minutes. Hurry!"

I hung up fast, as I would have if I'd been making an illicit warning call from a factory under siege by the Immigration and Naturalization Service.

I searched through my wallet to make sure I had the cards I'd need, thinking it was just like me to start this sting without checking on the props first. But they were there, because it was also just like me never to clean out my wallet. I'd used this gag a year and a half ago in the service of a completely different investigation. I stuck the cards in my pocket and strode up sunny Canal Street, fast but not as fast as I wanted to go. I held myself back to give Roland's employees time to disappear. By the time I reached the factory, just within the five minutes I'd warned the man on the phone it would take, it was a safe bet the place would be practically a ghost town.

At the grimy concrete building with the open-front cheap clothing store at sidewalk level, I straightened my jacket and started to run my hand through my hair to organize it, then realized that not only didn't I need to do that anymore, I actually couldn't. I set my face into a stony look and pulled open the door.

The elevator was down a short hallway whose ceiling and walls were decorated with peeling paint. Just inside the door, and again at the front of the elevator, boards showed through where the linoleum had been rubbed away under generations of impatient feet. I marched straight into the elevator, flashed one of the cards from my pocket, and demanded, "Lum's."

The elevator man, a middle-aged Chinese fellow who'd been sipping tea from the cover of his stainless-steel thermos when I charged into his domain, opened his eyes wide as he was hit by the jolt of fear my Jillian Woo, INS Inspector business cards usually inspire.

"Now!" I commanded fiercely, to forestall the possibility of his suddenly forgetting how to run the elevator.

He swallowed his tea, pulled the elevator gate shut, and threw the ancient lever that started the motor. He kept his fearful eyes on me, and I kept my steely ones on the walls moving past us behind the gate, all the long, slow way up to the fifth floor. When we got there he closed the gate and started down almost before I'd stepped out into the factory.

Roland Lum's factory, as it had been when his father had run it, was considered a model place, working there thought to be a plum job. That meant that the walls had been painted sometime in the last ten years, the toilet worked, the barred, rice-papered windows could be opened for ventilation, and there was heat in the paint-encrusted radiators. It didn't mean the whine and growl of the machines wasn't so loud and relentless that it was possible to hold a conversation; or that the air wasn't full of fine, invisible cotton dust that made you cough all day; or that you didn't work hunched over at the same machine doing the same painstaking, crashingly boring task for ten or twelve hours a day, six or sometimes seven days a week, trying to cram your lunch into ten minutes and your bathroom break into two because you're being paid by the piece and time is literally money.

The place wasn't huge. Two dozen industrial sewing machines pretty much filled it up, with the steam press over by the wall. The table where the thread-snipper usually sat was right next to that, because snipping the loose threads is the last operation before a garment gets pressed and hung in plastic on the pipe-rail racks. Thread-snippers are generally young; you need good eyes to do that job. Piles of fabric crowded the aisles, and rows of bare fluorescent fixtures pressed like cloud cover overhead.

The different machines, some stitching seams, some doing more demanding work like attaching collars or finishing buttonholes, would normally, in the middle of the day like this, each be whining and thumping at its own rate, as the operators changed bobbins and broke threads with their teeth. And the thread-snipper would be moving her endless pile of garments from left to right as she finished each, for the steam press or the skilled hand-finisher.

But the thread-snipper wasn't there. A lot of people weren't there. Just as I'd figured, Roland Lum's factory was almost deserted. Seven middle-aged women sat at new industrial sewing machines in a room set up for two dozen, looking for all the world as though they were so engrossed in their work they hadn't even noticed my arrival. A young man in the back, a hand-finisher whose talents probably netted him an extra fifty cents an hour, placidly skated an iron back and forth over the sleeve of a gauzy blouse. He, apparently, didn't notice me either.

Guaranteed to be citizens, all.

A fiftyish man whose skin hung as loose on his face as his vest and shirt did on his body stepped out from behind an ancient wood desk in the corner of the factory, to greet me.

"Yes?" he said in Cantonese, his face a polite blank. "Can I help you?" His was the voice I'd heard on the phone, the man I'd warned.

"INS," I snapped. I gestured at the near-empty room. "Where's everyone else?"

He looked around, as though taking employee inventory. "Everyone is here."

I gave him my best scornful look.

"Oh," he said, his eyes enlightened with sudden understanding. "The boss. He's away. He'll be back in about an hour."

"I'll bet he's away. Okay. I want their papers. Names, addresses. I want your time cards and payroll book. Get your records together, then send these people in one at a time. I'll be in there."

Without waiting for his permission, I turned and stalked into Roland Lum's office.

It was a cramped and messy half-enclosed space where a paper-piled desk sat surrounded by file cabinets and two old oak chairs. Papers were stuck to the walls and stacked on the file cabinets; some had settled like leaves on the floor. I knew the factory manager couldn't object to me being in here, because it was the only place I could talk privately to his employees, trying to get them to tell me the truth about how much they were paid and what hours they were made to work.

Of course, the employees who were left by the time I got here were the old-timers, the ones whose loyalty was to Roland and their steady paychecks, not to some *low faan* idea of worker solidarity. They would tell me, if I really were Jillian Woo, INS agent, that conditions were fine, hours were short, pay was good, and they had no complaints.

But I wasn't Jillian Woo. I was the daughter of a sweatshop worker. I grew up in this world, where Mr. Leng's greed and his willingness to exploit his workers, combined with my mother's stamina and determination, had sent my mother's five children to college. I didn't know what the answer to this sort of setup was, but I knew one thing. The vanished sewing ladies were losing money every minute I was here.

I moved past the open doorway and sat behind Roland's desk, because that was what the factory manager would expect me to do. Just a sense of what Roland was up to was all I wanted, some idea of what his life was about, what pattern in it had recently been broken in such a way that the solution seemed to be to hire Lydia Chin to chase a phantom Fujianese immigrant to Queens.

I looked around the office as though I were just taking up my own time until the factory manager sent the workers to me. I concentrated on the papers pinned to the bulletin board, hung from clipboards, and taped to the wall. Bills of lading for trucks delivering or picking up; lists of fabric, notes about future schedules. Old take-out menus, and four calendars. I let my eyes wander to the desk, where Roland had left himself scrawled memos, a crowded In box, and piled up mail, but none of that was interesting to me.

I wanted to find it, whatever it was, whatever hint or clue or idea this place could give me. Then I wanted to get out and let the ladies go back to making a living. I heard the manager out on the factory floor stopping women at their machines one by one to collect their work permits or their naturalization papers. My eyes searched the office again, walls and desk and floor. Nothing leaped out at me. The manager's footsteps started to head my way, as he brought me what I'd asked for. On their way up to the doorway to greet him, my eyes swept past the wastebasket in the corner.

And there it was.

My hint, my clue, my idea.

My manila envelope.

The one I'd last seen in Madison Square Park two days before, nestled on the top of quite a different trash basket.

TWENTY-ONE

I lunged and snatched up the envelope and stuffed it under my jacket. Then, standing, I grabbed the phone from the corner of Roland's desk. I had put on an impatient, angry face and was arguing with the dial tone in English when the factory manager stepped through the office door. He held in his hand a pile of cards and papers, and a stack of files. I frowned mightily at him, then went back to the phone.

"Absolutely not!" I told it. "You should have—no, *first!*" I paused. "Dammit!" I snarled, in a very un-Lydia-Chinlike way. "All right! I'm leaving now. I'll get there as soon as I can."

I banged the receiver down and glared at the startled factory manager. "I have to go back to my office. They have an emergency. Idiots!" I slung my bag over my shoulder. "I don't know when we can reschedule . . ." I muttered, as if to myself. Then I fixed him with my beady-eyed gaze. "Things better be in order when I come back. Unlock that exit door. And open the damn windows so they can get some air!"

I stomped from the office to the elevator gate. Pounding the button to call the tea-drinking operator, I glared around the factory for good measure. Everyone was carefully not looking at me. The elevator arrived. I got in and, glaring all the way, floated down to the worn linoleum on the ground floor. I was a block and a half up Canal Street before the glare came unstuck and my face burst into the grin I felt I deserved.

I called Bill again. Well, of course I did. Sometimes you need someone to bounce things off of, someone who thinks enough the way you do and enough differently that he can see where you're going and also where you're going wrong.

And sometimes you need to tell someone how clever you are.

He wasn't there. Again.

Annoyed, I called my own machine, but really just for form. I didn't expect anything from it.

I was wrong.

"Hi," the message went, Bill's voice clear in the single syllable. There were noises in the background, voices, people going about their business, not quietly. Something about the noises made the hairs on my arms stand up. Then I found out why. "I'm at the Thirteenth Precinct," Bill's message said. "With Harry Krch. I think you should come up. Call when you get this; I'll be here." He left the number and hung up.

"I'll be here." Something gave me the feeling that what he was really saying was, "I can't leave." I didn't know if that meant Bill had been arrested, but I knew it didn't mean anything good.

I called the number. They told me I'd reached the Squad Room. I asked for Detective Krch. I heard those same noises while I waited, then the phone was picked up.

"Krch."

"I'm Lydia Chin, Detective. My partner—"

"Hey, would you look at that, it's Lydia Chin. Why call so fast, Miss Chin? We could've waited another two hours. Take your time." Krch's rough voice dripped sarcasm.

I swallowed a very unpolitic reply and said, "I just got my partner's message."

"Oh, your partner? Who, Smith? Well, ain't that a surprise. And here I thought he was just some clazy Amellican trying to hit on you."

Krch's pointedly bad Chinese accent grated on me, but it had been my gag, so I supposed I deserved it.

"Is he there?" I asked.

"Smith?" Krch said innocently.

"Yes." I forced myself to sound calm and reasonable. "Is he there?"

"Uh-huh."

"May I speak to him?"

"I don't think so."

"Has he been arrested?"

"Arrested? You mean somebody might want to arrest Smith? What the hell for?"

"I don't know. If you haven't arrested him, I'd like to speak to him."

"Well, now, we haven't actually booked him yet, but he's being held on suspicion of being an asshole. But I'll tell you what, toots. You want to talk to him, you could come up here."

So I went up there, fuming all the way.

The Thirteenth Precinct is in a newish brick building on Twenty-first Street. That makes it very handy to the N train, and I was about half a block from the N myself, so I jumped on one. I was out of the subway and into the stationhouse ten minutes after I'd hung up the phone. No cab could have been faster.

Riding the few stops on the train, though, I thought it probably must have seemed like a long time to Bill. My machine put the time of his message to me about an hour ago, and who knew how long he'd been at the precinct before that? I didn't know why he was there, but I didn't think any length of time spent with Harry Krch could be classified as a fun morning.

The desk sergeant told me how to get up to the Detective Squad Room, which is always on the second floor of a stationhouse because that's how the detectives pull rank. "Take 'em up to the Squad," they say out of the corner of their mouths, and a suspected perp is hauled off to the elite level to sit in a holding cell until the Squad decides whether to book him. I wondered if that's where Bill was now.

It was, and it wasn't. When I walked through the open door past the THIRTEENTH PRECINCT DETECTIVES sign, I saw a roomful of cheap chrome-legged desks with fake wood tops, under a checkerboard ceiling of acoustic tiles and square fluorescent lights. The institutional-blue walls were covered with Scotch-taped wanted posters, memos, and announcements. At some of the desks detectives worked phones or poked at the keyboards of desktop computers; the Thirteenth had come into the computer age, but it looked like most of the detectives hadn't. One of those detectives, fingers actually flying at a fairly good clip, was Harry Krch. He didn't see me come in.

I stepped further into the room and looked to my left, guessing. I was right: hidden behind a partition was the lockup, placed out of sight like that so witnesses who made it as far as the Squad Room wouldn't see or be seen by alleged perps unless the detectives wanted it that way. The lockup was occupied, by Bill. He was lying on his back on the cell's single stainless-steel bench, smoking a cigarette and staring at the ceiling. But the situation wasn't as bad as it could have been. The cell door was standing open.

I stepped around the partition to the front of the cell. "Hi," I said.

At the sound of my voice Bill looked up. He swung his legs off the bench and mashed his cigarette out on the floor, where it joined about fifty others. I hoped they weren't all his. He came out of the cell, leaned and kissed me on the cheek. "Trouble," he whispered while he was there.

"And I thought you just liked it here. I found something," I told him quietly while I returned his kiss. "Are you okay?"

He nodded, and then Krch was upon us.

"Shit, isn't this heartwarming?" Krch stood a little too close to us, arms shut across his chest. Bill and I moved apart.

"Nice to see you, Suzie Wong," Krch said. I flushed hotly, angry with myself for letting that happen because I knew that's what he'd been aiming for. "Come with me. You stay here," he ordered Bill.

"No," Bill objected. "That wasn't the deal."

"We had no deal! Your girlfriend's here, let me see what she has to offer. If I like it, maybe we'll make a deal."

"What are we dealing for?" I asked. "I came to talk to Bill."

Krch stared at me with a mean little smile. "Oh, you did? Okay. I'll book him and send him downtown, and around midnight when they're through processing his butt and he gets his phone call, you can talk to him. Or you can come with me now. Somebody find Rossi for me, huh?" he said, raising his voice to the rest of the room. "I'm in number three. If Smith does anything besides sit there looking stupid, lock it."

"Krch—"

"Christ, Smith, shut up. What are you afraid of? She'll sell you out?"

Krch grinned. Then he turned and walked through the door without looking to see whether I was following him.

I met Bill's eyes briefly. He was close to an edge, the place where you know your anger is only getting in your way and knowing that only makes the anger worse.

"It'll be okay." I touched his hand lightly. "Just let me see what he wants." He didn't answer. As I left the room he was lighting another cigarette.

Number three turned out to be one of the interrogation rooms down the hall. Inside the room Krch dropped himself into one of the plastic chairs around the Formica-topped table and waited for me either to do the same, or not. I did.

"Hope he don't slug anybody while we're gone," Krch said, in a tone of voice that told me he hoped exactly the opposite.

"He'll be all right."

"Got one hell of an attitude, that guy."

"He doesn't like to be locked up."

"That's right," Krch grunted. "Bad memories, huh? Six months inside can be hard on a guy. You know what he was in for?"

"Misdemeanor assault," I said. "Not a felony, or he wouldn't have a license."

"Good lawyer," Krch grunted. "Drove a hard plea-bargain. The original charge was attempted manslaughter, you know. You might want to think about having a guy like that for a partner," he offered, as though I'd asked. "Bad temper, bad attitude. Bad luck. Well, I guess you know what you're doing." He smiled a sour smile.

"Yes, I do, thanks," I said.

But Bill was only my partner sometimes. And though he'd told me about his record the second case we'd worked together, to give me a chance to say, "No, thanks," I'd never thought it was any business of mine to ask what it was he'd done.

Not that there was any chance I'd tell Krch that.

Krch stuck his hands in his pockets and tilted his chair back. "All right," he said. "You're in deep shit. Both of you, but him more than you because he's uglier and I hate him more. Not that that means I won't nail you to the wall, too, sweetheart, unless you cooperate."

"With what?" I asked in as neutral a tone as I could manage.

"With me. Hey, Rossi," he grunted as the door opened. I swung my head around to get a look at Rossi.

196

In a sweatshirt and baggy jeans, without makeup, with a gun on her hip and a badge on her belt, her look was completely different, and she was so out of context that it actually took me until she'd closed the door behind her and stood leaning against the wall to recognize her. It was the way she held her cigarette, between the knuckles and not the fingertips, that sent me suddenly back to the bar at Donna's, where I was being warned away from Ed Everest by a woman named Francie whose last name I didn't know.

TWENTY-TWO

"Officer Francesca Rossi," said the young woman leaning on the wall. She acknowledged me with a small nod of her gamine head. "Anti-crime." She drew the last of the smoke out of her cigarette, then dropped it to the floor and crushed it.

Anti-crime officers are not detectives, but they're plainclothes cops, working undercover usually as decoys or in sting operations. It's one good route to moving up in the department, if that's what you want.

"Francie," I said.

"Oh." Krch widened his eyes as though he were impressed. "You and Officer Rossi have met?"

"You must know we have or you wouldn't have wanted me to come here," I said, trying to curb my distaste for the man and his style.

"Don't you believe it. It wasn't my idea for you to come here. It was Asshole's." He gestured vaguely in the direction of the room we'd come from, where Bill still sat in the cell I hoped was still unlocked. "I was all for just picking you up and tossing you in the can. That's what I had in mind for him, too, except I was gonna insist on having the pleasure of tearing up his license and feeding it to him one scrap at a time."

"What for?"

"What for? Being all over my cases like a fucking cheap suit!"

I wasn't sure what crime that constituted, but I had a feeling I'd better get more details before I said anything else.

"But," Krch went on, "your partner had this other idea."

"What idea?"

"He thought maybe you should come up here and we could work something out."

That Krch had agreed to that might mean that he didn't feel he had enough of whatever it was he had to actually get away with arresting us. Or it might mean something else. I waited.

Krch regarded me with bitter curiosity. "I should have known when I saw you with him in the park that some shit was going on." With a sudden jerk of his body he brought his chair forward, making a little crash as the front legs hit the floor. "But I had real shit to worry about!" he barked. "I got an investigation I'm trying to run, I got a shooter in the park—I got no time to worry about My Favorite Asshole and his new Chinese squeeze." He shook his head and said, as though to himself, "Big mistake, Harry. Because where you got Smith, you got trouble, every time."

He stopped and scowled at me.

"If you're waiting for me to say something, Detective, I can't until I know more about what's going on."

"Until *you* know what's going on? How about you telling *me* what the hell's going on?"

"I don't know what you mean."

"You lied to me in the park!"

"I don't remember that you asked me a question."

"I asked who you were."

"You asked Bill who I was," I corrected him. "He said he'd been trying to get to know me. That was true. We work together sometimes, but he doesn't know me very well."

Krch's color rose. "You called him a clazy Amellican!"

"Well," I said, "that's true, too, isn't it?"

Officer Francesca Rossi snorted something that might have been a laugh.

"Shut up, Rossi." Krch's red face edged into purple. Then he relaxed. He stuck his hands back in his pockets and tilted his chair

198

again. "Fuck the both of you, toots. You want to play the game his way, we don't have a lot to talk about."

"I don't know what we're talking about now," I said.

Krch opened his mouth, but Rossi was faster.

"We have an investigation going," she said. She pushed off from the wall and moved to the table, to a place across from me. "Ed Everest and his hookers." She pulled out a chair and sat.

"You know about that?" I looked from her to Krch.

"Citizens' respect for the police is boundless, ain't it, Rossi?" Krch growled. "What do you think, Miss Chin, we're not even as sharp as you two sorry-ass P.I.s?"

"If you know," I countered, "why is it still going on?"

"Why's what still going on?"

"Why is Ed Everest still running hookers?"

"Is he?"

"She just said—"

"Can you prove it?"

"I—"

"No, Miss Chin, you can't. We can't either. That's why they call this an investigation. And that's why it don't need jerks like you two screwing it up!"

"I shouldn't even have done what I did in the bar," Francie—Officer Rossi—told me. "Warned you away from Ed Everest. But you looked so exactly like one of the pathetic little suckers he pulls in. That was before the new haircut," she added.

Oh, well then, I thought.

"It was my good deed for the day, trying to save you," she said. "I didn't know who you were. I didn't even mention you to Krch until later, when—"

"Until later," Krch said.

Francie stopped.

I spoke to Krch. "That's what this is about? That you think we messed around in your Ed Everest investigation?"

"Not completely."

"Then what?"

"First, tell me what you know about Everest."

I thought about what to say to him, besides "who wants to

199

know?" or something equally mature. "Probably the same thing you do," I settled on. "He takes girls who want to be models, gets them in a position where they owe him, and starts them turning tricks."

"How do you know?"

"I actually don't. I'm guessing. Rumors you hear. And because he seemed anxious to spend a lot of money jump-starting my career, and I'm not model material."

"You went to him?"

"Just to look around."

"Just to look around. Be a little more open with me, Miss Chin; you might find it's a good idea. Why were you and Asshole investigating him?"

"I wish you wouldn't call him that."

"I don't care."

Well, at least we'd gotten that straight. "We weren't investigating him, really," I said. "We were on another case that went nowhere, but we ran across Everest in the middle of it. I got intrigued and wanted to follow it up. Just to see what would happen."

"You're just like him, aren't you?" Krch asked with a weary sigh. "You can't let things go, either. What a hot couple."

I didn't think there was any good answer to that.

"Go get him, huh, Rossi?" Krch said, unexpectedly. Francie stood and left the room. "What was the other case?" Krch asked me.

"It's not connected to Ed Everest," I said.

"Did I ask you that?"

"I was following someone. It put me at the bar. Everest came on to me, and I got interested. I don't like the idea of his taking advantage of girls' dreams any more than Francie does."

"Oh? You know all about what she likes?"

"She made warning me her good deed for the day," I said.

"She's a fucking saint. I want to know what the other case was."

I managed to swallow the "I don't care." "I'm too much like Bill," I said. "You know I won't tell you."

"Was Wayne Lewis part of it?"

Uh-oh, I thought. This water might be deeper than I know about.

Saving me from having to answer right away, the door opened, and Bill and Francie entered the room.

"Sit down," Krch told Bill peremptorily. Bill, the tight line of his jaw the only sign of what he was feeling, threw me a look as he sat. I told him with my eyes that I didn't know, no matter what the question was. Francie took up her old chair opposite.

"Lydia and I were just discussing Wayne Lewis." Krch said, leaning his padded forearms on the table, including everyone in his remarks, as if we were all at a seminar. "I was just asking her to explain to us why she and Ass—she and Pencil-dick here impersonated officers and broke into a crime scene." He turned to me again with an expectant look, as though I really might answer that.

"That's not what happened, Krch," Bill said shortly, "I told you that."

"Yeah," Krch answered, speaking in reasoned tones. "But in the absence of you telling me what *did* happen, I'm assuming you're full of crap and I'm asking your partner." He turned back to me, his face a caricature of polite interest.

"You know what happened," Bill said.

Krch swung back to him, "I'm not talking to you!"

"I was there. It was my idea."

"You're not doing yourself any favor saying that."

"Anyway, it's not true," I stuck in.

Krch turned to me again. "What's not?" he demanded.

"It was *my* idea," I said. "But we didn't impersonate anybody and we didn't break in."

"Oh, Christ, look at this, Rossi. They're gonna be heroes and protect each other." To me again: "I don't really give a shit whose idea it was, and I have a witness who says you said you were cops."

"Your witness is wrong."

"She let you in."

"The lady upstairs?" I asked. "I'm not surprised she didn't understand who we were. She was scared, and she'd been drinking. She absolutely insisted that we go in and look around because the door was open and the tape was torn. I thought we were being reassuring good Samaritans. Making her feel better until the cops came."

I thought that was pretty good, but Krch didn't look as though he'd bought a word of it. "Love it, don't you, Rossi? Good Samaritans. Then why didn't you stick around until the cops got there?" he asked.

"The place wasn't that interesting."

"No? What would have made it interesting?"

Bill cut in. "What the hell do you want, Krch?"

"I want to know why you two are everywhere I fucking look in the last three days! And I'm talking to your partner, so shut up." Back to me: "What were you doing in the park?"

"Having breakfast," said Bill.

Krch's eyes hardened. "Smith, so help me, if you fuck up my case—"

"I thought you were investigating Ed Everest," I said, struck by a thought. "What do you care about Wayne Lewis? Why do you even know he's dead? That wasn't in your precinct."

Krch looked at Francie Rossi, who hadn't said a word since she'd come back into the room. He seemed to be weighing something. He leaned back in his chair again and tipped it backward.

"Yeah," he said. "That's right. I was investigating Ed Everest. You know why?"

"No."

Krch rubbed his nose with a meaty hand. "Because what he's doing, nobody gives a shit. No, I'm serious. Couple of dolls selling a piece of ass, turning their paychecks over to Poppa, you think that's big news in this town? And don't give me that crap about taking advantage of their poor little dreams. They know what they're doing. And you can't tell me the girls in that life don't at least halfway like it. What's not to like?"

Francie and I exchanged glances, but he outranked her, so she held her tongue. And I thought about Dawn Jing, and held mine.

"Then why investigate?" Bill wanted to know.

"Because every now and then," Krch told us, "some horse's ass chews the Commissioner's ear off about some pet peeve. Then some schmuck cop gets stuck putting in overtime to take out the Commissioner's garbage. This Everest cocksucker was somebody's. The word came down, shut him down. But this wasn't any glamour case.

202

Hopeless. Not gonna make anybody's career. So you stick Harry Krch with it. You know why?"

Bill said nothing. I asked, "Why?"

" 'Cause," Krch answered me, "Harry Krch's got no career." He fixed his eyes on Bill. I wouldn't have wanted what was in his eyes directed at me. He said, "You know why?"

Nobody answered. He went on anyway. "Because an asshole P.I. who knew better than everybody else fucked up his career for him."

The room was silent. Krch stood slowly and walked around the table to stand behind Bill. He leaned forward and put his face next to Bill's ear. Bill drew a breath, but didn't turn.

"See," Krch breathed softly, "shutting down an operation like this, it's impossible. How're you going to do it? Everest keeps himself clean, you've got nothing on paper on him. But you can't get to the girls without him. And if you get to the girls, what are you going to do? Screw 'em and try to pay? You'd get laughed out of court with something like that." He rested his hand on Bill's shoulder, as if they were pals discussing the ballgame in a bar. Bill didn't move. Krch went on, in mild tones. "And the girls aren't going to talk. They know where the paycheck comes from, the nice apartment, all that. Look what it took to shut down the Mayflower Madam. They had to set up an entire squad, just for her. This one isn't that big, no one's gonna do that. The Department just wants to look like it's going through the motions in case anybody asks. So you give it to Harry, because you give all the dead-end shit to Harry. That's what Harry's for."

Bill was breathing steadily, rhythmically. His eyes were fixed on the wall ahead. Under the table his right hand was curled into a fist.

"And you give Harry one fucking undercover," Krch went on. "Some green girl. At least she's got energy. She figures the case'll be good experience for her, even though it'll go nowhere."

Francie looked at Krch. She seemed about to say something, but she didn't.

"Wait," I said, more to focus Krch on me, to give Bill some space, than because I wanted an answer to the question I was about to ask. "Ed Everest doesn't use white girls. He specializes. 'Exotics'· blacks and Asians. I saw his books of photographs. How close could Francie get?"

"Oh, no." Krch said. He took his hand from Bill's shoulder to wag a finger at me. I almost cheered. "I couldn't send in some one of you people or something for him to take on. That's entrapment, sweetie. He'd claim she was the first whore ever worked for him and he didn't know nothing about it. I had to send someone into his world, where he lives, to listen and ask around and build a case, not to stick herself in the middle of it. See, that's called investigating. You might not have heard of it."

"You're exhausting," I said. "Did you know that?"

Krch smiled a joyless smile. Francie started a more amused one, but squelched it.

"It's just as well this is how we did it, anyway," Krch said. "Rossi made friends around. That's how we got the miracle."

Krch leaned forward again to put his face an inch from Bill's. "The fucking miracle. See, the impossible case turned out not to be impossible. Maybe. Something that could pull a cop's career out of the shitpile and let him at least retire as a *cop*, if he pulled it off. Maybe." The last word was almost a whisper. As it trailed off, Krch slammed his palm on the tabletop. The sudden crash made us all jump. "And then suddenly Smith is everywhere I fucking look! I don't know what your connection with this case is, Smith, but if you screw it up I'm gonna cut your fucking balls off! Now, talk to me!"

In the cords in Bill's neck I could see what it was costing him to keep still. I wasn't sure how much longer he had in him, and I didn't think his grabbing Krch by his thick throat and throwing him against the wall was going to be a good idea.

"Detective," I said.

Krch straightened up. "What?" he snarled.

"When I got here," I said, shifting to look at him, "you said you'd been planning to have me arrested, and Bill, too, but Bill had this other idea, so you asked me to come up here to 'work something out.' All you've done since I got here is threaten us. If you want something, tell me what it is. If you don't, arrest me or I'm leaving."

Krch stared at me angrily for a few moments. Then he brushed past me and slammed out of the room.

I watched his back, then turned to Francie. "Where'd he go?"

She shrugged. "Get a cup of coffee. That's usually what he does instead of slugging someone." She looked at Bill. "You really grind his cookie, don't you?"

Bill drew a cigarette from his shirt pocket. "He has a right."

"No smoking room," Francie said, pointing to the sign on the wall. She took out a cigarette of her own, lit it and reached a cardboard coffee cup off the floor for them to share as an ashtray. "You really screw up his career, like he tells it?"

"No, he did," Bill said. "I just let everybody know."

"Why?"

"His career or a fifteen-year-old kid's life," Bill said. "Didn't look like much of a choice to me."

"Did you do the right thing?"

Bill didn't answer.

I said to Francie, "What do you mean?"

"The kid," she said. "He go on to be a brain surgeon or thing?"

"I don't know," Bill said evenly.

"Krch could have been a good cop."

Bill pulled on his cigarette. I looked into his eyes. They seemed troubled to me, but he wasn't looking at me.

The door opened and the man who could have been a good cop came back into the room.

He had a steaming cup of burnt-smelling coffee in one hand and a cigarette in the other. Great, I thought. Three to one. Krch sat down again in the chair he'd been in before, the one across from Bill.

"Okay," he said. He spoke through clenched teeth, growling out the words. "Here it is. Ed Everest don't only run hookers. He deals drugs. Not in a big way, just some pissy little stuff. To his girls, to other models. Nothing the big drug boys would be interested in. But enough, maybe, you could put pressure on one of the girls, maybe she'd give you Everest."

I looked to Francie. "A lot of people in that world do a lot of drugs," she said, shrugging. "It's how the models stay thin, for one thing."

"Now, we figured this was good," Krch said. "Me and Rossi.

Rossi was keeping her eyes open, and we were gonna choose our little informant and close in. Squeeze her a little, get something on Everest we could make stick. Everything was rosy."

Next to me, Bill stubbed out his cigarette. He seemed to me like a pot whose flame had been turned down just before the pressure blew the lid off: still simmering, but for now under control.

"I don't see what the problem is," I said. "We haven't done anything that should have any impact on that investigation."

"Someone did. Someone had a big fucking impact on it."

"Who?"

"Whatever son of a bitch killed Wayne Lewis. He was Everest's connection."

TWENTY-THREE

h," I said.

"Don't give me 'oh'!" Krch barked. All three cigarettes were out now, but the whole room hung heavy with tension and smoke. "Don't give me that shit!" He drained his coffee, then crumpled the cup and threw it across the room. It bounced off the wall behind my head. "You knew that. You knew about Everest, and you were at Lewis's."

"At the bar," I said to Francie. "At Donna's, when you told Andi Shechter that Wayne Lewis was dead. That's what she meant, wasn't it? 'I won't go to Ed.' For drugs?"

Francie nodded. "Cocaine, she does. A little heroin. A lot of them do, like I said."

"Uncooperative," I muttered, half to myself. "Unreliable."

"What?" asked Francie.

"An editor at *Vogue* said there was a note in her file. Uncooperative and unreliable lately."

"It happens," Francie said. "They start doing drugs to keep themselves thin. Then the drugs get to them, and they begin missing appointments and looking like hell when they do show up. Andi's getting close to that point. She's not doing drugs to help her career anymore. She's working to support her habit."

And her friends are helping, I thought, remembering a smoky evening at Donna's and folded bills passing from John Ryan to Andi Shechter.

"So fucking what?" Krch finally broke in. I was surprised he'd let the conversation go on this long. "That's not your damn case, Rossi."

"I had the feeling Andi knew who Wayne's connection was," Francie defended herself. "I thought I could follow it one step further back."

Krch scowled at Francie. She shrugged. "Only, Krch said to lay off."

"Not your damn case, Rossi," Krch said again. "We're not Narcotics. That's for the big boys."

"The information was hot and the lead could have been good," Francie retorted. "It was worth a try."

Krch's face disputed that, but he seemed to be saving that fight for a different time. He turned to me again. "Okay, so you knew about the connection, Everest and Lewis. I want to know how, and what you were doing at Lewis's."

"Until just now, we didn't know," I said.

"You expect me to believe that?"

"I don't expect anything except rudeness from you, Detective. But I'm telling the truth."

"Well, what do you know, Rossi, she's telling the truth but she thinks I'm rude. Shit."

"You are," Francie replied.

"Go to hell. Look, Lydia, Smith: here's my problem." He was back to the exaggerated facade of reasonableness. "Now Lewis's dead, other cops are interested. So far I don't think they've turned up Everest yet, or Lewis's other drug connections, but they will. There's whole goddamn lists of them; they'll figure it out. And in the middle of investigating Lewis's murder, someone'll lean on someone, and Everest'll fall. And Harry's big last chance will be fucked."

He looked from one of us to the other, almost smiling. "Now, that would be bad enough if it just sort of happened. But to have it happen with Smith in the middle of it?" Suddenly he lifted himself out of his chair and roared, "No way! You tell me what's going on! You give me something I can use to break this Everest thing, or so help me the two of you are looking at new careers and the inside of a cell if there's any little thing at all Harry can do about it!"

He loomed across the table, face purple and fists clenched, while the room echoed with his words and then with silence. Bill slowly stood.

"Sit down!" Krch ordered.

Bill shook his head. "There isn't, Harry."

"Isn't what?"

"A fucking thing you can do about it," Bill said deliberately. "All you have when you're through yelling and screaming is a half-drunk witness who says we were at Lewis's. That's trespassing at best if you could make it stick. And you know you can't. We're leaving."

"Bullshit!" Krch's face spread in a sickly grin. "Here's what I think: you're working for some sleazeball lawyer. His client's a drugged-up yuppie who knows something about Lewis's murder—shit, he probably did it—and you broke into Lewis's place to fuck up that investigation. How does that sound?"

"Like a load of crap," Bill said.

"But crap I can sell to the D.A.," Krch smiled. "I don't know. You might wiggle off. But I can try."

"But you don't think it's true, do you, Detective?" I asked.

"What the hell's the difference? I can make it look like it is." He smiled at Bill again. "What'd you do in Nebraska, Smith? Six months? I'd settle for that again. Three months for your partner, if she can convince anyone you were the brains—"

"Oh, knock it off," I snapped. "You know, Detective, you might try 'please.' "

Everyone looked at me. I kept my eyes steadily on Krch. He growled, "What the hell do you mean?"

" 'Please,' " I repeated. "It's a word people use when they're asking for help. Because we're going to help you."

The room was full of silence again. Bill melted back into his chair; Krch eventually did the same. Francie was hiding a small smile.

Bill lit another cigarette, and Krch did too. I toyed with the idea of asking if we could move this meeting to the park.

Krch, cigarette dangling from his lumpy lips, said to the room at large, "Would you look at this, she's going to help me. You want me to kiss your feet, or what?"

I congratulated myself on passing up my chance to tell Harry Krch what he could kiss. "I know you don't want to do it this way," I said. "You'd like it better if we were so intimidated we'd do anything you said. But that's not happening, Detective. This is the best offer you're going to get."

He grunted, then asked, "What's the offer?"

I could feel Bill's eyes on me. My case, my game, and he was playing it the way we always played, going along with what I was doing because I was doing it, the way I would have if the inspiration had been his; but I could see how tightly he was reining himself in, the effort it was taking to keep himself in that chair.

Well, this shouldn't take long.

"Everest was getting something from Lewis besides drugs," I told Krch.

"What?"

"Johns."

Krch's eyes narrowed. "What the hell do you mean?"

"They were in the same business. Not on the same scale, or the same level. And part of the deal that goes with this is that nothing you do goes any distance to bringing down the woman Lewis was working for."

"Was working for him, you mean."

"No, I don't. And I want a promise."

"I can't promise that. She might come out in the investigation of Lewis's murder. Hell, she might have done it. Who is she?"

"Do I look that stupid? And if she comes out in that investigation that's her problem. But I don't want her exposed because of anything I do, and that includes talking to you."

"How do I know anything you say is worth a damn?"

"I don't understand you," I said. "First you try to intimidate us into talking to you, and now when I'm ready to talk for free you don't want to hear it. Maybe we should leave after all."

I looked at Bill and we both started to rise.

"Screw you!" Krch barked. "Sit down. What do you have?"

"Promise?"

He shrugged. "If I can."

"Try," I suggested. I sat, but only on the edge of my chair. "All right. It's this: Lewis was working for this woman. He kept the books and arranged her dates." It was harder than I'd thought it would be using Dawn Jing's innocent-sounding words to describe her life. "She's very high-class, very exclusive. She turns dates down a lot. For a fee, Wayne Lewis was sending those guys to Ed Everest."

Krch and Francie looked at each other. "Same stock in trade?" Krch asked me.

"Maybe."

"Okay," Krch said. "So what good is this to me?"

"I can probably get you one or two names."

"From?"

"From my source." Assuming Dawn could remember one or two names of guys she'd washed her hands of. "Then instead of leaning on the girls who work for Ed, you can lean on the johns. I like it better that way anyway. It seems to me they're the real creeps and criminals in this kind of thing."

"Spare me the feminist crap, or whatever that is. I'll lean on anybody I can to get to Everest, and I don't really give a shit about him, either, between you and me. He's just a job I want to do. But a name some shaky P.I. gives me from a source she won't identify is no damn good, sweetheart. Thanks a lot anyway."

"No good in court. But you can squeeze the guy, tell him you'll expose him at home, at work, make him panic—you can't tell me you haven't done that kind of thing, Detective."

"Yeah, and you're just the bleeding-heart type to cry and whine when we do." He stared at me silently. I stared back, forcing my eyes not to blink and the muscles in my face not to move at all. "Okay," he said. "Feed me some names and we'll try it."

"I'll call." I nodded, and turned to Bill, ready to leave.

Bill was looking at Krch with a small, strange smile. "You know, Lydia," he said to me, not taking his eyes off Krch, "you don't have to do that."

"Do what?"

"Feed him names. It's a good idea, as a way to shut down Everest, going to the johns. But you don't have to get names for him."

"Why not?" I asked.

Krch, at the same time, said, "Why don't she?"

"Because," Bill said, "you have them."

Krch scowled.

I said, "He has what?"

"He has everything he needs," Bill said. "He has more than he needs, but he didn't know until you told him that that's what he had. Or maybe he didn't know how to work it."

Krch growled menacingly. "Shut up, Smith."

"Shove it, Krch. But I'll be glad to help you out. I have the manual at home. I'll drop it over."

I suddenly caught up. "He has that thing?" I asked Bill. "That Pocket Wizard thing?"

Francie's look showed she wasn't clear, either, maybe even less than I.

"What thing?" she asked. "What thing is that?" She shifted her look from Bill to Krch.

"I don't know what he's talking about," Krch snapped.

"Lewis's datebook," Bill told Francie. "Address book, daily calendar. A little electronic thing. It looks like a calculator. It's a relational database."

I stared at Bill. "Who told you about relational databases?"

"Little birds. I read the damn manual, what do you think?"

That seemed reasonable. But the big question remained, so I asked it. "What makes you say he has it?"

"Lists," Bill said. "He said there were lists of Lewis's drug connections. Where, Krch?"

Krch's face was dark with anger. "The fucking bastard had a computer! He had lists on disks. The detective on the case has them. Any interested cop can get a look. You just got to be smart enough to ask, and then smart enough to know what you're looking at."

Bill shook his head. "My partner's pretty smart, and she didn't see any lists."

"What the fuck do you mean, she didn't see?"

211

Bill just shrugged. I just sat there.

"Fuck the both of you!" Krch exploded. "Go to hell! Get the hell out of here before—!"

"Wait." That was from Francie, looking hard at Krch. "I'm part of this investigation; I'm in this, too. If there's some shit that's going to land on me, I want to know about it."

Krch stared at her, unbelieving.

She turned from him. "Tell me what you're talking about. From the beginning," she ordered Bill.

Good, Francie, I thought. Green, maybe, but I'll bet you make it.

Of course, it helps to have a willing witness. Bill nodded agreeably at Francie. "We were there. At Lewis's. Make whatever you want out of that. We looked around. We didn't mess with anything and we didn't take anything except a copy of Lewis's computer files and the manual to this Pocket Wizard thing. The thing itself was missing when we got there. We figured that was what was stolen when the tape was broken."

"And?" Francie's voice was still hard.

"And Krch was the guy who stole it."

"Smith, so help me—" Krch snarled.

"Krch, put a sock in it, huh?" Bill said. "I don't know what your problem is, anyway. You're the cops. Who am I going to go to with this, outside this room? I'm only laying it all out now because I think you always ought to share everything with your partner."

Well, I thought, what a lovely testimonial.

Francie wasn't impressed. "You're accusing a police officer of breaking and entering. And theft," she said.

"And concealing evidence," Bill said. "That was the point."

"Evidence of what?" Francie frowned at Bill.

"Not of something he'd done. Of Lewis's drug trade. That's what he thought he was doing, anyway. Because of what he just said, about other cops getting interested if they knew there were drugs involved."

"Because Krch and Francie knew about that because of Everest, but no one else did?" I asked. "To keep it from the other cops. To keep Everest for himself."

212

Krch rose, red-faced, sputtering. "You lying motherfucker!" His hands were thick, white-knuckled fists. "You son of a bitch! You're fucking under arrest, right now—!"

"Sit down, Krch!" That was Francie. "Goddamn it! He's right, isn't he?"

Krch stopped in midroar. His face darkened to a deep maroon. With his mouth shut like that, I was afraid he might explode.

"Sure I am." Bill kept his seat, and kept his eyes on Krch. "It was just routine, when you heard about Lewis, right, Harry? At your shift briefing, I'll bet. A homicide in a neighboring precinct, just something to know about." He glanced at Francie for confirmation of that, and he got it.

"And you knew it could ice your comeback. You knew the big boys would be interested, narcotics, if they connected it up. You and Rossi were close. You didn't want them to know."

Bill slid his hands into his pockets and tilted his chair back, just the way Krch had. He looked up at Krch, who was still standing, still purple. "You didn't even know what you were looking for. You probably hoped there wasn't anything. You checked the computer files, and there wasn't, but then you thought. Rossi was right about you, Krch. You would've been a good cop. You saw how organized Lewis was, and you knew he'd have records. He was that kind of guy. So you hunted, and you found what the other cops missed. You can work a computer, which is more than I can do. You could work that thing, too. You knew what it was. What you didn't know, until Lydia told you just now, was what's in it. That's what the lists are, Harry. Not just drug connections. Johns. And they're yours now. They're a gift."

Bill lowered the front of his chair to the floor. He stood. I did, too.

"So that's it, Harry," Bill said. "We're even."

Krch, jaw tight and eyes bulging, glared wildly at Bill. For a moment, nothing; then a sweep of his meaty hand threw over a chair. "Motherfucker!" he roared as it clattered against the table. He charged past Francie and out of the room.

The three of us left looked at one another. Everything Bill had said I was sure was true, except one thing.

I didn't think they would ever be even.

TWENTY-FOUR

I kept up with Bill for blocks as, pulling on the cigarette he'd lit the moment we left the station house, he stalked rapidly down Third Avenue. His legs are much longer, so mine worked much harder to move that fast. By Seventeenth Street, I'd had enough.

I clutched at his arm as he was about to step into the street with barely enough time to beat the light. "You have to slow down," I told him.

He snapped his head around with a startled look, as though he were surprised to find me there. He looked up and down the street, a man getting his bearings, finding his location in the world. Traffic started to move in front of us. "I'm sorry," he said.

"You don't have to be sorry. You just have to slow down."

"Okay." He threw the cigarette butt, which was nothing except filter now, into the gutter as the light changed. "Buy you lunch?" he offered, as we started legitimately—and more slowly—across the street.

"Sure."

"Anyplace you like around here?"

"You know what? Can we eat in Union Square?"

Four times a week the city runs a Greenmarket in Union Square. Farmers and bakers and cheesemakers come from all around to sell their vegetables and fruits and bread and herbed goat cheese rolled in ash. It's fun to go to, and the food's really good.

And it's outdoors.

Bill smiled, giving me a sideways look while we walked. "That must have been tough for you, all of us puffing like chimneys in there," he said.

"It wasn't tough," I answered airily. "Easy as pie. Just revolting."

We wandered through the market, picking this and that, and

then found an empty bench in Union Square Park. Squirrels who'd either already eaten the nuts they'd buried last fall or couldn't remember where they'd put them sat on their winter-skinny haunches waiting for us to drop crumbs from our crusty sourdough loaf or our extra-sharp New York State cheddar. Bill, with the pocket knife he always carries, sliced the bread, spread it with grainy mustard, and topped it with slabs of cheese. I opened our jar of pickled green beans and took one out to munch.

It was a perfect day for an early-spring picnic, the sun spreading yellow warmth under a sky of cloudless blue. Couples leaning against each other meandered by past secretaries briskly shopping in the Greenmarket on their lunch hour. Funny, I thought, extracting another tart and dripping bean from the jar, that this glorious sky color was called blue, the same as the muddy, dull color on the station house walls, in that windowless and smoky room we'd sat in for too long.

"What color were the walls in Nebraska?" I asked Bill.

He looked up from cutting a sandwich. "What?"

"When you were in jail. What color were the walls?"

He cleaned his pocket knife with a napkin and put it away. "Tan." His voice was almost normal; maybe someone who hadn't known him as long as I had wouldn't have heard the strange note in it. "In a certain light," he said, "right before it rained, the ground outside was exactly the same color."

He unfolded a napkin next to me and put a sandwich on it.

"I don't know what made me think it was okay to ask that," I said. "I'm sorry."

He shook his head. "It is okay."

"It bothers you to talk about it."

"No. It bothers me to have been there."

"Did you do what they said you did?"

"You know what I was there for," he said.

"I know what the charge was," I answered. "That's not the same."

A squirrel bounced up and sat practically on Bill's foot. Bill broke off a sandwich crumb for him.

"I beat the shit out of a guy in a bar," he said. "Do you really want to hear this?"

"Yes."

He looked around the park. Shadows of tree branches swept the paths. "I was set up," he said. "An investigation I was working was getting too close, so the guy I had my eye on hired some good old boys to start a fight. The point was to get me arrested, to keep me on ice for a while."

He threw another piece of crust to the squirrel. "I knew that. I goddamn knew it, but the little bastards pissed me off so much I couldn't keep a lid on it. There were two of them, dirty fighters, young, and I just had to prove I was better. To them it was just a Saturday night bar fight they were getting paid for. They'd probably have done it for free, and then bought me a beer when I got out of jail. To me it was something else."

I took a bite of my sandwich and waited.

"I *was* better," he said. "I messed up one of them so badly that when the sheriff finally came, the charge was felony assault. It took just about everything my lawyer had to bargain it down to a misdemeanor, and I had to agree to serve the whole thing."

The squirrel was back at Bill's feet now, with a friend. Bill tossed each of them a piece of cheese.

"Was he all right?" I asked.

"The guy? He was out the hospital in a week. I heard he got paid double."

"What happened to your investigation?"

"Vaporized. The suspect disappeared. The Cayman Islands, or something. Took all the money with him. My client couldn't prove a thing."

He took a swig of apple cider from the jar we'd bought. "Some partner, huh?" He didn't look at me.

"The best," I said, taking the cider and taking a swig myself.

Looking at the squirrels, he lit a cigarette. I expected a wise-guy answer, but I didn't get one.

What I got was a sudden thought. "Hey!" I yelped.

"What?"

"Me, too! Krch got *me* so mad that *I* forgot what I was there for."

216

"At the precinct? I thought you were there to save my butt."

"Only incidentally. I was there because that's where you were, and I needed to talk to you. We couldn't talk until I'd saved your, excuse me, butt."

"Talk about what?"

"This." I pulled my manila envelope, the one I'd found in Roland Lum's trash, out of my shoulder bag and handed it to Bill.

He took it the way I'd held it, handling it only along the edges so he wouldn't smudge any prints, although who was going to run prints on this for us, and where we would get prints to compare them to, I had no idea.

"I told you I found something," I said.

He turned the envelope over, scrutinizing the back, then the front again. "Where?" he asked.

"Roland Lum's." I told him my story, my visit to Mrs. Chan and how I invaded Roland's factory. "You're not the only one who gets set up," I finished. "I fell for Peng Hui Liang."

He turned the envelope over again, digesting what I'd told him. "You never really did," he said.

"I never really believed he wanted her for the reason he said he did. But I believed he was looking for her."

"And now?"

"Now I think she never existed. He was sending me on a wild-goose chase. He wanted me out of the way."

"Why?"

"Why? Because of this."

"What does this mean, though?" Bill mused.

"What does it mean?" I frowned at him. Maybe he was still too distracted by the memory of Krch, or of jail, to get with the program. "It means Roland stole the ransom. It means he either was the shooter or was working with him."

"And he knew about the ransom how?"

"John told him they were having a problem, and John told him about hiring me. Maybe John tells a lot more than he means to."

"Possible. But why set you up?"

"Because I was getting close."

"But you weren't."

That stopped me. "I wasn't?"

"You wouldn't have been, if Roland hadn't reappeared in your life with a drumroll."

"That first time, on the street? He probably wanted to know how much I knew. To see how close I was."

"Did you give him any idea then that you suspected him?"

"I didn't suspect him, then."

"Then why did he feel he had to invent this Peng Hui Liang thing?"

I squinted into the sunshine. "I see what you mean."

"You're obviously right about the money: Roland took it, one way or another. But there's more to this than that. You'd—we'd—never have even suspected that if Roland had just laid low. Something made it worth the risk for him to come out into the open. There's some reason Roland wanted you distracted and running around Flushing *now*."

"You mean," I asked slowly, catching on, "you think something else is going to happen?"

"It has to be that. Something he doesn't want you in the middle of."

"What?"

"I don't know."

"Oh," I said. "Great." I crumpled our napkins and swept our crumbs into a paper bag. I screwed the top back on the green beans. "Roland set me up and shot at me and stole our client's money and now he's got something else up his sleeve and we don't know what it is. This is great."

"Could be worse," Bill said. "At least we know it's coming."

"Terrific. Like a tidal wave. Come on."

I stood and jammed our lunch garbage into a trash can. Hah, I thought, trash cans. Sitting there on the path like innocent urban conveniences. You don't fool me.

Standing, Bill saluted me. "Okay, boss. Where to?"

"I left Roland stranded and probably steaming on the Upper West Side. Let's go call my machine and see if he had anything to say about it."

Bill took our leftover bread and cheese and beans over to the next bench where a bum was stretched out and snoring. He settled them under the guy's hand; the guy stirred but didn't wake.

We found a pay phone at the Fourteenth Street end of the park, a new and generous brick plaza where exuberant teenage boys shot the steps on their skateboards and did fancy spinning tricks for groups of teenage girls who ignored them. Blocking out the teenage-boy and traffic noises, I listened to the messages on my machine.

There were two. Neither was from Roland.

The first, almost predictably, was from Andrew. "Lydia," it said, "call me. I have something important for you." Uh-huh, I thought. Sure you do. Some new crackpot theory about little sisters, no doubt. I pressed the button for the next message.

"Lydia?" The woman's voice was hesitant, and hearing it made me grab for Bill's arm, so he'd pay attention, too. "It's Genna. They called again. They want more money, and—oh, God, could you call me? I really need you."

TWENTY-FIVE

ill looked at me, his eyebrows raised; while I was fishing for another quarter I told him who it was and what she'd said.

"This could be it," I said.

"Roland?"

"Don't you think so?"

"Yes." He handed me a quarter; I gave up the search of my own pockets and dropped it in the phone.

"Mandarin Plaid," came a female voice I didn't recognize. Maybe it was the young assistant with the thick red lips. I wondered where Brad was, but I had more important things on my mind.

"Genna Jing, please."

"She's out of the office. Can I take a message?"

"This is Lydia Chin. I'm returning her call. She said it was important."

"Yes. She said if you called I should ask you to keep trying, and to find out if there's anyplace she can reach you."

"I'll be back in my office in fifteen minutes. I'll wait for her to call. Do you know where she is?"

"No, I'm sorry. But I'll tell her you're waiting."

As I hung up, Bill said, "She's not there?"

"No. She wanted to know where to find us. Let's go back to my office. But let me call Andrew back first."

"This is new."

"What?"

"Returning Andrew's calls," he said, handing me another quarter.

"He says it's important." I tapped in the number.

"He's said that before."

"I know, and it's never true. I'm going to nip whatever it is in the bud and then we'll head to my office."

We didn't, though.

"Lyd? Where've you been?"

"Don't start that, Andrew. I've been working, at what I do."

"Don't get huffy. Where are you? Can you come over?"

"Now?"

"Yes."

"No."

"This will help you, Lyd."

"The last time you said that—"

"Oh, come on, Lyd. I made a mistake, I was wrong. Give me a chance, will you? This one is real."

"Help me do what?"

"I don't know. But it's about Genna and John. You'll want to hear it."

"Tell me now."

"No. It's not me who has to tell it," he added, probably getting zapped by my impatience vibes through the phone. "Come over."

"If it has to do with the phone call Genna got this morning, I already know."

"What phone call?"

"You mean that? You don't know?"

"Know what?"

I considered, and then sighed. "Okay, brother dear. We're in Union Square anyway. We'll be there in five minutes."

I pushed down the tongue on the phone, keeping the receiver to my ear. "We're going to Andrew's," I told Bill.

"We are?"

"Uh-huh. You have another quarter?"

"You're a pricey hobby." He handed me one.

"Put it on your expense report."

"You think the boss will pay?"

"No. She's too cheap. But you can take it off your taxes that way."

I called Genna's office back to leave Andrew's number instead of mine. Then we headed over.

It was literally a five-minute walk to Andrew's Twentieth Street loft, and another thirty seconds in the elevator. Regardless, Andrew was waiting impatiently at the elevator door when it opened on his floor.

"How come you called now?" was his first question to me.

"Now? Meaning five minutes ago?"

"Right."

"I just got your message. When should I have called?"

"That's not what I meant. I just wondered if you knew Brad was here."

I looked past Andrew to the angular sofa. Brad was there.

He gave me a half-smile, but the rest of his freckled face didn't buy into it.

"I had no idea," I told Andrew. "I called Genna's, but I didn't ask where Brad was. What's going on?"

Bill and I crossed the polished floor to the end of the room where the chairs and the sofa surrounded the white shag rug. Brad stood.

"Hi," he said, sounding uneasy. He wore a band-collared white shirt and suspenders with rocketships and asteroids on them. His muscular arms didn't seem to know what to do with themselves, whether to shake hands with us, or just hang there.

We said "hi" back, and there conversation stopped.

Andrew the social lion stepped in. "Brad had a situation," Andrew said firmly, looking at me and at Bill. "He handled it the way I probably would have. But given what's going on, I wanted you to know about it. He's willing to tell you, but only as long as it doesn't go any further than this room. Agreed?"

For some reason, both Andrew and Brad gave Bill a longer and, it seemed to me, more hostile look than they gave me.

"Okay," I said, answering for both of us. "If we can."

"No, really, Lyd."

"Andrew, how can I promise that?" I was uncomfortably aware that I was echoing Harry Krch. "What if you tell me that he killed Wayne Lewis? I have to know what it is before I promise."

"Oh, hey." Brad dismissed my admittedly overblown conjecture. "It's not anything like that. It's not a crime. At least, my part isn't."

"It may not even help us figure out what's going on," Andrew said, slipping an "us" in there the way my brothers all used to talk to me about "our" New Year's sweets, after they'd eaten theirs up. "But it sounded like something you'd want to know about."

"Okay." I gave in, after a glance at Bill, who didn't seem to object. "I like to know about things. And if it's really not a crime, I won't spread it."

We all sat, arranging ourselves on the sofa and chairs, making a nice square pattern of people around the kidney-shaped coffee table. Everyone waited for Brad to start.

"I'm from Washington," Brad said, looking at me and Bill as if to see how we were taking this. "State, not D.C. A small town, Timothy, two hours east of Seattle. Major Bible country, totally farmers and loggers. I'm the first person in my family in three generations to go farther than Seattle, and most of them won't even go there."

No one said anything. He went on, his words getting a little sharp.

"The point is, I'm not out at home."

Andrew glanced at me. It seemed like I was supposed to say something.

"Okay," I said to Brad. "I'm not surprised you're not. Andrew's not out in Chinatown, and that's a lot closer. But I don't get why you're telling us this."

"All this stuff that's going on," Brad said. "It doesn't make sense to me that it's connected to my problem. But Andrew said you two were the experts at this, not him or me, so I should just tell you and you'd know if it mattered."

My eyebrows shot up. "Andrew said that?"

"Well, sure." Something in my look must have made him want to elaborate. "I mean," he said, "he says stuff like that about you all the time. He's always telling me about your cases and all the cool stuff you do. That business at the museum? He dined out on that for weeks. Don't you know that?"

I looked at all the men in the room. Andrew was concentrating on a very important cuticle on his manicured fingernail. Brad was smiling uncertainly, waiting to go on. Bill was smiling, too, a tiny smile I'd have to talk to him about later.

"Amazing," I sighed. "What an amazing world. So," I said to Brad. "Do go on."

Brad touched the tips of his fingers together. "I don't go back home often," he said. "Not even once a year. But when I do, I leave the earrings home. I grow the beard in, put on a flannel shirt and do macho northwoods boy. I did it the whole time I was growing up. Mostly because of my mom."

Bill reached into his jacket for a cigarette and then stopped. He knows how Andrew feels about smoke in the loft.

"It would be a problem for your mom?" I asked.

"My mom . . ." Brad trailed off, then started up again. "My mom has the best plots in the garden set aside just for the altar flowers for the Mount Hope Evangelical Bible Church. Yeah, it would be a problem for my mom." His fingers smoothed his goatee. "It's not cool these days not to be out. But Andrew's not out to your mom, either."

"So you felt okay telling him about this, whatever it is?"

"Well, I didn't until he started asking me questions. Before that

223

I was telling myself that what was going on had nothing to do with me."

"What was going on?" I echoed.

"The stolen sketches," Brad said. "And the rest."

I shot a glance at Bill, then back to Brad. "How do you know about the sketches?"

"Please," he said. "Do you know how hard it is to hide anything from your secretary?"

Bill grinned at that. I decided to never get a secretary.

"Actually, that's why Genna called you," Brad said. "Or I guess she asked Andrew to. I discreetly reminded her that if she had a problem that had to do with the robbery—I didn't tell her I knew what the problem was—that Andrew's sister was a P.I. Because I hear about you so much." I looked at Andrew, but his fingernail must have been really absorbing. "What the rest of it is, besides the sketches, I don't really know—at least Andrew tells me I don't," Brad went on. "But he says it's bad. And everyone knows about Wayne. Though really, I don't see how that could be connected. But I thought it was time to come clean. Andrew said you'd be okay with it." He included both me and Bill in his look.

"With what?" I asked. "With your being gay?" I glanced at Andrew, surprised that that was even an issue.

"No," Brad said. "With how I dealt with the problem."

"What problem?" I asked. Then, genius that I am, I finally got it. "Someone was threatening to out you?"

He nodded.

"Blackmail?" I said.

He said, "John's mother."

Part of me was scandalized. The other part wasn't even surprised. "Mrs. Ryan?" I asked, redundantly.

"She wanted reports on what John was up to," Andrew said, unable to hold it in any longer. "Can you believe it?"

"I've met her," I said shortly. "She told me she paid for information about John, she just didn't tell me who. Was that how she knew about me?"

"That's right," Brad said. "I had to tell her things. That was the deal."

I shook my head. "What a creep she is." I looked at Bill. He didn't seem even a little bit surprised. But creepy things going on in families rarely surprise him.

Brad went on, "I did it, because I had to. My mom . . . But that didn't mean I had to actually *do* it."

"What do you mean?" I asked.

"Well, I had to tell her some things. Like about Genna hiring you. Things she could have found out some other way, and then I'd be in deep shit. But I didn't tell her why you'd been hired. I pretended I didn't know."

"Why does she want to know these things?" Bill asked, speaking for the first time since we'd sat down.

"It's Genna," Brad said. "She hates her." He shrugged uncomfortably, looking at Andrew.

"Because she's Chinese," I finished, so he wouldn't have to say it.

Brad nodded. "It would ruin her bloodlines," he said. "Blond hair, blue eyes—what a loss to the world, if that were to go."

"And getting the scoop on John?" I asked. "How would that help?"

"Not just John. Genna's business." Brad took a breath. "I saw what was going on. I put it together, and I stopped giving her everything."

"What do you mean?"

"I'd tell Mrs. Ryan something, and something would happen. She never told me she was doing it, and the one time I confronted her she told me to mind my own business. Can you imagine? Spy for me and mind your own business." He ran his hand up and down his goatee.

"Something would happen? What?"

"Different things. Always bad for Genna. The supplier who was suddenly out of the little silver buttons? I was the one who gave Mrs. Ryan his name. And the factory that got another, bigger client? There was no client, just Mrs. Ryan."

"Roland," I said quietly to Bill. He nodded, eyes still on Brad.

From the corner of my eye I saw the inquisitive look Andrew was giving me, but I pretended I didn't.

"There were other things," Brad said. "But like I said, as soon as I caught on, I started being selective. I gave her things to keep her busy, but nothing Genna couldn't handle."

"How do you mean?"

"Other people make silver buttons. I found a new supplier two days after that one backed out. There are other factories, too. I knew that wasn't really a problem. You see, she was trying to ruin Genna. She thinks John just likes the glamour and glitz of this fabulous life—" he and Andrew exchanged sardonic looks "—and if Genna's business fails and there's no more glamour he'll dump her."

"Will he?"

"No way! He's put everything into this. He's in it for the long haul."

"Why? What does he get out of it?"

"Get out of it?" Brad's eyebrows creased together. "Nothing. He just loves her."

It seemed to me that was heartfelt, and I was surprised at how glad I was to hear it.

"So you gave Mrs. Ryan things that would make her feel as though she was making headway, but wouldn't really hurt Genna's business?" I asked.

"You got it. Just to keep her occupied until after Genna's show. Once Genna's a hit—and you have to know she's going to be—there won't be much of anything Mrs. Ryan can do to stop her. Then outing me won't buy her anything and she'll go away. Until then, it's busywork for Mrs. R."

I looked hard at my brother. "How long have you known about this?"

"Oh, Lyd, give me some credit! I only just found out."

"How? Brad just got an attack of conscience and told you? I'm sorry, guys, but I have to know."

Brad, touching the tips of his fingers together under his chin, said, "I didn't just tell him. He called and asked."

"Excuse me?"

Andrew said, "I did. I thought about it, and I realized no one had talked to Brad, and it seemed to me that in his position he might know something. I really meant information, facts, not something like this. So I called. And I was right. Not in the way I thought, but I was."

I looked at Andrew, and he at me. It seemed to me those looks were different from any we'd ever given each other before.

Bill said, "Tell us about Wayne Lewis."

Brad's index fingers tapped the coffee table. "I told Mrs. Ryan that John and Genna had hired Wayne as show producer. A few weeks later he quit. She must have paid him off."

"Or blackmailed him," Bill said.

"Not unless she absolutely had to."

"What do you mean?"

"Blackmail is what she uses when money won't work. The button supplier and the factory, she just paid them. She tried to bribe me at first, but I laughed at her. That must've been a bad move. I guess it made her mad."

"I don't think she gets mad," I said. "She's too icy. I think she just switches tactics. She tried to bribe me, too."

"I didn't know that," Andrew objected.

"I didn't tell you. I think you were too busy yelling at me that night for something else, anyway. So you think Mrs. Ryan bought Wayne off?" I asked Brad.

"Sure. And I can't imagine how that could be connected to someone killing him. I don't really think it is. But Andrew said even if it wasn't, there's enough trouble already that I'd better just tell you about this." He looked from me to Bill. "Is it helping you at all?"

"I think so," I said slowly. "Though I don't know how." Actually, I had some idea how, but I didn't want to share it with Brad and Andrew before I'd gone over it with Bill.

"Listen," I said to Brad. "There's another thing. Genna got a call this morning—do you know about that?"

"A call? There were lots of calls before I left, but none that stood out. Who was it from?"

"The people who stole the sketches."

His face paled. "Oh, my God. Did I pass that on to her? What did they want?"

"I don't know. I was hoping you did. I—"

227

Andrew's phone rang, slicing through the loft like a sudden cold wind. Bill's back stiffened and his head went up. Mine did, too.

Which just goes to show how good our instincts are. It was Genna.

"She wants to talk to you," Andrew said, bringing the portable phone over to where I sat.

I grabbed it. "Genna? What happened?"

"Oh, God, Lydia." Genna's voice sounded thin and tight as a wire. "They called again. It's all terrible. I wanted to call you right away, but John—God, why did I *listen!*—anyway, I'm waiting for them to call but I don't know what I'm going to do, because I haven't got that kind of money—"

"Genna!" I said as sharply and loudly as I could, as I heard her words break into sobs. "Don't! Get control of yourself, Genna. Tell me what happened. How much money do they want?"

I heard Genna draw in a ragged breath. In a shaky voice she said, "A million dollars."

"A million dollars?" I practically shouted. Bill, Andrew, and Brad all stared; Andrew's mouth dropped open. Then everyone leaned closer to me, as though that would help them hear the words spilling jerkily into my left ear. "For your sketches?" I asked, unbelieving.

"No, not for the sketches, of course not!" Her voice got wilder. "Oh, Lydia, please help me! You have to go with me to Mrs. Ryan. Please, will you?"

"You're going to ask Mrs. Ryan for money?"

"She's the only person I know who has money like that!"

"Why would she give it to you?"

"She *has* to," she wailed. "They'll kill him if she doesn't."

I suddenly went cold. "Kill who?"

"John."

filled in Andrew, Brad, and Bill in rapid-fire shorthand as Bill and I got ourselves together and waited for the elevator.

"We're coming," Andrew said, as it arrived.

"No way." Following Bill, I stepped inside. "Don't argue, it's too serious. I'll call you as soon as I can. Really, Andrew." I kissed his cheek and pushed the DOOR CLOSE button.

Miracle of miracles, it worked.

The elevator had barely landed before Bill and I had shot out the door and were racing up the street and down the avenue to Genna's building. Her elevator was slower and the wait was excruciating, but we finally got to her floor. Genna was at the empty front desk, waiting for us, and she swept us into the conference room and yanked the glass door shut. None of us sat.

The conference room was more chaotic than last time, more fabric pinned to the walls, more boxes of buttons and buckles piled on the table. An armless, headless dressmaker's dummy leaned drunkenly in the corner, swathed in Genna's crinkly gold cloth.

"What happened?" I asked, as soon as the door was closed.

Genna's soft skin was ashen, her eyes red and her makeup smudged; but she was still beautiful. Her ruby-nailed hands twisted around each other as she said, "They called. This morning."

She stopped, as though that was information we could have done something with. But it wasn't. "And?" I prompted.

She swallowed, realizing she was going to have to go on. "I wanted to call you right away, but John—" Her voice broke, but she lifted her head and continued. "John didn't want to. He said you hadn't . . . hadn't done us any good the first time."

I couldn't argue with that.

She swallowed again. "He said he'd do it himself."

"Do what?"

"Make the payoff. They told us where to bring the money. He went to do it."

"How much money?" Bill asked.

She frowned at him as though she didn't understand the question. But she answered it. "Fifty thousand dollars. The same as before."

"Where'd you get it?"

"John got it. From his bank. Oh, what's the difference?" she burst out. "It all went wrong, and now they have John and they're going to kill him if I don't give them a million dollars!"

"What went wrong?" Bill pressed.

"Oh, *stop!*" Genna entreated. She turned to me. "Lydia, do we have to talk now? I'll tell you later. On our way. Because they said there's a deadline—"

"When?" I asked.

"Eight hours from when they called. Tonight."

I glanced at Bill. His eyes told me what he wanted. "There's time then," I said. "It will help if you tell us what happened."

Genna slapped the back of the chair next to her with a small, impatient gesture. She looked toward the ceiling, fighting back tears. "They called," she said, her words forced from a tight, constricted throat. "This morning. They said they were ready to deal again."

"Man or woman?" asked Bill.

She looked at him, not in a friendly way. "A man."

"Did you recognize the voice?"

"Of course not!"

"Go on, Genna," I said, to come between them.

She set her mouth and brought her eyes back to me. "They told us where to bring the money. The same amount as the first time." Flicking her eyes to Bill, she said, "We went to John's bank. He took it out, in cash the way they wanted, and he went to take it to them."

"Where?" Bill asked.

"The East Side. A phone booth at Thirty-fifth and Third. He was supposed to just leave it. He promised that was all he'd do."

I asked her, "That was when you called me the first time?"

She nodded. "After he left. I thought . . . I'm not really sure what I thought. Except that you could help. I wanted . . . I'm not sure." She seemed about to say something more, but she didn't. Her eyes wandered from me, to the window, to the fabric-pinned walls. Then, as though she'd been going on fuel she'd suddenly run out of, she slumped into the nearest chair. Her eyes brimmed with tears; she squeezed them shut, tried not to cry.

I sat down, too, so she wouldn't feel like we were looming over her. Bill pulled out a chair and perched on the arm. "What went wrong?" he asked, in a very gentle voice.

She opened her eyes to him with something like surprise. With a catch in her throat, she said, "He followed them."

"How do you know?" I asked.

"They said so. When they called. They were really mad. 'Twice,' they said. 'You tried to screw us twice. That's not very smart.' I tried to tell them we didn't have anything to do with that other time in the park, we didn't even know who took that money, but they didn't believe me. 'Anyhow it doesn't matter,' they said. 'Talk to your girlfriend, jerk.' Then they put John on. 'I'm sorry, baby," he said, 'But I was just so pissed that anyone would do this to you. I wanted to find them and break their necks.' "

Genna put her hand to her mouth and once again fought against tears. "Then—" her voice broke. She started again. "Then they took him away. And the man came back. 'So he thought he was Rambo, your boyfriend. Charging in here, what a jerk. But you're lucky.' I asked him why. I didn't feel lucky. 'Because his momma's rich,' the man said. He sounded to me as though he was smiling. I hated him. 'So you get another chance.' They told me not to tell the police. They'd probably be mad that I even called you. But if we'd called you in the first place John wouldn't have . . . anyway, they said to bring a million dollars to them in eight hours or John . . ." She lost her battle for control and broke down into sobs.

I rose from my chair, went and put my arm around her. Bill handed her a handkerchief. After a short while her shoulders stopped shaking. She wiped her eyes and blew her nose.

She seemed ready to talk again, so I asked, "Where? Where do you have to take the money?"

"I don't know," she said, in that deep, cloudy voice you get when you've been crying. "They said they'd call and tell me. So now," she blew her nose again, then looked helplessly at her hands, "I have to go see Mrs. Ryan. To ask her for the money."

My eyes met Bill's. Then I turned back to Genna.

"Maybe we should go to the police," I said gently.

"No! Lydia, we *can't!* They told me not to!"

"Genna," I said, "we think we know who's behind this."

She didn't answer at first, just stared. Then she whispered, "What? Who?"

"Roland Lum," I said. "The factory owner, in Chinatown? He's involved somehow. If he didn't steal the sketches, he probably knows who did. He knows something, anyway, and the police should—"

"No!" She shook her head wildly. "No police! I don't even care who it is! I just want John back." She pressed the back of her hand to her mouth. "I shouldn't have called you. I'm doing this wrong. Oh, God."

"No," Bill said, calm and reassuring. "No, it's all right."

She raised her eyes to his, probably more for the tone of his words than for their meaning.

"There's nothing the police could do now," he said. "They'd go to the factory and to wherever Roland lives, but you can bet he's not there. At best they'd be useless, at worst they'd alert him. Later, when we find out where the payoff is supposed to be, let's rethink calling them. But not now."

Genna nodded. She wiped her eyes again, then stood and began to pace the conference room, but stopped after a few steps, her face confused, as though her action made no sense to her. She stood, looking helpless and lost, surrounded by her work.

"Okay," I said, standing. "We'll go. Together."

Her smile was so full of relief and gratitude, I was embarrassed to have it shining on me.

"I'll wash up quickly," she said. She took hold of the door handle.

"Wait," Bill said. "Tell me one more thing."

She turned to him.

"The phone booth. Where?"

"Thirty-fifth and Third."

"You're sure?"

"You think I could forget that?"

"No, I'm sorry. What corner? Northeast, northwest . . . ?"

She looked quickly from me back to Bill. "Why?"

"I'll go there," he said. "Maybe I can pick up a trail."

"No! That's dangerous for John. That's how they caught him—
he was following them."

"I'm better at this than he is," Bill said matter-of-factly. "And
they won't be expecting anything from that end. I won't get too close.
But it could be important."

Genna looked at me. "Lydia? Do you think this is a good idea?"

"Yes," I said quietly.

Genna's eyes went down to the carpet. "On Third. The west
side of the street, up the block toward Thirty-sixth. In front of the
cleaners."

"All right. Let's keep in touch," Bill said to me. "My service,
your machine. What's Mrs. Ryan's phone number?"

Genna gave it to him. She went to the washroom to splash cold
water on her face and repair her makeup. Bill and I talked briefly while
he waited for the elevator.

"You think she'll give them the money?" he wanted to know.

"For her own son?"

"You're the one who met her."

"I can't believe she wouldn't. You think John's all right?"

He had no way to answer that question, and we both knew it.

"I'll see you later," he said. He kissed me quickly as the elevator door opened. Then he got inside and left.

TWENTY-SEVEN

Genna and I caught the next elevator. From the door
of her building, I dashed to Sixth Avenue and stuck my arm in the air.
A cab swerved across two lanes of traffic to screech to the curb for us.

Genna and I piled in the back and told the Sikh cabbie to take us to York as fast as he could. He grinned, and drove as if he'd been waiting for a challenge worthy of his skills all day.

"God, Lydia," Genna said in a tight, strained voice as the cab sped up Park Avenue. "Why did John do that?"

"You mean, why did he follow them?"

"Why didn't he just leave the money? What's wrong with him?"

Genna was perched on the edge of the seat, as though if she leaned back her weight would slow the cab down.

So, I realized, was I.

"I don't know," I said automatically, and knew I was lying as soon as I said it. I went on, telling the truth. "But I would have done it. Bill would have, too. Some people—I don't know, we can't hold ourselves back."

"You don't want to," she said, peering through the window as if she could stare the other cars, the ones that were delaying us, into nonexistence.

"What?"

"You don't want to. If you hold yourselves back you never get that rush. It's not that you can't keep out of trouble. You like it."

I didn't know how to answer that, or even if I had to. Or even if she was talking to me.

"But John's not like that," she went on. Our cabbie blew a blast on his horn and charged through a narrow gap in the traffic.

"He's not?" I was surprised. "I thought he was a hothead. That scene he made, when you wouldn't take his money—"

"No. He blows up at people, and he wants his way. But he looks before he leaps."

My thoughts went back to the bright and noisy interior of Maria's on Canal, and a pastry Roland Lum and I had shared. "That's not what I'd heard about him."

Genna shot me a look. "From who?"

Good point, Lydia, I mused. Consider the source.

The cab made a sharp right that threw me against the door and Genna against me. She and I didn't speak again until, after another few minutes of the kind of driving that leaves a lot of honking horns behind you, we slammed to a stop in front of Mrs. Ryan's York Avenue building. Genna threw the grinning cabbie a twenty, and we scrambled out without waiting for change. It was almost too bad, I thought, to reward that kind of driving; but he'd gotten us here.

The delicate side chairs were still lined up with nervous precision along the edge of the lobby carpet. Genna spoke to the concierge, who called upstairs, had a conversation we couldn't hear, and then waited an interminable time with the handset pressed to his ear. Genna tapped her foot and threw looks around the lobby as though she might find something there, something beyond framed prints of lighthouses and trout, something that might help.

The concierge finally hung up his handset. He said, "I'm sorry. Mrs. Ryan isn't in."

Genna looked at me, sudden fear widening her eyes. "Oh, my God. What do we do now?" she whispered.

"Yes, she is." I pushed past Genna and put both hands on the concierge's polished counter. "If she's not there, what was the long wait about? That was when the maid went to ask if she'd see us. Well, this is critical. It's about her son. Call her again."

The man fixed his eyes on me. They were blue, and bored. "Mrs. Ryan," he repeated, "is not in. To *you*."

"Call her again," I repeated, too. "Tell her Lydia Chin has been speaking to Roland Lum, Wayne Lewis, and the man who makes silver buttons." I didn't mention Brad; it didn't seem to me that Genna needed to hear about that right now. "Tell Mrs. Ryan her son John will know everything they told me in about five minutes if she doesn't let us up. Go ahead, do it," I demanded as he hesitated. "She'll thank you."

He spoke low into the handset, keeping his eyes on me but not letting us hear what he was saying. While he spoke to Mrs. Ryan, Genna spoke to me.

"Lydia? What are you talking about? What man who makes silver buttons? What do you mean, John will know everything in five minutes?"

"That part was the bluff," I whispered to her. "I'll tell you about the other part when we get a chance."

The concierge replaced the handset again. He looked at us with new respect, or at least new something. "East elevator," he said. "Twenty-third floor."

When we stepped out into the tiny, hushed lobby, the door to Mrs. Ryan's apartment was open and the sturdy woman who had let me in the first time was standing there waiting for us. That made three times in one day people had been waiting for me at elevators, I thought. I'd always thought it must be great to be eagerly anticipated everywhere you went. Now I wasn't so sure.

We stepped down the three steps into the formal living room. The room's huge mantlepiece was carved from gray-veined white marble, and furniture upholstered in blue silk sat regally on miles of ice-white carpet, but nothing in the room was as cold as the eyes of Mrs. Eleanor Talmadge Ryan, who waited for us at the far end.

She stood, silk-bloused arms folded, near where the glass of the French doors revealed an empty terrace and the wide spring sky and sparkling river beyond. Her eyes swept Genna coldly and perfunctorily, and then dismissed her with contempt. They came to rest on me, and I found myself wondering why she wasn't wearing a sweater over that thin silk blouse, in a room where I suddenly had to suppress a shiver.

"What can you possibly have been thinking?" She spat each word at me through clenched teeth. There was no preamble, no greeting.

"Mrs. Ryan—"

"I only instructed Joseph to allow you up because I was not prepared to have you make a public scene in the lobby. I have no such qualms about my own home. If you are not out of here and on your way in thirty seconds, I shall call the police."

She dropped her arms and stalked to the ornate desk that held the phone.

"That will be dangerous for John," I said.

"What? How dare you? Is that a threat?"

Her pale skin flushed crimson, but she put the phone down. I took advantage of the moment.

"Mrs. Ryan, John is in serious trouble."

"If John is in any trouble at all, I'm sure it's entirely the fault of

236

the company he's been keeping," she said, turning the ice-ray eyes on Genna.

Genna bit her lips together. She seemed about to collapse into tears.

"Mrs. Ryan," I said, "I think you're pretty despicable and I know you don't care much for me either, but we have no time for this. John's been kidnapped. They're demanding a ransom of a million dollars by tonight or they'll kill him."

Genna gave a tiny gasp when I said that, as though she hadn't heard it before.

Mrs. Ryan, however, did not gasp. Her eyes widened and a blast of arctic anger flew from them. "Why, you cheap chiselers!" she exploded. "Get out of my house!"

"Mrs. Ryan—"

"Can you really have thought I would believe that? My goodness, whatever happened to the subtle, diabolical Oriental?" She calmed down and smiled a frozen smile. "On the other hand, I can't imagine anyone else dreaming up a scheme this cold-blooded. Where is my son?" she inquired almost pleasantly. "Is he out of town, for just long enough for you two to think you could carry off this little plot? Disgusting." She picked up the phone again.

I saw fear on Genna's face, felt amazement on my own. "What are you doing?" I demanded.

"Calling the police," she answered calmly. "Not just to throw you out. To have you arrested for extortion."

You? I thought. Arresting people for extortion?

"No!" Genna burst, in a sob. She ran to the desk and wrenched the receiver from Mrs. Ryan's hand. "You can't! They'll kill him!"

Mrs. Ryan, her mouth curling in revulsion, stepped quickly away from Genna. "Helga!" she called loudly. "Helga, come in here!" She stepped back again, as though she were afraid Genna was going to strike her.

Genna, however, stayed by the desk, squeezing the receiver in her trembling hands. "You have to believe us," she begged. "They said they'd kill him. We had nothing to do with it. I'm afraid . . ." Her words trailed off with a catch as she wiped a tear from her cheek. She gave the receiver in her hand an uncomprehending stare, then, still looking confused, gently replaced it where it belonged.

"You're not even a good actress," Mrs. Ryan sneered. She seemed to have recovered some of her composure, although she kept a lot of white carpet between herself and Genna. "If there were any truth to this idiotic story, why wouldn't the kidnappers call me directly? Why are you here at all?"

Genna swallowed. "Because it's all my fault."

"Oh, how touching. And what am I supposed to understand by that?"

"John was helping me. He wouldn't have gotten in trouble if I hadn't needed him."

"He wouldn't have gotten in trouble, Miss Jing, if he'd never met you."

Just as I was about to say something I knew I'd be sorry for, the solid woman in the sensible shoes appeared at the head of the carpeted stairs. "Did you need me, Mrs. Ryan?" she asked placidly.

Mrs. Ryan fixed a stare at Genna and me. "Yes. These ladies are just leaving. Show them out."

"No." Genna raised her head and squared her shoulders. "Mrs. Ryan," she began in a creaky voice that got stronger as she went, "you have to listen. If you don't want to, then you'd better go ahead and call the police because I'm not leaving otherwise."

Good going, Genna! I cheered silently. "Of course," I put in, to help, "if the police do come, they'll be interested in how you knew Wayne Lewis, and whether your relationship with him had anything to do with his drug business."

Genna turned to me, her eyes open with surprise. Mrs. Ryan sent a wave of frigid air my way. I didn't look to see what Helga's reaction was, but after a moment Mrs. Ryan said to her, "Helga, you may go."

"Yes, ma'am." And calmly Helga went, showing not a shred of unsatisfied curiosity.

"Mrs. Ryan knew Wayne?" Genna turned to me. "What do you mean drug business?"

"Later," I said. "I don't think Mrs. Ryan wants to talk about Wayne right now. I think she wants you to tell her about John."

Mrs. Ryan's face was harder than the white marble mantle. She didn't speak.

"Mrs. Ryan," Genna began earnestly, "please, just listen. A few days ago someone stole sketches of my work for next spring. They wanted money. Maybe it was stupid of me to give it to them, but so many things had been going badly for me lately that I just couldn't take anymore. If things had been better, I'd probably have refused. Anyway, everything went wrong, and they never got the money. They called today and asked for more. John went to deliver it, but he didn't just leave it. He followed them and they caught him. That's why they called me, and that's why I've come to you."

Genna delivered this whole speech in tones entreating but controlled, looking Mrs. Ryan straight in the eye.

Mrs. Ryan was silent for a few moments after Genna was done. She folded her arms across her chest again. "Miss Jing," she said, in a voice like ice floes cracking, "the fact that your story has a beginning, a middle, and an end doesn't impress me in the least. But I believe we can strike a deal."

"A deal?" Genna sounded as though she'd never heard the word. "We're talking about John's life."

"I doubt that. But I'm prepared to give you a million dollars."

Genna blinked. "What?"

"If you're that interested in my money, you shall have it. We can call it a loan. An investment in your ridiculously named business. The loan will accumulate interest at a rate of ten percent per annum, but you need pay neither interest nor principal as long as you stick to the conditions."

"What conditions?"

"That you never see my son again."

"I—"

"If you do, Miss Jing," Mrs. Ryan's raised voice drowned out whatever Genna was trying to say, "the entire loan amount will become due immediately, and you can rest assured I shall make it my business to collect. In fact, I shall publicize the fact that you were willing to sign away the man you love for money."

Genna's face was pale with horror.

"Mrs. Ryan—!" I began hotly.

"You keep silent!" She turned on me. "This entire scheme was probably your idea. This woman and my son have been together long enough that if she were capable of inventing such idiocy on her own, she would have done so before this."

Mrs. Ryan strode around the desk and sat down behind it. She opened the writing drawer and pulled out a sheet of elegantly deckle-edged paper. Across it she quickly stroked a gold-tipped fountain pen. When she was through she handed the paper to Genna. Genna took it slowly and ran her eyes over it, only seeming half aware of what she was doing.

"That's not any kind of contract," I said, pressing my feet hard into the carpet to keep from dashing over, yanking the paper out of Genna's hands and tearing it up. "It wouldn't stand up in any court."

"I'm sure that's true," Mrs. Ryan answered. "If the case were argued to a conclusion. If Miss Jing could afford the legal assistance it will take to fight the lawsuit I'll bring the next time she and my son are seen together. I can keep a good number of lawyers in business for a very long time, Miss Jing," she said, smiling for the first time at Genna. "Can you?"

Genna numbly shook her head. She handed the paper back to Mrs. Ryan. Mrs. Ryan gave Genna a pen—not the fountain pen, but a ballpoint from inside the drawer—and Genna leaned over the desk to sign it.

"Genna!" I protested. "You can't sign that!"

She turned her head slowly to me. "I have to, Lydia," she said in a distant voice. "It's the only way to get the money for John."

"You may as well drop that fiction now," Mrs. Ryan snapped, seizing the paper the moment Genna picked up her pen. She slid it into the desk drawer, then locked the drawer with a golden key. Genna, breathing shallowly, watched the paper disappear.

Mrs. Ryan lifted the receiver from the phone and pressed in a single speed-dial digit. "Mr. Morse, please," she said after a pause. "This is Mrs. Ryan." Another brief pause, then, "Fine, thank you, Peter. And you? Very good. Peter, I need a loan. Large but short-term. One million dollars, and I believe it must be in cash." Another pause, during which she smiled condescendingly at Genna. Then she spun in her chair so that her back was to us, and she spoke in low tones. Genna, her eyes fixed on Mrs. Ryan's silk-clad shoulders, studiously avoided my gaze while the conversation went on. "No," I heard Mrs. Ryan say. "No, absolutely nothing. No, just an opportunity I can't pass up. I know it is. Pardon me? Yes, quite beautiful." She paused. "Yes, of course I have." She dropped her voice again and murmured some sentences I couldn't quite hear. Then, "We'll collateralize it from the Dreyfus—yes, thank you, Peter, I'm sure you would, but I can—very well, thank you, I appreciate that. Yes, I'm sure. Perhaps later in the week, over cocktails? You'll enjoy it. No, not anything we've discussed, something quite new. Yes, thanks. That would be fine. I'll be here."

She swiveled her chair around again, hung up the phone and stood. "Your 'ransom' money will be here in half an hour. My banker thinks I'm purchasing art on the black market. He's thrilled with the prospect."

"Mrs. Ryan," Genna said earnestly, having one more try, "what we've said is true. John's in danger. This money is for him."

"Miss Jing, you can continue with this ridiculous story for your own entertainment if you want, but it really doesn't make any difference to me. You'll get your money, and you'll walk out of my son's life. Then he'll no longer be in danger."

She smiled at Genna, a smile as cold and stabbing as winter sun flashing off snow. "You may wait in the foyer," she told us. "You'll pardon me if I don't sit with you. Helga will let me know when Peter's messenger arrives." She stood waiting for us to move, to herd ourselves back to the foyer.

And we did. We sat on striped-silk chairs while Mrs. Ryan stalked down the hall I'd been taken along on my first visit here. She disappeared, but the unruffled Helga appeared at almost the same instant, taking up a respectful post across the foyer from us. I was sure she was there to make sure we didn't stuff our pockets full of Mrs. Ryan's valuable knickknacks, but to Helga's credit she didn't stare at us, didn't seem to even notice us. She stood blankly eight feet from the door as though she had nothing else to do all day but await the arrival of one million dollars.

TWENTY-EIGHT

he million dollars came. It came in a rectangular package the size of a phone book, carried up by a mustached man in a uniform like the concierge's. Helga thanked him and brought us and the package to Mrs. Ryan, who was two rooms away in the wood-paneled study. Mrs. Ryan cut the brown paper wrapping to reveal the piles of green inside. She leafed through one package of bills, counting them, and then counted the packages. Then she taped the paper up again and held out the package to Genna.

"Now get out of my house," she said.

Genna's hands moved, as if trying to express something for which she had no words. I had words myself I was trying not to express. Genna's hands gave up; she took the package. Turn and leave, Lydia, I told myself, just walk away, and I was two steps into that when Helga reappeared in the doorway.

"Telephone, ma'am," she told Mrs. Ryan. "For the young ladies."

"You left this number?" Mrs. Ryan's eyes flashed angrily at Genna. "How dare you?"

Helga said, to the space between us, "It's young Mr. Ryan."

Genna's eyes flew open. Mrs. Ryan's mouth set.

I lunged for the phone.

"John? Where are you? Are you all right?"

"Lydia?" John's voice sounded strained but controlled. "I don't know where I am. I'm blindfolded. They say they've been watching and they know my mother's banker just sent over a package. They say it had better be their money."

"It is their money, John. Are you people listening? Are you on this line? Stay calm and tell us what to do."

Genna reached for the phone, to take it from me, but I shook her off and stopped her with a look.

242

"There's no one on the line but me, Lydia," John said. "It's a cellular phone. They said it's stolen, so you can't trace it. They told me to tell you that."

"What else did they tell you?"

"They say to tell you to bring the money. They said . . . they said soon."

"I want to talk to them."

"They won't let you. I'm supposed to give you instructions."

"All right." Roland would know that I'd recognize his voice if he spoke to me. This was no time to say anything about that, though, no time to let Roland know I already knew. We'd deal with that after the exchange was made. "Tell me where to go."

But before he could, the phone was wrenched from my hand.

"John?" Mrs. Ryan snapped into the receiver. "Where are you? What's going on?" Silence. Then, "Who are you? Put my son back on the line. Of course I don't, not a word—It can't—Wait! What—John? John! Yes, yes, all right." With no words and a look on her face I hadn't seen before, Mrs. Ryan handed the phone back to me.

"John?"

"Lydia?" I could hear John draw a ragged breath. "An abandoned building in Alphabet City."

"Are you all right?" I asked him.

"My mother didn't buy it, I guess," he said. His voice was tighter than before. "She needed convincing."

I shot a look at Mrs. Ryan. Her face was pale.

"Alphabet City," I said into the phone. "Where?"

He gave me a Third Street address. "You put the money in the basement, in the boiler room. Then you leave. They'll pick it up. Then they'll let me go."

"No."

"Lydia—"

"Tell them no. You and the money, at the same time. They walk away with the money when I walk away with you."

The murmur of voices came to me faintly through the phone. I strained to hear but I couldn't make anything out.

John came back. "They say no."

"Then I say no. Tell them there's no point in arguing this one. I'm not paying for merchandise I haven't seen."

"I'm the damn merchandise, Lydia!"

Genna and Mrs. Ryan were both staring at me. Genna's mouth was partly open. I turned away from them. "I know that, John," I said quietly. "I'm trying to save your life."

More murmuring on the other end of the phone. Then John said, "Okay. Come to the building, now. Alone. They say you know what will happen if you try anything tricky—"

"And so do they, if they do. Tell them that."

A sudden click. John was gone.

"What's happening?" Genna managed.

"I'm leaving." I hung the phone up and took the package from her. "I have to take them the money."

Mrs. Ryan's arms were folded across her chest as they had been when we came in, but now she seemed to be less containing herself than holding herself together. Or maybe she'd suddenly realized what a cold place this was that she lived in. "My son," she said to me, in a voice used to giving orders, not used to this. "If any harm comes to him, so help me—"

I turned and walked out of the room. Genna hurried after me. We left Mrs. Ryan standing in the study, finishing her threat to an empty room.

TWENTY-NINE

You can't come," I told Genna as we rode the elevator down. "It's too dangerous."

"I don't care, Lydia." Genna's eyes pleaded with me. "I'm not scared."

"Not just dangerous for you," I said. "For John. They said I should come alone. It's too risky, Genna. You can't come."

The elevator doors slid apart and we marched quickly through the formal lobby. Joseph the concierge watched impassively as the doorman pulled open the street door for us.

I surveyed the street for a pay phone. There aren't all that many on York Avenue. "Come on," I told Genna, and dashed down the block to the one I'd spotted, on the far corner. I dropped a quarter in and called Bill's number. I didn't expect him to be there, just hoped for a miracle, but I didn't get one; his service picked up. I had nothing really to say to them—tell him I'm making a ransom payment and trying to get a kidnap victim back safely, ask him to call me, maybe we can do lunch? I left a message that I'd called and that he should call Genna. Then I called my machine, and heard his voice.

"Lydia," he said. "Something. I'm following it up. I'll call again."

Beepers, I thought. After this is over, assuming everyone's still standing, Bill and I have to get beepers.

"What's going to happen?" Genna asked me. I guessed her whispery voice was as strong as she could make it.

"Here's exactly what's going to happen," I said. "When I get where I'm going, I'll give them the money. They'll turn John over to me. They'll leave and then we'll leave."

Boy, did that sound easy.

"I want to come."

"No. Go back to your studio."

"That's what John said! I wanted to go with him to drop the money and he said, go back to the studio. And look what happened!"

"Genna. No. Go on back. Keep trying to call Bill, and give me half an hour. If I don't call you, call Francesca Rossi at the Thirteenth Precinct. Tell her what happened. She'll send the cops."

"Lydia—"

"Genna!" I barked. I stopped myself, seeing her flinch. "I'm sorry," I said in a softer voice. "But please. You can't come. We don't have time to argue about it."

I hailed a cab and climbed in. As it pulled away from the curb, I turned and saw Genna out the back window, standing on the sidewalk, pale face staring after me. I turned away again. As storefronts and streetlights flew past, I was struck by the courage it had taken for her to do as I'd said, to not come, to go home and wait. Courage I didn't think I'd have had, if the strained voice on the other end of the phone had, for example, been Bill's.

Third Street and Avenue C was probably as picturesque right now, on a beautiful early-spring afternoon, as it ever got. That's what I was thinking when the cab dropped me at the corner, where grimy walk-up tenements, some abandoned and some not, were packed shoulder-to-shoulder as if, at the end of a weary day, they needed to borrow each other's strength to stand. A plastic shopping bag, ballooned by the wind, skittered by on the sidewalk as I walked up the block to the address I had.

I was on the north side of the street because the address was on the south side. I wanted a chance to survey the area, just to look around, just to see. I wanted to check the building out from top to bottom before I descended into the depths of it.

Across the street from the place I was looking for, I stopped and stood. The building I was going into was one of the abandoned ones, with plywood hammered into the holes where the windows had been and now, in places, knocked out again so pigeons and squatters could move freely in and out. The door lay flat on its back next to the gaping doorway. Not a place I'd have chosen to spend a spring afternoon, but a place I might have headed for if I'd needed to lay low—like for example if I'd kidnapped someone and was waiting for my ransom money.

I stood still across the street from this place, letting my eyes wander along the sidewalks, over the rooftops. No one seemed to be watching me particularly, unless this was a pretty sophisticated operation and the staggering junkie at the corner or the twelve-year-olds playing hooky from school to get in a game of stickball were part of it.

Good, I thought. That's that, then. Nothing to do now but just go on in there, Lydia. Just go on in.

I gripped the money package tighter, squared my shoulders, and went on in.

It wasn't a nice place. Stray cats and dogs, or maybe stray people, had left the pungent aroma of urine floating in the air above the thicker scents of molding food and rotting wood. I kicked an aluminum take-out container as I moved cautiously along the dank, dim

246

hallway. It scraped, something scurried into the shadows, and rice spilled across my shoe.

Yum. Okay, Lydia, I ordered myself, find the way to the basement. Maybe, I suggested, you could try looking under the stairs to the upstairs. I did that, and I found a door. I thanked myself very much and pulled it open.

"Who's that?" came John's shout.

"Lydia Chin," I answered. "I brought what I was supposed to bring." I don't know why I said it like that; I just had trouble yelling down the cellar steps, "I have a million dollars in a little package here."

"You're alone?"

"Of course I am."

"Come down," John ordered.

I creaked my way down the steps. About halfway down, the sunshine that had been willing to come a few tentative feet into the hallway refused to go on. After that the only light came from a thin line that leaked around the basement door, half off its hinges in the areaway under the sidewalk. Gee, I thought, I could have come in that way, if I'd only known.

"Back here," John's voice called, so when I reached the bottom I headed back there, away from the door and the thin line of light.

There was light in that direction, too, though, a softer yellow patch spilling across the dusty concrete floor from a room near the back of the building. I stopped and turned toward it when I got to the doorway it was spreading from. I didn't go in, because the lamp that was making it was pointed directly into my eyes and I couldn't see a thing.

"Well, look at this," Roland Lum's jaunty voice said, from somewhere beyond the light. "She really is alone." The light swung away. I blinked, and now I could see.

Before me, standing in front of a rusting hulk of a boiler, were two black-hooded, ninja masked figures, one taller, one smaller, both holding guns. Their shadows swayed under the swinging metal reflectored lamp one of them had just let go of. Seated beside them, blindfolded, hands tied behind him to the chair he was in, was John Ryan. Crusted blood stained his cheek.

Ninja masks. Ninja masks and black clothes. I thought of the

247

hard cobblestones of the West Village, and I wanted to rush over and slug whichever one of these figures was Roland Lum.

But I didn't. "I'm alone," I echoed calmly, standing balanced and relaxed. What I said was a little bit of a lie. My gun was with me, clipped in its holster onto my belt, covered by my loose jacket. Part of me wanted its reassuring weight, its cool smoothness, in my hand right now, but the other part knew that we were all safest if it stayed where it was. "I have the money," I said. I held out the package in both hands, so they could see that that was all I held.

The figure closest to me gestured with its gun at the other one, who came forward and took the package. Black-gloved hands ripped the paper, rifled through the packs of bills inside. The figure nodded.

"Okay," I said, keeping my tones controlled and reasonable, as though I'd just paid the agreed-upon price for a pound of perch and was ready to have it wrapped to take home to my mother. "That's the deal. Untie John now, and we'll leave."

"Oh, I don't think so," the shorter figure said. That was, it turned out, the one with Roland's voice.

John turned his blindfolded face toward the voice. "You—"

The figure's gloved hand smacked John sharply on the back of the head. "Shut up."

John didn't. "What—"

The figure hit him again, harder. John's head dipped; before he'd lifted it again black gloves had stuffed a filthy-looking towel into his mouth and taped it around with adhesive tape. John made stran-gled noises, kicking in his chair. The ninja-masked figure leaned heavily on John's shoulder, letting the gun dangle casually.

"People know where I am." I addressed the ninja masks with no change in tone. "They're giving me time, not a lot of it, and then they're going to call the police. If you keep to the deal, you have a chance of getting away, but if you don't, you won't."

The shorter figure shook its head. "Other way, I'm afraid. And it's your own fault. I tried to keep you out of it. I really did." The left hand, the one that wasn't holding the gun, peeled the ninja mask off. The face underneath was, completely unsurprisingly, Roland's.

"You knew, didn't you?" he said. His smile was half regretful, half pleased, like an actor in a play that had been panned except for

248

his own exceptional performance, singled out universally for praise.

I nodded. Keep it going, Lydia, run out the clock until Genna calls Francie, and Francie sends the Marines. "If you knew I did, why the masks?"

"We thought you might not be alone. We didn't see any point in advertising."

"Who's that?" I asked, pointing at the figure by his side.

"Forget it," Roland said. "You don't need to know."

"Did you shoot at me in the park?" I asked. "Or did you steal the sketches in the first place?"

"Why don't we just say I was doing great until you came along? I should have known you'd screw me up. But honestly, Lydia, I didn't know you were any good at this. All I remembered was that you were a pest. I mean, you were always underfoot when I was hanging out with old Elliot, but you didn't really make trouble, you were just annoying. You were even kind of cute, for a kid sister."

Annoying? I thought. *Cute?* I felt hot blood rush to my cheeks. Then, calm down, Lydia, I told myself. He has a gun. He can call you whatever he wants.

"But when I started screwing you up," I said, "you tried to scare me off? In the Village?"

"I tried." He grinned, shamefaced. "And you know, you fight okay. I didn't really want to hurt you, but maybe I should have. Scaring you sure didn't work. Does it ever?" he asked, as an afterthought, just friendly and interested.

"Not really." See, Lydia Chin can strut, too. "So then you invented Peng Hui Liang?"

The grin turned rueful. "I really thought that was going to work. I thought it would appeal to your white knight thing. Did nasty old Roland really knock up some poor FOB? Can Lydia find her and save her from him? Tune in next week."

"Then I was supposed to go running all over Queens so you could finish up. And then John followed you and this new opportunity fell in your lap." I pointed to John. Gagged and blindfolded, the tilt of his head told me he was following our words closely, nevertheless.

"Yeah," Roland said easily. "And you should have done it. Even

249

if you tipped to it. I went to a lot of trouble to get you out of the way. Maybe you should have gotten out of the way. Did you ever think of that?"

"I thought of it."

"Instead of sending me on a wild-goose chase all the damn way uptown and then screwing around in my factory."

When he said that, Roland's face lost its affability, went hard, as I'd seen it do in the restaurant at the waiter's mistake.

"It seemed like a good idea at the time," I said.

Something made a soft, scraping sound. All of us jumped a little, then relaxed. Nerves, Lydia, I thought, as my pulse raced. Rats in the shadows. Stay calm, please, or at least calm-looking.

Roland shrugged. "Well, I don't care. Factory's over. I hate that stupid place. Dust and the noise and the damn ladies gossiping, running like scared chickens from the INS. How'd your mom stand it all those years, Lydia?"

There was a simple answer to that, I thought: she had to. But it hadn't really been a question, and Roland went right on.

"And for what?" he demanded. "So my brother and my sister can come to me all the time, oh big brother, you have to help us out, you have the factory, I need tuition, I need to buy a house. You ask your brothers for money all the time, Lydia?"

"No."

"Because it gets on your fucking nerves, let me tell you," he went on, as if I hadn't answered. "If they think I'm ending up like my old man, busting my ass seven days a week and then popping off out of nowhere so my sister can drive a Benz and my brother can sit around a pool in Malibu, they're fucked."

"That's what this is? Your ticket out?"

"Damn right. And Lydia, it's too bad, but you're the only thing in my way."

"I'm not in your way, Roland. Take your money and leave."

Roland laughed. "And what? You couldn't leave it alone when you didn't know what was going on. You're sure as hell not going to just wave bye-bye now."

"It's your only chance, Roland. Leave now. I won't follow you."

"But you'll know. And you'll tell, because you're a good little detective. I'd offer you money, come in with us, but I don't think you'll do it. And besides," he considered, then shook his head, smiling, "I don't want to share."

He lifted the gun slowly until it was pointed right at my heart.

"You're not going to kill me, Roland."

"You're wrong, Lydia. The first one wasn't very hard. The second one's got to be easier."

The first one. "Did you kill Wayne Lewis?"

Roland smiled. "Of course I did," he said.

At that John began to kick again.

Roland's face snapped from friendly to furious. "Shut up, I said!" He lifted his gun and smashed it down by John's ear. John's head drooped. He started to raise it slowly, then let it drop again. He made a choking sound, but he didn't kick anymore.

Roland's expression relaxed, and the smile came back. I looked at John, now still in his chair, and then back at Roland. Of course you did, I thought. Now tell me *why*.

But I didn't say that. What I said, quietly but trying not to sound scared, trying not to sound as if any of this was anything out of the ordinary, was, "I meant it, about the police coming. You'd better leave now or you won't be able to get away." While I spoke, I breathed levelly and watched his eyes, watched as Sensei Chung had taught me, watched for the telegraphing flash of motion that comes fractions of a second before the punch or the kick or the shot, the flash that always comes from the eyes. If you're watching, that warning is sometimes enough.

"I guess you're right," Roland said. "I'm sorry, Lydia. Sorry for old Elliot. But I guess it's time to go."

Roland's partner lifted a gun, too, and pointed it at me, too. Left or right? I wondered. Which way to dive?

But I didn't have to decide. "Lum!" a male voice roared. A loud, resonant male voice. A beautiful voice. Bill's voice. "Both of you! Drop the guns!"

Roland started like a rabbit. I hit the ground, left, away from him. I yanked my .38 from its holster as Roland's shot howled through the basement air. Another answered. Roland ducked behind John, making him a shield. Roland's partner, left alone and exposed, fired

251

through the doorway. From the hall I heard a yelp, then another shot. The ninja-masked head snapped backward and the figure slammed against the rusting boiler, crumpling slowly to the floor.

The force of the crash loosened the ninja mask; it had slipped partway off by the time the figure hit the floor. Askew, it revealed full, pouty lips, and high, delicate cheekbones. At the temples, drifting out from the blackness of the hood, were wisps of glossy hair the white-gold color of morning light.

Andi Shechter.

"Lum!" Bill yelled, bursting into the thousand questions I was asking myself. "Give it up! The place is crawling with cops!" I knew that wasn't true. If the cops were here, they'd never have let Bill in. There were no cops.

"Screw you!" Roland screamed. "Drop your guns or I'll blow his fucking head off! Do it! What do I have to lose?" He raised his gun and fired a wild shot into the ceiling. Plaster splashed down around us as Roland cocked the hammer and pressed the gun to John's head.

"All right," I said. "All right!" I threw my gun across the floor, and stood.

"Whoever the hell you are!" Roland yelled into the hallway. "You do it, too! Do it!"

Bill said nothing, but stepped from the shadows into the light of the room, tossing his gun before him.

"Hands on your heads!" Roland barked, and Bill and I did that, standing helpless in the dusty room where Andi Shechter bled on the floor.

Roland switched the gun to his left hand and kept it hard against John's temple while his right pulled at the rope holding John's wrists. John's arms flopped down to his sides. He moved them vaguely, lifting one to hold his head. Roland hauled him out of the chair.

John in front of him, Roland began to edge out of the room. John moved clumsily, tripping.

"Lydia!" Roland ordered. "Pick that up and give it to me." He nodded at the brown paper package bursting with green stacks of bills that Andi had dropped. I knelt slowly, gathered it up, and passed it

252

to him. He squeezed it under the arm he was gripping John with and started to move toward the door again.

I was closest to Roland. I waited for Bill to make the move, to create the distraction that would draw Roland's attention so I could tackle him. I knew that's what was coming next.

But it wasn't.

From the darkness of the hall a woman's voice yelled, "Hey!" Not Roland's name, not a command, just "hey!"

It was enough for Roland. He shoved John back into the room, spun and fired two blasting shots in the direction of the sound.

John tripped and clutched at me for balance as I flew toward Roland. He made me trip, too, my knee crashing on the concrete before I righted myself.

A shot rang from the dark, from where the voice was. Roland made a sound of surprise. He staggered forward, then he fell.

A deafening silence filled the basement. For a second everyone, everything, was frozen.

Then I grabbed up my gun and pushed past John, who was pulling weakly at the tape around his mouth. I held my gun on Roland as Bill leaned over him, feeling his throat for a pulse. Bill shook his head and stood.

Eyes shining, smiling a strange smile, left arm bloody, Dawn Jing stepped out of the basement shadows.

THIRTY

In the life of East Third Street, police cars and ambulances were clearly not unusual enough to cause a lot of alarm, even on a beautiful spring afternoon. The small crowd that collected watched with mild interest, the way you'd watch a children's game from your front stoop, as the Crime Scene cops disappeared inside the building and, eventually, the paramedics brought Roland's body out, and then Andi Shechter's. They were covered, and then strapped down, as though even in death they might still be looking for a ticket out.

The Crime Scene cops came out after a while, too, with the spent shells Dawn and Andi and Roland had fired, and the ninja masks and the rope from John's wrists and the filthy towel and the million dollars, all bagged neatly in clear plastic bags. Roland's and Andi's personal effects were in other bags, just the small things everyone carries with them in the course of a regular day—wallets, tissues, combs, and keys, the things that are supposed to help you make your way from one day into the next.

John was already gone, semiconscious with a concussion, carried off with sirens and flashing lights to St. Vincent's Hospital. I'd called Genna right after I'd called the police, to tell her he was hurt but alive. I'd said to stay where she was, and that I'd call her as soon as I knew which hospital they were taking him to.

I hadn't told her Dawn was here. In the dusty air of the basement, Roland motionless as the concrete at my feet, I'd waited, looking from Bill to Dawn, for someone to explain this to me. Bill, crouching down to examine the gash in John's temple, had said simply, "Dawn knew where to come." I didn't consider that much of an explanation, but John was holding his head and moaning, Dawn was bleeding, and Bill said, "Later." That usually meant, "In private," and that was okay with me. So I ran upstairs, found a street corner phone, and called it in. Then I called Genna; by the time I was off the phone with her and headed back down the block, the howl of the sirens was getting close and the action had started.

Andi's bullet had sliced through Dawn's left arm. Once out on the street, she winced, then grinned as the paramedics sat her on a gurney and worked on her. "Doesn't hurt much," she said, in answer to someone's question. Then, to Bill, who'd given her the cigarette she was smoking while they wrapped her arm, she added, "And some of my dates are really into scars."

Bill smiled past his own cigarette. He was hanging out at the front of the building, strolling around, sitting on the stoop, rising again, strolling, but not far. He couldn't go far. He was waiting for the Ninth Precinct detectives who were grilling me to finish so they could start on him.

As soon as they'd come, we told them what had happened and why, but they seemed to be having a hard time believing us. "You mean to tell me," one of them, a thin man with jerky movements, kept asking, "We got three Chinese in the same shootout here and it's got nothing to do with gangs, tongs, like that?"

"Yes," I said wearily, for what seemed like the fifteenth time. "It was kidnapping. I told you. Talk to John. Talk to Genna. Talk to John's mother—she can tell you all about Chinese people."

"No reason to get snappy, miss," his heavier, slower partner said, although I could think of a few. "Tell us again what you have to do with it." He smiled reasonably and offered me a Life Saver. I couldn't decide which of them I disliked more.

I told them again, and then again. Finally they gave up, took my gun to be tested though anyone could tell it hadn't been fired, and converged on Bill.

They'd told me not to leave. I sat on the steps. As the ambulance took Dawn Jing away, I heard Bill say that he was working for me, that he'd come here in response to the message I'd left with his service, that he'd never met or seen Roland before but he knew I'd been suspicious of him for a while. They asked Bill about the Chinese gang angle, too, and they asked him a lot of other things while I sat, felt the breeze against my skin, and tried to think of nothing.

In the end they took us over to the Ninth Precinct and went through the whole thing again. They waited for the cops talking to John at the hospital to call in, and they compared Dawn's statement to Bill's, and Bill's to mine, and they left us each in different rooms for a while. Then they told me I could go, so I left the station house, crossed the street, sat on the curb, and waited.

It was another ten minutes before Bill came out. As the light blazed gold on the faces of the buildings, picking out windowsills and cornices, throwing barred, slanted shadows from fire escapes, he crossed the street to join me.

Crouching next to me, he took my hand. I hadn't realized how chilly the spring air had gotten until I felt the rough warmth of Bill's hand.

"You okay?" he asked.

I nodded. "You?"

"Never better."

"Sorry to hear that."

He smiled and dropped himself onto the curb beside me.

"Mrs. Ryan made Genna sign a contract," I said, watching the late sun glint off the windows across the street.

"A contract?"

"That was the only reason she gave us the money. It says that Genna borrowed a million dollars from her. If she never sees John again, she doesn't have to return it. If she does, she does. Mrs. Ryan says she'll take Genna to court and ruin her if she tries to get out of it."

"She made her sign that for the ransom money?" I could hear in Bill's voice that even he, Mr. Cynicism, had trouble with that.

"She didn't believe it was a ransom. She thought Genna and I had cooked the whole thing up. The kind of thing the Chinese do, you know."

Bill didn't answer. I hugged my knees to my chest and rested my chin on them. "You know," I said, "I didn't leave the address of that place with your service."

"I know."

"On purpose. So you wouldn't go racing down there before me, without the ransom money, and get yourself killed."

"I know."

"But you told the cops that's why you went there. Because of the message I left you. You couldn't have."

"I didn't," he said. "When I got there I wasn't even sure it was the right place."

"Why did you say that, then? And why did you come?"

"Dawn brought me. If I'd told them that, I'd have had to tell them how she knew where to go. And why I called her."

"Why did you?"

He looked across the street, too, to where the top floors of the buildings glowed in the dying light and the bottom floors were already in shadow. He said, "There's no phone booth at Thirty-fifth and Third."

Late afternoon light can play strange tricks. The buildings across the street suddenly took on an alien aspect, an unfamiliar and sinister quality I hadn't noticed before. "But . . ." I said. "Then . . . ?"

Bill looked at me and I looked at him, and we stood up and headed for St. Vincent's.

We talked it out while we walked across town into the red-striped sunset, and finished as we sat over espresso and perfumey Earl Grey tea in the Peacock Cafe, around the corner from St. Vincent's. In spindly metal-backed cafe chairs, listening to old recordings of an achingly beautiful operatic soprano, we went back and forth. Bill told me what he'd thought and what he'd done, the calls he'd made. I told him what Roland had said as we stood under the swinging light. We discussed what we didn't know and what we thought, now, that we did. We fell quiet, only the singer filling the space around us with music that, to me, was beautiful but meaningless, just as the tea I was drinking was warm and sweet but didn't reach the chill I felt inside.

We went on, to the hospital. They told us John Ryan was in stable condition and could have visitors, and they gave us the passes. We glided up to the third floor in the big, smooth elevator. The air smelled like Lysol, the floors were shiny, and conversations were hushed. Down the hall to the left we found John's room.

John was in the first bed, the one by the door. The other bed was empty. John had a drip in his arm, a bandage around his head, and a swollen purple bruise with a Band-Aid riding the crest of it on his cheek. He looked like hell, but he wasn't asleep. He turned slowly to the door as we came in.

"Lydia," he smiled weakly. "Smith. Hey, thanks." He closed his eyes, but opened them again right away. "God, how stupid does that sound?" he asked. His words were slow and soft, either from medication or from the concussion. "You saved my life, and I'm saying 'thanks.' "

"How do you feel?" I asked.

"Headache. I'll be all right. Run-of-the-mill concussion, they tell me. That guy was really crazy, wasn't he?"

"Roland? I guess he was."

"And Andi. Jesus, Andi. Poor kid. Is she——?"

"She's dead," I told him.

"God." He was quiet for a moment. Then he asked, "How's Genna? Is she okay with all this? Is she coming down?"

"I spoke to her a few hours ago, but not since. She was upset, but all right."

"Could you call her? Tell her I'm okay? I don't know what they're giving me here, I'm pretty sleepy, but I'd love it if she got here before I really go under."

He smiled again, and his blue eyes smiled, too. I wondered if his mother's blue eyes had ever smiled like that.

"Genna has a problem, John."

The smile faded. "What problem?"

"Your mother made her sign a contract agreeing to never see you again." I told him the story, the deckle-edged paper, his mother's coldness and her accusations.

"My God," he breathed. "My God. But," he stopped, creasing his brow, "now she'll get the money back, won't she? So the contract is void. If it ever was good."

"It doesn't matter if it's void or if it ever was good. Your mother can tie Genna up in court for years trying to get out of it, even though everyone knows Genna will win in the end. You can count on that being the end of Mandarin Plaid if she does."

John swore softly, under his breath.

"But that would make your mother happy," I said. "To destroy Mandarin Plaid. Because she thinks you're with Genna for the glitz and the glamour, and that if Genna's a failure you'll dump her."

John sighed. "I know she does. All that glitz and glamour. But it's not true."

"I know it isn't. And I know you know she thinks so."

John lifted his hand tentatively to rub his eyes. Then, realizing we were waiting for him to speak, he said, "You lost me. Who knows what?"

"You knew your mother was trying to destroy Mandarin Plaid. That she was behind all the things that went wrong—the vendors dropping out, Wayne Lewis quitting. She didn't want you to know, and you never told Genna, but you knew."

258

John waited a moment. Then, looking up at me, he said, "You're right. I knew what she was up to. She thought she was so smart, but it's her style, that knife-in-the-back stuff. I couldn't tell Genna. What I did was to run all around the city, trying to fix things." He laughed weakly. "My mother's always been disgusted with me because I've never worked. Her definition of work, you know, nine-to-five in a suit in a big glass building. Maybe up till I met Genna she was right. All I know is, I've never worked as hard as I did to try to keep her from destroying Genna."

"She was why Roland backed out after you had the factory lined up?"

John started to nod, but winced and thought better, apparently, of movement. "Right," he said. He added, "I thought I just about had him convinced to come back with us. I spent a lot of time talking to that guy. Shows you what I know, right? God, what some people will do for money."

"Let's talk about money, John," I said.

He looked up at me again. "Money?"

"Well, not that money. Not the million dollars, yet. The fifty thousand dollars for the sketches that you got from your bank."

"What about it?" He frowned again. "Where is it?"

"That's the question. Or it would be, if there were any such money."

He squeezed his eyes shut and then opened them again, as though he were having difficulty focusing. "What do you mean, if there were?"

"You had Genna wait in the lobby when you went to talk to the bank officer. You came back with an envelope, told Genna to go back to her office, and got in a cab. To go leave the money at Thirty-fifth and Third. Where there's no phone booth."

"No—? Sure there is. Where I left the envelope. And then, like an idiot, I stayed to see what would happen. Duh." He smiled again, weakly, engagingly. "Look, I don't think I can hold it together much longer. Thanks for—"

"No, there's not," Bill said, speaking for the first time since we'd come in here. His tone was mild, friendly even, but his words wove themselves together like a net settling over John. "I went there

259

to try to pick up your trail. There's no phone booth on Third at Thirty-fifth, or at Thirty-sixth. There's one at Thirty-fourth, but it's on a heavy-traffic corner, the kind of place you wouldn't tell someone to leave an envelope full of cash because it would be gone before you could get to it. There's a phone between Thirty-seventh and Thirty-eighth, but there was a drug dealer hanging out at it waiting for a call. The neighborhood says he uses it most afternoons. Not a good bet, either. And," he added, "neither of those two is anywhere near a dry cleaner."

"Third?" John frowned. "No, not Third. It was Second."

"Third," Bill said. "Genna was positive about that. I don't think that's the kind of mistake she makes. So—" John opened his mouth to speak, but Bill wouldn't let him get started "—so I called Citibank. I told them I was from Chemical and we suspected someone had been fraudulently accessing your account with us. I asked if there had been any large withdrawals in the last few days from any of your accounts with them. Not the amounts, so they didn't have to break a confidence, just any large cash movements. They told me no."

"I—"

"It wasn't there, John," I said. "I saw everything come up out of that basement in plastic evidence bags. I know what an envelope full of fifty thousand dollars looks like: I'd just put one down when someone shot at me, remember? Was that Andi? Or was it Roland? That's more his style, to do the cowboy stuff while someone else grabs and runs. Am I right?"

John raised his hand again to rub his eyes. After a moment he said, "Could you turn the light out?"

Bill went over by the door and did that. I didn't move. In the room's new twilight, the bed and the equipment cast soft, conflicting shadows from the light that drifted in through the window and through the glass in the door.

Bill came back to stand by the bed. John remained silent. Bill said, "When I knew there was no money and no phone booth, I called Dawn. I wanted someone who knew you, who might know how you'd think." He paused, then said, "Someone you'd once shown a building you owned. She remembered that building. She led me right to it."

Silence filled the room again. When John finally spoke, it was without anger, with great weariness. "I should tell you to go to hell," he said. "I should tell you you're crazy and to get the hell out of here. I could yell for a nurse. I ought to do a whole thing. But you know what?"

"What?" I asked.

He sighed, from deep within. "Screw it, that's what. I haven't got the energy. I can't do this anymore."

"Tell us what it is you can't do," I said gently.

"I guess my mother's right. I'm not good at much. I'm not even good at this."

"At what?"

"For a while," he spoke slowly, but clearly, as though he were explaining this not only to us, but to himself, "I actually thought I was. Good at something, I mean. At what Genna needed me for, at Mandarin Plaid. Not good enough to keep my mother from pulling her shit, but I never expected to be as good as my mother. Even my father was never in her league.

"But this idea. I thought this idea was good. Great. Awesome. Not mine, of course. But I thought it was brilliant."

"It was Roland's?" I asked.

"Sure it was Roland's. Roland was a genius. My mother offered him five thousand dollars to break his contract with us. He pushed her up to seventy-five hundred. He said he had this idea the minute she called." He coughed, then closed his eyes in pain. He opened them, though, and kept going. "I liked him, too. I thought he liked me. I thought we were partners. I didn't know he had any . . . I didn't know he was even thinking . . . shit! Son of a bitch. He was planning to kill me all along."

Anger flooded his drained face. With his right hand, the one that didn't have a needle and a tube in it, he pounded the bed.

I said, "You'd been planning to split the money?"

"Right down the middle."

"And Andi Shechter?"

"We brought her in at first just to grab the envelope in the park. She was my idea. I knew she needed cash."

"For drugs."

261

"Yeah," he agreed, as though needing cash for drugs was the same as needing cash to pay the rent. "She was going to get to keep what was in the envelope after the whole thing was over. She got off on it."

"Is that what you were talking about in Donna's that night? When she looked sort of meanly happy, and you didn't?"

"You were in Donna's?"

I nodded.

"Shit," John said. "You were on to us that long ago?"

"No. I just had a feeling you were up to something. Is that what that was about?"

"Yeah. And she wanted to tell me something else, too: my mother had called her to say she'd pay Andi to back out of Genna's show. Andi thought that was pretty funny."

Oh, yeah. Pretty funny. "And you gave her money."

"For the information. About my mother. That's how I knew what she was up to. I paid people to tell me."

My god, I thought. Like mother, like son.

I had another question. "If all Andi was supposed to do was grab the money the first time, what was she doing there today?"

"When we realized you were going to be bringing the ransom money, Roland said we'd better make it look good. So we called Andi. She was up for it. You were the dark horse, you know."

"What do you mean?"

"Roland was really impressed with you. At first he thought it was a great idea, having you involved. A pro—a pair of pros—would lend a lot of credibility to the thing. The bit about shooting at you in the park—that was so you'd get the idea these guys were crazy and dangerous. So when I got kidnapped everyone would be worried.

"But you two were better than he thought. He had to keep improvising to deal with what you were doing. But he said that made it exciting."

I didn't know how I felt about this, a compliment on my professional skills from an extortionist and would-be murderer, now dead, received secondhand from his wounded co-conspirator. "Andi Shechter," I prompted, to cover my confused thoughts.

"We offered her another fifty thousand," John said. "Just to stand there with a gun, for you. Shit, I didn't even know that gun was loaded. Roland's guns, both of them," he added. "So maybe I should have figured. It must have made it exciting."

"What were you going to do with the money?"

John looked at me as though he was surprised I was even asking the question. "Mine was for Genna," he said. "To get Mandarin Plaid going the way she needs, for a first season. Even with the investors, she hasn't got enough. She doesn't want to believe it, but it's true. She's undercapitalized. She won't make it without more start up cash."

Something came back to me. "That's why you were so mad when she used her own money for the ransom?"

"Right. The whole point was for her, to get money for her, not to drain her. She should have used mine."

Well, actually Dawn's, I thought, but I didn't want to go into that now. "What about Roland?" I asked.

"The money? Roland was going to use his to ditch the factory and set himself up. He wanted to open an import business—factories on the mainland, that's the coming thing, he kept saying. Labor's cheap and there are fortunes to be made. He just needed some capital to start. Shit, if I could have gotten my hands on my money legitimately, I'd probably have invested with him."

"Your money?"

"My father left me that money. *Me.* But my mother got to him and made him set it up as a trust. I can't touch a goddamn penny unless she gives it to me."

Someone passed by the yellow square of light shining in the glass in the door. I said, "So you decided to take it this way."

"It was *my* money."

"And the first theft? The sketches?"

John smiled, almost as though with a fond memory. "That was Roland's genius. He knew my mother wouldn't buy it if I just got snatched. She'd figure I was behind it, trying to get at my money.

"So we built this elaborate thing, where it would be plausible that I'd go running off to be a hero for Genna. And look, she almost didn't buy it anyway, did she?"

I shook my head, thinking about Mrs. Ryan in her huge white

living room, thinking about how my mother would react if someone called and demanded money for the return of Ted, Elliot, Andrew, or Tim. Or me.

"John," I said, "why did Roland kill Wayne Lewis?"

"Can you get me some water?" John asked. Bill found a plastic cup, filled it, and held it for John to drink.

"Thanks," John said. "Shit, my head hurts."

"I'm sorry, John," I said. "But—"

"No," John said, "I'll tell you the rest. I . . . None of this is what I wanted, you know. I just wanted to help Genna."

"I know," I said.

We waited for him to go on.

"Wayne," John said. "Genna had this crazy idea it was Wayne. I don't know what made her think that."

Bill and I exchanged looks.

"She didn't think that," I said.

"What?"

"She thought it was Dawn. She was trying to point us at Wayne to mislead us. So we wouldn't find out, and especially so you wouldn't find out, that Genna has a sister who's a hooker."

"Oh, God." John closed his eyes. "Is that true?" For some reason, opening his eyes again, he looked to Bill.

"Yes." Bill confirmed it for him.

John breathed deeply. "What did she think was going to happen if I knew that? Why did she think I'd care?"

"What did you think was going to happen if you told Genna about your mother? If you admitted that you didn't have any money, instead of trying to be her sugar daddy?" I countered. Why couldn't any of these people have told each other the truth? "Why did Roland kill Wayne?"

"I—" John looked as though he wanted to say something else, not what I was asking him, but he set his jaw and continued. "When I found out Genna had told you about Wayne, I called Roland. I thought he ought to know, just to keep up. I didn't know Wayne dealt drugs, but Roland did."

"How?"

"Roland was Wayne's connection."

264

"Roland? Roland dealt drugs, too?"

"Not in a big way. I had the idea it was more to show he knew the right people, you know? You come to Roland Lum, he'll help you out, that kind of thing."

"Did Andi know that?"

"Sure."

Which was why Andi didn't have to go to Ed, after Wayne was killed. And if Krch had let Francie Rossi follow through on that, Roland might have had the narcotics cops on his tail. This whole scheme might have been aborted. And Andi Shechter might be alive, right now.

Krch, I thought. Ed Everest. Someone had called the Police Commissioner to get the Ed Everest investigation started.

"Your mother," I said to John, who looked at me, waiting to hear the rest. "She was behind the cops looking into Ed Everest, wasn't she?"

"Yes," John said. He shifted his eyes away. "She'd heard rumors about Dawn, but she couldn't prove anything. She couldn't find her, because Dawn doesn't use her own name. My mother thought Dawn was still working for Ed, and that if she blew that up in a big scandal that would ruin Genna."

I was appalled into silence by the strength of Mrs. Ryan's obsession with destroying the woman her son loved.

"I still haven't heard why Roland killed Lewis," Bill said, pulling me back to the hospital room, to now.

"He was afraid that when you two went to Wayne, as soon as Wayne heard 'Mandarin Plaid' he'd tell you about being bought off by my mother, just to get you off his back before you dug up the drug stuff. Roland thought that once you knew that, you might start wondering who else my mother was paying off. He thought you might get onto us from there. I didn't know any of this until this afternoon," he added. "When I went to the building to meet them, and wait."

"That was it?" I said, feeling a little sick. "Wayne had nothing to do with any of this? Roland killed him in case?"

John gave me a long look. "You have no idea how much Roland hated that factory," he said.

Dusk had turned to darkness now in the street outside John's room. In here it was not much better, lit by what the street and the corridor could spare.

"What will happen now?" John said, sounding as though he was reluctant to hear the answer.

"I don't know," I told him. I looked at Bill. Your play, his eyes said. I went on, thinking out loud. "Roland and Andi are dead. Dawn shot them both."

"I thought you . . . ?" John turned his eyes to Bill.

Bill shook his head. "Amateurs. Andi couldn't have seen us; the only light was in the room right in front of her. She just panicked and shot. If Dawn had kept down, she'd never have been hit. She panicked and shot back. It didn't have to happen." Nothing showed on his face, but if you knew what to look for and you looked in his eyes, it was there. "I didn't know Dawn was with me," he went on. "I told her to wait outside. She told me she would. By the time I heard her behind me, it was too late to say anything. She knew that. It was pretty dark down there, but I know I saw her grin."

"What will happen to her?"

"There'll be an investigation," Bill said, "but it's pretty clear what happened. We'll have to testify. If her gun was licensed, she'll probably be okay."

"And the rest?" This question was to me, and we all knew what "the rest" was.

"From where the police stand now, this kidnapping thing is pretty straightforward," I said. I looked at John, thinking of Genna's hands clenching the telephone receiver in his mother's cold apartment. "They'll match one of Roland's guns to the bullet that killed Wayne Lewis, and that case will be solved and they won't care why." I stared out the window, looking for inspiration. "We could tell the police you were involved from the beginning. Or not," I finished. Great, Lydia, I thought. How's that for the decisive, definite, and self-assured P.I.?

John didn't say anything.

"If we do," I said, "I'm not sure you won't just worm out of it. I know your mother has a phalanx of lawyers who salivate over the prospect of a lot of billable time." He looked away from me when I said that, as though I'd discovered something true but shameful about his family.

"If we don't, though, it won't be to do you a favor. I think you're a lot like your mother. I can't believe you would do this to Genna."

"To Genna?" In the dimness of his room John appeared genuinely puzzled. "I did it *for* Genna."

"For Genna? Do you have any idea what a wreck she is by now?" I exploded. "The sketches, and waiting for another phone call, and then this happening to you? What she's been through! And so close to her first big show! You did it *for* her? God, men are such idiots!"

John looked to Bill, maybe for support, but Bill was looking at me. "What she needed was for you to be there helping her!" I ranted on. "Everybody has money problems. Those could have been worked out. She needed you *there!* But you had to be the mighty hunter. You had to go out and drag some goddamn woolly mammoth into the cave, when all she wanted was for you to help her build the fire. And the damn mammoth wasn't even dead, and it stomped all over her, and now you have no dinner *and* Genna's a wreck!"

John's face was a confusion of emotions. Bill's was more obvious: surprise and smothered laughter, an attempt to look as serious as the situation demanded, in the face of woolly mammoths.

"I'll have to think about it," I concluded, maybe a little feeble in content but strong in delivery.

John seemed to be about to make an answer to that, but the door swung open and Genna stepped into the room.

Holding the door to let the light in, she stopped and looked around. "What's wrong?" Her voice was quick with worry.

"Nothing," I said. "John's head hurts. He didn't want the light."

Genna let the door go, stepped to the side of the bed, and bent over John. She kissed him softly. "Baby," she murmured. "I was so scared."

"I'm sorry," he said. He lifted his hand to stroke her glossy hair. "It's okay now. Everything's going to be okay."

She took his hand in hers, kissed him again, and straightened up. She spoke to me. "You were going to call me. To tell me where John was. I had to call the police and ask them."

"I'm sorry," I said. "There were some things we had to go over. I needed to talk to him first."

Genna looked from me to John, seeming unsure of what to make of that.

I didn't want to say anything more, and I didn't have to. John spoke. "Baby," he said to Genna, "Lydia told me about my mother's contract."

"Forget about that. I don't care about that."

"You can't just blow it off like that. If she takes you to court you'll lose Mandarin Plaid."

"I don't care about that, either. I can go back to work for someone else. I don't need my own line. All I need is you."

Genna leaned down again and gently touched John's cheek. Their eyes met, and Bill and I were suddenly and unequivocally redundant.

"I'll call you," I told Genna as I opened the door to leave, but I couldn't tell whether or not she heard me.

She certainly didn't answer.

Out in the brightly lit hallway, on our way to the elevator, Bill and I stepped to opposite walls to let a linen-laden cart pass us. When we came together again, Bill said, "Is all that really true, about the woolly mammoth?"

"All right, so I'm not so good at metaphors," I grumbled. "It's not my fault. A genetic failing. One more thing the Chinese are supposed to be able to do that Lydia Chin can't manage."

"A disgrace to your race," Bill agreed. "A credit to your gender, though, if I may say so."

I looked at him in surprise. "You may say so anytime you like," I told him. "You mean that?"

"If what you said was true."

"Of course it's true. Why is it men just don't get it? Men all think they have to be Superman. Women all love Clark Kent."

"Really?"

"God!" I groaned. "Yes, really."

The elevator came, and we got in it. We had to squeeze; visiting hours were ending, and civilians were packed in pretty tightly with doctors in white coats and nurses in strong shoes.

"Glasses," Bill muttered as the doors slid shut.

"What?" I asked, but I couldn't turn around to look at him.

"Glasses," he repeated. The elevator arrived at the first floor and we spilled with the rest of the crowd into the lobby. We headed through the big sliding doors that would take us out into the street. "A boxy kind of suit," Bill said in a thoughtful tone. "White shirts and dull ties. Maybe even a briefcase. Will you help me shop?"

"What are you talking about?"

"Clark Kent. I'm going to start looking like Clark Kent. I'll be irresistible to women. I'll practice being irresistible to everyone else, and then I'll come back and be irresistible to you."

I stopped on the sidewalk and turned to face him. "There's only one problem with that idea."

"What's that?"

I stood on tiptoe; even still, he had to lean down for our lips to meet. Just before they did, I whispered to him what the problem was. "I already know you're Superman."

THIRTY-ONE

 ive days later I got a call from Genna.

I was at home, finishing up the straightening-the-drawers project I had started at the beginning of this case. The project had grown, seeping like a cloud of smoke into all corners of my room. I was in the back of the closet when my mother came to say there was a call for me.

There had been some unpleasantness with my mother over the Roland business. It might have been my fault. When she heard the story—not including the part about John's involvement, which no one but John and Bill had heard yet—she probably also heard, no matter how I was trying to hide it, the tiny note of I-told-you-so in my voice. Not that I'd actually told her so, but honestly, I thought it was reasonable to expect that my mother's relentless attempts at match-making might abate a little in the face of the knowledge that the most recent guy she'd tried to set me up with was an extortionist and would-be killer.

"Pah," she'd sniffed, when I was done with the tale. "A tragedy. Poor Roland Lum."

"Poor *Roland?*" I asked. "What about everyone else? Roland was the bad guy, Ma."

"Misled," she said. "From being alone. Because he didn't have a good Chinese wife. A Chinese wife would have stopped that white witch from enchanting him."

"White witch? Andi? Ma, she was just a dumb kid. Roland enchanted *her.* This whole thing was his idea."

She gave me a look I've seen before, the one where the squashed-together, turned-down mouth means Lydia Chin, in the opinion of her mother, will never understand anything about how the world really works. "Men like Roland Lum are full of ideas," she told me, with a touch of impatience, as though this was something I should already know. "Some are good, some are bad. They need a woman to tell them which are which." She shook her head at the preventable sadness of it all. "If only you had stayed in touch with Roland Lum after your brother went away to college," she said. "Then Roland Lum wouldn't have forgotten about you, Ling Wan-ju, when he got lonely. Instead he became confused, as a man will who has no wife, and he couldn't choose between his good and bad ideas."

I stood, amazed, in the living room as she wandered into the kitchen still shaking her head. She began to rinse bokchoy in the sink. I felt like I needed cold water splashed on me, too.

She had completely outdone herself. My mother had made this my fault.

So when she stuck her head into my closet that bright Monday morning, I thought she'd come to give me another installment of the long-running lecture on Why Lydia's Responsible for Everything. At least I remembered the morning as bright, though from where I was, in the Siberia of shoes, you couldn't tell. I was hefting sandals over my shoulder when the clothes on their hangers above me rustled and my mother's face appeared hovering like a wardrobe ghost between two shirts.

She looked around her as any ghost would who had materialized in the middle of an inexplicable and distasteful scene. "In the kitchen," she said. "Someone wants to talk to you."

"There's someone here?" I sat back on my heels, brushing dust from my face.

"Of course not, foolish girl. Who would I make wait in the kitchen?" She closed the shirts like a curtain and vanished.

Must be the telephone, then. Any distraction at a time like this. I followed her to the kitchen, where the red receiver—"More likely to bring good news"—dangled an inch above the floor. I picked it up and stretched it around the corner to the tiny front hall, where I would have at least the illusion of privacy.

"Lydia, it's Genna. Are you okay?"

"Me? I'm fine. How are you?"

"I'm sorry I didn't call you back when you called a few days ago. I was just . . . things happened. I needed to think. And everything was so crazy. But I called your office this morning and your machine said you weren't available for the next week. Andrew gave me this number. Is it okay that I called?"

"Of course it is. I left that on my machine because I'm not ready to take on another case right now. But I didn't mean you. I'd have called again but I thought you might want some space."

"Thanks. I did." There was a pause. "John's gone."

"What?"

I could hear her take a deep breath, readying herself to tell me her story. "They only kept him in the hospital overnight, but when I went to pick him up to take him home the next day, he'd already checked out. He left me a letter. He said he'd never been anything but trouble for me, and made a lot of trouble for everyone, but now he had a chance to make it up and he was going to do it. By leaving."

My mother stuck her head around the kitchen doorway to see what had gotten the gasp of surprise from me. I turned away, to hear Genna say, "But he's wrong. He's crazy. It's not his fault he got kidnapped. And what does he mean, he's been trouble? He's the one I counted on to *fix* things when they went wrong. What does he mean?"

"I . . ."

"His letter said to ask you, Lydia."

Oh, John. What a thing to do.

I decided, then, to tell her half the truth. "His mother, Genna. John's mother was behind the things that were going wrong for you. The things you counted on him to fix." I told her the whole story about that.

"Oh, my God," she choked, when I was done. "My God, what a horrible woman. And that's what he means by making it up."

"What?"

"The contract. If—if I don't see him again, I get to keep the million dollars. To start Mandarin Plaid off right. He said in his letter that he's going to tell his mother that everyone she knows will hear about the contract and how she breached it if she doesn't honor it."

"Then what he's done—his leaving—really is for you, Genna," I said gently.

"But I don't care about that! I don't care about my career, if it means losing him!"

"He does."

"What?"

"He cares about your career. And you do, Genna. He knows how much you do. He doesn't want you to have to make that choice. He's made it for you."

"That's what he said." She was almost whispering. "He said he was leaving because he loved me."

"I think that's true."

"But . . ."

I said nothing. When she spoke again, it was in a stronger, more controlled voice. As she had the first night we'd met in Andrew's loft, she pushed away weakness and focused on strength. "There's more, isn't there?" she asked. "More than he told me and more than you're telling me."

"What he's done is right," I said, gentle again.

"I don't know," she said, and I could almost see her shaking herself. "I don't know how to think about this. But John's letter asked

272

me please to go through with my show. For him. And I'm going to. And that's another reason I called."

"Another reason?"

"John left a list. Things I'd better not forget to do. Brad is being terrific, doing most of them. He's been almost living at the studio since Friday, just working all the time. He was wasted as a secretary. I never knew that until now."

Good, I thought. Good going, Brad.

"But there's one thing on John's list I need help on," Genna said. "From you."

"What is it?" I asked.

"Now that . . . Well, without Andi, I have no one to wear the gold gown."

The meaning of this did not sink in. "The gold gown?"

"You saw the fabric in the studio the first time you came up. I said the color would look great on you, remember?"

"On—Genna, you're not serious. You want me to wear the gown? In the show? That can't be what you mean."

"Why not?"

"Because I walk like a truck!"

My mother stuck her head around the corner again.

"You don't," Genna said. "You walk like someone who's going somewhere she really wants to get to. That gown would flow beautifully with your walk. For shoes we could—no, barefoot! God, what a great idea! You can wear it barefoot. Oh, Lydia, please?"

I said no. She said please. I said no. My mother watched.

Genna wore me out.

My mother, with no idea what was going on but with that mother's sixth sense for something that would please her more than it did me, smiled.

So there I was, the following Tuesday, in a small bedroom at the back of a huge, high, window-wrapped loft with views in three directions of two outer boroughs and another state. I was frantically trying to zip the gold gown without ripping it while the five other models—

the five real models—and the makeup people and the hairdressers and the young men whose job it was to find your shoes and bags and jewelry all ran back and forth like stampeding cattle.

Where we were it was complete chaos. But when it was time for someone to go out onto the just-built runway, somehow the curtain would part and the model, carrying the right bag, sporting the right pin, topped with the right hat and wearing the right shoes, would sashay out as though for all the world she had nothing else to do but stroll down this wooden tongue between the rows of seats.

Full seats. Genna was a hit. The fashion press was all here, and all the A-list types and hangers-on. Genna was in shock, as one after another of the people she'd sent tickets to with very little hope actually stepped out of the funky freight elevator. Her shock grew as she heard them wildly applaud one creation after another.

I was in shock, too, but a different kind. I couldn't believe I had agreed to do this, to go out there in front of all these people who rated clothes and makeup and bodies for a living, and stroll all the way to the end of a hundred-mile runway, turn around a couple of times so people could get a really good look at everything that was wrong with me, and then stroll back.

All these people. Fashion editors. Wholesale buyers. Magazine writers. Ladies who lunch.

Photographers, like my brother Andrew, who in his film-can-stuffed Abercrombie and Fitch fishing vest crouched at the side of the runway, one camera pressed to his face and another, plus two more lenses, dangling around his neck.

My mother.

Bill.

"Genna," I said, peeking through the curtains as another woman swept easily past them, displaying lots of attitude and not tripping over anything, "I can't."

"Of course you can," she said, disbelieving. "You go into basements where people are waiting with guns. This can't make you nervous."

"You have no idea," I said.

She sighed. "I wish John were here. He worked so hard for this . . ."

"For you, Genna," I said. "All the work he did was so you could have this."

"I miss him so much," she whispered, not looking at me.

"I know," I said.

To distract her, and also to try to keep my mind from noticing what my body was about to do, I asked a question I had meant to ask when we first met, but never had. "Why do you call your line 'Mandarin Plaid'?"

Genna turned away from the curtain. Her eyes were a little shiny, but she smiled. "I chose that name years ago, when I first started to dream about a line of my own. Because there's no such thing. In three thousand years of textile design, with so many complicated fabrics and all the complexity of Chinese design, we never used stripes across stripes: plaid. The simplest pattern of all, but it never came to us."

I was about to say something, but I'll never know what it was, because at that moment one of the frantic young men stage-whispered, "Gold! Go!" and the curtain was open for me.

So I went. No jewelry, no bag, no shoes. Just Lydia, walking like I was on my way to somewhere I really wanted to get to, seeing a blur of faces and hearing a roar of applause. The applause was for the dress, not me. I knew that. My job was to be here and invisible at the same time, to just keep going no matter what happened around me, to keep the illusion alive. I worked on that. Somewhere in that blur and roar I knew Bill was grinning and clapping, and somewhere else my mother. Without looking, I tried to find them.

In all of New York's Chinatown, there is no one
like P.I. Lydia Chin, who has a nose for trouble,
a disapproving Chinese mother, and a partner
named Bill Smith who's been living above a bar
for sixteen years.

Hired to find some precious stolen porcelain,
Lydia follows a trail of clues from highbrow art
dealers into a world of Chinese gangs.
Suddenly, this case has become as complex as
her community itself—and as deadly as a killer
on the loose...

China Trade

S. J. Rozan

CHINA TRADE
S. J. Rozan
_____ 95590-1 $5.99 U.S./$7.99 CAN.